THE ACADEMY

Also by Bentley Little

The Vanishing
The Burning
Dispatch
The Resort
The Policy
The Return
The Collection
The Association
The Walking
The Town
The House
The Store
The Ignored
The Revelation
University
Dominion
The Mailman
Death Instinct

THE ACADEMY

Bentley Little

A SIGNET BOOK

SIGNET
Published by New American Library, a division of
Penguin Group (USA) Inc., 375 Hudson Street,
New York, New York 10014, USA
Penguin Group (Canada), 90 Eglinton Avenue East, Suite 700, Toronto,
Ontario M4P 2Y3, Canada (a division of Pearson Penguin Canada Inc.)
Penguin Books Ltd., 80 Strand, London WC2R 0RL, England
Penguin Ireland, 25 St. Stephen's Green, Dublin 2,
Ireland (a division of Penguin Books Ltd.)
Penguin Group (Australia), 250 Camberwell Road, Camberwell, Victoria 3124,
Australia (a division of Pearson Australia Group Pty. Ltd.)
Penguin Books India Pvt. Ltd., 11 Community Centre, Panchsheel Park,
New Delhi - 110 017, India
Penguin Group (NZ), 67 Apollo Drive, Rosedale, North Shore 0632,
New Zealand (a division of Pearson New Zealand Ltd.)
Penguin Books (South Africa) (Pty.) Ltd., 24 Sturdee Avenue,
Rosebank, Johannesburg 2196, South Africa

Penguin Books Ltd., Registered Offices:
80 Strand, London WC2R 0RL, England

First published by Signet, an imprint of New American Library,
a division of Penguin Group (USA) Inc.

ISBN-13: 978-0-7394-9979-5

Printed in the United States of America

PUBLISHER'S NOTE
This is a work of fiction. Names, characters, places, and incidents either are the product of the author's imagination or are used fictitiously, and any resemblance to actual persons, living or dead, business establishments, events, or locales is entirely coincidental.

The publisher does not have any control over and does not assume any responsibility for author or third-party Web sites or their content.

This book is dedicated to Paul Smith,
whose tales from the trenches gave me nightmares.

Special thanks to Rachel Jackson-Smith,
who allowed me to use her name in this novel in
order to raise money for Golden Hill
Elementary School.

Prologue

"What do you wanna do?" Van asked.

Kurt shrugged. "I dunno. What do *you* wanna do?"

"I dunno."

The two teenagers leaned against the closed garage door, staring out at the street and looking before them at a long boring afternoon.

"Let's play some hoops," Van suggested.

"All right," Kurt agreed. Neither of them had been back to the campus since school let out, although the summer before, they'd practically *lived* there. This year, however, he had his driver's license, so they'd gone to the beach a lot, cruised for chicks (not that they'd found any) and generally taken advantage of his newly mobile status. Unfortunately, last week his dad had grounded him after getting the gas bills from Kurt's two credit cards, and for the rest of the summer they were once again relegated to doing things that were within walking distance.

The two of them grabbed a couple of cans of Coke from the fridge, then headed down the hill to the high school, bouncing the basketball between them on the sidewalk.

Van was hoping for a pickup game, but when they arrived, they were the only ones there. Kurt was glad. He hadn't played in a while and wanted to be able to get in a little practice before going against someone. "Let's play Horse," he said.

Van snorted. "What are you, three? Let's play Shit. Or Fuck."

"Fuck it is, then." Kurt took the ball, dribbled down the court, ran under the basket, threw the ball underhanded over his head and, miraculously, made it. He tossed the ball to his friend, who tried to copy his moves, but the ball hit the rim and bounced away. "F!" Kurt announced.

"Watch *this*!" Van called, going into Globetrotter mode and executing his fanciest dribbles.

But Kurt didn't watch. Instead, he looked toward the classrooms.

Something was wrong.

There was a chain-link fence blocking off the buildings in an effort to prevent vandalism. Behind the fence, he could see closed classroom doors and windows shaded by off-white institutional blinds. The sight of the shut-down school had made him feel happy last year, but now it made him uneasy. Even the field and the blacktop basketball courts put him on edge, their emptiness somehow emphasizing the fact that the two of them were all alone here.

And no one would know if something happened to them.

"Skills!" Van shouted.

Kurt looked over to see the ball bouncing underneath the basket. "Sorry," he said. "I didn't see it."

"What?"

"I was distracted."

"Automatic F!" Van told him. "And I get to go again! Pay attention this time." He dribbled the ball between his legs as he ran in a figure eight, then did a left-handed hook from the free throw line and swished it in.

Kurt grabbed the ball and attempted to imitate his friend, but on the first dribble the ball hit a crack on the asphalt and bounced back quickly at a sharp steep angle, smacking him hard under the chin and slamming his teeth together. "Shit!" he yelled, holding his jaw and letting the ball bounce away. He ran a finger around the inside of his mouth, checking for blood.

"U!" Van cried triumphantly.

"I'm not playing anymore, asshole! I quit!" Kurt tried wiggling his two front teeth with his finger and was grateful to find that they were still in place and unmovable. Out of the corner of his eye, he thought he saw motion, a furtive shadow the size of a skinny girl that darted between two of the buildings so quickly that he was not sure it was even there.

In the window of Mrs. Habeck's classroom, the shade was swinging from side to side, as though someone within the room had been peeking out and had quickly backed away.

"Let's get out of here," Kurt said.

"Fuck you," Van told him. He took a shot from the side. The ball bounced off the rim and he quickly rebounded and put it in.

Too embarrassed to let Van know that he was scared, Kurt stood there for a moment while his friend dribbled around the court and made a layup. He still wasn't sure *why* he was scared, but he was, and despite the fact that it was the middle of the day, and hot and sunny to boot, the fear seemed to be intensifying. He moved beneath a tree for the shade, leaning his back against the trunk, trying to think of a way to get his friend to leave.

A nut fell from the tree and hit him on the top of the head, bouncing to the ground. "Ow!" he yelled. The damn thing felt more like a rock than a nut. He pressed a finger into his hair, felt a bump starting already.

Another nut came speeding down and hit his forearm, a round red bruise appearing instantly on the skin.

On the blacktop, Van tripped and fell, landing hard and letting out a cry of surprised pain. "Shit!" he said, getting up and examining the knees of his jeans. Even from here, Kurt could see ripped denim and blood.

What the hell was happening? Maybe it was just his imagination, but it sure seemed to him as though the two of them were being attacked.

Another nut landed at his feet, missing him by an inch.

Kurt moved quickly away from the tree. "Come on!" he called out. "Time to bail!"

"No," Van said defiantly.

"Dude . . ."

"I said no!" There was real hostility in his voice, and Kurt was not sure where it had come from or what had brought it on. This wasn't like his friend. He tried to think of something to say to Van that would convince him to leave, something that sounded reasonable and not completely insane, but when Van purposefully turned his back on him, picked the ball up off the ground and started shooting at one of the baskets facing in the opposite direction, Kurt decided to leave with or without his friend.

The ball hit the edge of the metal backboard and came shooting back at Van, hitting him in the stomach and knocking the wind out of him for a second.

"I'm going!" Kurt announced.

"Fine," Van said without looking at him.

Kurt walked away. At the end of the teachers' lot, before the buildings blocked his view of the field and the courts, he turned around and looked back. Van was still shooting hoops, practicing his free throw.

It was the last time he ever saw his friend.

One

The letter came in mid-July and that was weird. Notification from the district didn't usually arrive until late August, and even before Linda Webster opened the envelope, she was mentally calculating her seniority, trying to figure out how far down the line she was, just in case the district had decided to cut positions and lay people off.

To her surprise, the letter had nothing to do with layoffs. Indeed, it said that the district projected an increase in enrollment this year and a need for two to three *additional* teachers per school. That was certainly good news. The real reason for the early communication, however, was to inform the faculty and staff of John Tyler High that the board had voted to consider its proposal to become a charter school. There would be a discussion of the subject at the next meeting on July 23, the following Monday.

Linda put down the letter and looked over at her husband. "They're talking about Tyler becoming a charter school."

Frank looked up from his computer. "What does that mean?"

"I don't know exactly."

"Does the letter—"

"It doesn't really go into any detail." She looked at the paper again and shook her head. "Charter school. There was no talk about this at all. I never even heard any rumors about it. But it mentions a 'proposal,' which means that Jody must have submitted something to the school board. It's just weird that she didn't discuss it with faculty and staff first to get our take on it. Or at least give us a heads-up. That's not like her."

"Well, it might help you get out from under the district's thumb."

He was right. In the last election, a slate of conservative fundamentalists had won a majority on the board and were now attempting to push through their bizarre and incomprehensible agenda, which included doing away with any and all Halloween dances/parties/celebrations, removing Harry Potter books from the libraries, stopping the teaching of evolution and canceling the breakfast/lunch program for low-income students on the grounds that it was not the schools' responsibility to provide social services. Attempts had been made by the principals of each of the district's six schools to argue on the new board's home turf. With the breakfast and lunch issue, in particular, they'd pointed out to the board that Jesus was a strong advocate for the poor. Not only that, but in doing away with the program, the district would lose federal funds. The board had not budged. And ever since, the schools and the district had been at loggerheads over a myriad of issues big and small. It would definitely be a relief to be free from the edicts of those fanatics.

"Or," Frank continued, "it might mean that they're going to contract out all of your jobs and hire some private company to teach the kids."

That was a possibility, too, and though Linda wanted to be able to discount it, the fact that the principal had been so closemouthed about changing

Tyler to a charter school made the idea not seem so far-fetched. She called her friend Diane Brooke, chair of Tyler's English department, to see if she'd heard anything, but Diane was just as in the dark as she was. Aside from the sketchy general information she'd read in the district's letter, she knew nothing.

"Doesn't that seem strange to you?" Linda asked. "You'd think Jody would've *mentioned* it."

"I know. And there had to be a ton of paperwork involved. You know the district. Which means that it's been in the pipeline for a while."

"Bobbi!" they both said together.

Bobbi Evans. Linda should have thought of her before. Not a thing went on in Tyler's office that the secretary didn't know about. Of course, Bobbi hadn't said a word about this either.

"I'll call her," Diane said. "Then I'll ring you right back."

Linda didn't even have a chance to go into the kitchen and get a drink of water before the phone rang again.

"Her machine picked up," Diane said. "I had to leave a message."

"I'm going to send out a global e-mail, see if everyone else is out of the loop or if it's just us."

"Are you including Jody in that?"

"It can't hurt. Maybe she'll let us know what's going on."

"What do you know about charter schools?" Diane asked.

"Not much," Linda admitted. "They operate independently from the district, right? They're almost like private schools?"

"In California," Diane said, "there are two main types of charter school. I looked it up online. In fact, that's what I was doing when you called. The one where a private company is brought in to run the place is usually used for failing schools in poor districts, which, obviously, is not us. In Orange County, charter schools are most commonly schools that are still overseen by the district but given a certain degree of autonomy. My guess is that that's where we're headed."

"Why do you think Jody would want to do such a thing? Doesn't that seem weird to you?"

"There are some good points. Textbook adoption, for one. We wouldn't have to go with the district's choice of textbooks, which, as you know, is horrible. We'd be able to pick our own. And we'd have more budgetary discretion. The theory behind charters is that individual schools know what's better for their students than the district does. On the other hand, there's probably a lot of potential for abuse with such a lack of oversight."

"So what's your gut reaction?" Linda asked. "Yea or nay?"

Diane sighed. "You know me. I don't handle change well. Better the devil you know and all that. You?"

"I should probably wait until I have enough information to know what I'm talking about, but it seems to me that no matter which way this thing plays out, it's going to mean job instability for someone. I hope I'm wrong, but I see negotiated protections going out the window."

Diane laughed. "Spoken like a card-carrying union member."

"Well . . ."

Linda did send out an e-mail to the rest of the faculty and staff after hanging up, but it wasn't until the next day that she began to receive responses. Nearly all of them commented on the seeming secrecy surrounding the proposed change and the fact that the principal had not mentioned anything about it to anyone, but a surprising number were already gung ho supporters of the charter idea. Frank was right—it was probably more a reaction to the school board than anything else, an opportunity to get out from under the board's thumb—but she couldn't help thinking that they shouldn't jump into anything right away, that a lot more study was needed before anyone made any permanent decisions.

Frank agreed. "You should talk to people from other charter schools, see how different the reality is from the promises, see what they like and don't like about it, find out, like you said, about job security and whether the protections you're afforded now will be cut or abridged. And you need to think about the long term as well as the short term. Yes, it would be nice to be free from that lunatic school board, but on the other hand, there's an election next year and the whole makeup of the board could shift. What would be in the ultimate best interest of the school? No one should be taking this lightly. This is a major decision."

She kissed him on the nose. "I love your logical, Spock-like mind."

"Just my mind?" he hinted.

"Tonight," she promised.

Linda spent most of the day answering e-mails and talking on the phone to other teachers. No one had heard from either the principal or her secretary, and though many messages had been left for the two of them, there'd been no response.

The charter proposal was public information and was posted as an addendum to the school board agenda on the district's Web site, but viewing the document provided more questions than answers. It stated that the petitioner's proposed charter followed state guidelines and had been certified as acceptable by the state board of education, that the implementation plan had been approved by the district's superintendent, that each of five mandatory educational goals had been met by the school over the requisite three-year period.

A charter had been written already? An implementation strategy had been submitted to the superintendent? This whole thing had been in the planning stages for the past three years?

It made sense that this had been in the works for a while, but Linda and everyone she spoke to were shocked to learn that they had been kept in the dark for so long while so much had been going on. According to the proposal, one of the reasons for switching over to a charter school was that the teachers would have more input; they would be able to collectively choose their curriculum rather than simply follow the district's edicts. If that was the goal, they were starting off on the wrong foot, because everyone she talked to was angry that they had not been consulted or even informed about what was happening.

Still, some of the teachers were in favor of trying to disassociate themselves from the board, and the idea of a more democratically run school, one in which they would have a say in regard to policy, was definitely appealing to them.

Linda was not so sure.

The chamber was packed, all the seats taken, teachers and parents lined up against the walls, more men and women spilling out into the hall. Such a turnout was rare enough during the school year; it was absolutely unheard of in the middle of summer. But both the *Orange County Register* and the local *Santa Mara Sentinel* had printed articles about the proposed charter school, and advocates for both sides had been fanning the flames in an effort to bring out their supporters.

Although, in truth, there didn't seem to be much organized opposition to the idea of a charter school save for some grumbling by the certified and classified employees' unions—and in conservative Orange County, union support was the kiss of death.

It was why Linda was worried.

Neither Frank nor Diane's husband, Greg, had wanted to come to the meeting, so she and Diane had carpooled, and though they'd arrived a half hour before the scheduled seven o'clock start time, the small parking lot was already full and they were forced to park on a side street nearly a block away. By the time they made it back to the district offices and up to the third floor, where the meeting was to be held, it was nearly seven and they were lucky to find two spots against the back wall near the doorway where they could stand. Looking around, Linda saw most of Tyler's teachers and recognized quite a few parents. She tried to eavesdrop on some of the surrounding conversations to get a feeling for the prevailing sentiment, but it was simply too noisy.

"Hey," Diane said. She pointed. "It's Jody and Bobbi."

The principal and her secretary sat silently in the front row, facing straight ahead, not acknowledging anyone or anything around them.

"Weird," Linda said. "Looks like they turned Stepford on us."

"Cover me. I'm going in." Diane turned sideways, sliding between the parents in front of her. "Excuse me. . . . Pardon me. . . . Sorry. . . . Excuse me. . . ." She made her way through the crowd to the front of the room, where she crouched down next to Jody's seat. She said something, but Linda could not hear what it was from back here, and from this angle it did not appear to her that the principal bothered to look at Diane or even respond. Seconds later, a look of stunned confusion on her face, Diane made her way back through the crowd.

"Well?" Linda prompted.

"She told me to mind my own business if I knew what was good for me."

"Jody?"

Diane nodded. The confusion on her face had been joined by anger. Other teachers nearby were moving in closer to hear what had happened.

"What did she say *exactly*?" Linda asked.

"Exactly that. 'Mind your own business if you know what's good for you.' In this low creepy voice. She didn't even look at me, just kept staring straight ahead. Bobbi, too."

"That's not like Jody," declared David Dolliver, the driver's-ed instructor.

"No kidding. That's why it freaked me out. It almost sounded like a . . . threat."

Yvonne Gauthier cleared her throat. "I believe it." Yvonne was Tyler's newest teacher, hired last year when one of the former math instructors decided not to return after her maternity leave ended.

All eyes turned toward her.

Yvonne fumbled nervously with her purse. "Don't get me wrong. Jody's been great to me, and I think she's a terrific principal. But when I was hired, she asked me if I had any kids or was planning to have any kids. I told her I was single, though it was really none of her business, and then I said that, yeah, I might want kids one day. She totally changed. Her face got completely serious, and her voice was low and . . . threatening, like you said. It *was* creepy. She told me that she'd been burned by my predecessor, who had lied and said that she never wanted to have kids, and that if I wanted this job, I had to promise never to become pregnant. So I promised. I lied, but I promised."

Ken Myers shook his head. "I've known Jody Hawkes ever since she was a VP at Santa Mara High," the history teacher said. "She's one of the kindest, nicest, fairest, most decent people I know. I can't see her ever behaving in such an unprofessional manner, let alone making threats like that."

"I *have* seen it," Yvonne insisted.

"Now I guess I have, too," Diane said.

There was a sudden stirring of the crowd, an increase in chatter followed by respectful silence as the last of the board members took his seat at the front of the chamber. The teachers' conversation was dropped as the meeting was called to order. Old business was quickly dispensed with and a few generic procedural items received cursory discussion and votes before the board took up Tyler's charter proposal.

The debate was surprisingly short given the number of attendees, but most of the people, Linda included, had come to listen rather than speak. Linda wished she had more knowledge of the topic, regretted that she hadn't done enough research to intelligently discuss the matter, but as she listened to Jody give her presentation and answer softball questions from the board, as she saw the sympathetic hearing given a group of parents who spoke in favor of the proposal and the hostile reception given the heads of the certified and classified employees' unions who spoke against it, Linda realized that the outcome of the Tyler petition was a foregone conclusion.

She should have been able to predict that, but she'd been looking at everything from the wrong angle. She'd been thinking the board might object to losing control over one of its schools, but she'd forgotten that the ultimate goal for its more ideological members was to keep the district's schools from adhering to state educational standards that were not "Christian" enough. And if weakening state influence entailed letting go of some of its own power, then so be it. Maybe Jody had even made some sort of promise or under-the-table deal with the board in order to get what she wanted.

With one dissension, the proposal was approved, although this did not mean that conversion to a charter school was automatic. The next and final step was to conduct a vote of all of Tyler's employees to determine whether a majority wished to be independent, or remain as is, under the district's aegis. If the change was ratified by the employees, those who did not want to work at a charter school could transfer to another campus within the district if there was an opening or if they could bump someone with less seniority. If it was not ratified, the charter proposal was dead in the water for the time being, and either the entire process would have to be started all over again or the idea abandoned.

After the meeting was adjourned, a mob of parents, students and local reporters crowded around Jody to congratulate her and ask questions about the plans for Tyler's future.

"Come on," Diane said. "Let's get out of here."

On the way home, they passed by the high school. The buildings were dark, black, and the rounded trees in front of the office blended with the contours of the structure to create a silhouetted shape in the gloom that reminded Linda of a hulking monster preparing to pounce. That was a weird thought, and not one that she'd ever had about Tyler before, though she'd been here at night countless times.

Linda glanced away, feeling cold, and it was not until they were several blocks away that she realized what had been wrong with the scene: not only were all the lights in the school off, but the streetlights on that side of Grayson were out as well, as though a blackout had hit only that one block. It made the school seem not only the focus of the darkness but the cause of it. She didn't like that, and though she knew life wasn't literature, the metaphor troubled her.

It was as if Diane could read her mind. "Things are changing," her friend said, and Linda was not sure if that was sadness or worry she heard in Diane's voice. It certainly wasn't anticipation.

"So what's your take on this whole charter school thing?" Linda asked. They'd been talking about Jody's behavior ever since the meeting adjourned, but they hadn't discussed the charter proposal.

"It really doesn't matter. It's going through despite what I think."

"But what *do* you think?"

Diane sighed. "I'll deny I ever said this. And it wouldn't have occurred to me even two hours ago. But the thought of giving Jody complete autonomy over the school scares the crap out of me. After what I saw in there . . ."

"At least school boards can be recalled," Linda agreed. "At least they're elected."

"So you don't buy our big switch to democracy either, huh?"

"Do I think we're all going to have equal say in how the school is run? Do I think it's all going to be one communal lovefest where all of our wishes are going to be granted? No."

"It's all there in the charter, in black-and-white. You heard Jody."

"Yes," Linda said, "I did."

Frank was in bed when she got home, watching a rerun of *Monk*. At least some things never changed, and she felt safe and comfortable as she brushed her teeth, took off her clothes and crawled in bed next to him. They made love, and though he was only halfway engaged and kept his eye on the television the entire time in order to see the end of his show, that was all right.

In fact, it was nice.

Two

Two days later, Linda received in the mail a heavy package consisting of two hundred bound photocopied pages with a title sheet that read "John Tyler High School Charter." There was also a cover letter and a numbered ballot on which were listed two choices: "Accept Charter" and "Reject Charter." The ballots were to be turned in at a mandatory meeting of all faculty and staff that was scheduled for Monday morning at ten.

Neither Diane nor any of the other teachers with whom she'd talked after the board meeting had believed that converting Tyler High to a charter school could be accomplished in less than a year. There were simply too many details to attend to, too many t's to be crossed and i's to be dotted. And although there'd been no mention of a timetable, they had all assumed that if the proposal was approved, the *following* school year would be the first under the new charter. However, as the cover letter made clear, the principal and the charter committee had every intention of implementing the changes *this* year and immediately shifting all administrative responsibilities from the district to the school.

Linda had never heard any mention of a charter committee before this, and she read the names of the seven members with interest. They were all teachers and staff members who she'd heard through the grapevine were gung ho about switching over. The principal's secretary, Bobbi, of course, and Janet Fratelli, the fascist librarian, as well as the math teacher Art Connor and the band teacher, Joseph Carr, two recent hires she recognized by sight but didn't really know. Then there was history teacher Nina Habeck, PE coach John Nicholson and art teacher Scott Swaim, all instructors with whom Linda had had run-ins over the past few years, Nina because of her insensitive treatment of a learning-disabled freshman girl who'd ended up in tears after a humiliating lecture in front of the rest of her class. This did not bode well, and Linda called Diane to get her take on the situation.

"Jody may have kept mum about this charter thing to us, but she obviously has a whole transition team in place and a plan that's rarin' to go," her friend said. "My opinion of that woman has done a complete one eighty over the past week. I swear, if you had told me last semester that I would feel anything but gratitude and admiration for her, after the way she turned this school around, I'd've said you were crazy. I considered her a friend!"

"I know," Linda agreed. "As far as I was concerned, Jody was the best principal I've ever worked under. And who knows? Maybe she still is. But it's definitely disturbing to find out that she was covertly planning a coup the whole time she was pretending that it was business as usual."

"You know," Diane pointed out, "we were two of the biggest complainers about the school board, especially after the election."

"Which is why it's so weird that Jody didn't confide in us. I mean, this wasn't some big state secret. There was no *reason* to keep this under wraps. And it seems to me that by getting the input of the teachers, she could have made an even more effective case for secession. But the way she went about it . . ."

"Does not seem promising," Diane agreed.

"Exactly."

"Maybe we're wrong," her friend offered. "We will be getting away from the district's craziness, so it could be that this really will be better for the school. Maybe it's *not* a power grab and Jody's just passionate because she believes so much in this."

"Maybe," Linda said doubtfully.

"You're right," Diane responded. "It's a power grab. All hail the queen."

The charter itself was an intimidating, densely detailed document written in nearly incomprehensible legalese that had to have been cribbed from somewhere else or generated by a lawyer. There was no way that the principal or her secretary had come up with it. The charter not only spelled out the chain of command and hierarchical levels of authority that would be installed in the reorganized school, but enumerated a dizzying array of new rules and regulations that would apply to both students and staff. To Linda, it seemed nightmarishly Orwellian. If the goal was, as stated in the cover letter, to get out from under the stifling dictates of the district and put the emphasis back on teaching, this sure was a funny way to go about it. The district's bureaucracy was nowhere near as complex or byzantine as what was being proposed for the charter school.

One subparagraph in particular caught her eye: "Agreements made between employees' associations and the district will neither apply to nor affect charter school employees. Any union or employees' association seeking to represent charter school employees in their dealings with the charter committee must first gain the approval of the charter committee, which has the right to terminate any agreement, arrangement or understanding at its discretion."

Linda read the words again. Was that even legal? She called the union headquarters and asked to speak to Lyle Johns, president of the teachers' association, who told her that no one knew whether it was legal, and that was why the union was fighting so hard to prevent ratification of the charter. "You can see why the board okayed this," he said. "They've always had an antiunion agenda. Our job now is to get word out to the Tyler teachers and make sure they know the consequences of voting for the charter."

"But the meeting's *Monday*," she said. "That's when we're going to vote. No offense, but if you're trying to get the word out, you're doing a pretty poor job. I called *you*. I haven't heard word one from the association. No e-mails, no phone calls . . ."

Johns seemed confused. "We've sent out e-mails to all members in the district. We even have people canvassing neighborhoods to inform parents so *they'll* put pressure to bear. This is the biggest threat we've ever had to face. Not only could it significantly weaken our association and affect our negotiations with the district, but it could leave all of the employees at your school unprotected and without recourse. We're pulling out all the stops for this campaign."

"Something's wrong, then," Linda said. "The message isn't getting through."

"I'll find out what's happening at this end, but, like you say, the vote's Monday. We're down to the wire here. Could I e-mail you some information and have you forward it to the teachers at your school, just in case?"

"Of course."

"We've got to get the word out."

"They can really do this? Nullify our collective bargaining agreement and eliminate protections?"

"We'd fight it in court, with backing from the state association, but similar restrictions have been upheld before. Charter's a whole new world. There's not much precedent. My guess is, we'd lose."

Linda was shocked. But when she started calling other teachers to tell them about it, she was even more shocked to learn that most of them didn't care. Diane, fellow English instructors Ray Cheng and Steve Warren, woodshop teacher Alonso Ruiz, French teacher Mary Mercer, social studies teacher Suzanne Johnson and Linda's other loyal allies saw the folly in getting rid of the only firewall they had against harassment and unfair disciplinary actions, but there were a lot of newer teachers without tenure who were actively antiunion, and there were other teachers in the middle who didn't care one way or the other. Still, she dutifully forwarded the e-mailed information, hoping that at least some of it might sink in.

She arrived early for the big meeting on Monday. Jody and her supporters had gone all out, because not only was the multipurpose room festively decorated, its walls hung with posters from various companies who had apparently promised to donate goods and services to the school should it become independent, but there was a long table piled high with doughnuts, drinks and various types of fruit. As each person walked through the door, he or she was presented with a packet that included articles and editorials about charter school accomplishments as well as copies of studies purporting to show that charter schools fared better academically than more traditional educational institutions. There was no way anyone would be able to read even a fraction of the provided material in the time allotted; the teachers were just supposed to be impressed and cowed into submission by the sheer bulk of it.

"Nice to see that we'll be able to discuss issues and vote in a balanced, fair and unbiased environment," Diane noted drily when she arrived ten minutes later.

Linda, who had been wandering around, mingling and eavesdropping on conversations, told her friend that from what she'd observed, the outcome was too close to call. "Although a lot of teachers seem to be skeptical, so that's a good sign."

People were starting to sit down as ten o'clock approached, and the two of them found seats near the front of the room. Diane squirmed uncomfortably in the plastic chair. "At least they could have found some adult chairs," she complained.

"There'll be plenty of money for that if we become a charter school," Linda said mock-helpfully.

"I wish you would keep your snide comments to yourself," Bobbi said from behind them. They both turned to look at the secretary, who was scowling as she made her way down the row toward the center of the room. "Your attitude is not appreciated."

"Oh, I'm sorry," Diane said sweetly. "I was under the mistaken impression that we lived in a free country. Of course, I only teach English and not history, so I probably don't know about such things."

Bobbi gave a disgusted snort and moved away.

"You know what?" Diane said loudly to Linda. "I don't feel very welcome here. I think I'm going home."

Bobbi hurried back. Her face was flushed, and there was anger in her eyes. "This is a mandatory meeting."

Diane stood, dropping her packet on the seat of her chair as she adjusted her purse. "Then I guess you'll have to type up a memo chastising me and put it in my box."

"*Everyone* has to vote today!"

Diane said nothing but simply stared at her.

"I'm sorry," Bobbi said, her tone suddenly conciliatory. "It's just that I've been putting in a lot of hours, doing a lot of work—"

"Don't worry about it," Diane said coolly. She turned her back on the secretary, picked up her packet and sat down in her chair.

Linda smiled as Bobbi walked away. "You're cruel," she said to her friend.

Diane grinned. "Feels good to stay in practice."

The meeting began once everyone had arrived. Most of the teachers around her were eating doughnuts and fruit—*Bribes,* Linda thought—as Jody strode to the front of the room and picked up the microphone from its stand on the podium. The principal started by welcoming everyone back and giving those who hadn't been there a thumbnail sketch of the school board meeting. She was pleasant and upbeat, friendly and approachable, the Jody Hawkes of the previous year rather than the hard, determined woman they'd encountered last week at the district offices.

Linda glanced around her as the principal spoke. *What is going on here?* she wondered. They were teachers and support staff. How in the world had they gotten stuck in the middle of this campaign? How had the fate of the school ended up in their hands?

Jody was beaming broadly. "I am going to enumerate some of the changes that will occur if we become a charter school. If you agree with them, let me know."

"Here it comes," Diane whispered. The crowd, done for the most part with snacking, was now listening intently.

"When we adopt our charter, we will become the masters of our own destiny, no longer dependent on the whims of the school board for educational necessities."

"Yes!" a handful of people yelled. Linda looked around. Bobbi, Janet, Art, Joseph . . .

The charter committee.

"We will have a democratically run workplace, with every faculty and staff member involved in the decisions affecting their jobs."

"Yes!"

They'd planned this, she realized with a sinking feeling in the pit of her stomach. They'd rehearsed what they were going to do.

It was a good plan, too. It worked. As with any audience, participation begot participation, and they got others to join in with their vocal show of support. After each of the principal's exhortations, more teachers jumped on the bandwagon, and the crowd's response grew louder and more fervent with every round.

"We will find ways to cut costs and use the savings to increase the pay of our employees!"

"Yes!"

"We will purchase *new* textbooks and *new* computers for every classroom!"

"YES!"

"We will make sure that parents become more involved!"

"YES!"

"Parents will be required to donate either time or money to their students' classrooms!"

"YES!"

"Ten hours or a hundred dollars!"

"YES!"

"Each quarter!"

The fervent chanting reminded Linda of an episode of Amy Sedaris' subversive TV show *Strangers with Candy,* where Sedaris' character, Jerri Blank, was brainwashed by a cult whose identically attired members sang the song "Welcome Table" at the drop of a hat. That's what this felt like to her, a cult meeting, and she imagined herself suddenly jumping up, stomping her feet, clapping her hands and singing at the top of her lungs: "I'm going to sit at the welcome table! I'm going to sit at the welcome table! I'm going to sit at the welcome table one of these days!"

Linda giggled.

Unfortunately, the chanting stopped just at that moment.

From behind the podium, the principal frowned at her. To her right, both Janet Fratelli and Ken Myers leaned around Diane to give her disapproving looks. That made her giggle all the more, and suddenly she couldn't stop. Like a little kid in church thinking about boogers and poop, she found herself convulsed with laughter that was far out of proportion to the situation, the setting and circumstances amplifying the humor far beyond what it deserved to be.

Diane hadn't caught her giggles, but she was smiling in support, as were several other teachers. The principal decided to ignore them all. Jody spoke more loudly into the microphone, announcing that everyone had had time to go over the charter and related materials and should, by this time, have formed an opinion about the way in which John Tyler High School ought to proceed. "Are there any questions before we go on?" she asked.

A slew of hands went up.

"I don't have time to answer all of your questions," Jody said. "But I'll try to—"

"Why *don't* you have time?" Diane asked. "It seems to me that if we're to make an informed decision, we should have all the facts at our disposal. Unless you're too busy and have something more important to do than convince us that your charter proposal is worthwhile."

Jody's face tightened.

There was a murmur of agreement from the audience.

The principal smiled stiffly, trying to put her best face forward. "Of course," she said. "I will be happy to answer any and all questions you may have."

Unfortunately, the questions were almost uniformly bad: softballs that made Jody look good and that she easily hit out of the park. There were a few legitimate concerns brought up but not many, and for those inquiries the answers were consistently vague. Diane asked whether tenure would be affected by a changeover, and Linda asked whether teachers could be fired without recourse. The principal informed them (smugly, Linda thought) that those issues would be determined at a later date. The way she phrased her response allowed people to think that the decision might be voted on and decided by majority opinion, but Linda had a sneaking suspicion that that was probably not going to be the case.

When there were no more hands raised, Jody smiled. "Very well, then. We will now vote on whether to accept or reject the charter. Raise your hand if you are in favor of becoming independent from the district and ratifying the charter as presented."

"I thought we were supposed to turn in written ballots—," Steve Warren began.

"There will be no secret ballots," the principal announced. "I want to know where everyone stands."

Linda looked around at the teachers nearby. There was surprise and confusion on the faces of several, but not the defiance she would have expected nor the sense of outrage.

She stood. "If our school is really going to be a democracy, if we are all to have a say in what goes on here and vote on issues that concern us, then we should have a secret ballot." She fixed the principal with a level stare. "This implied threat that anyone who does not vote the way the administration wishes will be remembered later and possibly retaliated against is antithetical to everything you claim this move is supposed to accomplish."

Antithetical. That was a good word, and she was impressed with herself for coming up with it on the fly. The way it flowed smoothly off her tongue made her reasoning that much more effective, gave intellectual heft and legitimacy to her argument.

Out of the corner of her eye, she saw Bobbi writing down information—her name and the nature of her transgression, no doubt—and Linda started through the crowd toward the secretary, pushing her way between various teachers' legs and the backs of the seats in front of them. "What are you writing there?" she asked. "Let me see."

Bobbi quickly bent over, hiding her clipboard with an encircling hand like a smart student attempting to protect test answers from the prying eyes of less-prepared classmates. "No!"

"I want to know what you're writing."

"That will be quite enough!" Jody thundered from the stage.

A collective intake of breath issued from the mouths of faculty and staff, a sound of shock, and the principal seemed to realize instantly that she'd gone too far. The look on her face was now one of blanched comprehension. Linda moved back to her seat, fixing her with a calm, level stare. "So much for democracy, huh? And you're right, Jody. That *will* be quite enough. Let's vote."

The principal appeared flustered, was not able for several seconds to formulate or express her thoughts. Finally, she cleared her throat, adjusted the microphone and repeated her initial call for a show of hands.

"Let's fill out our *ballots,*" Linda said, still standing.

There were nods all around, murmurs of agreement. "I need a pen," Steve Warren announced loudly. He kept his eyes on Jody.

"Very well." The principal smiled in an effort to be accommodating, but Linda could sense her frustration and hostility, and she only hoped that it was equally obvious to everyone else. At Jody's behest, Bobbi retreated for a moment to the rear of the room, returning with a box of pens. The secretary walked down the right aisle and passed them out to each row. The teachers, office staff and other school employees immediately filled out their ballots and folded the sheets of paper.

"Pass your ballots to the right," Jody said. "Bobbi will collect them and tabulate the votes. You may keep the pens."

Linda stood again. "I think we need two pairs of eyes, just to make sure there's no cheating."

"This is why I wanted to have a show of hands," Jody said sweetly. "Transparency." She smiled. "You can help count ballots, if you like. And, of course, we will double-check them just to make sure there have been no errors."

Giving Diane a significant look, Linda made her way to the end of the row and helped Bobbi collect the sheets of paper. The two of them then carried the ballots to a table at the back of the room and, as everyone crowded around to watch, began to count.

Linda finished tallying the results of her pile and then switched off with Bobbi. She and the secretary calculated their results independently and came up with the same numbers. Just to make sure, they did it again. The results were the same.

The ayes had it.

Three

"So what does this *really* mean for us? More work? More money? What?"

The janitorial staff—three full-time employees and two part-timers—stood in the empty cafeteria facing Enrique, the head custodian, who was focused rather too intently on putting sugar in his coffee. Carlos suddenly had the feeling that Enrique was just as out of the loop as they were, that he didn't know anything more about what was going to happen than the rest of them did.

"I have no idea," Enrique told them.

At least he admitted it.

"Just do your damn work the way you always did."

"But I need to know how this is going to affect *us,*" Mike pressed. "Right now, I can transfer to another school. Until this thing's official, we're still with the district. And if things look like they're going south, I can bail. But once we switch over, that's it. I'm stuck. We're *all* stuck. And maybe we're screwed. I just want to know where we stand."

"I don't know," Enrique said. He glanced around at the gathered custodians. "Any other complaints?"

Carlos and Rakeem looked at each other. "We don't like working here at night," Carlos said.

"Get another job," Enrique told them. "Anything else?"

"It's not that we don't like to work," Carlos explained. "We just don't like to work *here.* At *night.*"

"*Maricón,*" Enrique said dismissively.

Carlos tried to describe the situation in more detail, but the head custodian was having none of it. He ignored Carlos and began going over the items he'd written down on his clipboard. "Just sit there and be quiet," he ordered. "I have a lot to go over today."

The meeting ended early, before the day shift even ended, and since he wasn't scheduled to start work for another two hours, Carlos drove back home, called Maria to make a date for Friday, boiled some hot dogs for his dinner and watched the last half of *Escape from New York* before heading back to the school.

The sun was setting as he pulled into the staff parking lot, and the quad was dark with long shadows by the time he reached the janitorial-supply shed. Rakeem was waiting for him next to the cleaning carts. Carlos could tell from the expression on his face that he was unhappy, and he knew why before the other man even spoke.

"Shit. Why'd you have to say anything?" Rakeem asked.

"Come on, man. We talked about it."

"That doesn't mean you had to tell Enrique. Now we're on night shift till the day we fuckin' die."

"You *knew* I was gonna tell him. You *wanted* me to tell him."

"Yeah, well . . ."

" 'Sides, you didn't say nothing. Anyone's stuck on night shift, it's me. You're free and clear."

"Nah, bro. Wherever you go, I go. We're partners."

"Partners?"

"Yeah."

"You just don't wanna work with Mike."

Rakeem grinned. "This is true."

They flipped a coin for jobs, the way they always did, and Carlos lost. That meant Rakeem got to clean the office, the library and the downstairs classrooms, while Carlos had to take care of PE, art, band and the upstairs classrooms. "Great," Carlos mumbled.

Rakeem laughed loudly. "Have fun!"

Carlos pushed his cart across the quad, acutely aware of the silent, empty rooms in the minimally lit buildings around him. The clacking of the wheels and the rattling of the tools and cleaning supplies in the cart sounded loud, too loud, and he found himself hunching down a little, as though trying to minimize his presence and not draw attention to himself. Something had happened to the school over the summer. He'd worked here for eight years, the past three on night shift, and he had never had any qualms about being alone on the campus after dark. He wasn't a little kid, after all. But suddenly it started seeming to him that there was something odd and unnerving about this place, a creepiness he couldn't quite pinpoint but that made him feel very uncomfortable. Rakeem had noticed it, too. They'd even talked about it, although not directly at first. Carlos had casually mentioned one night, in an offhand manner, that he had been startled in one of the classrooms by a loud thump on the wall and when he'd gone next door to investigate, he hadn't been able to find the source of the noise. Rakeem had revealed that he'd nearly jumped out of his shoes a few nights prior when a pile of textbooks on a teacher's desk fell of their own accord, joking that he'd spilled his cleaning fluid and had ended up having to clean up his own mess instead of just the students'. When they found out a week or so later that both events had taken place in the same room, and that each of them had heard and seen *other* strange things around the school, they dropped all pretext of nonchalance and compared notes. Sure enough, they'd both experienced weird sights and sounds all over the campus. Which was why he'd wanted to tell Enrique—although he didn't really know what he'd expected his boss to do about it.

Now, of course, the head custodian thought they were the two biggest pansies on the planet. And the other workers were probably laughing behind their backs—or even planning some type of prank to scare them.

Rakeem was right. He should have kept his big mouth shut.

Carlos winced as the cart went over a crack in the concrete, clattering loudly. He glanced quickly around.

What was he afraid of?

That *something* hiding in the dark would know he was here.

Carlos pushed his cart up the slight incline to the music room. Using his master key, he opened the door and walked inside, flipping on the lights as he did so. Maybe it was his imagination, but the lights in the classrooms didn't appear to be as bright as they had been last year. None of the fixtures had been changed, but it seemed as if all over the school the illumination was dimmer than it had been before summer. He tried to tell himself that it was intentional, part of an effort to save electricity and cut down on energy expenses, but he couldn't make himself believe it.

Like members of the football team and the cheerleading squad, the kids in band returned to school a few weeks earlier than everyone else to practice. Carlos scanned the low risers on the left side of the room. Most of the instruments had been put away or taken home, but as always, a couple of them had been left out, and right in the center of the practice area, leaning against a metal folding chair, was a tuba. Carlos' gaze stopped on the instrument. Overhead lights glinted off the circle of gold metal that surrounded the black hole at the center of the large horn, and there seemed something mesmerizing about the sight. He found it hard to pull his attention away. He kept staring at that dark opening, and it was as though his gaze was being drawn *inside* it, his mind swirling down like water in a whirlpool.

He forced himself to look away. He felt chilled, frightened, and he decided that if he did not see any visible trash on the floor or furniture, if there were no major messes to clean up, he would leave. There didn't really need to be any mopping or dusting done. The room would survive one night without a thorough cleansing.

Mmmmmmmmmmmmm . . .

Carlos jumped at the sound. It was a low sustained note, and for a second he couldn't place it.

Then he realized it reminded him of someone blowing on a tuba.

He glanced quickly in that direction, but the instrument remained where it was, untouched, unmoving, its dark center in the midst of that gleaming gold seeming ever more eerie.

Mmmmmmmmmmmmm . . .

The noise continued, as though the invisible player possessed an unlimited breathing capacity and was planning to blow on the oversized horn forever.

Slowly, a drumbeat started, though there was no drum to be seen. Together, the sound of the two instruments blended and coalesced into a funereal dirge.

"Fuck this shit," Carlos said aloud, hoping tough words would prove to whoever—

whatever

—was in here that he was not scared.

But just the acknowledgment that he thought someone or something *was* in here, that he didn't believe the noises he was hearing were simply random night sounds, made him even more afraid, and with that unpausing dirge in the background, he turned tail, pushed his cleaning cart out of the music room and locked the door behind him. He left faster than he would have liked—it was obvious he was running away—but it still felt good to be outside again, out of the confines of that creepy chamber.

He hadn't brought his walkie-talkie, he realized.

What the hell was wrong with him? How did he expect to contact Rakeem if something . . . *happened*?

He stood there, listening, and was relieved to hear, from the area in front of the office, the squeak of Rakeem's cart and the other man's off-key voice as he rapped along to the music he heard on his headphones. Feeling not exactly foolish but decidedly less skittish than he had only a few seconds prior, Carlos glanced around the quad and decided to start his rounds with the PE department. The gym and connected sports buildings were out by themselves at the north end of the campus, separated from the other classrooms by the tennis courts and the pool, and though he usually left that area to the last, he didn't want to be out there by himself later at night. He'd rather get it over with in the early evening and spend the rest of the time doing the classrooms with Rakeem close by. If things went well, maybe he'd even get up the nerve to clean the music room.

He thought of the tuba and the slow beat of that invisible drum.

Maybe not.

The night air was cool. A soft breeze ruffled his hair as he made his way around the north edge of the quad to the open corridor that led between the social science classrooms. The corridor looked long. Much longer than usual. Like one of those movie scenes where the camera pulls back and makes an ordinary distance suddenly seem stretched out impossibly far. Ahead, through the arched opening at the opposite end, behind the darkened tennis courts and the fenced-in pool, the rounded bulk of the gym loomed before him.

Enrique was right, Carlos chided himself. *Maricón.*

He forced himself to continue on, walking forward at an even pace as though nothing in the world could faze him. He needed to get over these jitters or he'd have to find a new job. He couldn't spend every night at work scared of his own shadow.

If he could only get on day shift . . .

Carlos reached the PE department—what the school administration called the "sports complex"—and was about to go into the gym and give the wooden floor a once-over when he paused by the girls' locker room. All through his junior high and high school years, that tantalizingly off-limits chamber on the other side of the gym wall had been the holy grail for him and his buddies, the one place on earth they most often speculated on and fantasized about. Even now, the locker room had not entirely lost its allure, and whenever he went in to scrub the concrete floor or mop the tile, he couldn't help but think of all those hot young bodies in here during the day, naked, showering, dressing, undressing.

But something was wrong tonight.

There were voices coming from the locker room and there weren't supposed to be. Any summer practice had ended hours before, and at this time of evening, the PE department should have been as silent as a tomb.

Tomb.

Shit. Why had he thought of that word?

Carlos shivered. Sound could do weird things here in the PE department, he rationalized. The big echoey gym with its exposed beams and high ceiling, the tiled bunkerlike showers, even the coaches' offices with their windowed half walls, all distorted the resonance of voices and often made them sound as though they were coming from a room or section of building that they were not. So while there wasn't supposed to be anyone in here at this hour, it was entirely possible that one of the coaches had left a radio on in an office or something. There could be a perfectly innocent explanation for the fact that he heard people talking in the girls' locker room.

But he didn't think so, did he?

No.

Carlos tilted his head, put his ear closer to the crack between the double doors. He could hear both male and female voices, and there was something about their tone that made him pause, that kept him from opening the door and peeking inside to discover the source. They were not *just* talking; there were moans and yelps, grunts and gasps. It sounded like an orgy, but not one that he would ever care to join. Yes, he heard cries of pleasure and the light rhythmic slapping of skin, but there were other sounds as well, disturbing sounds, and male laughter that was harsh, cruel and far too loud. He tried to make out words, did his best to decipher what was being said, but everything was muffled. The only thing clear was that brutal laughter.

It sounded like his dad.

Carlos' heart tripped in his chest, its beat stumbling as he recognized the familiar cadence. His father used to laugh every time he'd hit him—which was often—

but he had not thought of that in years. Right before the old man had left for good, he'd beaten him with the buckle end of a belt and they'd both been naked and his dad had had a boner. Carlos had never told anyone about that, had successfully tamped down that memory and had not even recalled it himself until now, but the pain and humiliation caused by that act were still there and still stung, and they prompted him to take out his master key and yank open the locker room door.

Silence.

Silence and darkness.

He had not imagined what he'd heard, and he turned on the lights, holding tightly to the handle of a broom, ready to use it as a weapon should he encounter any sort of threat.

He walked forward slowly. At first glance, the locker room appeared to be empty, but he checked in the coaches' offices and went up and down each aisle anyway, looking for signs of anything amiss. He didn't expect to find anything—didn't *want* to find anything—but halfway down the center row, on the low flat bench between the two banks of temporary lockers, lay a pile of wet bloody towels.

From somewhere in the shower area came the sound of a loud slap, followed by a girl's scream.

And that deep harsh laughter.

His dad.

Carlos ran back the way he'd come, his fingers hurting from clutching the broom handle so tightly. He didn't bother to close or lock the door behind him, or even take his cart. He simply sped as fast as he could away from the "sports complex," running past the empty tennis courts, and through the open corridor between the social science classrooms—

Where he nearly knocked over Rakeem.

"Jesus!" Rakeem yelled. He had finished with the office and was heading over to the first-floor classes.

Finished with the office?

That was a one-hour job on a good day. It had been only about ten minutes. Carlos examined Rakeem's face, looking for any indication that something out of the ordinary might have happened. "You okay?" he asked.

"Sure." Rakeem would not meet his eyes. "What are *you* running away from?"

He wanted to tell the other man what he'd heard, what he'd seen—if anyone would believe him, Rakeem would—but there'd been a hint of derision in Rakeem's voice when he'd asked the question, and despite his suspicion that Rakeem had encountered something in the office, he thought about his partner's earlier admonition against talking to Enrique.

Carlos wiped the sweat from his forehead, breathed deeply. "Nothing," he lied. "Nothing. Everything's cool."

Four

"It's gonna be a long fuckin' day, dude."

Brad Becker turned to see his friend Ed Haynes behind him on the sidewalk. Ed was out of breath, so he'd obviously been running, but he'd already fallen into the slow, unhurried shuffle he favored when in public and was pretending that he just *happened* to have arrived at this section of concrete at the same time Brad himself had.

He smiled. Ed always tried so hard to be cool, but that was something that was just never going to happen. The two of them had been best buds since third grade, when they'd found themselves in the same class and discovered that they were both fanatic *Star Wars* fans, and in all the time he'd known Ed, his friend had never fit in with any crowd, had always been the geekiest guy in any gathering. Of course, he wasn't the most happening person himself, was just an ordinary, average member of the faceless majority. But Ed was not only a natural victim; he rubbed people the wrong way—and seemed to revel in it. Many times over the years, Brad had had to rescue his buddy from almost certain ass kickings by nearly every type of kid at school. Even girls.

This year would probably be no different.

"Heads up!" someone yelled, and from within a pack of students speeding by on bicycles came an apple that splattered on the sidewalk at Ed's feet.

Brad grinned. "And so it starts."

"Fuck," Ed said.

The two of them trudged forward toward Grayson Street and the school. Brad sighed. "It was a short summer, Charlie Brown."

"No duh. We're old. The years are going to start speeding by from here on in. Blink and you'll be middle-aged. Turn around again and you'll be ready for retirement."

"I won't even be eighteen for another month. *You* won't be eighteen until April."

"Still."

They turned the corner and saw, on the next block over, a yellow school bus turning into Tyler's parking lot.

"I hate school," Ed said.

"It's not so bad."

"My mom said that if I ditched any classes this year or drank alcohol at any parties or basically behaved like a normal high school senior, I wouldn't be able to buy that car I've been saving for."

"What a coincidence. Mine, too."

"Strange, isn't it, how our moms hate each other's guts, are complete opposites politically, but are exactly alike?"

Brad laughed. It was true. Ed's mom, a hard-core Rush Limbaugh Republican, refused to recycle or conserve energy because she didn't believe there was any such thing as global warming. Brad's mom, a dyed-in-the-wool liberal Democrat, refused to recycle or conserve energy because she considered the emphasis on such individual actions part of a conservative plot to keep the government from doing its duty and solving the problem itself. Neither of them bought into the think-globally-act-locally mind-set that their kids had learned at school and tried to bring home.

The two women were also simpatico when it came to donating money to charity. To Ed's mom, making donations was like paying taxes—she worked hard for her money; why should she give any of it away? To Brad's mom, it was another conservative plot—people *should* be taxed, and if individuals donated money, it kept *everyone* from having to make sacrifices.

The ironic end result of all these grand philosophical stances was that both moms acted the same in an unexpectedly large number of cases.

Like now.

"Ed, Ed, gives great head!" Larry Dodgeson shouted from a car filled with other jocks.

Without looking, Ed held up his middle finger.

"It's gonna be a long fuckin' day," he said again.

At school, Ed had to go to the office to straighten out a mistake on his class schedule, so Brad stopped off at the lunch area to see if any of his other friends were around. The cafeteria wasn't even open, and no one he liked was hanging around Senior Corner, so he walked through the quad, talked to a few kids he hadn't seen since last year, and met up with Ed again by the lockers. He had the same locker he'd always had—at Tyler, they were assigned to students as freshmen and remained theirs until graduation—and though there was a built-in combination lock, he put on his own as well, slipping its curved bolt through the provided opening after tossing in his backpack.

Ed's locker, one row down and two to the right, still had a big "EH" drawn on it in marking pen, though the lockers were supposed to have been cleaned during the summer.

The letters "EH" not only were Ed's initials but

stood for "educationally handicapped," a euphemism for students with learning disabilities.

Some people just couldn't get a break.

Ed took his lunch out of his backpack and put it on the small shelf near the top of the locker. "You heard about Van, didn't you? Van Nguyen?"

"What about him?" Brad said.

"He got kidnapped or something. There's a poster by the office."

"I saw that, too!"

Brad turned around to see Myla Ellis approaching from the walkway that led to the parking lot. His pulse quickened. At the end of last year, he and Myla had been kind of, almost, sort of semi-dating. She'd spent most of the summer with her father and his new wife in Denver, and though they'd e-mailed each other almost daily, there'd been a shift in the tone of her messages sometime in the middle of July. They'd suddenly become less personal, more formal, and he'd followed suit. He half assumed that she'd met someone over there in Denver, but he didn't ask, because he didn't want to know. She'd been back at her mom's for over a week already, but he hadn't called her and she hadn't called him, and right now Brad didn't know where they stood. He wiped his sweaty palms on his pants in as surreptitious a way as he knew how.

"Hey, Myla," Ed said. "Did you find a new boyfriend in Denver?"

Leave it to Ed to just blurt it out. Brad reddened, but he watched her face carefully to see the reaction. Myla blushed. "Of course not." She kept her eyes focused exclusively on Ed. "Did either of you?"

"No!" Brad said quickly.

She met his gaze for the first time, a look of relief on her face. "I thought—"

"No."

"*I* think you two have some issues to discuss. I'm out of here." Ed held up a hand. "Later days."

"See you in math," Brad said. He met his friend's eyes, hoped his gratitude showed on his face. He turned back toward Myla. "So . . . what's your first class?"

"PE."

"At eight in the morning? That's rough. Let me see your schedule." Before summer started, they'd both tried to arrange it so they'd have as many classes together as possible. Now they compared printouts. Sure enough, they each had third-period biology, fourth-period English and sixth-period economics. Their hands touched accidentally, and both quickly pulled away, folding their lists of classes and putting them back in their binders. Brad's skin tingled. All the feelings he'd had for Myla last semester were still there, though he'd known that already. "So you didn't meet anyone else—?" he began.

Just at that moment, the bell rang. Students started rushing to get to their homerooms, but the two of them remained where they were.

Myla shook her head. "Why would you even think that?"

He wanted to explain, wanted to talk it out, but she had to get all the way across campus to PE, and he had to go to the next building over for Spanish. "We'll discuss it later," he said. "You'd better get going. I'll see you in biology."

The disappearance of Van Nguyen was big news all over the school. It was mentioned in the morning announcements, and each teacher read a statement to his or her classroom from Van's parents and the police. The boy disappeared about a month ago after playing basketball at the school with his friend Kurt Jensen. They were going on the assumption that he was abducted, and everyone was warned to watch out for strangers, suspiciously parked vehicles or anything out of the ordinary.

Brad was surprised he hadn't learned of this until now. It had to have been on the news or in the newspaper.

He must have just spaced it out.

Kurt was in the same second-period Algebra II class as he and Ed, and Brad wanted to ask him the details of what had happened. So, apparently, did everyone else. A huge crowd gathered around him as Kurt entered the room, but he made it clear that he wasn't talking. He seemed genuinely freaked by what had occurred—even now, a month later—and he kept repeating that the police had told him not to talk about the case, although Brad knew that had to be a lie. There was something in the boy's refusal to speak that made him uneasy, and he had the feeling that there was more to the disappearance than either Kurt, the police or Van's parents were telling.

His friend Brian Brown was on the student newspaper, and Brad decided that when he saw him, he would suggest to the reporter that he interview Kurt for a story on the kidnapping.

"You think he's dead?" Ed whispered when Mr. Connor turned his back and started to write on the blackboard. "Seems like something would've turned up by now if he wasn't."

"I don't know," Brad said. He looked out the window of the classroom and saw a PE class shooting baskets on the outdoor courts at the edge of the field. From this angle, the gray metal backboards resembled nothing so much as tombstones on poles.

He didn't like those basketball courts, he decided.

And he wished he'd signed up for tennis.

* * *

At lunch, Brad and Myla met up with Ed by the lockers before heading over to Senior Corner. Since they were all seniors now, they thought it would be fun to eat at the small grassy area that they'd been barred from entering since freshman year. But the jocks and the cheerleaders had taken over the picnic table in the center as well as every available inch of space on the three-foot-high wall surrounding the spot, and they were unable to find a place to sit.

They ended up eating in their usual place, on one of the tables outside the cafeteria. Myla's friends Cindy, Reba and Cheryl were also there, and though neither Brad nor Ed was a big fan of the student-council girls, at least they *were* girls, and it was cooler hanging with them than with the dateless losers who would otherwise have been their lunchtime companions.

Brad ate his turkey sandwich and thought about the day so far. Math sucked, biology was okay and Spanish was Spanish, but he was excited about English. Besides having Myla in the class and being able to sit next to her, he'd been inspired by Mrs. Webster's choice of reading material. They were going to be tackling Günter Grass, Kurt Vonnegut and John Fowles this semester, and something about those choices made him feel smart and adult, as though he was really being prepared for college.

Ed was eating his lunch: Nacho Doritos and a Dr Pepper. "So," he asked, "how do all of you on the student council feel about this charter thing?"

When no one answered and it became obvious from the expressions on their faces that they were afraid to express an opinion, he added, "Because I think it sucks."

"Is your mom going to volunteer?" Brad asked. "They're supposed to volunteer *forty* hours."

Ed snorted. "My mom? Shit no. She's planning to blow it off. Although my guess is she'll have to pay the fine. She's pissed off about the whole thing." He did a dead-on impression of her. " 'I pay taxes to support public schools and now they expect me to work there, too? Or pay tuition like a private school?' " He grinned. "I told her to think of it as a user fee. She damn near attacked me.

"My mom loves user fees," he explained to Myla. "Hates taxes but loves user fees. Hmmm," he said, stroking his chin as if in deep thought. "Maybe I'll tell her it's called an 'education tax.' That should get her good and riled up."

"My mom *says* she'll volunteer," Brad said. "We'll see if that happens."

"It does seem weird," Myla offered, "that they can charge people to go to a public school. It seems illegal to me. Isn't everyone entitled to a free education? And what about poor kids? What if their parents work and don't have time to volunteer, yet they can't afford to fork over the four hundred dollars a year?" She shook her head. "Four hundred dollars. That's a lot of money." She looked over at Cheryl, the Associated Student Body president. "Maybe we should bring this up in a meeting, see if we can do something about it."

The other girl looked uncomfortable. "I don't think that's really our place."

"Not our place? The students elected us! It's our job to look out for their interests!"

"I ran for treasurer because it'll look good on my résumé," Reba said. "I'm not out to change the world. If parents don't like having to volunteer or pay money, let them go to the administration and do something about it." She paused. "Besides, I think it's good that parents are being forced to become more involved."

"Yeah," Cindy agreed.

"*Forced* to volunteer," Ed said. "Isn't that one of those 'jumbo shrimp' things? What're they called?"

"Oxymorons," Brad said.

"Yeah. Like 'effective student council.' "

"Why are you even here?" Reba said with disgust. "Find your own table."

Ed gathered up his lunch sack and tipped an invisible hat. "Ladies," he said by way of farewell.

Brad smiled and got up to follow his friend. "See you sixth period," he told Myla.

"Period!" Ed repeated loudly.

"Eww!" Cindy and Reba cried out together.

Brad laughed as they took their food to another recently relinquished table on the other side of the lunch area. "Making new friends everywhere you go."

"It's my job. How did Myla ever get caught up with those bitches? In fact, how did she ever get caught up in you? She's way out of your league, you know."

"She was elected; that's how she got hooked up with them. As for me, I guess she just has an eye for quality."

"Yeah. Right." Ed craned his neck to look over Brad's shoulder. "What's going on over there?"

He turned to see a crowd of students gathering around the outdoor basketball courts. There were always a few fanatics who actually spent their lunch hours shooting hoops on the asphalt, but this was different. It was obvious that something had happened. One kid ran back toward the lunch area, shouting for a friend of his to come and see what was going on. "A bird, man! It just flew right into the backboard! And two more right after it! Boom, boom, boom! The second one actually bounced off and went through the hoop!"

Ed looked at Brad. "Did you hear that? Freaky. Let's check it out." He stood.

Brad shook his head. "I've seen dead birds before. I'm just going to finish my lunch."

"Back in a sec." Ed hurried off to join the growing crowd, but Brad did not even turn to watch.

Because he was afraid to watch.

He was not a superstitious guy, and maybe his mind was just running along these tracks after hearing the story of Van's disappearance. He didn't know Van all that well, but it was possible that he was more affected than he thought by what had happened to the boy. Whatever the reason, the basketball courts made him uneasy, and he remained in place, eating the banana he'd packed for dessert, while more and more students rushed over to see the suicidal birds.

Five

Although Linda arrived at school over an hour early and figured she'd be the first person on campus, Jody was already there. Not only that, but the principal, instead of being in her office, was standing alone at the far end of the empty hallway when Linda went upstairs to her classroom. The sight of the other woman gave her a start, and Linda laughed to cover her nervousness. "I didn't expect to see anyone here," she called out.

Jody said nothing but stared silently for another beat, then turned and walked down the stairs to her right.

Weird, Linda thought. But as far as she was concerned, the principal had been acting weird ever since this charter thing had come up, ever since that school board meeting. It was as if the open, flexible, easygoing woman with whom she'd been working for the past several years had been replaced by an identical clone, a soulless pod person, an evil twin. She thought of how Jody had looked at the opposite end of the hallway, surveying the corridor before her. It reminded her of something, and as Linda unlocked and opened the door to her classroom, she figured out what it was: a prison warden. Standing solemnly against the far wall, the principal had looked like a warden inspecting rows of cells in a jail, and although the school year had just started, Linda wondered if that might prove to be an apt metaphor.

She walked over to the windows and looked down at the quad below. On the sidewalk between the trees, she saw Jody striding purposefully toward the office, looking neither left nor right but keeping her focus straight ahead. The campus was empty save for her—no other teachers, no students, no staff—and Linda was glad that the two of them worked in separate buildings. She did not want to be alone with that woman.

As though sensing her thoughts, Jody suddenly stopped walking and swiveled around, looking directly up at the window. Linda blanched and backed up, not wanting to be seen, *afraid* of being seen, though she knew such a reaction was stupid and childish. It was only when she reached her desk that she realized she'd been holding her breath, and she let out all the air in a great whoosh.

Her heart was pounding crazily, as if she'd just had an encounter with some deadly beast, and she could barely hear over the thumping of blood in her temples. She was trying to listen for the sound of doors opening or footsteps in the building, worried that Jody might be coming back.

Worried?

Why should she be worried? She was in her classroom, doing her job. The mere fact that she was hiding, trying to stay away from the windows, listening for footsteps, was ludicrous. Frank would be laughing his ass off if he could see her right now.

But try as she might to see the ridiculousness of the situation, she could not fully disengage herself. She did not know why, but she was nervous, frightened, and it took her several more minutes to gather enough courage to move forward and look out the window once again. She half expected Jody to be standing in exactly the same spot, unmoving, staring up at her, but when she glanced down, the quad was empty.

Her gaze moved on to the small one-story building housing the office. Even before today, the vibe in the office had been strange this year. Although it was not something she would ever admit to anyone, she felt uncomfortable just going in there and checking her mailbox each morning.

Most of that was due to Bobbi. The secretary acted almost like a coprincipal these days. She'd gotten a title change and a subsequent pay bump—officially she was now "administrative coordinator" rather than "secretary"—and it had definitely gone to her head. Her job was still to answer phones, type memos and act as Jody's toady, but she seemed to think she was ruler of all she surveyed. "Power corrupts," Steve Warren said when the subject arose, a sentiment echoed by several other teachers, and that about summed it up.

For Linda, the office had become a very unpleasant place. Bobbi really had been taking notes at that initial staff meeting, or so it seemed, and she was definitely holding grudges. Whenever Linda went in to pick up her mail or use the copier, the secretary—

administrative coordinator

—would stop whatever she was doing and simply stare. Any phone conversation was instantly put on hold, all chatting with the other secretaries, clerks or administrators halted, and the woman would glare silently at Linda until she was out of the office. Linda had taken to going in with Diane or another friend in order to check her mailbox, and as cowardly as it was, she'd sent her TA down yesterday morning to make copies of a homework assignment.

Now it was going to be even worse.

She looked over at the office building and tried to imagine what Jody was doing in there right now. What stuck in her brain was the strangeness of the woman's behavior at the end of the hallway and the creepiness of the way she'd stopped on the sidewalk to stare up at the window. The image in Linda's mind was of the principal sitting perfectly still in a completely darkened office, smiling evilly, glowing eyes focused on nothing that could be seen by mortal eyes.

Shivering, Linda turned away. She really did have work to do this morning. And the quicker she got down to it and stopped overdramatizing every little thing that happened to her, the better off she'd be.

A carton of books had come in yesterday—class copies of Kurt Vonnegut's *Cat's Cradle*—and it was sitting next to several reams of paper that she had yet to unpack. She put the paperbacks in her bookcase, then placed the paper in the supply cabinet. The nighttime custodians had erased everything on both blackboards, though she'd left a note instructing them to leave it all as is, and she painstakingly rewrote everything all over again before settling down at her desk and treating herself to a breakfast bar.

It seemed quiet all of a sudden. Too quiet. She hadn't really noticed while she'd been busy and moving around, but now that she was sitting still, the silence seemed oppressive. She was acutely aware that she was thc only person in the building, and she walked over to the door and locked it.

She needed some noise. She kept a portable CD player on a shelf behind her desk. Not an iPod or one of those small devices with attached headphones, but a cheap boom-box-looking thing she'd picked up at The Store several years back. She put in a reissued Nazz CD that Frank had given her for her birthday in June, and although she'd intended to spend this time making lesson plans, she found herself just sitting there and listening to the music. As a teenager, she'd owned the original vinyl album, and now hearing it again, she was brought back to those days. Even then, it had been a relic of another era, the music of an earlier generation, but that had been part of its appeal. She'd never dated much until her senior year in high school, and after her best friend, Maddy, had moved in the middle of ninth grade, she'd felt lonely and isolated. It was music that had saved her, that had let her know she was not alone. Particularly music from the late 1960s and early 1970s. She'd spent hour after hour in her room by herself, listening to records, and those songs had spoken to her. Albums like *Nazz* had not only understood and reflected back her feelings but promised something better. Art from an earlier age, it had contained the innocence of that time period but had also pointed the way to a tomorrow that was better than today.

Listening to the same tunes now made her feel slightly sad, but it was a sweet sadness, and it made her think about the importance of art, and how much music and literature had meant to her over the years. That gave her an idea, and she decided to set aside her lesson plans for the day and have a discussion in each of her classes not about what they were studying but why. In these test-mad days, where parents were concerned about educational competition with other countries and politicians downplayed anything that did not lead directly to a specific job track, she thought it would be a good idea to talk about the importance of subjects that fed the soul rather than the résumé.

Her first class of the day was twelfth graders, and that was perfect. They were the ones about to go out into the big wide world, and they were the ones who most needed to think about the why of things rather than just the what.

She shut off the music and unlocked her door. The campus was coming alive now. She heard voices and footsteps in the hall, and when she glanced through the window at the quad down below, she saw that it was filling with students. Soon they would be coming in to class.

She was safe.

That was an odd reaction.

But an honest one.

She'd discovered this morning that she did not like being alone on campus anymore, and Linda decided that maybe she'd talk to Diane and the two of them could start carpooling together every day instead of just every once in a while.

The students were in their seats by the time the second bell rang. There was one absence—a girl named Olivia whom she could not yet put a face to—and after the announcements and the pledge, Linda told everyone to put down their pens and pencils. They were just going to talk for a while. No note taking.

She leaned against her desk. "What is the purpose of art?" she asked the class, and was met by a sea of blank faces.

"I thought this was an *English* class," Antonio Gonzalez piped up.

"I'm not talking about art in terms of painting or sculpture, but art in general. The visual arts, of course, but also music and"—she spread her hands dramatically—"literature. As in . . . English!" She looked again around the room. "So why do we need art? What do you think it is about human beings that makes art a necessary and important ingredient in our lives?"

The conversation did not go the way she'd imagined. In fact, it wasn't a conversation at all. More like a monologue. Or a lecture. She ended up *telling* them why art was important, though her goal had been to lead them to discover it for themselves. Linda told herself that maybe it was too early in the year for something free-form like this. The kids were just getting to know her; she was just getting to know them; the sense of trust and intimacy that would be theirs later in the semester had not yet been established. But then she realized that she did know most of these students. Three-fourths of them had been in one of her junior or sophomore classes. Unfamiliarity with one another was not a legitimate excuse.

No, the fact was that her students simply didn't want to be led along the path she was trying to take them. Her entire premise seemed foreign to them, and by the time second period rolled around, she had abandoned her attempt at discussion and returned to her original lesson plan.

It was discouraging, how little kids today thought about anything beyond the facts and figures placed directly in front of them. For all the commercials, movies and television shows stressing the importance of thinking outside the box, very few young people possessed the ability to do so. And schools were not teaching those skills. It was a world of standardized learning now, and as an educator she was expected to teach to the test so their school's scores would go up and they would get more money. It almost made her think that maybe this charter experiment wasn't such a bad idea if it gave teachers more latitude to introduce alternative methods of instruction.

Back in her day, a knowledge of obscure trivia was

the key to intellectual respect, and she and her friends had attempted to one-up each other by finding the most arcane minutiae about literature or music and dropping them casually into conversation as though they were something that everyone should know. Such behavior had been silly but also exhilarating, as they'd explored new worlds and delved deeply into subjects to which they had not previously been exposed. Of course, she'd learned as she got older that it was the experience of art that mattered, not the useless tangential facts that proved to peers that one had read a book or been exposed to a specific work. There was nothing phonier or more pretentious than someone posing as an intellectual by aping the opinions of others. But these days, the Internet seemed to have rendered even that trivial pursuit obsolete as students looked up information on a need-to-know basis, using it when necessary but making no effort to retain any of it. They lived in a Wikipedia world, where knowledge was no longer required and only the ability to access it mattered.

Maybe she was wrong. Maybe this was better.

But she didn't think so.

At lunch, Linda went to the teachers' lounge, as she always did. The lounge was located in a windowless room adjacent to the Little Theater, which had always been an inconvenient pain in the butt to everyone except the drama instructor. But now she was happy about the lounge's out-of-the-way location, because it meant that the administrators remained in the office to eat. And her goal this year was to avoid Jody as much as possible.

Steve Warren and Ray Cheng were sitting around one of the tables when she arrived, unwrapping their lunches. Yvonne Gauthier was heating up a Lean Cuisine in the microwave. Coincidentally, they were talking about the importance of art.

Had students in their classes brought it up? she wondered. Maybe her attempted discussion this morning had had some effect after all. The thought cheered her.

Her colleagues, however, were in the same frame of mind that she'd been in after first period, discouraged by the current generation's cultural illiteracy. Steve shook his head. "There's no intellectual currency anymore. The whole system's breaking down. Used to be that if you name-dropped the right authors and musicians, books and movies, you could fool everyone into thinking you were smart. Kids today don't even know enough to know what they don't know. References just fly over their heads, and they're not impressed by anything. It's depressing."

"Movies used to be cool," Ray admitted. "Foreign films, old comedies. Very impressive, especially for a first date."

"Remember, in the early seventies, when we were in high school?" Steve asked. The two of them had grown up in Anaheim and had known each other forever. "Remember how we used to go to that revival theater and see Marx Brothers movies and W. C. Fields and Laurel and Hardy?"

Ray nodded.

"Remember how *old* they seemed?"

Ray chuckled. "Yeah."

"Well, there was only, like, a thirty years' difference between us and them. The movies from that time, the *new* movies like *Holy Grail, Tommy* or *Annie Hall*? Those are just as far away to students today as W. C. Fields was to us."

"You're right," Ray said as he did the math. He shook his head. "Shit. We *are* old."

The conversation faded away as more teachers entered the lounge, and Linda missed the chance to jump in and add her own two cents' worth. Suzanne Johnson mentioned to someone, in a voice filled with barely concealed disgust, that she needed to ask Jody for a day off next week to attend her brother-in-law's wedding. Before this semester, they'd never had to ask permission to use personal days.

"Has anyone seen Jody this morning?" Linda asked. She was curious if anyone else thought that the principal was behaving strangely.

There were shaking heads all around.

"I saw her before third period," Yvonne offered. "She was walking into the library."

"Seems like she's been MIA more often since we turned charter," Suzanne said. "Anyone else notice that?"

"Maybe she's busy," Steve suggested.

"Doing what?"

"I don't know. Charter stuff."

Linda wanted to share what had happened this morning before school started, what she'd seen, what she'd felt, but the truth was, she hadn't really seen anything, and her feelings would sound just plain stupid if stated aloud. Her anticharter sentiments were already well-known, so anything she might say that did not have facts to back it up would probably come off as sour grapes.

And might very well find its way back to the principal.

It was hard to tell where sympathies lay these days.

Mary Mercer walked into the lounge looking depressed and out of sorts. "Hey, Grumpy," Ray said. "Where's Snow White?"

"Shut up," the French teacher told him, and her tone of voice made it clear that she was not in the mood to joke around.

Linda walked over to her. "What is it?"

"I don't know. Nothing, I hope."

"What?"

"Nothing."

Mary swung her eyes toward the couch, where Nina Habeck and Ken Myers were discussing the new history textbooks, and Linda understood that the French teacher didn't want to talk in front of them. "Later," she said softly, putting a hand on Mary's arm.

Later came after school in the women's restroom, where she came across Mary dabbing at her red eyes with a tissue in front of one of the mirrors over the sinks.

"All right," Linda said. "Spill it."

The other woman just looked at her.

"Come on. There's no one else here."

She shook her head.

"Mary."

"It's . . . Dennis. I . . ." She took a deep breath. "I'm sorry. I can't. It's just too . . . too tabloid TV."

"What is it?" Linda asked softly.

Mary blinked into the mirror. "I found e-mails. On his computer."

"No!"

"Yes! Some whore named Tina." She dabbed at her eyes again. "I mean, maybe it's nothing—maybe I'm overreacting. . . .

"No," she said firmly. "I'm not. I read those e-mails and they were what they were."

"Explicit?"

"Oh yes." Mary's eyes held a hopeful, questioning look that made her appear almost childlike. "But a lot of people do that these days, right? I mean, a lot of times it's just fiction, fantasy. They're not actually having affairs with the people they chat with. They're just . . . writing. Right?"

"I wouldn't put up with it," Linda said honestly.

"I can't live with it either. That's what's got me so upset." She looked like she was about to cry again.

"Have you confronted him?"

"Oh, I couldn't do that! He'd know I read his e-mails. He'd know I broke his trust."

"Broke *his* trust? He's sneaking around behind your back writing sex letters to strangers."

Mary looked down. "I know."

Linda stared at the other teacher. She had no advice to give, no words of wisdom, and the terrible truth was that deep down she was just thankful it was not happening to her, that she did not have to face such a problem. "What are you going to do?" she asked.

"I have no idea."

"Even if you don't want to admit you were spying on his e-mails, you need to get this out in the open. You need to talk it out."

Mary reached over and touched her arm. "Thank you, Linda."

"For what?"

"Listening."

By the time she arrived home, Linda had a headache. "So how ends your first week at the charter school?" Frank asked from the kitchen as she stepped through the door into the living room. He was grinning, but Linda found nothing funny about the question, and the look she gave him wiped the smile completely off his face.

He walked around the end of the counter, wiping his hands on a kitchen towel. "That bad, huh?" he said sympathetically.

She sighed. "No, not really. But it's definitely different from last year. And not in a good way." She skipped her after-school session with Mary, but told him about Jody's creepy behavior, her own failure to engage the kids in an off-topic discussion, and the general feeling of unease that she had about Tyler, including the cold shoulder and hostile stares she received every time she went into the office.

"Like I said before, you could transfer to another school if you really feel that strongly about it."

Linda shook her head. "I'm not sure I can, actually. It may not be allowed under our charter. Besides, this is my school. I'd rather stay and fight than just run away and abandon it."

"I didn't realize you were so patriotic."

"Despite all your talk, you didn't move to Canada during the George Bush years, did you?"

"No," he admitted.

"Same thing."

"There's no chance that you could be laid off or fired, is there? I mean, you're obviously on their list, and you have little or no recourse—"

"If they ever tried something like that, I'd have them in court so fast their heads would spin. They have no cause. I'm a good teacher, I have ten years of positive evaluations to prove it and I have witnesses from both sides of the aisle. They don't have a leg to stand on."

"Still . . ."

"What brought this up?"

Frank sighed. "Word is that they're going to be outsourcing a lot of the company's IT functions. So my job's not exactly secure. And at least one of us needs to be gainfully employed."

"Are you sending out résumés?"

"Not yet. This is just scuttlebutt. It might not even be true. Who knows? Maybe it's the exact opposite, and I'm in line for a raise or a promotion. In which case, putting feelers out would stop those chances cold. So I'm just going to wait and see."

She kissed him and tried to smile. "We both will," she said.

Six

Kate Robinson sorted through the contents of the white folder-sized envelope that Tony had brought home from school and left on the kitchen counter for her. An appeal to parents to join the PTA . . . a discount offer from a private company offering math tutorials . . . a notice that Back-to-School Night was coming up and that attendance was mandatory for all parents . . . an ad for Target . . . a Coca-Cola coupon.

When she'd first received notification near the end of summer that Tyler High was going to become a charter school, Kate had been happy. She'd been reading about the academic successes of charters in the *Los Angeles Times,* including an editorial suggesting that even more schools in the L.A. district should be granted charter status, and she thought it a good thing that Tony's school was following suit. Now she was not so sure. She didn't like the commercial tie-ins that were popping up, the growing emphasis on fund-raising and other peripherals that had little or nothing to do with education.

She also didn't like the fact that parents were now required to donate either their time or money to the high school. She and Tony's father had been forced to sign a contract stating that they would volunteer to work at Tyler for a minimum of twenty hours each semester. If they did not sign it, Tony would have to attend one of the district's traditional high schools: either Washington, which was in a bad area, or Fillmore, which was on the other side of the city and very inconvenient to get to in the morning. Such a thing seemed illegal, making parents sign a contract to a public school, but it was up to parents with more money and initiative than she to try to fight it.

One of the papers in the envelope was for Tony, not her, and it was a pledge of allegiance to the school. Starting next week, said the attached memo, they were going to be replacing the traditional flag salute with this more site-specific version. She read the words:

I pledge allegiance
to the school
of John Tyler High.
And to the principles for which it stands.
One student body, under Charter,
With rules and regulations for all.

That, she decided, was very odd. She read the pledge again. It was fairly generic and didn't say much, but there was something about it she didn't like, an underlying assumption that the school was more important than anything else and that students' allegiance should be to Tyler High rather than to the nation.

That didn't sit right with her.

Kate finished looking through the envelope. Tony's art teacher, Mr. Swaim, had sent a note home asking if parents could help out by coming in tomorrow and, following his instructions, prepare the materials for various projects his classes would be working on later in the week. He needed two parents from each period.

Since assisting would help satisfy her volunteer requirement, she quickly e-mailed the instructor that she would be happy to show up and do whatever needed to be done, and he e-mailed back later that evening that she should meet him at the art room a half hour before school started at eight.

The next morning, she drove while Tony walked. He was at the stage where he didn't even want to acknowledge that he *had* parents, and he made her promise that they would arrive separately and that she would pretend not to recognize him if she saw him on campus.

All volunteers were required to check in at the office, and Kate stood in an unexpectedly long line before signing her name in a log and receiving a "volunteer pass" from one of the secretaries. Not knowing where the art room was, she asked directions, and when she made her way to the west side of the campus, she was surprised to see quite a few adults standing on the small patch of grass outside the classroom. There were over a dozen women and one man waiting for the art teacher—it made sense: two parents from each period, seven periods total—but seeing so many made her wonder what they were all going to do. It certainly didn't take fourteen people to cut construction-paper shapes or punch holes in cardboard or do whatever simple prep work the instructor had planned.

The parents seemed to be divided into two distinct cliques: a group of stay-at-home moms who had apparently known one another forever and who acknowledged her arrival with cursory insincere greetings before returning to their talk of scrapbooking; and a smaller but even more annoying pack of tattooed alterna-parents who completely ignored her existence. She ended up bonding with a grandmother named Lillian who was happily sorting through the contents of an oversized canvas bag, looking for her crochet needles. They talked as easily as old friends until the door to the art room opened and the teacher bade them all come inside.

"You know," the older woman confided, "I'm not sure if my being here even counts. According to my granddaughter Megan's contract, her *parents* are supposed to volunteer. I don't know if I'm allowed to substitute."

"Talk to the people in the office. They should be flexible on something like this."

"*Should* be. But that doesn't mean they *will* be. So far, my daughter is not very impressed with this charter school, and I have to say I agree."

One of the alterna-moms, a ferret-faced woman wearing camouflage pants and a faux Ramones tour T-shirt, pushed past them into the room and gave Lillian a bitchy look of disapproval. Kate was about to say something, but her new friend must have guessed her intentions because she met Kate's eyes and shook her head with a sad smile, imploring her to let it go.

Once they were all inside, the door closed behind them, Mr. Swaim spoke quickly. "I'm teaching seven art classes this year, from Beginning Painting and Drawing to Advanced Pottery. Ordinarily, that would mean that I'd have seven separate sets of curricula, but since Tyler High is now a charter school, I've been given the leeway to institute interdisciplinary course work." He held up a hand in anticipation of complaints. "I will still be teaching drawing in the drawing class, painting in the painting class, pottery in the pottery class, et cetera. But, periodically, I will be combining lesson plans and having the students produce artwork from the same source in their various media. First up will be the human form. To this end, I am looking for women willing to pose this Friday for each of my seven periods."

"Pose?" one of the alterna-moms said.

"Yes."

"In—?"

"In the nude, yes."

Kate stared at the teacher, stunned, not sure she'd heard what she thought she'd heard.

"Those are our *children*!" exclaimed an outraged scrapbooker.

"Don't worry," Mr. Swaim assured her. "I won't be asking *you* to pose." He addressed the other parents. "Those not posing I would ask to prepare materials for another upcoming project in which—"

"I'm telling the principal." The mother who had voiced the complaint turned suddenly and left the room, followed by three others of her group. Kate stood rooted in place and looked over at Lillian, who appeared as shell-shocked as she herself felt.

Mr. Swaim cleared his throat. "As I started to say, those who are not chosen to pose for a class will be prepping materials: cutting drawing paper to size, refilling glue bottles, measuring clay, mixing paint."

"*Chosen* to pose?" The ferret-faced woman stepped forward. "How are you going to pick?" She smiled slyly. "Do you want us to audition?"

"As a matter of fact, yes. This is why I asked you to meet me here before school." He pointed to the lone father, to Lillian and to one of the scrapbooking moms who had inexplicably remained. "You are out. The rest of you, take off your clothes. Panties, too."

There was a mass exodus from the room. Kate's heart was pounding crazily with fear and embarrassment—

he wanted to see her naked

—and she hurriedly followed Lillian and most of the other parents out the door. From the corner of her eye, she saw that the ferret-faced woman and two other alterna-moms had remained behind. One was already pulling her T-shirt over her head.

"I don't . . . ," Lillian began, then shook her head, at a loss for words.

"That guy's going to be fired," Kate said firmly. "I'll make sure of it. That's illegal, what he's doing."

She and Lillian followed the parade of outraged parents to the office. When they walked in, the principal was already standing next to the front counter, being yelled at by those first four parents who had stalked out of the art room outraged. The woman looked calmly over at Kate, meeting her eyes. Kate had never met the principal before but knew instantly that she did not like her. She operated on instinct, trusting her initial reactions or her woman's intuition or whatever you wanted to call it, and she knew immediately that Principal Hawkes was one of those inflexible, intractable I'm-always-right-and-you're-always-wrong bitches that she had made it her personal mission to avoid whenever possible. A quick glance over at Lillian told her that the old lady had the same reaction.

But Kate pressed forward, joined the crowd and stated that not only was Mr. Swaim asking moms to pose naked in front of their children's classmates, but he wanted them to *audition* by taking off their clothes. "Right now," she said, "there are mothers stripping in his room!"

The principal nodded noncommittally as the parents expressed their anger. Finally, when there was a pause, she spoke. "I understand your concern, and if any of you choose not to participate in Mr. Swaim's project, I completely understand. And you *will* get volunteer credit for the time you spent on campus this morning." Her expression hardened. "But I'll tell you right now that one thing I will *not* do is impinge on the academic freedom of my instructors. One of the reasons we became a charter school was to get away from the school district's small-minded micromanagement and avoid outside influence on our curricula. I'm not about to let a group of prudish parents dictate artistic standards to our highly trained and eminently capable staff." She glared at them. "You can transfer your children to other classes, provided we have the room. That is your right. But if the sight of a bare breast in an artistic setting is so upsetting to them at this age, then they are going to have a very difficult transition to adulthood."

"It's not just a bare breast," Kate said angrily. "He wanted us to take off our underwear. Do you understand what that means? Fifteen- and sixteen-year-old boys will be looking at women's crotches. Vaginas. Does that seem appropriate to you?"

"I—"

"*Vaginas*. The vaginas of their mothers or their friends' mothers. In class. With your support. Tell me now, do you think that's okay?"

The principal's eyes met hers, and Kate did not like what she saw in those dark brown orbs. There was a hardness that she had expected, but below that, beyond that, was something deeper and darker that she did not understand and that for some reason frightened her. "As I said," the principal reiterated in a voice surprisingly calm, "you are free to transfer your child to another class if you feel that Mr. Swaim's class is not a good fit. Our office staff will be glad to assist you." She smiled insincerely. "If there is nothing else, I must get back to work. Please excuse me."

And with that, the principal was gone, leaving the parents even angrier and more distraught than when they'd first come in. The person at the nearest desk, a slim conservatively attired woman with the plastic smile of a religious convert or a commissioned salesperson, stood up and walked over to them. BOBBI EVANS, her name tag read, ADMINISTRATIVE COORDINATOR. "How may I help you?" she asked.

Kate was the third mother to transfer her child out of Mr. Swaim's art class—to an elective titled The Blue and the Gray, about the Civil War—and she walked out of the office feeling both stunned and angry. Lillian had already left, since, as a grandmother, she had no jurisdiction over her granddaughter and needed to get her daughter to come to school and make any changes to the girl's schedule, and Kate headed out to the parking lot alone. The office was supposed to call Tony in and inform him of the substituted class, but Kate had no faith that anyone there would do so, and she vowed to check with her son when he arrived home and make sure the transfer had gone through.

As she reached the parking lot, Kate saw another woman walking from the classrooms to the cars and recognized her as the ferret-faced mom who had remained behind in Mr. Swaim's class to "audition." The woman recognized her as well, and she looked over at Kate, smoothed her fake T-shirt over her fake breasts and smiled proudly.

Seven

A group of eight or nine students was gathered in a circle around the flagpole when Brad, Myla and Ed arrived at school. All the students, boys and girls, were holding hands, their heads bowed. Mr. Carr, the band teacher, was leading them in prayer.

"I thought there was supposed to be separation of church and state," Ed said loudly as they walked past.

". . . and bless the unbelievers," Mr. Carr intoned for his benefit, "that they might know Your goodness and take strength from it."

"I hate religious assholes," Ed said.

"Hey!" Myla objected. "I'm religious!"

"You know what I mean."

She stopped walking. "No. I don't."

Ed looked toward Brad. "Help me, dude."

"I think he means the hypocrites." Brad gestured to the group of students in the prayer circle behind them. "Like them."

Ed nodded. "Exactly."

"Not all of them are hypocrites."

"Come on," Brad said.

"What do you mean, 'come on'?"

"You can't be serious."

"I'm very serious. Ashley goes to my church, and she's great."

Ed snorted.

Brad found himself getting annoyed. "They're passing around a petition to post the Ten Commandments in the library."

"So?"

"So why does it always seem that the people who want the Ten Commandments posted everywhere are always pro–death penalty and prowar? I mean, 'Thou shalt not kill.' That's one of the big ten, right?"

"Yes," Myla said cautiously.

"So killing's bad, according to them. But if you kill someone, then *you* should be killed, because it's wrong to kill. Of course, if there's a war and the government tells you to kill people in another country, then you can kill all you want. Men, women *and* children. In fact, the more foreigners you kill, the better. If you kill a lot of them, you'll even be rewarded with medals. But, of course, when you come back, you can't kill anymore. If you kill someone then, you should be killed. Because killing's bad."

Myla shook her head. "It's not that simple."

"Isn't it?"

Ed grinned. "Ever think of trying out for the debate team? You got a knack, dude."

Myla started walking. "I don't want to talk about this anymore."

Cindy and Reba were standing by Myla's locker when they reached it. Both frowned as they noticed her companions. "We have to find Cheryl," Reba said. "Something's come up."

"What is it?"

The two student-council members said nothing but looked over at Brad and Ed.

"We get the hint," Brad said. He touched Myla's shoulder, giving it a soft squeeze. "I'll see you later."

"Now, how are we going to disrupt the Harvest Festival?" Ed said loudly as they walked away.

"Asshole!" Cindy yelled after him.

"Is that the best you can do?" he called back.

"Leave 'em alone," Brad said. "What are you, in third grade?"

"They started it."

"Not really."

"Well, they deserved it."

Brad grinned. "I'll give you that one."

They walked to their respective lockers, putting in and taking out what they needed, then met up again at the corner of the building. There was still another ten minutes until first period, so they walked out to the quad. Over by the library, Myla, Cindy and Reba had found Cheryl and were engaged in what appeared to be a heated discussion.

"So," Ed asked, "are you guys ever going out on, like, an official date?"

"Saturday," Brad said.

"All right!" Ed held up his hand in an embarrassing high-five position, but Brad ignored it. Ed dropped the hand. "You want my advice?"

"About what?"

"You want it or not?"

"Okay, tell me what you're going to tell me."

"Whip it out. In the middle of the date. Whip it out. Chicks love that. They see a big hairy one dangling down in front of their face, they can't help themselves. They have to suck it."

Brad rolled his eyes. "Yeah, great plan, Ed. Tell you what, I'll save that one for you. And if you ever *get* a date, maybe you can try it out and see if it works."

Ed shook his head. "The sense of humor is the first thing to go."

The truth was, Brad *didn't* have a sense of humor when it came to Myla. He was serious about her, and their relationship—whatever it was—was not something he took lightly or was able to joke about. It was meaningful to him, significant, and though he knew it was too early for him to feel this way, he did, although that was not something he was about to share with Ed. Or even Myla herself.

In the quad, a crowd had gathered, dozens of students standing close together, all of them looking intently toward Senior Corner. There was none of the shouting or excitement that would have accompanied a fight, but Brad couldn't tell *what* was going on. No adults were anywhere to be seen, and he and Ed changed direction, pushing their way through the outskirts of the crowd until they were close enough to see what everyone was staring at.

It was the school mascot. Or, rather, the school-mascot costume usually worn by some overly enthusiastic rah-rah at each pep rally and sporting event. The tiger costume had been filled with an unidentified brown substance that looked a hell of a lot like shit, and its arms and legs were spread-eagled and staked to the ground. Flies were everywhere, their buzzing so loud that it could be heard over the baffled conversations of the crowd.

Ed whistled. "Fuck howdy with a dick water sandwich à la mode."

Brad turned toward him. "You've been saying that same stupid phrase since grammar school and it makes no sense whatsoever. What the hell is that supposed to mean?"

Ed looked back levelly. "How would I know? I was in grammar school when I thought of it."

"Then don't say it."

"I like the way it sounds."

"I bet it's Washington," said a tall heavyset girl in an unflattering Idaka dress. "We're playing them Saturday." There was a chorus of assent from all around.

This didn't look to Brad like a harmless prank by students from a rival school, but he didn't say anything. There was an uncharacteristic grimness to what had happened to the mascot costume, a seriousness underlying the incident that belied any benign interpretation. Despite their stated opinions, the onlookers seemed to sense it, too, their subdued tone and noticeable lack of amusement at what should have seemed hilarious—that obnoxious tiger stuffed with shit, what could be more appropriate?—testimony to the solemnity of the occurrence.

But if it wasn't a rival school, who *had* done it? And why?

One of the custodians arrived to clean up the mess, and the students began to walk away. Watching would be just a little too gross, and Brad knew that he might gag if the contents of that costume were confirmed. The bell rang at that moment, and he nodded a farewell to Ed. "See you second period."

"Later."

After class, they met up again by the lockers, stopped to chat with Stewart Bigley, who claimed to have news about the mascot costume but didn't, and were late getting to math. To Brad's surprise, Mr. Connor, standing in front of the class, didn't lecture them for their tardiness but simply gave them a disapproving look as they sat down in their seats.

The teacher scanned the room. "Now, I know you all want to talk about Mr. Dolliver and what happened, but I'm here to tell you that in *this* class we are not going to waste time with idle speculation. This is an algebra class, and we will be studying algebra, the same way we do every day. Now I want you to do problems five through fifteen on page twenty-three. When everyone has finished, we will correct them together. You have ten minutes."

Dolliver? *What* had happened? Brad glanced over at Ed, who shook his head and shrugged his shoulders to indicate his own bewilderment.

Connor kept the lid on and didn't give anyone the chance to talk, and it wasn't until after the bell rang and they were walking out the door that Brad was finally able to ask Joey Maswick what had happened.

"You didn't hear? They found kiddie porn on his computer."

"No shit?"

"Yeah. Little naked boys and stuff."

"*Gay* kiddie porn?"

"That's what I heard."

Ed's eyes widened. "Fuck howdy."

Brad gave him a hard stare.

"I guess he's suspended or whatever until they sort it all out, but I don't think he's coming back."

"I don't think so either," Brad said.

Ed shook his head. "He doesn't seem the type. Not that you can always tell, but . . ."

Brad had the same reaction, and as the three of them walked down the hallway, that seemed to be the consensus of everyone they encountered. In the quad, he looked over at Senior Corner. The mess had been cleaned up, but the small section of grass was still empty of students.

No seniors on Senior Corner.

He had never seen such a thing in the three years he'd been going to this school, and he found the sight troubling. The disquiet must have shown on his face, because when he met Myla outside biology, she immediately asked him what was wrong. "Nothing," he said. But that wasn't true, and she knew it, and they ended up getting into a fight.

He spent his lunch with Ed, watching crows and sparrows slam into the blacktop backboards as raucous students cheered them on.

Woodshop.

Last class of the day.

Ed walked past the drafting room and past metal shop, then slowed as he reached the long section of windowless wall before the woodshop door. Yesterday, he'd arrived early to class, and though the door had been open, the teacher was nowhere to be found. That had been scary. Woodshop was a magnet for some of the toughest and meanest kids in the school, students looking to graduate by doing as little academic work as possible, and quite a few of them hated his guts. Luckily, the three worst offenders were busy tormenting Wayne Dickey by the band saw and Mr. Ruiz arrived before they noticed Ed. But it had been a close call.

Today, he walked past the doorway as though he were on his way to auto shop and merely taking a casual peek as he passed by. But he saw Mr. Ruiz standing by his desk, saw no sign of bullies and quickly stepped inside.

Safe.

Todd Zivney and his buddies came in moments later, punching one another and laughing at a cruel prank they'd pulled on some kid in the halls. Zivney had been one of Ed's chief torturers since eighth grade, the leader of his little gang of thugs, and Ed watched warily as he swaggered past Mr. Ruiz and sat on one of the worktables, awaiting the bell. Zivney scanned the room from his perch, and for a second, their eyes met. Ed looked quickly away, heart pounding.

"Mr. Zivney," the teacher said loudly. "Please get

off the table and sit down on your stool. I do not want to have to tell you this every day."

The bully just looked at him, making no effort to comply.

"Mr. Zivney?"

The whole class was looking at him now, and Ed noticed for the first time that there was some sort of patch on the sleeve of his shirt. It looked official, almost like something a policeman or security guard would wear. *What was it?* Ed squinted, looking closer. The patch depicted a growling tiger, the school's mascot, flanked by twin palm trees, with a silhouette of Tyler's buildings in the background. He recognized the logo. It was the same one printed on the school's letterhead.

He thought of that mascot costume stuffed with shit. It had been one weird fucking day, and it didn't look like it was going to chill out at the end here either.

Zivney was staring silently at the teacher, refusing to budge.

"You're going to the office," Mr. Ruiz announced, taking out his referral pad.

Zivney hopped off the table. "No. I'm not." There was something threatening in the way he said it, and in the way he started across the concrete floor toward Mr. Ruiz's desk.

Ed's stomach lurched, his heart pounding.

"I don't have to listen to you. I'm a Tyler Scout now." He pointed to the patch on his sleeve, pulled out a badge from his pocket. "I've been empowered by Principal Hawkes to enforce rules and regulations with students *and* teachers."

"You're not making any sense."

"Oh yeah? Principal Hawkes called me in for a meeting this morning and made me a deputy! It's *my* job to make sure *you* do *your* job. And if you don't . . ." The sentence trailed off ominously.

The teacher's face was red and angry. He ripped a referral off the pad. "Please take this to the office, Mr. Zivney."

The boy lifted his chin defiantly. "You gonna make me?"

Mr. Ruiz stood. "Yes, Mr. Zivney. I will."

"Come on, old man. I'll deck ya!" Zivney slipped the badge back in his pocket and put up his fists.

"Let's take it outside," the teacher said.

"No."

Ed found it hard to breathe. This was not good. Mr. Ruiz was the only thing standing between himself and certain annihilation. Without the teacher's protection, he was dead meat. He looked over at Wayne, saw a panic on the other boy's face that mirrored his own. Most of the kids in class looked frightened, but Zivney's buddies were laughing excitedly and elbowing each other.

Suddenly, the boy lunged. His right fist flew forward . . . and missed. Mr. Ruiz neatly sidestepped the attack and punched Zivney in the stomach. Not hard. Just enough to let the student know that he *could* hurt him if he wanted to.

That should have been the end of it.

But it wasn't.

Zivney stumbled, nearly hitting his head on the corner of the teacher's metal desk. He was grimacing, breathing hard and sucking in air loud enough for everyone to hear. Instead of going after the teacher with his fists again, he scrambled around to the side of the room and grabbed a length of two-by-four from the discard pile. Mr. Ruiz picked up another, longer two-by-four from the floor next to his desk. Warily, the two circled each other in the open space close to the door. Ed thought of a poster he'd seen in a horror-movie book for a film called *Fight with Sledgehammers.* It was from the early nineteen hundreds and had to be really primitive, but the images his mind conjured from that title had always stayed with him. Now his woodshop teacher and a student were about to whale on each other with boards, and he had the same sick queasy feeling in his stomach that he'd gotten when he'd first thought about that movie.

Screaming crazily, his face red and filled with rage, Zivney swung at the teacher, putting so much strength behind it that the board made a swishing sound as it cut through the air. Mr. Ruiz wielded his own board like a sword and parried. The force of Zivney's swing caused his two-by-four to bounce back at him at an odd angle. He was struck on the side of the head by his own board and fell flat on the cement, landing with a hard thud, the two-by-four dropping onto his back.

Ed thought for a moment—

hoped

—that he was dead, but Zivney moaned, struggled to his feet and stared about dazedly, as though unsure of where he was.

The teacher looked at Rick and Mitchell, Zivney's friends, who were no longer laughing. "Take him to the nurse's office," Mr. Ruiz ordered. He picked up the referral from his desk. "And give this to the principal." He was nearly out of breath, and Ed was afraid for a moment that Mitchell and Rick would double-team him and kick his ass—he saw the hatred on their faces—but the students did as they were told, and as soon as they left, the rest of the class gratefully settled into their usual woodworking routines.

Ed had been planning to make speaker boxes for the back of his car this semester—not that he *had* a car yet . . . or speakers, for that matter—and he proceeded to sand a piece of maple that yesterday he'd crosscut to length. But his mind was not on the project, and several moments later, after Zivney's friends had returned from the office and Rick had accidentally on purpose bumped into him, causing the handheld sander to veer off the board and onto the table, he stopped. He liked woodworking—and he was good at it—but he couldn't put up with this for an entire semester. Mitchell and Rick were starting to work on their own projects, and Ed went up to Mr. Ruiz and asked the teacher if he could have a hall pass to go to the office.

"What's the matter?" the instructor asked. "Don't you feel well?"

He didn't want to say the real reason, but he didn't really have a choice, so he lowered his voice. "I think I'm going to transfer to another class."

He'd expected the teacher to try to talk him out of it. But Mr. Ruiz seemed to instinctively understand Ed's plight. The instructor nodded, gave him a reassuring smile. "We're going to miss you," he said, writing out a hall pass.

"It's not—," Ed began.

"I know," the teacher said.

Ed walked across campus feeling as if a great weight had been lifted off him. He passed Cheryl in the hallway between the science and social studies buildings. The student body president did not acknowledge him, but he grinned at her and said, "Hey, Cher! How's it going?"

"Drop dead," she muttered as she walked past.

"I retract my invitation to the homecoming dance, then. You're out."

"In your dreams, loser."

He laughed.

There were fewer students in the quad than there should have been. Quite a few seniors didn't have a seventh period, and in previous years a lot of them had hung around Senior Corner, waiting for their friends to get out of school and hassling any underclassmen who happened to pass by. Today, however, the quad was deserted save for himself and a girl he didn't know who was heading from the Little Theater toward the restrooms.

Maybe the administration had made a new rule that students couldn't loiter on campus after their classes ended. It would be a stupid rule—but he could definitely see it happening.

A lot of things were different this semester.

Almost none of them good.

Ed reached the office and pulled open the tinted door, walking inside. Instantly, the buoyant lightness he had felt after leaving woodshop vanished. He stood there for a moment, acclimatizing. There was something creepy about the office. He'd noticed that the other day. The lights seemed too low, for one thing, and there were shadows in the corners that shouldn't have been there in the daytime. But there was something else as well, something he couldn't quite put his finger on, and he walked forward slowly, almost cautiously. He handed his hall pass to the secretary at the front desk. "I'm here to see my counselor." He found when he spoke that his voice was quiet, subdued.

"Who is your counselor?"

"I don't know. I'm a senior, so I guess it's Mr. Hill."

"Mr. Hill is no longer at the school," the secretary informed him, and the way she said it made his arms break out in gooseflesh. "Your new counselor is Ms. Tremayne." The secretary pointed down a short hallway. "Room B."

A TA walked by silently, carrying a stack of interoffice envelopes, looking blank and dull, almost tranquilized.

Zombified.

That was even more accurate, and he shivered as he saw another TA pass by, a vacant expression on her face.

The secretary was staring at him—*suspiciously?*— and he quickly thanked her and walked around the front desk, through the open area behind it and toward room B. Short as it was, he still didn't like the hallway. He didn't like the entire office. The counselor, though, seemed fairly normal, and when he knocked on the frame of her open door, she smiled and bade him come in.

"Hello," she said, extending her hand in greeting. "I'm Ms. Tremayne."

He wasn't used to shaking a woman's hand, but he did so, acutely aware of how slender her fingers seemed, how soft was her skin. He sat down on the chair at the side of her desk.

"How can I help you?"

"I want to transfer out of my seventh-period class."

"What's your name?" Ed told her and she typed it into the computer on her desk. "You wish to get out of Woodshop Two?"

"Yes," he said gratefully.

"May I ask the reason?"

Ed hesitated. "I'd rather not say."

"I need a reason."

"There are some bullies in the class. They don't like me. They've hated me since junior high."

"The instructor should be able to—"

"One of them picked a fight with the teacher today. He's probably in the nurse's office right now." Ed leaned forward. "Look. Mr. Ruiz said it's fine if I transfer out. He understands and he's all for it. If you could just help me find another class . . ."

The counselor looked at him for a moment, then nodded. "Okay," she agreed, and he could tell from her tone of voice that she felt sorry for him. She pressed a key on her computer. "Do you have any preferences? Woodshop's an elective, so I assume there's nothing you *have* to take. Is there anything that you *want* to take, anything specific that you'd like to study?"

"What's available?" he asked.

"Seventh period? Not much." She swiveled the screen in his direction and he looked over the list of classes. "Not much" was right.

"How about library TA?"

Ms. Tremayne frowned. "You have a solid college-prep schedule. Do you really want to dilute it with a TA position?"

"I'm *not* signing up for Healthy Cooking."

"You don't have to have a seventh period," she pointed out.

"I want the credits. Besides, library should be an easy A. It'll boost my grade point average."

"Okay," the counselor said. "But you'll need a parent's permission."

"Call my mom's cell." He gave her the number.

Five minutes later, he was on his way back to woodshop with a transfer form for Mr. Ruiz to sign. He brought it back to the counselor, who gave him another form to bring to Mrs. Fratelli in the library. "Have her return this to me," she said. "And good luck."

Ed smiled. "Thank you."

He walked out of the office into the short dark hall. Across from him was the closed door of the principal's office. For some reason, he didn't even want to *look* at that door.

"Ed?" Ms. Tremayne said.

He turned around, faced the counselor.

"You have any problems, you come to me," she said. "That's what I'm here for."

He nodded, smiling. "I will," he told her. "And thanks again."

He walked over to the library.

Ed had hung out in the library a lot in junior high, trying to avoid getting beaten up, but since coming to high school, he'd fallen out of the habit. Part of it was the librarian, a cold angry bitch who could have played Miss Gulch in a remake of *The Wizard of Oz*. But part of it was the library itself. Unlike the friendly, single-roomed structure back in junior high, Tyler's two-story monstrosity was an intimidating building inside and out, a blocky architectural eyesore that stuck out amid the school's surrounding Spanish-style buildings like a rock among flowers. The interior was dark, with brown brick walls, brown carpeting, tinted gray windows and recessed lighting that was too dim to offer anything more than the most basic illumination. A narrow staircase in the precise center of the library connected the upper and lower floors, which were crammed with high bookcases set too close together. On the upper level, study carrels lined the walls, and on the first floor, several round tables occupied the open area in front of the checkout desk.

Ed stood in front of the closed double doors. So *why* exactly had he decided to work here as a TA? Ms. Tremayne was right. He didn't need a seventh period. And he could have signed up for photography, which actually wouldn't have been half-bad.

He stared up at the darkly tinted windows of the library and realized that he didn't know why he was here. That worried him. Something about the office seemed to have affected his decision making, influenced him, and while he hadn't felt it at the time and still couldn't recall it, the results spoke for themselves. He would never have signed up to work at the library if he'd been thinking clearly.

You have any problems, you come to me. That's what I'm here for.

He could go back to the counselor again, transfer to yet another class. But after a moment's thought, he decided against that. He wasn't a brave guy, but he was a curious guy, and he wanted to see how this would pan out. Besides, his thoughts were starting to go off in wacky directions here. Sure, the office had seemed a little strange, but to think he was being *affected* or *influenced,* as though he were in some horror movie, was just crazy.

And if being a TA sucked, he could always transfer.

He pushed open the library door. Despite the dimness, the air felt warm instead of cool. Uncomfortably so. He'd forgotten about that, but it was yet another reason that he didn't like coming in here.

The study tables were empty, and there was a girl he didn't know—another TA—installed behind the checkout desk and staring at him. He didn't see the librarian or anyone else around, so he walked up to the girl and held out his transfer form. "Is Mrs. Fratelli here?" he asked.

An uninflected emotionless voice came from somewhere in the murky area behind the counter. "Is that Mr. Haynes?"

The girl looked at him. "Are you Mr. Haynes?"

His counselor must have called to announce that he was coming. "Yeah. Ed Haynes. I'm going to be a TA."

The girl showed not a flicker of interest.

"Send him back to my office," the voice called.

Ed's eyes had adjusted to the darkness, and he saw now that behind the counter was what looked like a large alcove containing three walls of metal shelves on which were piled various books. Two empty pushcarts stood next to the shelves on the right. In the wall without shelves was a door, and although the door was closed, it was clear that this was where the voice was coming from.

"Mrs. Fratelli is expecting you in her office," the girl said, gesturing toward the door. She pulled up a section of the counter that revealed itself to be a gate.

Ed walked past her. "I know," he said. "I heard her."

The girl frowned at him, but it was a reaction he was used to, and he didn't really care. Something about the bland officiousness of the TA annoyed him, and he could tell right now that the two of them were not going to be friends. He just hoped that there was another student working here this period, someone he could get along with who might make the hour more fun.

He knocked on the closed door.

"Come in," Mrs. Fratelli said.

The librarian's office was small and cramped and cluttered, but what his gaze focused on was a framed soft-focus photo on top of the paper-strewn desk. It was of Mrs. Fratelli. Her hair was teased out, she had on way too much makeup . . . and she was wearing nothing but a lacy red bra and thong.

"May I have your transfer form?"

He looked up from the photo into the hard, severe face of the librarian and *he* saw that *she* saw where he'd been looking. He was embarrassed but pretended not to be, handing her the form and waiting for her response.

"You wish to be my TA?" she asked suspiciously.

"Yes," he lied.

Mrs. Fratelli glanced at the page, paused for a beat, then signed on the bottom line.

She gave him a cold mirthless smile. "Welcome to the library."

Eight

Frank forgot to set the alarm, and they both awoke late, scrambling to get dressed and out of the house, although for Linda it didn't really matter, since it was a staff development day and there'd be no kids on campus.

Or at least she *thought* it wouldn't matter.

But, like everything else, in-service days had changed since they'd become a charter school, and the previous lackadaisical attitude toward attendance was no longer in evidence. Instead, Bobbi was installed at a table outside the doorway of the Little Theater, where she noted each staff member's arrival time and issued name tags to all who entered. She clicked her pen, as Linda approached, looking down at the list before her. "Name?" she asked, as though the two of them had never met before.

"Jesus Christ . . ." Linda started to push past her.

"Hold on a sec." Bobbi quickly sorted through the last few squares of clip-on plastic atop the table. "Here you go."

"I'm not wearing a name tag," Linda said.

Bobbi grew indignant. "You have to! It's mandatory!"

"I'm not going to. It's stupid." She walked into

the building, leaving the secretary—*administrative coordinator*—sputtering behind her.

Not everyone was here, but most of the staff was, and she grabbed a seat in the back row next to two of the PE teachers, trying to be as unobtrusive as possible. On the stage, Jody was standing in front of a podium, talking into a microphone. Linda frowned. The podium was new, and not only was it adorned with elaborate carvings, but portions of it were embossed with gold and silver. The principal's voice, she noticed, was coming out of new state-of-the-art speakers.

Linda looked around the room, trying to find Diane. The two of them had put in a request for a mere twenty additional ninth-grade textbooks due to the large influx of freshmen this semester, but Jody had turned it down, citing a scarcity of funds. "We might be able to get those books for you later in the year," she told them, "but the charter committee needs to go through our budget more carefully and determine our priorities. We have a fixed amount for the entire year; we can't just go back to the district and ask for more."

Apparently, though, there was enough money in that still-fluid budget to buy a fancy new podium and speaker system.

Priorities.

The principal was talking about the benefits of working for a charter school as opposed to a traditional public school, emphasizing the academic freedom that such an arrangement offered, and stressing that controlling a budget at the school rather than the district level would leave more money for pay raises and various incentives. Linda shook her head. What was all this for? Hadn't they been through it already? Tyler *was* a charter school. Jody didn't have to keep selling them on the idea.

Although maybe she did.

Looking at the expression on the principal's face, Linda saw a desire—no, a *need*—to convince the rest of them that they were part of the greatest and most important movement in the history of education. She was trying to create converts. She didn't want them to just work at the school; she wanted them to *love* it, and she wouldn't be happy until every last one of them expressed their undying loyalty to Tyler High.

There was nothing scarier than a true believer.

Linda sat quietly, listening. Before the school got charter status, Jody's statements in meetings had been blessedly brief, but now she was going on and on, and Linda wondered if they were in for some sort of Castroesque filibuster.

The principal continued talking, but gradually the tone of the speech changed, became less promotional and more confrontational. Removing the microphone from its stand, she stepped away from the podium and began pacing the stage. "By law," she said, "in order to maintain our charter status, we must improve student achievement as measured by standardized tests. Granted, we will not be up for renewal for another five years, but we must establish a workable plan to reach this goal. As I see it, and as the committee has discussed, there are two ways for us to boost Tyler's overall average. We can work hard to bring up the test scores of as many students as we can, particularly those at the lower end of the scale. Or"—she stopped pacing and smiled—"we can weed out the academically challenged and force them to transfer to another school, thus retaining only the most high-performing students."

Toward the front of the theater, several teachers cheered.

The charter committee?

"We can make Tyler into not only the top-scoring

school in the district but in the county, the state, the country!"

More people cheered this time.

Linda was stunned. The purpose of a school was to educate children, and her job was to do her utmost to teach every student in her classroom, be he good, bad or indifferent. In fact, she received the most satisfaction from seeing the light go on in the eyes of a student who claimed to hate reading but suddenly discovered the joys of literature through the power of a book that she had assigned. She was shocked to the very core of her being that Jody would even suggest cherry-picking students in order to boost the school's overall test scores, and she quickly looked around to see who was in agreement with this horrifying idea and who was not. She'd always believed that crowds brought out the worst in people, that a mob mentality could override the better instincts of most individuals, and she thought that even more so now. On their own, many of the teachers cheering the principal's proposal were good people and caring educators, but together, following a leader, they surrendered any pretense of independent thought and became a frighteningly pliable entity that could be used for any purpose.

Now Jody was talking about punishing parents who took their children out of school for doctors' appointments, dentists' appointments or, worst of all, family vacations. "It is their responsibility to schedule these appointments at a time that does not conflict with school hours!" she announced. "From now on, failing to do so shall result in a day's in-house suspension for the child and a fine of fifty dollars for the parents!"

There were cheers, but not quite as many this time.

"Under no circumstances shall there be any makeup tests or independent study for students whose parents remove them from school."

"So let it be written, so let it be done," muttered Paul Mays, the EH teacher, from the row in front of her.

Linda had to smile, though the situation was anything but funny. She'd always hated staff development days. Most of the teachers did. But whereas, in the past, the dopey seminars they'd attended and the useless consultants they'd listened to had all had at their core the best interests of the students, it seemed now that their in-service days were to be spent in strategy sessions that made students and their parents into enemies to be conquered.

Linda hadn't seen anyone else come in after her, but the last few stragglers must have arrived because Bobbi had left her post and was walking down the theater's far right aisle and up the steps to the stage. She said something to Jody and then stood respectfully behind the podium.

"Listen up!" the principal announced, placing the microphone back in its stand. "We have something special planned for the rest of the morning. All of the vendors assisting us with fund-raising this year have graciously consented to showcase their goods and services so that you may be aware of what is available. As you know, each classroom has a quota that it is expected to meet, and each instructor may choose the fund-raising options that best suit his or her needs. There will be presentations in the gym. Please feel free to stop by each booth or table, and ask all the questions you want."

Linda raised her hand, but when the principal looked at her and did not call her name, she blurted out: "Will we need a name tag to get into the gym? Because I seem to have lost mine."

"She never *got* her name tag!" Bobbi shouted, rushing forward. "She refused to wear it!"

Several teachers chuckled.

Jody held up a hand to silence Bobbi, who was red-faced and furious. "You will still be allowed inside," she promised. "And I think you will be very favorably impressed."

"Very funny," Diane admitted, catching Linda outside the building a few minutes later.

Linda laughed. "I thought so."

"You've made an enemy for life, though."

"And she wasn't already?"

"Good point."

"What is going on with this school?" Suzanne said, meeting up with them. "Am I the only one who thinks all this emphasis on fund-raising is a crock? I mean, aren't we supposed to be *teachers*?"

"You're preaching to the converted," Diane said.

Like a herd of lemmings, the faculty and staff walked en masse through the center of campus to the gymnasium.

"Do you think anyone would notice if I just hid out in my room and corrected papers?" Suzanne asked.

Diane looked around mock-furtively. "Be careful. Bobbi's not only counting heads—she's monitoring conversations. Your pay could be docked for a statement such as that."

"That's probably not as much of an exaggeration as you intended," Linda pointed out.

"I thought that even as I said it."

All of the gym's doors were open, and when they walked inside, the sight that greeted them looked like a cross between a carnival and a trade show. There were tables and booths, balloons and even a band. Several of the salesmen were trying to compete with one another by using remote microphones, and there was one display under a large white canopy that featured two shimmying women in bikinis.

"What the hell is this?" Diane marveled.

They walked from one exhibit to another, picking up pamphlets and catalogs, samples and bribes. The sheer breadth of options was overwhelming. They could send their students home to sell everything from magazine subscriptions and holiday decorations to resort time-shares and life insurance. There were even prizes offered to those students who sold the most and to the teacher whose classes raised the greatest amount of money. Linda stopped to look at a table piled high with miracle cleaning products. This entire concept did not sit well with her. The kids in her class were students, not salespeople, and they should be concentrating on their schoolwork rather than fund-raising.

"Did you see the portable tent?" Bill Manning, the biology teacher, asked excitedly, passing by. "It fits in a school backpack!"

"I think I'm done here," Linda said, hefting her plastic Store bag filled with freebies.

"Me, too," Diane said.

Suzanne had gone back to her classroom, and the two of them walked past a shrill-voiced man conducting a no-stick frying pan demonstration and out the door. Linda looked up into the sky, taking a deep breath, suddenly aware of how claustrophobic it had seemed inside the gym. She turned around and saw teachers flocking around booths, trying various products, hurrying to catch another demonstration. "Shouldn't students be rewarded for doing well academically rather than for selling . . . crap?" she asked.

"The kid who sells the most magazine subscriptions gets a limo ride," Diane said. "Did you see that? And whoever sells the most books gets to go to Familyland. During school hours!"

"Ridiculous."

They started walking back toward the classrooms. The PTA was catering a lunch at eleven thirty, and after that was an afternoon's worth of speakers, but until then they could catch up with whatever they needed to do.

Diane glanced behind them to make sure no one else was nearby. "You heard about Michelle's husband, didn't you?"

"Yes! Oh my God, I couldn't believe it!"

"Did you hear how he died?"

Linda shook her head.

"Choked on his own vomit."

"Was he drunk?"

"Oh, no. Food poisoning. He fell asleep in his chair, in front of his computer, with his head leaning back, and asphyxiated when he threw up. It seems that he tried to clear his throat and get it out of there, but he couldn't do it." She shook her head. "What a horrible way to go."

"And Michelle found him?"

"No. Their son did."

"How old is he?"

"Ten."

"Wow." Linda was silent for a moment. "Choking on your own vomit when you're not drunk. That's pretty rare, isn't it?"

"Yeah, I guess it is."

"Are you starting to notice a pattern here?"

Diane frowned. "Pattern? What do you mean?"

"Mary's getting a divorce. Coleen's moving because her husband is being transferred to Texas. David got caught with kiddie porn—"

"Which I *still* can't believe."

"—and now Michelle's husband is dead. Dead! Doesn't it seem to you that all of the bad things are happening to the teachers who opposed the charter?"

"I've heard of conspiracy theories, but this takes the cake."

"I'm serious. Look at it objectively. Our side's being decimated and Jody's allies are getting off scot-free."

Diane stopped walking. "Listen, this is crazy. I'm right with you on all the anticharter stuff, but what are you saying, that Jody's putting some kind of curse on teachers who oppose her?"

Linda sighed. "I don't know."

"Well, I do know. And that's just not happening."

"You don't think things are a little . . . weird this semester?"

Diane smiled. "It would be weird if things *weren't* weird."

"Come on. The new pledge of allegiance?" She held up her bag, using it to motion behind them. "All *that*?"

"Yes, things are weird," Diane admitted. "But they're *explainable*. They're not . . . supernatural, or whatever you're suggesting."

Linda lowered her bag. "I hope you're right," she said, though she was still not convinced. "I hope you're right."

Nine

Myla's mom let her borrow the minivan, and for that, she was grateful. Despite what she told Brad when he teased her, she wasn't quite as comfortable with most of the other student-council members as she made it seem, and this semester she'd even been feeling a little distant from her friends. It was probably from spending so much time with Brad and Ed, but she'd found herself increasingly irritated with Reba and Cindy's annoying gossipy chatter, so much so that sometimes she actually dreaded seeing them. Cheryl was all right, but Myla still didn't want to carpool with her. She wanted to head straight home after the meeting, and she knew her friend would want to stop by Starbucks or Del Taco and hang out awhile.

Myla wasn't sure why they had to have their meetings at night anyway. Last year's council had met at lunchtime, and everything seemed to have run smoothly. She suspected that it was because Cheryl's lunches were consumed with early lobbying for homecoming queen, and because she wanted the chance to cruise around on a school night in the new VW that her absent and guilt-ridden daddy had bought her for a "senior-year present." Student-council meetings offered perfect cover.

There were only a few cars in the parking lot, and Myla pulled next to an Explorer that she recognized as Reba's dad's. She shut off the engine and the headlights, but left the radio on as she sat there and waited for someone else to show up. The campus was dark, and as she looked out the windshield, she thought that maybe she *should* have carpooled with Cheryl. Lights were on in the parking lot, but they were a strange muted orange and offered little illumination. There seemed to be *no* lights on in any of the buildings, and she could see only a dim faint glow from some indistinct light source within the quad.

She sat through one song. Two. A commercial.

According to the clock on the dashboard, it was eight already. The meeting was supposed to be starting. There weren't enough cars in the parking lot for all the council members to be here. Where was everybody? It occurred to her that some of them might have walked or taken a bike, and some of them may even have parked on Grayson Street on the other side of the campus, which was actually a lot closer to the multipurpose room where they would be holding the meeting than where she was now.

She had to walk all the way across the school grounds to get to the meeting.

Myla took the key out of the ignition, shutting off the radio, causing the lit dashboard to go black. The world was suddenly silent. Getting out of the van, she locked the vehicle's doors. She wished she'd brought a flashlight. There was one somewhere in the van that her mom kept there for emergencies, but she didn't know exactly where it was, and she didn't have time to look for it. She was late already.

Myla stepped over the curb, starting down the walkway that led into the center of campus. She didn't like the echoing sounds her footsteps made on the cement or the way that indistinct light shining from within the quad ahead of her made the surrounding trees and buildings look unfamiliar and threatening.

She glanced back at the van, parked next to Reba's dad's Explorer and close to a light-colored Prius. At least there'd be other people walking with her to the parking lot on the way back.

She quickened her step.

At the last minute, she opted not to walk through the quad but to take a longer route around the cafeteria and lunch area. Seconds later, when she glanced between the buildings and saw a small dark form rush past the front of the library, she was glad she had.

There was a noise from the quad that sounded like a box of tools falling to the ground from one of the second-floor windows.

She ran.

Turning the corner, the open door of the multipurpose room, with its warm light and visible crowd, was like a beacon, beckoning her. She stopped running and slowed her pace, not wanting to walk into the meeting out of breath. She was a little surprised at how spooked she'd gotten on the walk here and how absurdly relieved she felt to see other people again. Even other council members.

The meeting was not yet in session. Several of the students had still not arrived, and those who had were scattered about the oversized room. Cheryl, Cindy and Reba were standing by the flag, and Myla headed over to where they were talking.

"What do you think of Mr. Nicholson?" Cheryl asked as she walked up.

She wasn't sure what they were discussing. "As a teacher?"

"No . . . as a man."

"Eww!" Cindy and Reba squealed.

"Quiet down!" Cheryl whispered, looking anxiously about.

Myla felt cold. It had to be a coincidence, but she'd had a dream about Mr. Nicholson last night. A nightmare. The PE teacher had been naked and wielding a bullwhip, standing at the front of the gym snapping it at the girls of the school, all of whom were undressed and milling about like cattle. Flecks of blood were flying every which way, but none of the girls seemed to care, not even the ones hit, and only Myla was making any effort to escape as the whipcracks grew louder and faster and Mr. Nicholson started to laugh.

"Reba likes that new kid in band—," Cheryl explained to Myla.

"Francesco," Reba said.

"—so we were talking about dating and guys and stuff like that."

Cindy giggled. "But Mr. Nicholson?"

"Shut up," Cheryl said. "Conversation's over." She walked up to the front of the room, where Mr. Myers, the adviser, was sitting and where a long table had been set up with enough chairs for the entire student council. "The meeting is about to start!" she announced, and everyone took their places. Two council members had still not arrived, but either they weren't going to show or they were so late that it was not right for the rest of them to wait any longer, and Cheryl picked up the gavel in front of her seat and used it to rap loudly on the table. "I call this meeting of thc Associated Student Body council to order!"

Myla glanced at Roland Nevins, sitting on the left side of her. He had a Tyler patch sewn or ironed onto the sleeve of his shirt—an embroidered version of the school logo—and as Cheryl ran through the rules of order, Myla examined it more closely. She'd seen someone else wearing one of those patches yesterday, and she'd wondered then what it meant. "Excuse me," she said, and though she'd spoken softly and hadn't meant for anyone else to hear, everyone turned to look at her, and even Cheryl stopped talking. "Why are you wearing that patch?" she asked Roland.

"Principal Hawkes gave it to me," he said proudly. "It means I'm a Tyler Scout. It is my job, and the job of all sworn scouts, to make sure that the rules are followed."

"What rules?"

"The rules and regulations specified in the school charter. And if we see infractions, we report those to Principal Hawkes."

"Oh. Like the Hitler Youth," Myla joked.

Nobody laughed. Even her friends remained stone-faced, and looking around the room, she felt as if a cold finger were being run over her spine.

"Sometimes," Roland said, and there seemed to be some sort of hidden import in the grave way he intoned the words, "we are empowered to take care of the problem ourselves."

"Okay!" Cheryl said, changing the subject, the shift so jarring that Myla nearly jumped. "This is our first meeting, so let's go over our individual jobs and obligations. Cindy? I expect you to be taking notes on this so you can type up the minutes of our meeting. Next time, you will also need to print out an agenda."

They discussed their roles and responsibilities for several minutes, Cindy dutifully writing down what each of them said, and then Cheryl tabled the discussion and asked, "Any new business?"

They were all silent for a moment, looking at one another, each unsure of what exactly they were supposed to do.

"I've gotten a lot of questions about the cell phone

situation," Myla said finally. "Everyone's asking me why phones won't work on campus."

"Students aren't allowed to use cell phones on campus," Cheryl said primly.

"I know that. Which is why I didn't notice the problem myself. But then I did try to call out, and I couldn't. . . ."

Even as she spoke, most of the other council members were taking out their phones and checking to see if *they* could call out. Myla did it herself, just to make sure it was still a problem and hadn't been some freakish fluky thing. She quickly punched in her mom's number. Sure enough, there was one clearly audible ring, then a much lower, barely perceptible ring, then a quiet click, then nothing.

"Huh," Cheryl said, looking at her own phone, surprised.

"I know we're not supposed to use phones on campus, but what if there's an emergency? Or a national disaster? The phones need to work."

"Maybe it's, like, a science project or something that's interfering with the signal," Reba offered.

Everyone ignored her.

"I'll ask Principal Hawkes tomorrow and will get an answer for you by our next council meeting," Cheryl said.

Myla smiled. "Or you could just tell me when I see you."

Cheryl banged her gavel. "Next item."

"I'm not sure this is within our purview . . . ," Roland began.

Purview? Myla thought. *Awfully big word for Roland Nevins.*

"But I think—I mean, *we* think, me and the other scouts—that there need to be a few more restrictions set in place for ASB-sponsored activities. We need these events to be successful, so we need to make sure that they're not disrupted or sabotaged by . . . well, *you* know the kinds of kids I'm talking about."

There were nods all around, though Myla was frowning. *She* didn't know.

"We could tie it to parent volunteer hours," Cindy suggested. "Kids whose parents volunteer a certain number of hours by the time of the dance or the Harvest Festival or whatever it is can go; otherwise they can't."

"I'm thinking an increase in ASB fees," Cheryl mused. "I think forcing students to purchase an ASB card to attend events, and charging, say, a hundred dollars in ASB fees in order to get the card, should pretty well weed out the riffraff."

"No," Myla said firmly. "Discriminating against poor kids is not a good way to . . . to . . ." She shook her head. "I don't even know what you're trying to do. It sounds like you want to keep certain students away from things that should be open to everyone." She looked to the adviser for support, but Mr. Myers was staring blankly at the far wall, seemingly oblivious.

"I think what Roland is suggesting," Cheryl said, speaking slowly and enunciating clearly, as though talking to someone with comprehension problems, "is that the dances we put on, the Harvest Festival, the play, whatever, would be more successful, and more fun for those participating, if we restricted attendance to students who really *wanted* to be there."

"The people who want to be there *are* there," Myla argued. "The ones who don't aren't."

"That's not a foolproof plan," Roland said.

Cheryl agreed. "We need additional safeguards."

The discussion devolved from there into proposals for instituting exclusionary policies on a whole host of subjects. Myla stayed out of it, but none of it seemed ethical or even legal to her. For one thing, she didn't think the student council was supposed to be making rules or passing resolutions that applied to the whole school like actual laws. And for another, although she still wasn't sure exactly whom these rules were aimed at, they definitely seemed discriminatory. She kept stealing glances at Mr. Myers, but the adviser appeared to be paying no attention whatsoever to what was going on.

It was nearly ten o'clock when the meeting was finally adjourned, and Myla walked back to the parking lot with Reba. They both waved good-bye to Cheryl, who headed in the opposite direction toward Grayson Street.

"Mr. *Nicholson*?" Reba said after they were out of earshot. "That was kind of creepy."

Myla nodded. She'd been thinking the same thing. "It was," she admitted.

"That guy weirds me out, to be honest with you. And Cheryl thinks he's sexy or something?"

Myla glanced to her left, past the lunch area to the gym and the locker rooms. On the adjoining lawn, light shone from an open doorway or window, creating an elongated rectangle on the grass.

Mr. Nicholson's office?

A chill tickled the back of her neck.

It had to be a janitor, cleaning up after hours. She tried to remain focused on the parking lot ahead, but her eyes glanced once more toward that rectangle of light, and she imagined the PE teacher in there, naked, as he had been in her dream, beating a cowering group of female students as drops of their blood speckled his body with each crack of his whip.

She started walking faster.

Reba kept up. "I don't like to be here at night,"

she said. "Especially this year. It seems different. Have you noticed that?"

Myla quickened her pace. "Yes. I have."

Something sighed in the bushes to their right.

By the time they reached the parking lot, both of them were running.

After dinner and a movie, they'd gone to a park to . . . park. Not the most original idea, and one that at least one other couple at the far end of the lot had also had, but Brad had been thinking about it all night—through the enchilada plate, through the Steve Carell flick—and it was the goal toward which he'd been working all evening. Last year, they'd made out a little, but something seemed to have happened over the summer. They were more comfortable with each other, less inhibited, and as soon as the ignition was off, Myla took the initiative and kissed him with the sort of hungry passion he'd always dreamed about but had never before experienced.

Now his hand was down her unzipped jeans, pressing against the outside of her obviously moist panties. Breathlessly, she pulled back, pushed his arm away and began to zip up.

"What's wrong?" he asked. "What is it?"

"Nothing."

He leaned in once again. She gave him a quick kiss, then pushed him firmly back. "That's all," she said.

He was understanding—frustrated but understanding—and he leaned back against the driver's-side door and watched while she buttoned her blouse, although he couldn't help letting out a self-pitying sigh, hoping she'd feel sorry for him and relent.

She did not.

Their make-out session had left both of them thirsty, so on the way back, Brad pulled into the drive-thru of a Taco Bell and ordered Myla a Sprite, himself a Pepsi.

Myla was text messaging in the seat next to him, and she closed her phone, looking up. "Could you swing by the school before you take me home?"

"Why?"

"Just for a second," she said.

"We spend all week there. We were there yesterday, and we'll be there Monday. We deserve to have the weekend off."

"I want to see something."

"What's going on?" he asked suspiciously. "Something's up. Who were you texting?"

"I need to see something, but I'm afraid to go by myself." She flipped her eyelashes in a show of exaggerated girlishness. "Unless I'm with someone big and strong like you."

He laughed. "You've got the wrong guy."

"Please?"

"All right. I don't get it, but all right."

They picked up their drinks from the window, then pulled onto West Street, driving past the Ralphs shopping center and into the residential area beyond.

"It's Cheryl," Myla said finally when they turned down Grayson. "She has this . . . thing for Mr. Nicholson."

"Holy shit. And she's there with him right now? At school? That's what she told you?"

"No," Myla admitted. "But she's not answering; she's not there. And on Saturday night her phone is *always* on. No matter what she's doing."

"And now you think they're hooking up. At night. At school." Brad shook his head. "That's a pretty big stretch. Don't you think if something like that *was* going on, they'd pick someplace safer?"

"It's just a feeling I have." She put a hand on his

arm, and he realized that there was no reason they *couldn't* stop by the school. It wasn't *that* late.

"Okay," he said. "Let's check it out."

She gave him a quick kiss on the side of his cheek. "Thank you."

"You know, speaking of creepy, Ed says the librarian has one of those glamour shots of herself on the desk in her office—and she's wearing sexy lingerie!"

Myla grimaced in disgust. "Mrs. Fratelli?"

"The very one."

"That's wrong on so many levels."

The buildings of the school were looming up on their right, and he pulled over to park in the twenty-minute drop-off zone. He cut the ignition, switched off the headlights. "All right. What's the plan?"

Myla was looking between the classrooms toward the center of campus. She seemed nervous all of a sudden.

No, not nervous, he thought. *Scared.*

He touched her shoulder. "We can leave if you want. We don't have to—"

"No," she said. "We'll just do a quick check. To make sure."

Again the nervousness.

Fear.

"Let's go by the PE area. His office, maybe."

They got out of the car, locked the doors. "What's the plan if we find them?" he asked. "Are we supposed to turn them in? Tell them to knock it off? What?"

She obviously hadn't thought of that. "I don't know," she admitted. "We'll figure that out when it comes up. *If* it comes up."

Hand in hand, they started down the corridor next to the English classrooms, heading for the walkway that led to the sports complex. He'd been here at night before for various special events, but never when it was empty like this, and he had to admit that it did seem a little spooky. The only sounds were their footsteps echoing on the cement, and it seemed as though there should have been more lights on than there were.

"Do you have a flashlight?" he joked.

Myla's only response was to grip his hand tighter.

He found himself thinking of Van Nguyen, who had disappeared from the school in broad daylight. He looked around, saw nothing but shadows and places for someone to hide. It would be so much easier to kidnap someone here at night.

Kidnap? Was that what he really thought?

No. It was nothing that simple. He remembered the birds flying into the backboard on the blacktop. There was something about the school, about Tyler itself, that—

Something banged on the locker next to them.

Myla screamed, and both of them jumped. Grasping her hand so tightly that his fingers hurt, Brad pulled her off the walkway, away from the lockers, backing quickly onto the narrow strip of grass that ran between this building and the next. He glanced around in all directions, even up on the roof of the adjoining building, looking for someone who could have thrown a rock or shot at the lockers.

The noise came again, a loud sharp bang, as though a baseball bat had slammed against the metal, and this time they could *see* where the noise originated.

Something was inside one of the lockers.

The rectangular metal door was still vibrating.

The two of them continued to back away. Brad looked to his left. If they ran down the strip of grass, parallel to the walkway, they could make it back out to the street and escape.

"That's where my locker is," Myla managed to get out.

She was right, but he saw almost immediately that though it was *near* her locker, it wasn't the same one.

Then he noticed something even worse: the locker didn't belong to anyone. It had no lock on it.

The noise was louder this time, and the bottom left corner of the locker door stuck out. It had been struck so hard from the inside that the metal had bent.

"Let's go!" Brad said, but before they could even start to run, the locker door flew open—

—and nothing was there.

He wasn't sure what he'd been expecting—a small hairy beast? an evil dwarf?—but it hadn't been . . . anything. Not that his mind was any more at ease. The fear within him was powerful and instinctive, and a split second after that locker flew open, they were off and running. Bounding onto the sidewalk, they dashed to the Toyota and got in, locking the doors.

"Cheryl's on her own," he said, starting the car.

It had been a joke. Sort of. A quick quip under pressure. But as they sped down Grayson past the back half of the school, he saw what looked like two figures—a male and a female—passing under a light at the edge of the stadium. He didn't say anything to Myla, though, and it was not until they turned onto Yorba Avenue and Tyler High was no longer in his rearview mirror that he finally stopped hearing the pounding of his panicked heart in his ears.

Ten

On Monday, Kyle Faber was gone.

He was not in class and not on her first-period attendance list. Linda could not say she was unhappy about that—he was probably her worst student, a problem both behaviorally and academically—but his sudden unexplained absence disturbed her. It was almost as though he'd been deleted, erased, with no indication that he had ever existed, like some disappeared dissident in a totalitarian state.

There was another mysteriously missing student in her third-period class—another troublemaker—and when she stopped by the department office between third and fourth periods to check on the status of tenth-grade textbooks that had still not arrived, she learned that Diane and Steve Warren also had students who no longer seemed to be enrolled in school.

"Do you think—?" she began.

"I *know,*" Diane said. "Jody said they were going to do this."

"But so fast?"

Steve smiled wryly. "I guess charter schools *are* more efficient."

Still, the absences gnawed at her, and at lunch she gathered up her courage and went into the office, looking for answers. Bobbi frowned at her as she walked in, but Linda ignored the disapproving stare and walked over to the cubicle of Elena Moore, the attendance clerk. She'd never had that much contact with Elena, but every time they'd encountered each other, they'd always chatted easily and gotten along. So it was a surprise to see the attendance clerk look up at her and scowl angrily. "What do *you* want?"

Linda was taken aback, but she tried hard not to act as flustered as she felt. Bobbi, she knew, was watching. Jody could very well be watching, too. "I, uh . . ." She forced herself to smile. "I'm just trying to find out about a couple of my students who've been taken off the attendance roll—"

"The rolls have been purged," Elena said shortly.

Much to the clerk's annoyance, Linda sat down in a chair next to her desk. "What exactly does that mean?"

"What do you mean, 'What does that mean?' "

" 'The rolls have been purged'? What about the students? Did they move? Have they transferred to other schools? Where exactly are they?"

"That's none of your business," Elena told her. The voice was still antagonistic, but she kept sneaking furtive glances at Bobbi, and Linda understood that the attendance clerk was afraid.

Maybe that was why she was hewing so closely to the party line.

Perhaps if she could get Elena away from here, talk to her one-on-one . . .

She looked into the clerk's eyes. No. The fear was there, but behind it was the will of a true believer. This was not the Elena she had known.

This was not the *office* she had known.

Now that she was here, Linda shifted uncomfortably

in her chair, trying to figure out what had changed. Obviously, the people had undergone a cultlike transformation. But that was not all. There was something wrong with the building as well. She felt uneasy being in it and was still not sure why. She glanced around. There was a new carpet, an ugly one, although that hardly would have affected her perception to such a degree. The plants were gone, the pothos and ficus that had been in pots and hanging baskets, and the windows were tinted so darkly that no one could see in *or* out. The recessed bars of fluorescent light in the ceiling glowed not the typically antiseptic white but a more sickly greenish yellow. None of these things individually would have been so disturbing, but taken together, everything was off just enough that the entire scene was skewed, which was probably the reason why she felt so ill at ease.

No, it wasn't.

No. It wasn't.

Something else was at work here, something that could not be seen but could only be felt. It was not the physical placement of objects within the room that made it so unsettling but the living essence of the office itself. As crazy as that sounded.

Still, she kept the false smile on her face. "So you can't tell me what happened to my students?"

"No, I cannot. That would be a breach of confidentiality. But don't worry," Elena said shortly. "They'll be replaced."

"What do you mean, they'll be replaced?"

"Our funding still depends on enrollment even though we're a charter school. We can't afford to let the count go down."

"But—"

"Principal Hawkes has arranged to bring in some

high achievers to help tilt the balance." Elena's smile was cold and hard. "Your test scores will go through the roof."

This was not what Linda wanted to hear.

The attendance clerk turned away, sorting through a stack of forms on her desk, and Linda understood that she was being dismissed. It was just as well. She was starting to perspire. The office seemed far too warm. It also seemed hard to breathe, and though she had never before been claustrophobic, it felt as if the walls were closing in on her and the room were shrinking. She stood, heading out of the office the way she'd come, and it was all she could do not to run out in a mad dash for freedom.

Outside, the open air felt wonderful, and she bent down, put her hands on her knees and breathed deeply, like a runner who had just finished a race. She glanced back at the office and though she could see nothing through the dark tinted glass, Linda had the feeling that she was being watched. She hurried into the crowd of milling students and did not relax until she was in the teachers' lounge and the office was hidden from her behind closed doors.

The next day, two more of her students were gone, both of whom could most charitably be described as academic underachievers. Another boy, Luke Vernon, came to fourth period late, turned in his textbooks and angrily told Linda that he had been expelled.

"For what?" she asked, incredulous. Luke wasn't one of her best students, but he was squarely in the bell portion of the curve and he certainly wasn't a behavioral problem.

"Made-up reasons," he said. "Coach Nicholson said that I refused to follow directions and was being insubordinate because I walked on the six-minute jog/walk, and he wanted me to run. It's part of the president's physical-fitness test, and it doesn't even count toward our grade. And it's called the jog/*walk*. You can do either."

It came to her then: he wasn't good in PE.

Jody was weeding out not just those students who didn't perform well academically but those who did not do well in *any* class.

Don't worry. They'll be replaced.

"I'll be back," Luke promised. "My dad's a lawyer. And once he hears about this, he's going to sue the school."

I hope he does, Linda thought, but she could not say such a thing aloud. She took his textbooks, signed him out and wished him luck.

After Luke left, Linda looked out over her class, noting the empty seats, feeling discouraged. She thought for a moment. "We're going to do something different today," she said. "A creative-writing exercise."

Groans greeted her announcement, but not as many as she would have expected. Several students actually looked at her expectantly.

Her mood brightened a little. Maybe she was making progress.

"When I was in high school, one of my English teachers played a fun game with us. She turned out all of the lights, played a piece of instrumental music—sometimes it was classical, sometimes rock, sometimes jazz—and had us listen. Afterward, we had to tell her what images the music conjured in our heads. We're going to do a variation on that here today. Only I'm going to ask you to write down your impressions instead of saying them aloud. You might write a story, a poem or a descriptive paragraph. You could even write down individual words that correspond to what you feel when you hear the music. It's up to you. Now, I'm going to play three pieces. I'll play them each twice. The first time, I want you to just close your eyes, listen and let your mind go. When it's done, I'll play it again, and at that time I want you to write. Ready?"

The students nodded, closing their eyes.

She chose three instrumentals that she enjoyed and that happened to be in her CD stack here in the room: a Rick Wakeman song her older brother had turned her on to when she was a kid, a Keith Jarrett improvisation she'd discovered on her own and a Daniel Lentz composition she'd first heard in a music-appreciation class in college. She started with the Wakeman piece, "Anne Boleyn" from *The Six Wives of Henry VIII,* and although everyone was supposed to remain quiet and reflect individually on what they'd heard, the second the music stopped, the students started talking.

"It reminds me of a bad acid trip," Roland Nevins said. Several other kids nodded sagely in agreement.

"It makes me think of being raped," Tiffany Leung offered.

"Yeah," another girl said. "Exactly."

Linda frowned. These were not the responses she'd been expecting, and she found the students' observations more than a little disconcerting. Her goal with this exercise was to get them to use their imaginations, and the last thing she wanted to do was dictate the type of response they should have to the music, but the piece was supposed to be a musical portrait of Henry VIII's most famous wife, and the dark descriptions that were being expressed were definitely at odds with what she perceived as the lyrical tone of the music.

What bothered her most was that the kids seemed to be speaking from experience.

"Being raped *while* on a bad acid trip," Tiffany said definitively.

Linda looked out at the faces before her as she pressed the replay button on her CD player. All the students who'd spoken up, she realized, had those Tyler patches on the sleeves of their tops or shirts.

"Start writing now," she announced. "You have until the song is over, and then we're going on to the next one."

The situation was repeated with the next two pieces she played, and once again it was the students with those patches who seemed to be the ones expressing strange and seriously off-center opinions.

She'd heard from some of the other teachers that the patches indicated their wearers were "scouts," part of some new hall-monitor program Jody had set up. That was fine; there'd always been students in school who had been given the opportunity to police their peers to a greater or lesser extent. But she suspected an ulterior motive on the part of the principal. Something was up here, and she found herself wondering exactly how and why these particular students had been chosen.

The class continued to write their impressions of the Daniel Lentz piece.

She was very curious to read what they had written.

At lunch, Diane said she had some paperwork to catch up with. Since she was on a diet anyway, she was going to skip eating and work in the department office, so Linda went with Suzanne to the lounge. She had just heated up some leftover spaghetti and was starting to eat when Paul Mays, the EH teacher, stormed into the room and slammed down his briefcase on the table, startling Suzanne and causing her to spill her coffee. Linda quickly grabbed a handful of paper towels and began soaking up the mess. All the teachers in the lounge looked over at the angry EH instructor.

"They're putting up walls around the campus. Did you hear that? I can't get enough textbooks for my class, and they're putting up a nine-foot wall because Enrique is too lazy to clean graffiti off the buildings. This is a high school, for God's sake! There's going to be graffiti."

Linda hadn't heard anything about this. "What do you mean, a wall?" she asked. "Like a chain-link fence?"

"No. A brick wall. Which of course will soon be covered with . . . graffiti!" Paul grimaced.

"They could use barbed wire," Alonso Ruiz suggested. "It would keep people out and you can't write on it."

Everyone looked at the woodshop teacher.

"I'm just saying," he mumbled embarrassedly.

"Is the point to keep people out . . . or keep people in?" Linda wondered aloud.

Paul sat down heavily. "A brick wall. I can't believe it. Linda's right. It'll be like working in a prison."

"Jody could use her new 'scouts' as guards," she suggested.

"You laugh now," Alonso said, "but that might be on the menu."

"I'm not laughing."

"I'm not either," Paul said. "I'm pissed. Jody and her stupid committee have turned down every single request I've made this semester. Even for necessities. But they can waste who knows how many thousands of dollars on a brick barrier that's going to enclose the whole school? Just because Enrique's too goddamn lazy to do his job?"

"I don't think that's why you can't get books," Suzanne said quietly. "I think they're trying to phase out the EH program to bring up test scores."

"What?" Now Paul was screaming. He jumped out of his seat. "Where's Art? Where's Joseph? Where's Nina? I want to talk to one of those assholes on the charter committee! I want some answers, goddamn it!"

"I think part of it *is* Enrique," Trudy Temple said. "The other day, in the gym, he refused to clean the gum off the bleachers when I asked. I had to get Hung to do it." She nodded at Paul. "*I'm* pissed because I can't get my girls new volleyballs, yet, like you say, they have money for this fence."

"I'll ask Carlos or Rakeem about it," Ray Cheng promised. "I know they're not thrilled with Enrique these days. They'll tell me what's going on behind the scenes."

"I think they're both on night shift," Alonso said.

"Mike, then."

As if on cue, Mike walked into the lounge. The custodian walked straight to the sink, where he started washing out his coffee cup, and was about to get something out of the refrigerator when he noticed everyone looking at him. "All right," he said, facing the group. "What's going on?"

"The wall," Paul said angrily.

Mike held up his hands in a gesture of surrender. "I had nothing to do with that. Out of my jurisdiction."

"Whose idea was it?" Paul asked. "Enrique's? I heard that he thinks this'll keep kids out and cut down on graffiti."

"He does have a bug up his butt about graffiti," Mike said. "But this order came from the top. I don't know—maybe Enrique had something to do with it. Maybe he told Principal Hawkes that we needed it or something. But she's the one made the decision."

" 'Principal Hawkes'?" Linda said. "You're not a student. You don't have to call her 'Principal Hawkes.' Call her Jody. Like that pig in *The Amityville Horror.*"

"Linda!" Suzanne said, laughing.

"We're all friends here."

Mike was smiling. "We all think the wall's a stupid idea. All of us except Enrique." He turned around, took a half-filled two-liter bottle of Mountain Dew out of the refrigerator and poured some of the drink into his coffee cup. "And there's going to be *more* graffiti because of the wall. It gives the kids a bigger surface to tag on." He put the bottle back into the refrigerator. "You ask me, Principal Hawkes . . . uh, Jody . . . suckered Enrique with that graffiti argument. I think she wants a wall so she can lock the kids down here."

"I think you're right," Linda said.

Mike waved, heading toward the door. "Gotta go. Maybe Enrique can disappear for hours on end, but the rest of us gotta take up the slack." He put a hand to his mouth and widened his eyes in mock surprise. "Oh! Did I say too much?" Grinning, he walked out. "Later."

Linda's food was cold by now, but the lunch hour was passing quickly, and she took a bite of her spaghetti. She turned toward Paul. "The wall aside, Suzanne might be right about dismantling the EH program." Between bites, she explained about her missing students and the plan she'd heard about replacing them with ringers. "I think Jody's remaking Tyler into her idea of a perfect high school."

Paul scowled. "Well, I won't stand for it. She's got a fight on her hands, whether she wants one or not."

"Good!" Linda said. "I'm with you." She looked around as the other teachers nodded their support. "We're all with you."

Before going back to class, she stopped by the women's restroom. Pushing open the door, she saw a flash of movement on her right. Then Bobbi bumped against her, practically pushing her into the doorjamb on her way in. Linda expected to hear an "I'm sorry" or "Excuse me," but the other woman continued forward, heedless.

Maybe it was an emergency, Linda rationalized. But Bobbi didn't head into one of the stalls; she walked over to one of the sinks and began leisurely patting down her hair while looking at herself in the mirror.

Linda felt a small twinge of anger at that. *She bumped into me on purpose.* "Hey!" she called out.

Bobbi glanced over at her. "I did not get your completed fund-raising estimates."

"No. You didn't."

"I need them today. I needed them yesterday."

Linda smiled, saying nothing.

"You will have them on my desk by this afternoon or disciplinary action will be taken."

"I'll take it into consideration."

Bobbi whirled on her. "You will do it! I am this school's administrative coordinator. It is my job to make sure that you comply with all rules and regulations. I am *above* you in the campus hierarchy—do you want me to show you the flowchart?—and when I tell you to do something, I expect you to do it. Believe me, I can make life very difficult for you."

"You know," Diane said from the closed stall, and Linda was surprised to discover her friend was in there, "I don't think I'm getting you a present for Secretary's Day this year."

"I am the administrative coordinator!" Bobbi shouted. "I am not a secretary!"

Linda leaned forward. "Bobbi? I think Jody needs

someone to take a memo and make some coffee. Do you think you can hurry along and do that for her?" She smiled, batting her eyelashes.

She thought for sure that the woman was going to slap her. The rage on that face was unlike anything she had ever seen, a furious distortion of features that made her appear almost deranged. But instead of lashing out, she stalked away, slamming the door against the wall as she threw it open.

Diane giggled.

Linda went into the far stall to use the toilet. When she emerged, her friend was standing in front of a mirror, putting on lipstick. "That was funny," she said.

"Wasn't it?"

"Crawls out of a hole and thinks she rules the world."

"What do you think Her Royal Highness will do if I fail to turn in my estimates?"

"Give you thirty lashes.'

"She'd sure like to."

Diane paused. "Listen," she said. "All joking aside? You really should turn those things in. As department chair, I've been getting pressure on this. Jody's likely to take it out on both of us."

"What can she do? We have tenure."

"Have you read our charter's fine print? I'm not sure tenure even applies in this brave new world."

Linda frowned. "You're not caving, are you?"

"Of course not. Never." Diane sighed. "But I think, from here on in, we're going to have to pick and choose our battles."

Linda was late getting back for fifth period, and there was a new student standing next to her desk when she arrived. She told the rest of the class to read silently for ten minutes—they were halfway through *Cat's Cradle*—while she got the new student settled.

She read the sheet he handed her. His name was Brandon Cowles, and he was transferring from Washington High.

Washington High?

That was a magnet school for science.

He was one of Jody's ringers, Linda realized, and although she knew it was wrong and petty of her, she found herself hoping that he was a poor student in English. She would love to be able to give one of Jody's handpicked replacements a failing grade. The boy also had an air of privilege about him that she found more than a little off-putting. Still, she smiled as she issued him a book and assigned him a seat.

When she decided that she'd given the students enough reading time and started to ask questions about the novel, Brandon was the first to raise his hand.

Damn it, he was smart.

She looked impasssively over the rows of students before her and called on someone else.

"I want to speak with the principal. Right now!"

Libby Vernon glared at the officious bitch who tried to pass herself off as the school's public face. She'd dealt with bureaucracies before, and she knew that the only way to get anything done was to go straight to the top and not waste time and energy dealing with flunkies. She'd forgotten the bitch's name already, but she squinted at the name tag pinned to her flat chest. "Bobbi," she ordered. "Get your boss."

"I'm the administrative coordinator—"

"I don't care if you're the emperor of China. I want to talk to the principal!"

Clearly insulted and angry, the other woman turned on her heels and strode briskly away, walking across the open area behind the front counter and down a short hallway into an office. She emerged a moment later with another woman in tow, a well-dressed, dark-haired woman who looked like the wife of a Midwestern politician. The principal. There was a nasty expression on Bobbi's face, nasty and almost triumphant, but Libby didn't have time to analyze the look because the principal was there, offering a well-manicured hand to shake. "I'm Principal Hawkes. How may I help you?"

"My son. Luke Vernon. He's apparently been—"

"Expelled," the principal said.

"I want him reinstated. Now."

The principal fixed her with an insincere smile. "I'm sorry, I cannot do that."

"Luke has never been suspended or even had detention. He's never been in trouble before at all. And now he's been *expelled*?"

The smile remained frozen. "According to our physical education instructor, your son refused to follow directions and complete the assignment given him. 'Gross insubordination,' I think, is the term the instructor used."

"Insubordination? What is this, the army?"

"No, Mrs. Vernon. It is a high school."

"That's not even a cause for keeping him after class, let alone expelling him. Besides, it's the teacher's word against Luke's, and I'll take Luke's every time. So unless you want a lawsuit on your hands"—she leaned forward—"I suggest you rescind that expulsion pronto and put my son back in his classes before he falls even farther behind due to your *gross* incompetence."

"Why don't we step into my office for a moment," Principal Hawkes offered. "We can discuss this matter in private."

"I'd just as soon discuss it right here." She glanced around the room. "We'll need witnesses for our lawsuit. By the way," she said, "my husband's a lawyer."

"Come into my office. I'm sure we can find an amicable way to resolve this issue." Still smiling, the principal motioned for her to walk behind the counter.

"Fine."

Libby followed the principal through the open area and into the short hall that led to her office. The second she passed through the doorway that framed the truncated corridor, she hesitated, caught her breath. It suddenly felt as though all the oxygen had been sucked out of the atmosphere. The air was not appreciably colder—there were not even any visible air-conditioning ducts—but goose bumps popped up instantly on every inch of exposed flesh. Her heart was pounding. The passage might be short and well lit, but it was creepier than any long dark hallway she had ever seen.

No, it wasn't creepy, exactly.

It was wrong.

Yes. There was something wrong with the brief hall, and when she forced herself to walk again and follow the principal, Libby felt slightly off-balance, unsure on her feet.

Jody Hawkes pushed open the door to her office and led the way inside.

What was this? Libby stepped forward slowly. Behind her, the door closed with a muffled click. The room was unlike anything she had ever seen. It certainly wasn't what a high school principal's office should look like. Her eyes took in the purple-striped walls, the dirty broken furniture, the lone window smeared with mud. Beneath her feet, the floor was cracked concrete. From the ceiling hung a single bare bulb on which was drawn a frowning face. There was the smell of rotten fruit in the air.

The principal strode to the other side of her scarred and lopsided desk. From the jumbled pile of odds and ends atop it, she withdrew a bamboo cane. She used it to point at a rickety, rusted folding chair in front of Libby. All trace of conciliation was gone from her voice. "Sit your ass down," she ordered.

Libby did as she was told. She'd come in here angry and out for blood, full of righteous indignation, but after going through that hallway and seeing this incomprehensible office, she felt cowed and effectively subdued. The balance of power had shifted, and she looked up at the principal, who was still standing on the other side of the desk and holding the cane.

"Your child was insubordinate!" the principal thundered.

Mention of Luke brought back her courage. "I want him reinstated."

"Silence!"

Libby shut up.

The principal walked slowly around the side of the broken desk, twirling the cane in her hands. "I will give your child one more chance," she said coldly. "*One.* But if his score on the president's physical-fitness test does not improve, he is out of here." She leaned forward. "And there *will* be consequences."

That sounded like a threat, and although Libby would have gone into attack mode if that statement had been made when she'd first walked into the building, she now accepted it without protest, grateful that the principal had nothing more to add. She was afraid of the other woman, and not even for Luke was she willing to face her wrath.

"Now get out of my office," the principal said, pointing the cane at her. "And don't come back."

Libby stood quickly and hurried out, down that horrible short hallway into the larger open area. Was that officious little bitch smirking at her? She didn't know, didn't care. All she wanted was to escape, to get out of this building and as far away from the principal and her hellish purple-striped room as possible. She felt like a coward, a traitor to her son, but fear and self-preservation overrode love and loyalty, and she strode so quickly across campus to the parking lot that she nearly knocked over a timid young girl hurrying to class, clutching her books to her chest.

She did not breathe easily until she was in her car and off school property, speeding down the street away from Tyler High as fast as the law would allow.

Eleven

His parents weren't there when Ed came home from school, and they still hadn't returned by the time dinner hour rolled around. For the past two years, he'd gotten nothing but grief from them about the importance of eating together, his mom going on and on about how teenagers who ate meals with their parents were more successful academically and less likely to use drugs or get involved with gangs. Now *they* were the ones who were not here.

Maybe they're dead. Maybe they were killed in a car accident.

He pushed the thought out of his mind. What would make him even think such a thing?

Working at the library.

Yeah. That would do it. Ed walked into the kitchen. Mrs. Fratelli was, without a doubt, the freakiest person he had ever met. The other day, he had come across her licking something small and black off her index finger. He hadn't asked what she was doing, but she volunteered the information anyway. "I like to pull out my eyelashes and eat them," she said. "They taste salty."

He'd nearly gagged, but had managed to leave her

presence without commenting or reacting or drawing attention to himself. He'd had a dream that night that he'd come upon her in her office and she'd been breaking the arms off a dead infant lying on her desk. "I like to pull their arms out and eat them," she said. "They taste salty." It was one of those dreams where after he woke up, he wasn't sure if he'd dreamed it or it had really happened, and to his mind, that said more about the librarian than anything else.

Mrs. Fratelli also seemed to have a strange hold on the other students who worked as library assistants. It was not something he could even pretend to understand, but with the exception of himself, all the boys and girls who worked in the library, in all periods, had the same dour, subdued, almost anesthetized demeanor as Mrs. Fratelli herself. It was almost as though she had hypnotized everyone—except him.

Then why, he often wondered, did she keep him around?

He was not sure he wanted to know the answer to that question.

Rummaging through the kitchen cupboards, he found an open, half-empty box of Cheez-Its, and he took it out, shoving half a dozen of the little orange squares into his mouth. He grabbed a can of Coke out of the refrigerator and headed back out to the living room. He'd finished his homework, so he turned on the TV, flipping the channels until he found something worth watching.

It was dark out now. And his parents still weren't home.

The phone rang. He picked it up immediately, heart pounding. "Hello?"

There was a mechanical click and then the recorded voice of his school principal: "Good evening, parents.

This is Jody Hawkes, principal of John Tyler High School. I want to remind you that our Back-to-School Night is this Thursday. We will be—"

Ed hung up the phone.

It rang again immediately.

He picked it up, and once more there was a mechanical click, followed by the principal's voice: "How dare you hang up on me?" It was a recording, but the voice sounded angry. Startled, Ed hung up the phone again.

Immediately, it started ringing.

He backed away, feeling frightened, though he knew he couldn't be harmed by a phone call.

There was a beep as the answering machine picked up, and then another recording of Principal Hawkes' furious voice, low and dangerous. "Pick up the phone, you little shit. I know you're listening."

He backed into the kitchen, peeking around the corner, afraid even to be in the same room as the telephone.

"You will never graduate," the recording of Principal Hawkes' vicious voice promised. "I'll make sure of that."

Ed found that his hands were shaking. What exactly did she mean by *that* remark? That she was going to make sure he didn't have enough credits to graduate?

Or that she was going to make sure he was dead before the end of his senior year?

There was a click and then silence as the message ended. He waited several minutes, hiding in the kitchen, just in case the phone rang again. But when it became clear that the calls were over, he stepped carefully back into the living room, keeping his eye on the red blinking light of the answering machine. Even that light seemed eerie and intimidating to him, the way it kept flashing like a robotic eye, but it also told him that he had captured the message, that he had proof, and he walked over to the end table and pressed the PLAY button. Instead of Principal Hawkes' angry voice, however, there was only a muffled hum that sounded like the engine of a boat as heard from underwater.

The front door opened, and he nearly jumped out of his skin. It was his parents. His mom put down her purse while his dad closed and locked the front door. They both looked tired and demoralized.

"Where were you guys?" he demanded.

"Don't ask," his dad said.

"We were in an accident," his mom responded. "Or at least we thought we were in an accident."

Ed frowned, confused.

"It was by your school," his dad explained. "We were late to begin with because some jackass had slashed both rear tires on the Buick. Had to get towed to Sears and get two new ones. Cost me a damn fortune. Last time I'm taking my business there. On the way back, there was some kind of construction on Madison, so I took a shortcut down Grayson. Right in front of your school"—he shook his head—"this kid ran out into the street. *Right* in front of the car. I swerved, but . . ."

"We hit him," his mother said.

"Or we thought we did. I mean, we heard the bump, *felt* the bump, and I slammed on the brakes and jumped out, but . . . there was no one there. Nothing there. Not even an animal or a rock or a branch or . . . anything."

"We saw that boy, though," his mom emphasized. "He ran right in front of the car, a foot away from us, and we hit him."

"We *didn't* hit him," his father said, annoyed. "He wasn't there. There was no one there." He looked bewildered. "There wasn't even a dent on the fender."

"But we felt it."

His dad nodded. "We felt it." He exhaled deeply. "Anyway, that's why we're late. I pulled over, walked up and down the block, even knocked on a few doors to see if any of the neighbors had seen anything. Nothing." He grimaced, turned to his wife. "I don't want to talk about it anymore. What's our plan for dinner?"

As he watched his parents trudge tiredly toward the kitchen, Ed saw, out of the corner of his eye, the flashing red light of the answering machine, and he couldn't help thinking that their holdup had been intentional, that everything had been a setup, that they had been delayed because someone had *wanted* him to hear that angry, threatening recording.

But why? What point did it serve? And why go to so much trouble for such a small pointless thing?

He didn't know, but he believed it.

And it scared him.

"I'm not lying, dude! It's the truth!" Ed kicked a dead leaf on the sidewalk in frustration. The leaf crumpled into tiny brown pieces.

Brad shrugged his shoulders, not sure of what to say.

"I believe you," Myla said quietly.

Brad looked at her in surprise. Ed's story was completely ridiculous. Maybe he did really believe it had happened, but that just meant that he'd been half-asleep or on medication or . . . something. Because what he'd described was impossible. A prerecorded message did not have angry prerecorded follow-ups. And there was no way the principal had sat there calling Ed and *pretending* to be a recording.

"I got that same message," Myla said. "About Back-to-School Night."

"Everyone did. But there was no recording of Principal Hawkes swearing at the people who hung up." Brad looked at his friend. "Sorry."

"I *heard* it. And it scared the shit out of me."

"Look," Brad said, "I'll admit that there's something weird going on at this school." *Haunted* was the word he had in mind, although he was afraid to say it aloud. "But it's the school, not the people. And not the principal. I mean, she's . . . she's . . ."

"She's what?" Ed prompted. "She's the person in charge of this freaky place. And her job title does not guarantee that she's not a psycho. There are plenty of doctors, lawyers and fine upstanding members of the community who turned out to be thieves, murderers or worse!"

Brad smiled. "Or worse? What's worse than a murderer, Ed?"

"You know what I'm talking about."

Myla fixed Brad with a hard stare. "After what we saw, you're telling me you're still not open-minded enough to believe that what Ed said happened?"

Ed frowned. "What did you see?"

"You didn't tell him?"

"I guess I forgot," Brad said. But of course he hadn't forgotten. He'd been avoiding that hallway ever since, even in the daytime, and he was wary of every locker now, including his own. But just thinking of talking about it, even to Ed, made him feel stupid, and the truth was that he'd been embarrassed to mention it.

Both Myla and Ed were staring at him.

"You're right," he said. "You caught me." He turned to Ed, told him what had happened when he and Myla had stopped by the school after their date.

"Fuck howdy! And you wouldn't believe that I got a threatening message from the principal?"

"Well, I just couldn't see how it could work. I mean, I know the school has the cheapest-ass equipment possible, and it didn't seem like it could redial the same number with a different message when it was programmed to send the same recording to everyone." The explanation sounded lame even to himself.

"Yet ghosts could fly out of a locker and chase you off campus?"

"Yeah," he said weakly.

"That makes a lot of sense."

Brad smiled. "I should move to Missouri."

Myla dropped her voice as a group of jocks walked by. "You heard about the art class, didn't you?"

Ed grinned. "I sure did." He nudged Brad with his elbow. "I wish I would've signed up for art this semester."

"No one's supposed to know this, but Sean Bergman tried to kill himself over the weekend. He's in Fairview right now, under observation. That was his mom they drew."

"How do you know this?" Brad asked.

"I got an e-mail yesterday. Everyone on student council did." She looked at him significantly. "From the principal."

"And that's supposed to mean . . . ?"

"Think about it."

"Why does the student council get told stuff like that?" Ed asked. "What are you guys supposed to do about it?"

"You've got me," Myla admitted. "Ask Principal Hawkes."

"I'd rather not."

Brad was still confused. "So the principal's responsible somehow?"

"Not exactly," Myla said. "But she knows about this art class—she must have approved it—and even though Sean tried to commit suicide, she's still not shutting it down. She doesn't even care."

Ed slapped a hand on his shoulder. "There's your principal. That fine upstanding citizen."

"Hands off, homo." Brad moved away from him.

"Cheryl wants us to keep the Sean thing quiet," Myla said. "I think she just feels privileged that Mrs. Hawkes is e-mailing us. She doesn't want to rock the boat. *I* think we should let everyone know. Especially parents. If they put pressure on the school . . ."

"Tell the school paper," Brad suggested. "I could talk to Brian—"

"Don't tell anyone!" Ed said. "We've got naked moms here. We don't want to put a stop to that!"

They both looked at him.

"Fine," he said. "Fine. I'm the asshole. I'm the dick. Do whatever you want."

Traffic was getting thick as students hurried past in both directions. Brad didn't have a watch, but he could tell that it was almost time for the bell to ring.

"The whole fucking place is going crazy," Ed said. He pointed to where a group of day laborers was digging up a section of lawn on the edge of campus. "And what's with this wall they're putting up? Did Hawkes e-mail you about that?"

"No," Myla said. "We got a special presentation, complete with a computer rendering of what the school will look like after it's done. Apparently, there's been a lot of vandalism and graffiti this year, and the administration decided to put up the wall to keep troublemakers out of the school on nights and weekends. And to discourage truancy during school hours. It'll be a lot harder to ditch if we're all locked in here."

"It's going to be like a prison," Brad said.

"That's what we told her. Even Cheryl complained about it. But they got some architect to design it, and there's going to be new landscaping, and it's supposed to blend right in."

"How tall's it going to be?" Ed asked.

"Nine feet, I think."

"Oh yeah. That'll blend right in," he said sarcastically.

"Break it up here!"

Brad jumped at the sound of the voice. Ed and Myla did, too, and there was a chorus of laughter as Todd Zivney and two of his tough friends moved in on them. "What are you talking about?" Zivney demanded.

"Your mom," Ed said.

Zivney shoved him, nearly knocking him down. "We're here on official business, asshole." He pointed to the Tyler patch on his sleeve. "It's against school rules for you to make fun of the school on school grounds."

"Lot of 'school's in that sentence," Ed noted.

One of Zivney's friends moved forward, but Brad blocked his way. "What do you want?"

"It was reported to us that you were talking trash about Tyler."

"Yeah. So? It's a free country."

Zivney grinned. "Not here, it isn't."

"I'm on the student council," Myla announced. "I'm the vice president. I outrank you."

"Oh yeah?" Zivney sneered. His friends laughed.

The bell rang.

"Yeah," Myla said. "And, believe me, I'm going to report this harassment." She used a finger to push against Zivney's patch. Hard. He winced but tried not to show it. "If I have anything to say about it, you're going to be kicked out of the scout program so fast your head will spin."

"You *don't* have anything to say about it," Zivney told her, but he and his friends were already leaving, heading to class. He pointed at Ed as he backed up. "This isn't over."

"Funny. That's just what your mom said." He ducked behind Brad, but the three scouts had turned away and were halfway down the hall.

Brad punched his friend's shoulder. "What are you trying to do? Get me killed?"

"At least we know one thing," Myla told them. "We'd better start being careful about what we say in public."

There was no time to talk further. The hallway was nearly empty, the second bell was about to ring and, saying quick good-byes, the three of them hurried off to their respective classes.

Spanish was boring, as usual, although the next class, math, was anything but. Brad and Ed arrived at almost the same time and saw Mr. Connor carefully writing the word "DEATH" on the blackboard in big block letters. As the class filled up and the bell rang, the teacher continued to write, augmenting his white chalk letters with red chalk horror-show blood that dripped from the cross-stroke of the T.

Finally, Mr. Connor turned to face them. His cheeks were red, his forehead was sweaty and the front of his light blue shirt was stained with a spreading Rorschach of perspiration. He smiled humorlessly and looked at each of them with bulging too-wide eyes. Using the piece of red chalk still in his hand, he pointed to the word on the board. "*Death,*" he said. "If it were up to me, that would be the punishment for every student who does not get a hundred percent on my tests." He glanced wildly around the room. *"That means all of you!"* he screamed.

As unobtrusively as possible, Brad looked sideways. Ed, already doing the same, widened his eyes slightly to acknowledge the craziness of what was happening.

Mr. Connor leaned forward. "If I had my druthers, each and every one of you would be slit open, crotch to gullet, and left to stare at your innards as you died." He straightened, put down the piece of chalk, ran a hand through his hair to straighten it. "But, fortunately for you, our school charter forbids it."

The law, too, Brad wanted to say, but he was afraid to move a muscle, let alone speak up. He stared straight ahead.

"I don't think you realize how lucky you are to be attending a charter school. Our charter not only protects you. It grants you rights and privileges far beyond those afforded students in other schools. If this were an English class, I would have you write essays on what the charter means to you and have you tell me how grateful you are. But," he said, and once again there was a hint of wildness in his eyes, "this is an algebra class. Algebra Two. And the charter mandates that you learn a specific curriculum this semester." He started to pace in front of the blackboard. "The problem is that you have so far demonstrated neither the aptitude nor the ambition to master that curriculum. You are a spectacularly mediocre class."

"Death!" he screamed, pointing at the word on the board. "That's what you all deserve!"

Zorida Marin, in the last row, burst into tears.

"There will be no crying in this classroom!" he shouted at her, and her sobs ceased instantly.

"Now," he said, his voice calmer, "we will spend

the rest of the period discussing what the charter demands of *us* and what *we* can give the charter."

Forty minutes later, the students emerged from the class silently, seconds before the bell rang. Mr. Connor had let them out early, but none of them dared speak, and they merely looked at one another as they exited into the hall. Then the bell did ring, and students were pouring out of the adjoining rooms, laughing, talking, yelling.

"I don't even know what to say to that," Ed admitted.

"There's nothing *to* say," Brad told him.

Ed nodded, and the two of them separated, heading into the crowd and off to their next classes.

Twelve

Back-to-School Night sneaked up on her this year. In fact, it seemed to sneak up on everyone. Linda had no idea how that had happened. For one thing, the event was later than usual—four weeks after school had started rather than the usual two—and for another, Jody had been pestering them about it in e-mails and voice mails and memos left in their mailboxes. That should have meant that they'd be *more* prepared than they were ordinarily. But all day Thursday, teachers were skipping lunch and showing videos during class as they tried desperately to get their rooms ready for the evening.

Carpooling with Diane, Linda felt woefully unprepared herself. It shouldn't have mattered, since, ordinarily, very few parents attended Tyler's Back-to-School Night. It was well-known among teachers that nearly all parents showed up for Back-to-School Night at the elementary level, there was a big attendance drop-off in junior high, and by the time their kids reached high school, hardly anyone showed.

But as Diane pulled into the parking lot and the two of them looked in vain for an open space, it was clear that that was not going to be the situation this year. Start time was still forty-five minutes away, yet they were forced to drive around to the opposite side of the school and park on the street.

"I guess I should have worked a little harder on my bulletin boards," Diane said drily.

Linda shook her head. "This is amazing."

Every light in the high school seemed to be on, and both around the perimeter of the school and down the corridors that led to the center of campus, they could see men and women milling about, pointing at rooms and familiarizing themselves with the layout of the buildings. They got out of the car and walked through the crowd of parents to the office, where Jody had informed the staff they were all required to sign in. There was a skeleton staff on duty—Bobbi and Janet—but she and Diane ignored them both, signing in silently and not speaking until they were once again outside.

Linda surveyed the quad. "I wonder where Jody is."

"She's out there somewhere," Diane intoned in a hushed dramatic voice. "Somewhere in the dark, dark night."

Linda laughed.

"Let's go. I really do have some last-minute decorating to do." They began walking. "Meet in the department office after it's over?"

"Sure."

Although their classrooms were in the same building, Linda's was upstairs and Diane's down, so they parted at the stairway. "It's going to be a busy night," Diane predicted.

"That'll be a nice change of pace," Linda said, starting up the steps.

But while the campus was teeming outside, the stairwell was empty and so was the hallway on the second floor.

Save for a lone figure standing at the far end.

Jody Hawkes.

She stood exactly where she had before, and while the doors of several other classrooms were open, teachers inside, none of them came out, and it was as though the two of them were alone in the corridor. Jody smiled at her, an inexplicably wide and off-putting grin. Then, just like last time, she turned and walked down the opposite stairway.

Feeling ill at ease—which was doubtless Jody's intention—Linda unlocked and opened her classroom door. Flipping on the lights, she saw that everything was in place, where she'd left it. But there was a terrible odor in the room. The place smelled like a cat box, and she walked slowly around the periphery, sniffing, trying to determine where the stench was coming from. Finally, she narrowed it down to the book corner, where she kept the volumes of her class library, and after a little more investigation, she came upon a copy of *Leaves of Grass* lying flat across the tops of several other books. Dried excrement extruded from between the book's pages.

She wasn't sure if the shit was cat or dog or human. She didn't care. Grimacing, she picked up the book by a corner and carried it out into the hall. There was no trash can up here, so she hurried downstairs and outside, tossing it into a barrel next to a tree in front of the building.

Linda returned to her room. The evening was cold, but she opened all the windows that were operable in order to air out the place. She was pretty sure she had some deodorizer somewhere in her desk, and she dug through the drawers until she found the aerosol can. Spraying it all over the room, especially in the book corner, she thought about what had happened, wondering who could have done it.

Jody?

Was that why the principal had been smiling?

No. Even as creepy as she seemed to be these days, Jody would not have defecated in a book. Although just imagining the logistics of such a thing made Linda smile herself, and she laughed out loud at the thought of the principal squatting over the open pages of *Leaves of Grass.*

Her first period's parents started arriving soon after, and though the smell was not entirely gone, no one mentioned it. As always, Back-to-School Night was structured like an ordinary school day, with parents attending their children's classes in the same order as the students did, albeit for only ten minutes each. By the time the first bell rang, every seat in her room was filled, and for the most part it remained that way for the rest of the evening.

There was something unnerving about that. For the first time since she'd started teaching at Tyler, Linda had a chance to speak with the parents of nearly every one of her students. That was great, of course. And all of them seemed interested in how their children were doing so far. But there was a tension underlying their presence. They were being coerced into doing this, and beneath the legitimate concern for their kids' welfare was a barely restrained animosity, the coiled resentment of totalitarianism that people naturally felt toward institutions that dictated and enforced arbitrary rules and requirements.

She was supposed to take attendance and turn into the office the names of any families that did not show, but Linda had no intention of doing that. Only a few parents did not attend, and those who couldn't make it probably had very good reasons. Even if they didn't, she wasn't about to inform on her students' mothers and fathers. For all she knew, Jody was planning to expel the sons and daughters of any parent who didn't come tonight.

And she refused to be a party to that.

In her last class, her sixth-period class, one of the dads kept fooling with his iPhone—or trying to. Finally he gave up. "Excuse me," he said. "Is there some reason I can't get a signal in here?" He looked suspiciously around as if the walls were lined with lead.

"That's true of the whole school," Linda told him. "We don't know why yet, but it's being looked into."

"What if my son needs to get ahold of me?" a mother asked. "What if it's an emergency?"

"That's a good question," Linda told her. "You should bring that up with the principal."

The class emptied out quickly after the final bell—it was eight thirty, after all, and a weeknight besides—and Linda closed her door, intending to tidy up a bit before meeting Diane down in the department office. She turned back toward her desk.

And saw a student sitting in the front row of the classroom.

Her heart practically leaped into her chest, and she let out a short, startled cry. The room had been empty only seconds ago. She was sure of it. She had escorted the last father out the door.

There had been no kids in her class all night.

Yet there one sat now, a boy, in the front row, facing forward, staring at the chalkboard.

He had not moved a muscle when she'd let out her involuntary cry, had not been surprised by her short scream, had not turned to look and see what was happening. Even now, he remained completely silent and still, and she saw with something like horror that while she hadn't noticed it at first, his clothes were dusty and of a style that had been old when her grandparents were young. His hair was not blond, as she'd originally thought, but white.

A spider hung from a thread on his collar and scuttled down his back.

And still the student remained silent, unmoving.

Staring at the blackboard.

Linda ran. She opened the door and bolted down the hall, not bothering to turn off the lights, not locking the door behind her. The sound of her frantic footsteps alerted Steve and Ray, who both hurried out of their classrooms to see what the commotion was all about.

She'd fled on instinct, running away without a plan or thought in her head other than the necessity of escaping, but as soon as she saw the two teachers, she stopped. "There's someone in my classroom!" she said breathlessly. "An intruder!"

Intruder?

That was an odd word. But it was better than "ghost," which was what she was really thinking, and it got Steve and Ray moving. They sprinted back to her classroom and walked inside. "Hello!" she heard Ray call. "Anyone here?"

She knew then that the student was gone—if he had ever been there at all—and though her gut was telling her to flee to safety and get out of the building, she gathered her courage and walked back to her classroom, peeking in. Steve saw her and shrugged his shoulders. "There doesn't seem to be anyone here."

"He was sitting in that seat there." She pointed.

"An *intruder* was *sitting* in a seat," Ray said skeptically.

She couldn't explain what she'd seen: the unmoving boy, the old clothes, the white hair, the spider. There was no way they'd believe any of that—and there was no way she could convey the feeling of terror the utterly still student had engendered within her. So she told them about the despoiled book and how she'd tossed it outside. "I think he was the one who did it," she said. "The guy I saw."

"The intruder."

"I don't know why I called him that. I'm sorry! I didn't mean to make you come in here—I wasn't trying to fool you. . . ." And she started to cry. She couldn't help herself. All her fear and frustration came out in entirely uncharacteristic tears, and she wiped them angrily from her face.

Steve and Ray stood there awkwardly.

"I'm sorry," Ray said. "I didn't mean—"

"It's all right," she told him.

"We could look some more," Steve offered. "Maybe he's hiding."

She waved him away. "Let's just get out of here," she said.

Embarrassed, the two men shuffled past her into the hall. She shut off the lights and closed the door, locking it.

"I believe you," Ray said. "I'm sorry if it seemed like I didn't."

"Yeah," Steve added.

Linda shook her head. She knew they were lying, but she didn't want to discuss it with them. She knew what she'd seen—

a ghost

—and all she wanted to do right now was go downstairs, find Diane and get out of here. She used a finger to push away the last of her tears and forced herself to smile. "It's okay," she told them. "It's been a long day. I'll see you tomorrow."

But before going into the department office to meet with Diane, she walked outside the building to look up at the windows of her room. She saw movement in the darkness, a hazy white bobbing in the black gloom, and she turned quickly away, walking past the trash barrel where she'd thrown *Leaves of Grass,* and back into the building, where her friend was waiting.

The school was crowded. The lights were all on.

And Myla was scared.

There was no rational reason for it. She knew that. But even as she stood behind the baked-goods table, collecting dollar bills and handing out brownies, Myla felt nervous. Reba, next to her, did not seem to notice anything amiss, and neither did the girls from the pep squad or Idakas who were helping out at adjoining tables. The boys from the Key Club were selling sodas across the way, and parents and teachers were everywhere. Yet she might just as well have been sitting alone inside a haunted mansion. For that was the way she felt: anxious, frightened, vulnerable.

The worst thing was that she desperately had to go to the bathroom. She'd been holding it for a long time, planning to tag along with Reba or one of the other girls if they had to go. But no one did. And it was starting to become an emergency.

She told herself that the campus was so crowded there were bound to be other women or girls in there—parents, teachers, students—but logic had nothing to do with the way she felt, and she didn't want to walk down that long hall and go into that bathroom unless she was with someone she knew.

What exactly was she afraid of?

She didn't want to think about it, didn't want to make those fears concrete.

Myla pressed her thighs together, bit the inside of her cheek. She took a dollar from a mother, handing over two chocolate-chip cookies. If she waited any longer, she was going to wet her pants, and even as scared as she was, she knew that she had to walk over to the bathroom now.

"I'll be back in a minute," she told Reba. "I need to use the restroom." She glanced around. "Does anyone else need to go?" she asked hopefully.

No one did, and she moved out from behind the table, made her way through the crowd and started down the hallway to the nearest girls' room. The crowd thinned out as she headed away from the quad. *Why can't the restroom be closer?* She knew the classes around her were filled with mothers and fathers checking in with their children's teachers, and she even passed several pairs of parents on the way, but after the noise and bustle of the tables, the corridor felt long and empty. The fear and dread she'd been experiencing all evening long intensified, and she was sure that if some practical joker jumped out at that moment and yelled "Boo!" she would die of a heart attack.

She reached the girls' room not a moment too soon, hurrying into the first stall in what was practically a crouch. Her heart was pounding, and she was aware that something about the restroom seemed off, but she didn't allow herself to think about it until she was finished. That was less than a minute, however, and even before flushing the toilet, she became conscious of the fact that she was the only one in the bathroom and that she couldn't hear any noises from outside. The tiled room was totally silent save for the amplified beating of her own heart. She quickly flushed, pulled up her panties and jeans and pushed open the swinging metal door. To her left, the light above the far stall was flickering, the bulb ready to go out, and the jittery illumination cast eerie swirling shadows over the back half of the restroom.

Myla quickly hurried away from that strobing area, toward the sinks—

And saw something in the mirror.

It was only a glimpse. If that even. A rapidly moving

shape, small and dark and formless, that dashed behind her and disappeared.

Before she could run away, the door opened. And in walked a teacher. Mrs. Gauthier.

Myla was filled with relief. She turned on the water in the nearest sink, soaping up her hands. The teacher smiled at her, said hello, then walked back to the far stall and closed the door.

The far stall?

Myla's heart started pounding. Why would she choose to go in that darkened corner rather than one of the closer, more well-lit cubicles?

It wasn't any of her business. She should just finish washing her hands and leave. But she turned her head to the left, saw that intermittent light, those swirling indefinable shadows, and was filled with a sense of dread. There was no noise, no sound coming from the stall at all. It was as though Mrs. Gauthier had walked in and disappeared. On impulse, Myla crouched down, just to make sure the teacher's feet were visible under the metal barrier.

They weren't.

Panic set in. She didn't know what to do. Should she call out the teacher's name? Should she go and get help? Should she check the stall herself?

No. That last one was out. She was not walking back there. She was not even going to ask the teacher if anything was wrong. In her mind's eye, she saw Mrs. Gauthier crouched on top of the toilet, grinning insanely in that flickering light, waiting to leap on and devour whoever opened the stall door.

Devour?

It did not seem as far-fetched as it should have.

From the corner of her eye, she saw movement in the mirror again.

Myla ran.

She pushed open the door, sped down the corridor and did not stop running until she had reached the quad and was once again in the midst of a crowd.

"What is it?" Reba asked, staring at her as she made her way back behind the table. Myla could tell from the expression on the other girl's face that she probably looked exactly the way she felt: frightened and completely rattled.

She took a deep breath. "Nothing," she said. "Everything's fine." She forced herself to smile, and glanced over the stack of wrapped brownies on the table. "So. How are we doing?"

"I swear to God, I'm going to quit this fuckin' job." Carlos looked over at Rakeem, who was taking down a butcher-paper banner that had been taped to the outside wall of the library.

Everyone else was gone and the campus was quiet, but the quad looked like it had been hit by a tornado. Trash was everywhere, and the tables they had set up for the PTA and various clubs so they could sell drinks and goodies had been piled one on top of the other until the wobbly stack was higher than he was.

Rakeem laughed. "They're jus' kids, man. They're jus' playin' around."

"Yeah, but we have to clean up their mess." Carlos looked down at the ground. His eye was caught by a photograph that lay between a discarded Lay's potato chips bag and one of the metal legs of the bottom table. He picked the picture up off the cement. It had the faded, washed-out look of a 1970s Polaroid, but it was of tonight's festivities.

Sort of.

He recognized the front of the office and saw groups of milling parents on the sidewalk, but there was something else—or rather some*one* else—on the roof of the building. The colors in the photo were bleached, and the figure stood in the darkness above a shining spotlight on the building's edge, so it was hard to make out specifics, but Carlos saw what appeared to be a bearded man wearing an old-fashioned coat staring down at the parents below.

Feeling suddenly cold, he glanced over at the office, saw nothing there, then hurried up to Rakeem, holding out the photograph. "Hey, man. Look at this." He pointed to the figure on the roof.

The other custodian froze. "Where'd you get that? Who took it?"

"I don't know," Carlos admitted. "I found it over there, by the table."

Rakeem took the photograph, looked at it carefully. "I seen that man before," he said, and his voice was hushed, scared. "He peeked in at me once when I was cleaning the office. I saw him through the window, standin' there in the dark. I woulda gone out and told him to get off the property, but I could see that he wasn't really there. He was more like a reflection."

"Reflection?"

Rakeem hesitated. "Ghost."

"Why didn't you tell me?"

The other custodian shook his head. "I don't know. Embarrassed, I guess."

Carlos understood. He'd done the same thing. More than once.

"I thought I saw him again one time." Rakeem pointed at the photo. "Right there. On the roof like that. But when I looked again, he was gone, and I couldn't tell if I imagined it or not." He exhaled loudly. "Guess not."

"You think someone *wanted* us to find this picture?" Carlos asked.

"Wouldn't surprise me none. Lotta weird shit goin' down these days."

Carlos nodded.

"You know, I don't like to clean the office anymore. Just like you don't like the sports complex." Rakeem grinned at his friend's surprised expression. "Oh, yeah. I know about that. In fact, the only reason I do the office is habit. And 'cause it's close to the classrooms. But there's also not that much to clean these days. The principal's office is off-limits. Everything down that little hallway is. Basically, all I have to take care of is that one big room and the supply closet."

"Why you tell me this now? To rub it in?"

Rakeem glanced down at the photo again before looking up at Carlos. "Because I think it's gettin' dangerous. I don't think we should split up anymore. I think we should work together."

"It's gonna take longer."

"Maybe, maybe not." Rakeem handed back the picture. "But it'll be *safer*."

Carlos pointed toward the stacked tables. "You wanna give me a hand with that?"

The highest one was above both of their heads, but they could reach the legs, and they each grabbed two, lowering the table to the ground. Even before they'd brought it all the way down, though, something slid off the tabletop.

Another photograph.

Carlos placed his end of the table on the cement and picked up the picture. This one, also faded and washed out, looking at least thirty years old, showed Rakeem and himself, from just a few moments before, talking by the front of the library. It appeared to have been taken from atop the stacked tables.

Behind them, in the shadows, barely visible, was the bearded man.

"Shit!" Carlos cried, dropping the photo.

Rakeem picked it up, then looked around frantically. Carlos did, too, but there was no sign of the ghostly figure.

They met each other's eyes. "What you wanna do?" Carlos asked.

There was no discussion of how the photo had gotten there, who had taken it or what exactly it was. They were already way beyond that. "I'm gettin' the fuck outa here, and tomorrow I'm goin' to the district. I'm transferrin' to another school. No way I'm puttin' up with this shit."

"I don't think we can transfer," Carlos began. "Enrique said—"

"Fuck Enrique! And if I can't, I can't. I'll just quit and go somewhere else. But I'm not stayin' in this place another fuckin' minute."

"Me either," Carlos said.

"Let's go, then."

They'd both parked in the far lot near the sports complex, which meant that they had a long way to walk. Carlos would just as soon have gone out to the street and walked around the block, but Rakeem had already started off through the center of the quad, and Carlos followed him.

Once out of the quad and by the lunch area, he hazarded a quick look back. The shade in one of the classroom windows was swinging, as though someone inside the room had been peeking out at them and had moved away so as not to get caught. He walked faster.

Something dwarfish and dark darted between the lunch tables away from the cafeteria entrance.

Carlos heard laughter, low masculine laughter. Not the giggle of a child or something that would have corresponded to the small speeding shape, but a deep terrifying chuckle that seemed to come from something much, much larger.

"Ow!" Rakeem cried out. He'd bumped his knee

on the edge of a brick planter, and he must have bumped it pretty hard, because he was holding the knee with both hands and hopping on the other leg.

Only the planter hadn't been there before. Carlos knew every inch of this campus intimately, and while this rectangular brick construction contained mature established geraniums and looked to have been there for decades, he recognized that it was in a previously empty spot. Of course, Carlos told himself, Enrique and the principal had approved a lot of landscaping changes recently. This could very well be one of them.

But he knew that was not the case. He had walked by this area earlier and there'd been no planter in place.

"Come on," Carlos prodded. "Let's get out of here."

"Son of a *bitch,* that hurts!" Limping, Rakeem followed Carlos past the lunch tables.

And promptly tripped over a rock.

Rakeem was the most coordinated and athletic guy he knew. For him to be suddenly so clumsy and awkward was not only weird but unbelievable. Now his *other* leg was scraped and in pain, but Rakeem continued to hobble toward the parking lot.

A tree branch fell in his way.

This was getting ridiculous. There was no wind, no remotely logical reason for the branch to have fallen from the carefully maintained sycamore, and angrily, Carlos strode ahead of his friend. He attempted to pick up the branch, wanting to break it in half and heave the pieces as far as he could, but it was heavy, and the best he could do was to shunt it off to one side.

Behind him came a loud crash. Rakeem shouted, "Fuck!"

A metal trash barrel was rolling out of the darkness toward the other custodian, with another one hot on its heels.

The school was attacking him.

It was a stupid thought. A crazy thought. But that didn't mean it wasn't true, and Carlos grabbed his friend's arm and helped him hobble out of the way. If he could just get Rakeem off campus, the man would be safe.

The barrels rolled past them.

Then stopped.

And sped backward.

They both went down, knocked over like human bowling pins, and Carlos was surprised by the *force* of the rolling barrel. When it hit his legs, the impact was tremendous. It felt as though he'd been struck by a car, and he flew several feet in front of the trash receptacle, the bones in one leg audibly cracking, pain engulfing the entire lower half of his body. Then the barrel rolled over him, forcing his head onto the concrete, crushing his right arm. He was screaming in agony, but even with all that was going on, he realized that his was the *only* scream. Rakeem was not making any noise at all.

Dimly, he was aware of the fact that the barrels were still rolling. He heard the hollow echoing sound of metal on cement. Beneath the cacophony of his own screams, he also heard a strange low tone that at first he couldn't recognize but that his rattled brain finally recognized as a note being blown on a tuba.

Mmmmmmmmmmmm . . .

When he shakily lifted his head, he saw Rakeem lying unmoving on the ground. Behind Rakeem, he saw Enrique's motorized cart, speeding toward them from the sports complex, lights off. Was Enrique in it? He couldn't tell.

And he would never know.

The last thing he saw was the tire that crushed his skull.

Thirteen

The campus looked beautiful in the morning. The custodians must have been there all night cleaning up the mess, and Linda vowed to thank Carlos and Rakeem when she saw them.

She walked slowly across the quad. Thinking about the custodians, it occurred to her that she hadn't asked any of the classified employees how they felt since Tyler became a charter school, and she decided it was high time she took an informal poll among the non-teaching staff. They were probably just as angry and disappointed as she was. More so, perhaps, since they no longer had any supplemental help from the district and had more than doubled their workload. Theoretically, they, too, were supposed to have an equal voice in this great experiment in democracy, but the truth was that their opinions mattered even less to Jody than did the teachers'. And since there'd been no talk of those promised raises since the changeover, she was pretty sure the custodians and other classified employees were pretty dissatisfied with the way things were going.

Enrique, driving up the sidewalk in his motorized cart, saw her and gave her a fake smile. "Hello, Mrs. Webster."

"Hi, Enrique," she said. "When you see Carlos and Rakeem, could you tell them what a great job they did last night? The campus looks beautiful."

The custodian's smile grew. "Well, thank you, Mrs. Webster. But I'm the one who cleaned up last night. Carlos and Rakeem don't work here anymore. They quit."

The surprise must have shown in her face because Enrique chuckled. "No great loss. They weren't hard workers. Now I can hire men who'll do a *good* job.

"*And* who'll respect the charter."

If she'd been suspicious before—how likely was it that two full-time custodians with seniority would quit at the same time?—that last statement was the icing on the cake. If Carlos and Rakeem had quit, it was because they'd been forced to do so. More likely, they'd been fired because they refused to toe the party line, although Jody and Enrique had no doubt devised some made-up reason for their dismissal.

"Well, anyway, the school looks nice." Linda walked past the head custodian. The truth was, the campus no longer did seem quite as nice to her, and the good mood she'd been in until now had been ruined. She looked straight ahead, not slowing her pace until she heard the cart take off behind her. Stopping, she looked up at the second-floor windows of the building before her. Even though it was daytime, she was still nervous about returning to her classroom. Diane and Frank, not to mention Ray and Steve, had almost convinced her that she hadn't seen what she thought she saw, but the image of that immobile white-haired boy was still fresh in her mind, as was the fear she'd felt. She'd even had a nightmare last night about the encounter, and in it she had seen his face. She'd awakened at that point, drenched with sweat and on the verge of screaming, and she was thankful that all details of that terrible visage had disappeared with the dream.

"You want me to go in with you?"

She turned at the sound of the voice. It was Ray.

"Come on," he said. "I'm going up, too. We'll check out your room."

It was nice of him, and the fact that he didn't try to make her feel silly gave her confidence. She accompanied him up the stairs, and together the two of them gave her room a cursory search. There was nothing unusual, nothing out of the ordinary, and feeling more relieved than she was willing to admit, Linda thanked him for his help.

"That's what friends are for," he told her.

She smiled. "I've heard that." She began going over her lesson plans for today and was just starting to write her first period's assignment on the board when Ray returned.

He looked disgusted and upset. "Linda?" He said no more, merely beckoned her with his finger, and she followed him to his room, a sinking feeling in the pit of her stomach.

Someone had left a pile of feces on top of his desk.

Linda gagged, moved back outside the doorway.

"Well, at least we know you're not crazy," he said, trying to make a joke of it.

She looked at him. "You thought I was crazy?"

"Of course not. Bad joke." He looked back at his desk and grimaced. "I need to call the janitor, get this out of here."

"Take your kids to the library until they get it cleaned," Linda suggested.

"Are you kidding? The Fascist won't let us in without at least two days' notice."

"Just show up."

"She'll bite my head off!"

"Let me get this straight," Linda said. "You're not afraid of ghosts, but you're afraid of our librarian."

"That's about the size of it, yeah." He frowned. "Ghosts? Is that what you thought you saw?"

"I don't know. Maybe."

Ray glanced toward his desk. "No ghost did that. Disgruntled student would be my guess." He walked over to the phone on the wall. "I'd better report this."

Linda headed back to her room. "Good luck," she said.

Just in case, she gave her own room a more thorough search, but she could detect nothing peculiar, nothing that had been moved or taken, and with a sense of relief, she continued writing the assignment on the board.

In the middle of second period, a TA from the office arrived. The entire class looked up from their books at the intrusion, and the girl walked self-consciously around the first row of desks to hand Linda a sealed envelope. "Back to work," Linda told the class. Groaning, they returned to their books while the TA left.

She opened the envelope. Inside was a memo from the principal, dated today:

Dear Ms. Webster,

I request that you come to my office immediately after your last class this afternoon. There are several important issues I would like to discuss with you.

Thank you for your cooperation.

It was signed by the principal, and a "CC" in the corner alerted her to the fact that Bobbi had been copied on this as well.

Linda read it again. She didn't like the formal tone

of the memo, nor the fact that the request had been made in writing, and during break she went down to the department office and called Lyle Johns, president of the employees' association, and told him that she wanted a representative from the union to accompany her to the meeting.

At lunch, she discussed the memo with anyone who would listen, trying to get as many opinions as she could. Nearly everyone expressed puzzlement save Joseph Carr. The band teacher sat on a couch in the lounge with an enigmatic smile on his face and refused to participate in the conversation.

"Hey," Ray finally asked him. "When's your next steering-committee meeting?"

"It's the *charter* committee, not the *steering* committee, and I'm afraid that information is privileged."

The other teachers looked at one another with raised eyebrows.

"Excuse me," Alonso said. "We're all supposed to be the captains of this ship. We all have a stake in how this thing turns out, and we all have a vote. You can't keep secrets from us."

Carr did not respond. That mysterious smile remained on his lips, and he turned his attention toward Linda. "We have discussed *your* case," he told her, "but I can't say anything about it."

"My *case*?" she said. "What is my *case*?"

Chuckling, Carr pointed to his watch. "Oh, look at the time." Standing up from the couch, he headed toward the door. Nobody said a word until he was gone.

"Bring a union rep with you," Alonso advised, and there were nodding heads all around.

"Don't worry," Linda told them. "I'm going to."

Boyd Merritt, the rep, met her in the English department office after sixth period to look over the memo. "It doesn't give us much to go on, does it?" he admitted. "Do you have any idea why the principal would want a meeting with you?"

Linda shook her head. "I've been anticharter from the beginning, and I know she carries a grudge. But other than that . . ." She shrugged her shoulders. "That's it. I can't think of anything I've done. Certainly not anything I can be disciplined for."

"Well, we'll just go in and see what happens," Boyd told her. "But let me do all the talking. This is kind of a test case, and for all we know, Ms. Hawkes picked you at random just to teach us a lesson. She's been itching for a showdown ever since your charter went through. She might just be trying to throw her weight around."

"Maybe so," Linda said. "But I was *not* chosen at random. She doesn't like me, and if she can find some way to get rid of me, she'll do it."

"That's why you need to let me do the talking."

The campus was quiet, too quiet, as the two of them walked across the quad to the office. In previous years, seventh period had been a loose, amiable hour, a social time for many seniors, who often didn't have a last-period class and who hung around the campus, waiting for the bus or their friends or simply socializing. But stricter rules were in place this semester, and there was a coldness to the quiet campus that Linda found uncomfortable as they strode up the walkway. She glanced between the library and one of the classroom buildings at the front of the school where the wall was going up. She might have been walking through the grounds of a prison or a mental hospital.

Both seemed apt metaphors for Tyler High.

They reached the office, opened the front doors and walked in. Suddenly everything stopped. It was like a scene from a movie, something filmed in slow motion.

Typing fingers froze; hands halted in their passing of papers; conversations ceased. Then the principal came roaring out of her office in the back. "Get him out of here!"

Boyd held up a hand, indicating that Linda should not respond, but she was not about to let this outrage go unchallenged. "He's my union rep," she told Jody as the other woman approached the front counter. "I'm not going into a meeting with you without him."

The principal smiled, looking remarkably sharklike. "I'm afraid that won't be possible. The charter specifically prohibits union representation of any Tyler employee."

"It does no such thing," Boyd said calmly. "I have a copy of your charter right here in my briefcase. It requires approval of the charter committee to discuss matters *before* the committee—a stipulation that our lawyers do not believe to be legal—but it makes no mention of union representation of employees in disciplinary hearings before the principal."

"There've been some amendments since then," Jody informed him.

This was the first Linda had heard of it. "We never voted on any amendments," she said.

"Even if you had, they would not be recognized or valid," Boyd explained. "The school board and the state approved a specific document, and it cannot be changed after the fact. You must abide by the charter you submitted."

"There's where you're wrong," the principal said with barely concealed contempt. "Article sixteen, paragraph GG, subparagraph twelve, specifically grants the charter committee the right to amend at their discretion any school rules pertaining to personnel matters, irrespective of district policy." She smiled. "And they have done so."

"It is illegal under California law to ban union—"

"Get out of here now," Jody said, still smiling. "Or I will have you thrown out."

Boyd took out his cell phone. "I'm not moving a muscle. And, moreover, I'm going to—"

The cell phone was snatched from his hand. Linda whirled around to see two Tyler Scouts standing directly behind them. Somehow, the two tall beefy boys had opened the office door and entered without either of them noticing. These scouts did not merely have patches on their shirts but were wearing full uniforms. They looked vaguely militaristic, with creased brown pants, lighter brown shirts and some sort of small badge affixed to the shirt pocket. Although they didn't have side arms, their thick belts contained squarish pouches that resembled holsters. There were still patches on the scouts' sleeves, more elaborate and detailed versions of the ones that had been proliferating over the past few weeks.

"Escort him off campus and make sure he does not return," Jody ordered.

The two boys grabbed Boyd's arms, turning him around.

"Don't say a word!" he told Linda. "This is illegal!

"*You* are in big trouble!" He pointed at Jody as the scouts led him off.

"I don't think so," the principal responded. She waited until the doors had closed and then fixed Linda with an amused gaze. "Shall we go into the conference room?"

"The conference room?" Linda asked. "What about your office?"

"Not my office," Jody said. She smiled cryptically. "Not yet."

Linda was still fuming about the union rep—she was going straight to the teachers' association headquarters after this and filing a formal complaint—but she refused to give Jody the satisfaction of acknowledging her anger, and she walked behind the counter. She had no intention of saying a word during this meeting. She was going only to listen, to hear what the principal had to say. She would report everything back to the union.

Jody picked up a folder from Bobbi's desk.

Rather than going down the short hallway to the principal's office—and she *didn't* want to go down that hallway—Linda followed the other woman to a door to the right of the hall that led to the conference room. Jody opened the door and a motion detector turned on the light. There was a new table in the center of the room, Linda saw. It looked like mahogany. As did the stylishly designed chairs. On one otherwise bare wall was a flat-screen TV. "Nice," she said. "I guess this is why we don't have the money for new books, huh?"

Jody ignored the comment and motioned for her to sit down in one of the chairs, taking a seat on the opposite side of the table.

Linda folded her hands on the tabletop and sat there silently, waiting.

"Did you hear about Yvonne Gauthier?" Jody asked casually. "Our illustrious math instructor? She quit. Right in the middle of Back-to-School Night. Turned in her resignation effective today, without giving me even two weeks' notice. Bitch."

"Bitch?" Linda said. "That's a very unprofessional thing to say, don't you think?"

"She left us in the lurch, she's gone and I don't have to be nice to her." She smiled. "Unlike with you."

"I'm not going anywhere," Linda said sweetly.

"We'll see." Jody opened the folder and started sorting through the papers in front of her. Seconds later, Bobbi walked into the room and sat down in an adjacent seat. "Okay," Jody announced. "Now we can start."

"Wait a minute," Linda objected. "I'm not allowed to have a witness, yet you have one of your people sitting in on the meeting?"

"You make it sound as though this is going to be adversarial. Do you know something we don't?"

"I'm here in my capacity as administrative coordinator," Bobbi said. "I am not a witness."

"Oh, I'm sorry." Linda offered Bobbi as placid a smile as she could muster. "I thought you were here in your capacity as secretary. In fact, I was going to ask if you could get me a cup of coffee before you started taking notes. Do you think you could do that, please? Black. No cream, no sugar."

"That's what I'm talking about!" Bobbi said, slamming her palm down on the table and looking imploringly at the principal. "That's the attitude I'm talking about!"

Jody held up a hand to quiet her down, but her smile was forced, and it was clear she'd lost a little ground.

Hands still folded, Linda waited.

"Now, I realize," Jody said, "that you were not in favor of Tyler High becoming a charter school, but you did choose to remain here rather than transfer to another school in the district, and that means that, like it or not, you are required to follow the same rules as everyone else." She tapped the papers in front of her. "But according to these reports here, you have been consistently insubordinate since the beginning of the semester."

Linda wanted to protest; her natural reaction was to defend herself. But she needed to follow Boyd's advice and remain silent.

"During our first in-service day, I was informed that

you refused to wear your name tag as required. All other attending staff members wore theirs. You did not."

Bobbi smirked.

"You also neglected to turn in class sales estimates for our fund-raising drive. And either you did not take roll last evening or did not submit your sheets to the office, so we cannot accurately tabulate how many parents attended Back-to-School Night, a mandatory function."

Linda did not respond.

"Individually, these lapses might seem inconsequential. But taken together, they show a pattern of insubordination that is very troubling.

"The question is," Jody said, "should you be subject to disciplinary action?"

Bobbi smiled. "I believe she should."

The suggestion of a frown passed over the principal's face, and Linda could tell that she wished she had not invited the other woman to participate. Linda looked from one face to the other. Bobbi clearly saw this meeting as a huge boost to her power and prestige, but she was out of her depth, and Jody was embarrassed. This was a reflection on *her*. And for Bobbi, Linda hoped, it might be the beginning of the end.

"What do you think should be done? Would it be better, do you think, to forget these infractions and start over with a clean slate, with the understanding that from here on in there would be no more similar incidents?"

"No!" Bobbi said.

The principal looked at her coldly. "I was not speaking to you."

Bobbi shrank back.

"Well?" Jody pressed.

Linda looked at her. "No comment."

"You would prefer to be disciplined?"

"No comment."

Jody was suddenly all business. Linda had the impression that she had just been given a test and that her answers were not the ones the principal had wanted. Or expected. "I will be placing a written reprimand in your file. You will, of course, have the opportunity to respond and that will be placed in your file as well." She stood. "This meeting is over."

Linda finally spoke. "I expect a copy of that written reprimand."

"One will be placed in your box." Jody closed her folder, picked it up and walked out of the conference room, Bobbi following deferentially after.

Linda remained seated, not for any particular reason, but because she wanted to mess with Jody's head a bit. The principal didn't seem to like it when things went off script, when people acted as they weren't supposed to, and since she was probably expected to leave with the other two, Linda stayed in place, looking around the room, thinking.

The truth was, when Jody had said the word "disciplined," Linda's mind had gone to a far different place than "written reprimand." She'd thought of beatings and torture and incarceration, and it was actually a bit of a surprise to discover that her punishment was so light and so . . . ordinary. It made her realize how off the charts was her perception of the school. That didn't mean that she now thought things were normal here. It just meant that Tyler's transformation was not as far along as she'd believed.

But she had no doubt that it would get there.

Finally, she stood and walked out of the conference room. No one in the office looked at her or spoke to her, and it was not until she was outside that she stopped and exhaled deeply. She had not felt as claustrophobic in there as she had before, but she'd still been nervous, and once again she was grateful to be outside.

From the other side of the office building, from the expansive lawn that fronted the school, came the sound of voices chanting. The voices were male, so they were not cheerleaders', but they could have come from the pep squad or the choir or a music class. Somehow, though, Linda knew that this was nothing so benign, and, curious, she followed the sidewalk around the building.

She was greeted by the sight of several rows of high school boys marching across the length of the lawn. They were Tyler Scouts, what she'd started to think of as the principal's own praetorian guard, and what shocked her was how *many* of them there were. She'd seen the scouts here and there, of course, in her class and on campus, but she'd never even thought about their numbers. If pressed, she would probably have guessed there were around ten or fifteen, all total, girls included. But there were a good fifty or sixty boys on the lawn, all of them marching in strict formation and shouting out unintelligible words in a martial cadence. Like the students she'd seen in the office, they were wearing complete uniforms rather than just patches on their sleeves, and seeing all that brown moving in unison sent a chill down her spine and made her think of Nazis.

She saw no adult supervising them, no leader or coach, but as she watched, they broke into smaller groups of six or seven each, as if they were being ordered to do so by someone she could not see. They were obviously in training, though for what she did not know, and they began to fight, group against group. It could have been wrestling or self-defense they were practicing, but there seemed to be a chaotic lack of rules as well as an unbridled ferocity to the boys' attacks that made her think of commercials she'd seen on TV for Ultimate Fighting championships.

They were hidden from the street by the now partially constructed wall, and she wished that passersby could see what was going on. For she had no doubt that if members of the general public spotted high school boys hitting, punching and kicking one another with such focused intensity—and under the school's aegis—they would be up in arms.

In the skirmish between the two groups of students closest to the office, two boys were ganging up on one, kicking him hard in the side as he tried in vain to roll over and stand up. A kid from one of her classes, Nolan Reese, kneed another in the groin.

She was about to walk into the fray and order them to put a stop to this—she was a teacher, after all, and seemed to be the only adult around—but as quickly as it had started, the fighting stopped. With a surprising economy of movement, the students were back in formation and marching across the lawn. Although many of them were no doubt in great pain, none of them limped or appeared even slightly out of step with their peers.

She didn't want to see any more. The sight sickened her, and though she tried to imagine what possible use Jody could have for the scouts or what purpose they could serve within the context of an educational environment, she could not come up with anything.

The final bell had not yet rung, so she returned to the English department office and began correcting papers as she waited for Diane. School ended. There was a cacophony of voices, footsteps and other unidentifiable sounds as students surged through the halls toward freedom, and five minutes later her friend arrived.

"I didn't expect to see you here," Diane said. "How did the meeting with our fearless leader go?"

Linda explained about the reprimand, and the amendment banning unions that Jody and her cronies had surreptitiously added to the charter.

"That's bullshit!"

"That's what I said. I'm stopping by the association headquarters after this to find out what can be done."

"We have to let everyone know."

"And we have to tell them to be careful. They're changing the charter without telling us, and they're not even giving us updates."

Diane's mouth was set in a straight line. "Well, that's going to stop. We need accountability. I'm head of the English department, and I'm going to get all the other department heads—"

"Except those on the charter committee."

"—except those on the charter committee, and we're going to demand that we be kept abreast of any changes. As I understand it, keeping us in the dark is against charter rules."

"Unless they changed that, too."

"This is getting out of hand."

"I saw something else weird," Linda confided. "You know how I said those scouts came and took Boyd away? Well, they were wearing uniforms, full uniforms, not just patches on their sleeves. And after I came out of the office, before I came here, I saw a whole troop of them training on the front lawn, first marching in formation, then going through some sort of fight exercises or conflict preparation. There were no teachers there, though, only the kids, only boys. Seniors mostly, by the look of them. I don't know what exactly the point of it all is, but it seems to me that Jody's putting together her own private security force."

Diane frowned. "How many of them were there?"

"That's what freaked me out. A lot. How many kids are at this school? Two thousand? Figure half of those are boys. Well, nearly a hundred of them are now scouts. And I'm sure that number's growing. They're being recruited, like the military, and they're *behaving* like the military. It was like they were getting ready for battle or training to quell a riot. The whole thing gave me the creeps."

"What about the girls?" Diane wondered. "Do you think she's starting a similar program for the girls?"

"No doubt. I have girls in my classes wearing those patches, too. But I don't know what they're up to or what Jody has planned for them."

"I'll talk to the other department heads about that, too." She grabbed a pen and a piece of paper from the desk. "In fact, I'm making a list of questions we need answered. And I'm going to point out to everyone that there's a lot less communication between administration and staff than there was *before* we had the charter—which is exactly the opposite of what we were promised."

"Good," Linda said.

"Speaking of that . . ." Diane stopped writing and took a blue sheet of paper from the metal in-box on the shelf above the desk. "Did you get the memo about merit pay?"

"I don't know. Maybe. I forgot to check my mail."

"Well, it's out. The idea's been scrapped."

"No great loss." Linda had been against merit pay from the beginning. The idea that teachers should be rewarded by how their classes performed on standardized tests was ludicrous. Obviously, those instructors heading the advanced-placement courses would rack up better scores than those teaching the remedial classes, and those who taught to the test would have students who scored better than those who were more freewheeling and, to her mind, more interesting. Merit pay rewarded conformity and compliance.

"That's not the point," Diane said. "It's the same root problem as the lack of communication. After all those promises Jody made, she's reneging on nearly every single one of them." A mischievous smile played across her lips. "Besides, as department chair, I could have stacked the decks in our favor, given us all the smart kids. We'd've made out like bandits."

"You wouldn't!"

"Of course not. I'm just saying." Diane sighed. "The frightening thing is what she's offering as incentive instead of merit pay."

"What?"

"Loyalty pay."

Linda stared at her. "You're joking."

"I wish I was." With a dramatic flourish, Diane handed over the blue memo and Linda scanned it quickly. "As you can see, it says that those staff members who are sufficiently proficient in kissing Jody's ass and obeying her every whim, *and* who sign a 'loyalty oath' that she's going to be passing around, will be eligible for a monthly bonus on their paychecks."

"I thought loyalty oaths were illegal. Weren't they outlawed in the 1950s?"

Diane started writing on her list. "Another question to ask."

"I'll ask the union about it, too. I'm going to stop by the association's office on my way home and see what they plan to do about all this."

"Want me to come?" Diane looked up.

Linda shook her head. "I'll call you tonight and let

you know what comes of it. You get busy with the other department chairs and try to put some pressure on Jody and that charter committee."

"This is turning into one big headache," Diane said.

From outside the building came the sound of footsteps marching on concrete as a seemingly endless parade of Tyler Scouts passed by.

"It's a nightmare," Linda said.

Tired, Linda dropped her purse on the hall tree. "I'm home!"

Frank sat up on the couch, where he'd been lying down and watching CNN. "Hey!" he called. "How'd things go? See anything weird in your classroom?"

"No . . . ," she said slowly, sitting down next to him. "But I'm a test case."

"I have no idea what that means."

She told him about the memo that had been delivered to her in class, the disciplinary meeting with Jody, the fact that she was denied representation. "I stopped off at union headquarters after school. They were already up in arms about what happened and have meetings scheduled with lawyers and people from the state organization. They're acting like this is it, the big showdown, and it's going to decide once and for all the rights of unions and associations to represent the employees of charter schools. They're ready to go all the way to the Supreme Court with this because either way it plays out is going to have lasting consequences for California teachers."

"Jesus."

She sighed. "It's been a long hard day."

"What do you say we go out tonight? We'll have a nice dinner at a nice restaurant, and you can relax and forget all about this."

She placed her head on his shoulder. "That's

thoughtful of you, but I couldn't forget about this if I tried. Why don't we just order pizza and eat in and watch a movie? Preferably a comedy."

He put an arm around her. "Anything you want."

"Wow. I should be harassed and threatened and reprimanded every day if it's going to get me treatment like this."

"Maybe you will," he said.

"That's what I'm afraid of."

Fourteen

Sean Bergman sat on his bed, staring at the blank wall of his bedroom. Downstairs, from the kitchen, he could hear his mom and dad discussing something. He couldn't make out specific words, but he could hear their tones of voice, and he knew they were talking about him.

He tried not to listen, concentrated on the wall. He'd wanted to tack posters on that wall. Movie posters. His friend Max, who used to work at a Blockbuster, had taken a stack of them when he'd quit, and he'd let Sean have three or four for himself. But his mom had never let him put them up. She hadn't liked the movies he'd picked. Old exploitation flicks would have been okay, or horror or kung fu or something by Quentin Tarantino, but the posters for popular mainstream films that he'd chosen were not acceptable to her, not hip enough. So, in defiance, he'd left the wall blank.

Sean glanced down at the bandages on his wrists, flexing his fingers. Ever since he'd gotten out of the hospital, he'd been doing that. A lot. He told himself it was exercise, but it was more like a ritual, a compulsion. He flexed his fingers again. The adhesive tape felt tight on his skin, but below that, the still-healing cuts hurt, and he remembered how it had felt when he'd sliced into his wrists and the blood had begun to flow. In his mind, he saw now what he'd seen when he'd made those incisions—his mom, naked on top of a table in front of Mr. Swaim's class, holding her breasts, spreading her legs and smiling out at the students ready to draw her—and once again he was filled with shame and humiliation.

Did his dad know what his mom had done?

Sean wasn't sure. He certainly hadn't brought it up, but maybe the doctors had. Or maybe his mom had even come clean, although she'd no doubt put her own spin on it in order to justify her actions.

Would his dad even care?

Again, Sean wasn't sure. His parents had always prided themselves on not only being cooler than all of the other parents but being cooler than his friends as well. Every once in a while that ended up working out, but for the most part it was just embarrassing. More than anything else, it made him feel as though he were a third wheel. It had always been clear to him that they were uncomfortable in the roles of mother and father, that the responsibilities of parenthood put a serious crimp in their lifestyle. Half the time, he thought that they'd be happier if they'd never had him.

They were selfish. He'd known that instinctively, but it was not something he'd been able to articulate until now, and he found that he was looking forward to discussing it with the new psychiatrist he was supposed to see.

Downstairs, he no longer heard the bored drone of his dad's voice, but his mom's shrill annoyance came through loud and clear, even if the words didn't.

Had she given even a second's thought to how *he* would feel if she posed nude in front of his class?

Obviously not.

He remembered the way he'd felt, sitting in his seat, when Mr. Swaim had not let him leave, when the teacher had forced him to sketch *all* of his mom's body instead of just her head and shoulders, as he'd originally attempted.

"Your old lady has a nice twat," Todd Zivney had said after class. He grinned. "She keeps that thing trimmed, doesn't she?"

And that was only the beginning of it. At lunch, nearly everyone he saw commented on his mom's body, even people who hadn't been in the class, even people he didn't know, and by the end of the day all he wanted to do was hide. But he didn't want to go home. The thought of seeing his mom made him feel queasy, and he had no idea what to say to her. He could hide out at one of his friends' houses until his dad came home, but he didn't want to see his friends either, didn't want to answer their questions, didn't want to endure their looks. Even more overwhelming was the thought of returning to school tomorrow and spending the whole day as an object of attention.

He didn't want to do anything, Sean realized.

He didn't want to be anywhere.

He didn't want to be.

It was then that he'd come up with the idea of slitting his wrists, and while he was kind of glad now that he had not succeeded in his attempt to kill himself, he was kind of not. He was stuck in some sort of limbo where he didn't really know what to do or what he wanted, or what not to do or what he didn't want.

He heard his mom's too-precise footfalls coming up the stairs and down the hall to his room. Sean experienced a flare of panic, and briefly considered getting up and doing something, pretending to be busy, but the feeling passed as quickly as it had come, and he remained on his bed, staring at the wall.

She came in, not knocking—she never knocked—and stood before him. She didn't speak for a moment, but if she was waiting for him to break the silence, she was out of luck. He continued to look past her at the blank wall where his movie posters should have been.

"What were you thinking?" she finally demanded.

He shrugged, said nothing. He flexed his fingers, feeling the tape tighten, feeling the cuts burn.

"I'm on three committees this year," she said accusingly. "How am I supposed to give them the attention they deserve if all of my time is taken up with taking care of *you*?"

The way she said *"you,"* in a voice filled with resentment and disgust, made him wonder if she would have been happier if his attempt had been successful.

Then you shouldn't've showed my class your crotch. Which, by the way, Todd Zivney said was nicely trimmed.

It was what he should have said but didn't. Instead, he kept looking at the wall, unable to meet her gaze, unable to look upon her at all.

"How do you think I feel, having a son who did something like that, huh? Do you know how embarrassing that is?"

He should have turned those questions around on her, but he didn't. He flexed his fingers harder, opening them wider, closing them tighter.

She moved closer, bent down, looked into his eyes. He had the feeling that she knew what he was thinking, or, more accurately, that she was thinking the same thing. She smiled but not in a nice way, and stood up straight.

"The razors are in the bathroom," she said as she walked away. "Feel free to use one."

* * *

Bill Manning stood in front of the classroom, grinning. He felt good about Tyler's chances in the academic decathlon. He thought they might even have a shot at going to Washington, D.C. Before this year, the school had never even placed in the *district* competition, let alone state, let alone the nationals. But never before had he been given free rein to do whatever it took to whip his team into shape.

Whip his team.

With a loud swish, he cut through the air with the black leather riding crop he held in his hand.

Nervously, some of the students looked up. Others glanced over surreptitiously, their heads still bent over their books and papers, their eyes on him. Most continued studying, too frightened, too *whipped,* to risk his wrath.

He swung the riding crop again, cutting the air, his smile growing wider.

Outside the window, the sun was going down, the light turning orange. Fall was here, and soon it would be getting dark before they finished these practice sessions.

There were a lot of things he could do in the dark.

Mr. Manning looked up at the clock. It was almost four thirty, almost time to end the study break and get back to the serious business of drilling. Usually, he gave them half-minute warnings and then loudly counted down the last ten seconds, but this time he waited in silence, keeping his eye on the clock. Five minutes . . .

Four minutes . . .

Two minutes . . .

. . . *ten, nine, eight, seven, six, five, four, three, two . . .*

One.

He whirled around, using the crop to point at Angela Yee. "Nucleotides contain two types of nitrogenous bases! What are they?" he demanded.

"Pentose and purines!" she shouted out.

"Wrong!" Angrily, he slammed the riding crop on her desk, barely missing her fingers. "Purines and pyrimidines!"

Angela started to cry.

"What's the matter, wittle baby?" He leaned down, pushing his face mockingly in front of hers. "Are we cwying because we're dumb?"

She sat up straighter, sniffled, made a concerted effort to stop crying. "I'm not dumb," she assured him. She wiped away a stray tear. "I can handle this."

"No, you can't!" he yelled at her. "And you *are* dumb! You're just about the most ignorant, worthless piece of shit it's ever been my misfortune to coach!" He swung his riding crop again, and this time it hit her. She cried out as the tip slammed into her shoulder. "Maybe you'll remember better next time."

He walked slowly down the central aisle of the class. "In the vascular plant body, the primary tissues are . . . *what*?" He slammed his crop down on Kirk Newcomb's desk.

"Primary xylem and primary phloem!"

"Yes."

The drill continued this way as he walked through the room, picking students at random, berating them and hitting them if they answered his questions incorrectly, bestowing halfhearted praise if they got them right. Finally, everyone had had a chance to answer at least one life science and one earth science question. He returned to the front of the classroom. It was going to be a long, hard slog, but with his help and hard work, they were going to make it. If not . . .

He swung the riding crop hard, listening with pleasure as it sliced the air.

He faced the decathlon team. "Now, let me make one thing perfectly clear. We are in this thing to win. We are not competing so we can come in second place or third place or get a little pat on the head and an honorable-mention certificate. Does everyone understand me?"

"Yes!" they answered in unison.

"Good! Now, I expect you to ace the district, take state and win the nationals! If you do *not*—!" He dropped his voice. "If you do not, if you falter anywhere along that path, you will be punished. Severely. Not only will you never enter another decathlon again; you will never be *able* to enter another decathlon again. I will beat you until your writing hands are crippled, your fingers so broken they can never hold a pen or tap a keyboard. I will strike your head so hard that you will be lucky to find yourself in an EH class. I will make sure that you will never again be in a position to embarrass either myself or the school. Do I make myself understood?"

"Yes!" they answered.

He smiled broadly. "Then that's it for today. Now go home and study. I'll see you here again tomorrow."

Mrs. Temple blew her whistle. "One . . . two . . . three . . . go!"

Cheryl put her heart into it. She had helped design this routine, and while it was difficult, especially for some of the newer, younger cheerleaders, it would be worth it in the end. This was the kind of routine that won trophies, that inspired movies.

"—the Tyler Tigers sure are great!" they concluded, doing the splits sequentially from left to right.

"Hmmmm," the cheerleading coach said. "Let's try it again from the top."

Cheryl didn't know about the others, but she tried

even harder this time, jumping higher, yelling louder, moving with more definition. Still, Mrs. Temple wouldn't give them a pass. "Let me see that first kick again," she ordered.

"Something's wrong," the coach said when they'd finished. She stood there, thinking, as they watched her. "It's that bulky material beneath your skirts," she decided. "I think it'll work better if there's nothing there."

The girls looked at one another, not sure they were hearing what they thought they were hearing.

"Take 'em off, girls!" she ordered. "I want to see bush!"

They were practicing in the stadium, on the field, in front of the stands, and Cheryl looked around to make sure there were no other kids watching, especially not those dweeby little pervs from the tennis team. Although, now that she thought about it, what did it really matter? These stands would be *filled* Friday night, and everyone in them would be able to see when she kicked high and jumped.

The thought gave her a little thrill of excitement.

No one had started to take off her underpants. To her right, Yolanda Martinez stood there like a block of wood, her legs unconsciously pressed together. The girls beyond looked at one another, nervous and embarrassed. Lindsey giggled. To her left, Carrie was hesitating. "I will if you will," she told Cheryl.

"Girls!" the coach shouted. "Now!"

Cheryl unfastened the underwear from the skirt and pulled down her panties underneath. The air felt cool between her legs all of a sudden, and as Carrie took off her own underwear, she did a high kick, flashing the stands.

Moments later, they were all bare under their short skirts.

"Try it again, girls!" Mrs. Temple ordered.

They did, and even the shyest of them admitted afterward that the flow was a lot smoother, the kicks and drops not nearly so jerky and mechanical.

"Excellent job!" the coach told them. "Now go home and make sure you get a good night's sleep. We have a lot of hard work to do before the game, and I want you rested and rarin' to go. Oh, and Yolanda?"

The girl stopped, turned.

"Trim that thing, will you? It looks like a goddamn rain forest down there."

Fifteen

He had no friends in his last-period Government class, so Brad spent the minutes before the teacher arrived reading *The Magus,* this week's assignment in English. He loved English. Mrs. Webster was a great teacher, and somehow reading the books she wanted them to read, discussing them, hearing her opinions on them, made him feel smart and intellectual, as though he were already in college rather than still in high school. It was a personal feeling, private, a feeling he hadn't shared with anyone, not even Myla, who was in the class with him, and somehow keeping it to himself made it seem all the more special.

But English was the only course he really enjoyed this semester.

And Government?

This was definitely one he could do without.

Mr. Myers walked in, and Brad closed his book. He'd gotten stuck in the front row, so even though he hated the class, he had to at least pretend to pay attention or else the teacher would be all over his ass.

Mr. Myers went over to his desk and dropped off a folder he'd been carrying. "We're going to the library today," he announced as the bell rang. Chatter among the students subsided, stopped. "I'll be passing out a list of topics. Pick one and do a report on it. Five pages, three sources. Books and periodicals only, no Web sites. I want footnotes and a bibliography."

Sheets were dropped off at the head of each row and passed back. Brad looked over the list. As he'd suspected, the ideas were all boring, but he quickly raised his hand and nailed down "Why the First Amendment Is Important," probably the least objectionable topic. Everyone else followed suit, and in a few moments the entire class was ready to go to the library and start working on their papers.

Suddenly, the door of the classroom opened, and in walked two uniformed scouts. Moving in lockstep, they approached Annabelle Ivers, who sat in the back row looking down at the battered bestickered notebook she always carried with her. As usual, Annabelle was wearing her goth regalia—black boots, black dress, black lace, silver skull jewelry—and above her almost Kabuki-white makeup, her dyed black hair had been teased into a Tim Burtonesque rat's nest. She did not bother to look up as the two boys stopped and stood on either side of her desk.

"We got a report about you," the first scout said.

Brad did not recognize either of them, but they both had the square-jawed clean-cut appearance of dedicated jocks.

"You're breaking the dress code," the second one told her.

Annabelle still didn't look up. "There *is* no dress code," she informed them.

"There is now." As one, the two boys grabbed her arms, lifting her up and out of her seat.

"Hey!" she cried.

The first scout snickered. "Where'd you get those clothes, your mom's closet?"

"Yeah, what do you think this is, 1988?"

She tried to fight but couldn't, and they pulled her out of the room as though they were comedic cops in a movie, holding her arms as her feet dragged behind her on the floor. Brad and the rest of the students looked quickly toward the teacher, shocked that he would allow this to happen in his own classroom, but he was smiling pleasantly as though nothing out of the ordinary were going on. "Bring your books," he said. "We won't be coming back to class. You'll be leaving directly from the library."

"Those two guys just came in and dragged Annabelle out of the room," Gary Chen said.

Mr. Myers nodded. "Yes. Now let's get ready to go."

"What about her books?" someone else asked.

"Don't worry," the teacher said. "She'll be back."

"But you said we're not coming back," Gary pointed out. "We're leaving directly from the library."

"Every minute you waste talking about Annabelle is a minute that you could be using to work on your report. Now come on, let's go."

Didn't one of the constitutional amendments have something to do with unreasonable search and seizure? Brad thought. He should have chosen to write about that one.

Following the teacher, they went down the stairs, out of the building, across the quad to the library. Too cool to walk in a single-file line, they moved in sprawling formless groups that were spread out but traveling in the same general direction. Brad walked alone, near Gary, who was also by himself, and a new transfer student whose name no one knew. He looked up at the square forbidding block that was the library building and couldn't help smiling to himself as he thought of Ed working in there.

"I want you all to be quiet once we're inside," Mr.

Myers warned them. "If either Mrs. Fratelli or I have to speak with you, points will be deducted from your grade on this assignment." He opened the door for them. "Now walk over to the two tables in front of the history aisles. Those are ours. Put down your books and backpacks, then go to the computers and take turns looking up books and articles that pertain to your topic. There may be other classes in here as well, so you may have to share."

There was a quiet rush as students hustled into the library, dropped their things off at the tables, then jockeyed for position at one of the four computers. Brad knew that the library's history section was arranged by subject, so instead of waiting for his turn at the computers, he walked down the first aisle, reading spines, until he found a group of books on the Constitution and the First Amendment. It was a gratifyingly large group of books, and he pulled them down one by one, checked through the indexes, then chose the two that seemed most promising.

He was taking notes, and half of his class had returned to the tables with their own research materials, when Ed came by pushing a wheeled cart filled with books that needed to be reshelved. Brad grinned at him. "Having fun?"

"Yeah. I got a book here for you." He tossed a hardback on the table and pushed the cart past. Brad looked down at the title: *Creative Flower Arrangement.*

He laughed.

"Hey!" someone said. "Heads up!"

From the second table, a book flew out and hit Ed in the back. He winced in pain, then bent down to pick it up.

"That's why his mama named him EH!"

Brad saw Rick Schlaegel laughing, and, standing, he picked up his own book, walked by as though he was going to return it to the shelf and "accidentally" used it to hit Rick in the back of the head.

"Ow!" Rick cried out.

Around him, everyone giggled.

"Sorry," Brad said. "Didn't see you there."

"Yeah, right. Your ass is grass, Becker."

"Anytime, pussyboy."

"Later," Rick promised darkly.

"He won't be able to make it later," Ed confided in a whisper. "He'll be too busy fucking your mom."

Rick jumped up and grabbed for Ed.

The teacher was suddenly right there. "Do we have a problem, Mr. Schlaegel?"

Rick sat down docilely.

Behind the instructor loomed Mrs. Fratelli. The librarian was looking at the two tables as though they were populated by cockroaches, and the black expression on her face caused everyone to immediately return to work. Still standing, Brad went into the history aisle and hid, pretending he was looking for another book.

A few moments later, when he was pretty sure it was safe, he went back to his seat. Opening one of his texts to the page indicated by the index, he started taking notes. A few moments after that, he saw Ed at the far end of the room, pushing his cart into one of the aisles, and he picked up the book on flower arranging and brought it over to him.

Ed took the volume. "You didn't have to do that, you know."

"He deserved it."

"What do you think you are, my protector or something?"

"I did you a fucking favor. Show a little gratitude, will you? I just let him know that he can't get away with shit like that."

"Actually," Ed said, "he can. Besides, I'm used to it." He looked at his friend. "You should know that by now."

"Yeah, I guess so," Brad admitted.

"I'm not sure why," Ed went on, picking up a book from his cart, "but I guess I'm some kind of natural victim. I don't think I'm especially dorky or weird-looking or anything. But . . ."

"You have a big mouth," Brad pointed out.

"This is true."

"For what it's worth, Myla doesn't think you're *that* big of an asshole."

"But is she going to set me up with one of her friends?"

"Would you *want* one of her friends?"

"That's a point," Ed conceded. He placed a book on the shelf, made its spine even with those on either side of it. "But to be honest, dude, at this stage I'd take just about anything. Hey, how *is* your mom these days?"

"There's that mouth."

"Right. Sorry." Grinning, Ed picked up another book from the cart. "You'd better get your ass back. Myers'll shit a brick if he sees you standing around talking to me instead of working on whatever you're supposed to be working on."

"Don't worry. I'm going to stay a little after class, let him know how conscientious I am."

"Good plan. I'll stop by after I get off."

"Get off?" Brad widened his eyes in mock shock. "You're going to get off here in the library? What if someone catches you?"

"Go to hell."

Laughing, Brad walked back to his seat at the table. Mr. Myers frowned at him, but the teacher didn't say anything and Brad immediately started poring through a book and writing down facts about the First Amendment, making sure he did so with a serious and dedicated look on his face.

Annabelle Ivers returned near the end of the period, the goth girl delivered to Mr. Myers in the library by the same two scouts who'd dragged her out of the classroom. She was no longer wearing any jewelry and her hair was combed in a modified pageboy. Her black clothes were gone, replaced with clean khaki pants and a beige T-shirt on which were printed the words PROPERTY OF TYLER HIGH.

Did that refer to her or the T-shirt? Brad wondered. Because not only Annabelle's wardrobe had changed. Her attitude was entirely different as well. She was still quiet, but not in a sullen, disassociated way. She seemed meeker, almost submissive, and when Mr. Myers asked her to sit down in a specific chair, she did so politely and without complaint. Brad glanced around at the other kids in his class. They were all looking about in an effort to confirm that the surprise they felt was shared by everyone else.

The bell rang soon after, and the students around him gathered their belongings and walked out in a surprisingly subdued manner, obviously more affected by the mystery of Annabelle's transformation than he would have thought. Brad himself waited until Mr. Myers finished talking to Mrs. Fratelli and left, before he put away his own materials. There were two books he wanted to check out, and he took them up to the front counter, where a blank-faced blond girl sat staring into space, making no effort to leave even though school had ended. He handed her his ASB card and the books, and she silently scanned them and pushed them back.

Turning around, he saw Ed coming toward him

down the center aisle, and he walked over to meet his friend.

"What's with her?" Brad whispered, motioning back toward the front counter.

"They're all like that," Ed confided. "All the TAs. Except me of course."

"It's like she's hypnotized or something."

"That's what I thought, too."

"Do they act like this all day long, in their regular classes, or is it only in the library?"

"You got me," Ed said. "They're not anyone I know, and I've never seen any of them outside of this building."

Brad found that creepy. He imagined a workforce of whey-faced zombies living permanently in the library and doing Mrs. Fratelli's bidding, that girl at the counter remaining there morning, noon and night, sitting motionless until someone needed to check out a book. But, of course, that couldn't be possible because Ed was here, too, and he was just a regular student who'd transferred from another class to become a TA.

Brad stopped himself. He wasn't questioning the idea that zombies could work in the library; he thought it seemed illogical just because Ed was a TA as well?

That alone spoke volumes about this semester.

"Aren't there, like, assistant librarians?" he asked. "Adults?"

"There's supposed to be one, Miss Green, but I've never seen her."

"Don't you think that's weird?"

The answer was so obvious that Ed didn't bother to answer but merely gave him a "What do *you* think?" look.

"You know," Ed said, "there's a thing here in the library called 'Special Collections.' Upstairs. It's apparently filled with stuff that's been donated to the library but that students can't check out."

"What's in there? Antique books?"

"Porn, I'm thinking. But I don't have access to it, so I don't know."

"You wish," Brad said.

"You're right. I do. But I'm not just talking out of my ass, and it's not as far-fetched as it might seem." Ed glanced over at the front counter, then motioned for Brad to follow him. "Remember those books I was putting away?"

"Yeah."

"Well, I found one on my cart that wasn't supposed to be there." Ed kept walking, turning down one aisle, then another. The library suddenly seemed bigger than it should, and for a brief second, Brad felt something like vertigo. "It didn't have any call letters. And the freaky thing is that I don't remember putting it on the cart when I was sorting. It just *appeared* there." Ed stopped, reached up. "I didn't know what to do with it, so I put it here." From the top shelf, he brought down a slim volume bound in brown, with neither words nor pictures on its cover. "Check it out."

Brad took the book from his friend. Glancing through its pages, he saw words in a language that might have been French, and old overexposed black-and-white photographs of children who were maimed, deformed or afflicted with gruesome diseases of the skin. "What the hell is this?"

"That's what I was wondering. Flip to the back of the book."

Brad did so and saw photographs of a beautiful woman, completely naked, her body contorted into painful-looking but decidedly erotic poses. "Jesus."

"Yeah."

"So what are you going to do?"

"I just saved it to show you." Ed put the book back on the high shelf. "Tomorrow, I'm going to show it to Mrs. Fratelli, see what happens. My guess is she'll take it to Special Collections."

Brad looked up and down the aisle. "I've never liked this library. And now I *really* don't like it."

"I don't either," Ed admitted. They started walking back the way they'd come, zigzagging between the stacks. "It's like a maze in here," Ed said. "There's a basement, too. Did you know that? I didn't." He shook his head. "I actually got lost in here one time. It doesn't make much sense, but I did, and Mrs. Fratelli had to find me and lead me back to the front counter. The place isn't really that big, but sometimes it seems confusing."

Brad knew what he meant and was about to say so when they reached the main aisle and practically ran into a group of students who seemed to be heading toward one of the two study rooms against the east wall. Nathan Whitman, as obnoxious and arrogant as he always was, tried to press past them, using his shoulder to push Ed aside.

"Uh, the library's closed," Ed told him.

"We always have our Bible study meetings here. Mrs. Fratelli said we could."

"Church, state," Ed said.

"It's after school."

"Church, state. Church, state. Church, state."

"You are going to hell," Ashley Hallett told them.

"Just for the thoughts I have about your sister each night," Ed agreed.

"Your soul is not a joke!" another girl chimed in.

"No, but you are," Ed replied. He leaned close to Nathan and held a hand to the side of his mouth as though whispering an important secret. "We were just looking at a book back there, and you can see pictures of this woman's twat." He did his best Borat impression. "Niiiiiiiice."

Mr. Carr, presumably the club's sponsor, walked up. He frowned at Brad and Ed. "What's going on here?"

"Nothing," Brad said, starting to walk away.

Ed stayed his ground. "I was just trying to explain the concept of the separation of church and state, but Nathan-boy didn't seem to understand."

"I will thank you to leave our study group alone," Mr. Carr said. "Any more harassment on your part, and I will tell both Mrs. Fratelli and Principal Hawkes." He placed a hand on Ed's shoulder before moving on. "I will pray for you."

Brad and Ed headed in the opposite direction, toward the exit. "Why do they always want to pray for me?" Ed wondered.

"They want God to turn you into the type of person they think you should be. They want him to make you just like them."

Ed snorted. "Yeah. Like that's going to happen."

Outside, the campus was almost completely empty. In previous years, quite a few kids had remained after school, hanging out with their friends, making out with their boyfriends or girlfriends, biking, skateboarding. But Tyler cleared out fast these days, and whether it was a conscious decision or just instinctive, most students were spending as little time as possible on campus.

But not the scouts.

There they were, marching back and forth on the lawn in front of the school, and Brad and Ed walked in the opposite direction. Even without the official sanction of the school, those bullies and jocks were their natural enemies, people the two of them had always made an extra effort to avoid. And now that the principal had given them permission to physically enforce the school's rules and regulations, they were downright dangerous.

"Assholes," Ed said, looking over at them, but he said it quietly, not wanting any of them to hear, although they were so far away that it was doubtful they could hear him even if he shouted.

Laborers were working on the wall, music from competing Spanish stations blaring from the tinny speakers of cheap radios placed upon piles of bricks, and Brad and Ed had to walk around a fairly long section before finding an open space where they could get out to the sidewalk. Two of the workers close by were talking loudly, trying to be heard over the music, and though Brad's Spanish was poor even after three years of classes, he made out the words "afraid," "bad" and "ghost face."

"Let's go to McDonald's," Ed said. "My treat."

Brad's surprise was so great that he forgot about the workers. "Your treat?"

"I found five bucks in one of the study carrels," Ed admitted.

"And you didn't report it or put it in the Lost and Found?"

"Hey, finders keepers, losers weepers. You want some fries or don't you?"

"Yeah," Brad said.

"All right, then."

They started walking toward the golden arches down the street, but before they reached the corner, Brad looked back at the workers he'd overheard. Both of them were still talking.

And it might have been his imagination, but he thought they both looked scared.

* * *

Despite the hard line she'd taken with the student council over . . . well, nearly everything, and the fact that she'd been so angry with Cheryl after the last council meeting that the two of them had ended up screaming at each other and had not spoken for five straight days, Myla still considered Cheryl her friend, and it was she who took the initiative in making up. She e-mailed an apology, left a voice mail message on the other girl's cell phone and waited for Cheryl outside her first-period class in the morning. Though she hadn't responded, Cheryl *had* gotten both her e-mail and her voice mail, and after a few awkward moments, the fight was over.

Reba and Cindy had stayed away from both of them during the feud, and while they were all ostensibly friends again, there was a tightness and tension to their exchanges, and they now avoided talking about a lot of subjects so they wouldn't end up arguing. The time they spent together was a lot less than it had been, too, and while she knew part of it was natural, the result of diverging commitments and boyfriends and the usual social changes that occurred senior year, part of it wasn't.

Part of it was something else.

She felt sad about the old gang breaking up, and she knew her friends did as well, but there didn't seem to be anything any of them could do about it. Still, she made an effort to counter the drift and connect, and on Wednesday, she even went with Cheryl to cheerleader practice. Afterward, they were planning to go to the mall, window-shop and eat an early dinner at the food court, just like they used to do last year.

Myla sat on the bottom row of the stadium seats, watching the girls practice. The truth was, she'd wanted to be a cheerleader when she was in junior high. She wasn't coordinated enough to ever make the squad—she wasn't confident enough to even try out—but it had been sort of a secret dream of hers. Her tastes and priorities had shifted since then, and cheerleading no longer held much interest for her, but she didn't have the disdain for it and for the girls that Brad did. Sitting here, watching them flex and stretch before starting their first routine, she even admired their skills and abilities.

And then they kicked up their legs.

Myla looked quickly away, shocked and flustered. She could feel the heat on her face as her skin reddened with embarrassment. Glancing up again, her eyes went to Mrs. Temple. She thought, or was *hoping,* that this was a prank pulled by the girls on the squad, some sort of rude but good-natured joke on the cheerleading coach. But a few of the girls seemed uncomfortable and embarrassed themselves, while Mrs. Temple was all business and not at all surprised by the sight.

"Okay!" the coach said. "That was pretty good! But we need to work on synchronization. Hayley, you came in half a beat behind at the beginning, and, Jasmine, you were a little too quick with your kick. We're looking for precision here. On the first kick, especially, I want to see those skirts fly up at exactly the same time. This is the money shot, folks. All right, let's try it from the top!"

The practice seemed to drag on forever, and it was nearly dark by the time it was over. Some of the girls followed Mrs. Temple into the locker room to shower and change, but Cheryl merely pulled a pair of underwear out of her bag, put it on and joined Myla in the stands. "What do you think?" she asked.

Myla didn't know what to say.

"That first routine was mine. And the last one, too. I choreographed them both."

"I could . . . see you," Myla said finally. "At the games, *everyone* will be able to see you."

Cheryl nodded happily. "Yeah."

"What if your mom or dad watches that?"

"Oh, they don't go to the games."

"What about someone else's parents? They could tell your mom and dad. Wouldn't you get in trouble?"

She shrugged. "The school would get in trouble, not me. I'm just following orders."

"But how can you do that?" Myla asked.

Cheryl looked dreamy. "I just tell myself that Mr. Nicholson will be watching," she said.

On Friday, Myla and Brad went out. There was a football game at school, which was where she'd told her parents they were going, but neither she nor Brad was a football fan. And Tyler High was the *last* place she wanted to be at night.

She thought of Cheryl, pantyless, kicking her feet high in order to give the crowd a show, and shivered.

"You cold?" Brad asked.

She shook her head no and snuggled against him. They'd gone to the beach for their date, which was a little weird for her. Despite being raised in Southern California, a mere twenty miles or so from the ocean, she was not much of a beachgoer. When she *did* go, it was always with her family, and being here now with Brad made her feel grown-up somehow, although there was also an irrational twinge of guilt, as though she were doing something she shouldn't.

They sat on a bench above Corona del Mar, listening to the crashing of the waves below. There was moonlight on the water and the salty smell of the sea in the air. An exotic-sounding bird sang in one of the bushes near the edge of the bluff.

"I don't want to go to the Harvest Festival," she admitted.

He shifted on the bench to look at her. "You have to. It's sponsored by the ASB, isn't it?"

She nodded. "I know. But I'm afraid."

"Why? There'll be plenty of people there."

It was hard to put into words. And when they were here at the beach, so far away from school, her reservations seemed, if not exactly trivial, at least unconvincing. "I just have this horrible feeling that something's going to go terribly wrong."

Brad held her. She wondered if he was thinking about that locker.

She was.

Myla took a deep breath. "And I don't like the fact that they're trying to keep people out, that they want to make it just for themselves and their friends, like one of those restricted country clubs." Anger pushed away the apprehension. "The festival used to be for everyone—now it's only for the privileged few. That really pisses me off."

"Then don't go."

"No, you're right. I have to go. We're sponsoring it. I'm even listed as one of the organizers on the flyers and posters."

"Well, I'm not going," he said. "There's no way I'm paying those outrageous fees just so I can play some stupid games and win some crappy prizes."

"I can get you in," Myla said. "Ed, too."

"It's the principle of the thing."

"But that's just what they want, don't you see? That's what I've been fighting so hard against. They want to have an exclusive party where no one else can come."

"I thought you said you were scared."

"I *am* scared," she said. "But that's why I have to go. And that's why you and Ed need to go, too. If something happens, we need to be there. We need to witness it."

He nodded slowly, and she knew he knew what she meant.

They were silent for a few moments.

"Are you afraid, too?" Myla asked softly. She hadn't meant to embarrass him; she was just wondering, and she thought they were close enough that he would be honest and tell her the truth, especially after what they'd been through together. But when he didn't answer right away, she quickly assumed he was a more macho, less enlightened guy than she'd originally believed, and she was about to do the usual high school girl thing and apologize to salve his ego.

He surprised her, though. "I don't like to go to that school at night," he admitted.

"I don't think anyone does," she said. She snuggled closer to him, happy that he felt safe enough to tell her that, and soon afterward, they left the bench and returned to the car.

In the darkness of the backseat, they started kissing. She was nervous at first, because there were people occasionally walking by on the sidewalk next to them—other couples, mostly—but after a while the windows were so steamed up with condensation that no one could have seen in even if anybody had wanted to.

And this time, when he tried to slip his hand beneath her panties, she let him.

Sixteen

Kate Robinson had come to dread the white envelopes.

Tony went into his bedroom to work on the ridiculous amount of homework that was assigned to him each night, while Kate sorted through the envelope's contents. Various ads for chain stores and restaurants. An army recruitment flyer. A Jogathon sign-up form, with a suggested pledge total of two hundred dollars or more. A request that each family with a child attending Tyler High sell a minimum of three hundred dollars' worth of magazine subscriptions to friends, neighbors and coworkers in order to help fund the school's music program. A plea for parents to volunteer for a campus-beautification committee.

She dropped the pile of papers and the white envelope on the coffee table. Never, in the twelve years Tony had been going to school, had she encountered anything like this. On a weekly basis, Tyler High made appeals for her time and money. And it never stopped. The school was like a big vacuum, sucking parents dry, demanding ever more from them. She thought about her own high school days. Her parents had never contributed a dime to her school, nor had they been asked to. And volunteering? Aside from the occasional room mother, no parents volunteered. No one had *needed* to volunteer.

And that had been true at Tony's schools, too.

Until this year.

Until Tyler became a charter school.

Kate looked at the pile of papers on the table, then got up and went into the kitchen to start dinner. Her impulse was to throw all those papers away, but some she was supposed to sign and send back, to acknowledge that she'd received and read them, and she didn't want Tony to get flak because she wasn't following the rules. She'd sort through them later and do what she needed to do.

They ate homemade hamburgers for dinner—turkey burgers, actually; she was trying to make slightly healthier food these days—and halfway through the meal, she noticed that Tony wasn't talking. She was chattering enough for both of them, telling him about her horrible new coworker at the title company, which was why she hadn't noticed his silence at first. But there came a lull in her soliloquy, and when Kate looked over at her son, she saw the same sullen expression she'd seen so often on his father's face. She was not about to let him turn into his father, and rather than let things slide, she decided to address the situation head-on. "What's the matter?" she asked.

"Nothing." He refused to look up from his plate.

"Tony."

"I said it was nothing!" His voice was a little too defensive, a little too loud.

"You can't keep things bottled up inside—" *Like your father,* she wanted to say. "It's not healthy. Whatever it is, you can tell me. You can talk to me about it."

"It's you! All right?"

Kate blinked. "Me?" This came as a complete surprise.

"Yeah."

"I don't understand."

"You never help out at my school! Why can't you sign up for something? Sell soda at the football games or tickets for the Harvest Festival? Why can't you work in the library?"

"What brought this on? If I remember correctly, I was a room mother when you were in fifth grade, and you were so embarrassed by my existence that you begged me, crying, never to volunteer at your school again."

Tony shifted uncomfortably in his seat. "Yeah, well . . ."

"Well, what?"

"Well, I guess I changed my mind."

"Oh you did, did you? And why's that?"

He looked at his plate. "Some of my teachers might've . . . mentioned it."

"Mentioned what?"

"That you haven't volunteered as much as you were supposed to." A torrent of words poured out, hurt and angry. "They made fun of me in class! Mr. Connor pointed me out and said you're the only parent who doesn't pull her own weight! Mrs. Habeck said in front of everyone that part of my homework was to get you to be more responsible! I'm not going to be able to even go to the Harvest Festival this year because you haven't volunteered enough!"

Kate was taken aback. "I'm . . . sorry."

"Yeah, well, sorry's not good enough." There was that look again, his father's look.

She reached across the table, touched his hand and was gratified when he didn't pull away. "I'll take care of it," she said. "I promise." She looked into his eyes, and it was not his father's angry gaze she saw there but a worried hopefulness she recognized from when Tony was a little boy. "I promise," she said again.

He did pull away, but he nodded.

There was a PTA meeting the next morning, she knew, and though she'd never attended one before, Kate was determined to go to this one and complain about the outrageous demands being placed upon the kids and their parents, particularly working parents. The constant pressure of the white envelopes was bad enough, but when students were harangued in their classrooms by their teachers over their parents' perceived unwillingness to volunteer enough time or donate enough money to the school, well, that was completely unacceptable.

After dinner, she fished out the notice from the pile of papers on the coffee table. The meeting was at ten o'clock in the multipurpose room, and in the morning she called her supervisor, let him know that she was taking half a personal day, and drove to the high school. She was there ten minutes early, and to her surprise she was the first one to arrive. The door was open, but the room was empty. She'd expected someone to be setting up coffee and cookies on a table, and figured the PTA officers would be conferring among themselves before everyone else arrived, but she was the only one there.

Not that she cared.

The truth was, she didn't like a lot of the other parents she'd met at Tyler. There was a weird competitiveness among many of them, and within the insular world they inhabited, their status was far too dependent on the achievements of their children. There was a constant jockeying for position, with their kids' grades, sports and extracurricular activities all used to determine who was top dog. And of course, no one had normal kids; none of *their* children could possibly be average. They were all gifted or special or exceptional—despite the fact that nearly all of them would eventually end up getting regular jobs and living in suburbia and having ordinary lives just like their parents.

She didn't play that game and had little tolerance for those who did, but Kate knew that she was going to have to get at least some of the other parents on her side if she was going to effect any kind of change, and she started thinking about ice-breaking topics of conversation as she sat down on a metal folding chair in the back row.

A few minutes later, the PTA moms arrived en masse, as though they'd already started the meeting somewhere else and were coming here to conduct the last part of it. She recognized Helen Adams, Jason's mother. Their boys had been friends back in junior high, though they hung out with different crowds in high school. And over there was Andrea Hagen. And Barbra Watkins.

Only . . .

Only none of the women looked the way they usually did. They were "tarted up," as her own mother would say. Far from the Betty Crocker / Carol Brady stereotype she'd been expecting, the women walking into the meeting were wearing tight jeans and halter tops, minidresses and spiked heels. Makeup was thick and garish. Tattoos were exposed. She felt like the frumpiest hausfrau on the planet as she sat there and watched the rest of them pass by.

The women ignored her, one and all. Talking among themselves, they sat together in the first three rows, putting an end to any thoughts she might have had about chatting a few of them up ahead of time. Why had she decided to sit way back here?

Three other women arrived, sitting with the group.

She wasn't a naturally outgoing person, but gathering her courage, Kate stood and made her way toward the front of the room. She found an empty spot next to Helen, and sat down, giving the other woman a friendly smile. "Hi," she said. "How's it going?"

Helen ignored her, turned away and started talking to the woman on the other side of her.

Not knowing how to react (in old movies, didn't women just huffily say, *"Well!"* and turn away?), Kate sat for a moment in silence. Another woman, this one very obviously wearing no bra under a tight pink T-shirt featuring a sparkling green marijuana leaf, sat down next to her. Kate was about to say hello and attempt to start a conversation when the meeting started. A woman in the front row stood up, faced the seated mothers and without preamble began running down a list of topics they needed to address this week.

It wasn't a meeting so much as a lecture, and in its speed and brevity was almost a parody of those hyperefficient proceedings conducted by high-powered businesspeople. Kate had thought she would get a chance to talk, but there was no opportunity to bring up unscheduled subjects, and before she knew it, the meeting was over. Seconds after the closing announcement was made, the women around her were standing and starting for the aisle.

"Wait!" Kate said loudly. "I have something I want to say!"

She was greeted by a crowd of hostile frowning faces.

"Who do you think you are?" the PTA president demanded. Chairs were pushed aside, and the president was suddenly right in her face. Kate found herself surrounded by an encroaching circle of women.

Kate held her ground. "My name's Kate Robinson. I came to this meeting because I wanted to talk about all of the time we're supposed to volunteer and all of the money we're supposed to donate. It's getting ridiculous, and I think most parents—"

"This is the first PTA meeting you've been to," the president said.

"Yes."

The woman looked angry. "I recognize your name. You didn't sign up for the mother-son dance like you were supposed to. And you didn't donate anything for our bake sale on Back-to-School Night."

"Those are all voluntary," Kate said frostily. "So far as I know."

"You're not a team player!" Helen said, leaning close. "You don't know what it means to support the school."

One of the other mothers shoved her, causing her to bump into a different woman. The woman shoved her back. Within seconds, she was being buffeted back and forth, and it was all she could do to remain upright as she was pushed first one way and then another by the increasingly irate crowd. Long fingernails scratched her upper arm. The sleeve of her blouse was ripped. Someone pulled her hair.

"Knock it off!" she cried, but it sounded more like a plea than a demand.

Barbra slapped her face. Andrea yanked the strap of her purse.

Kate fought back. She slapped Barbra even as one of the other mothers tried to pull her off-balance, and she jerked back on the strap of her purse. Seeing an opening between two of the women, she stumbled forward, ramming a halter-topped bimbo out of the way and giving the PTA president a gratifying elbow in the gut.

Then she was free and running for the door. She expected to be chased, anticipated the sound of high heels rat-tat-tatting on the floor behind her as the president yelled, "Get her!" But nothing like that happened. Beneath the harsh rasp of her own breathing, she heard only a few muffled laughs, and then she was out the door and on the sidewalk and making a run for her car.

A few students were out of class and watched as she sped by, but Kate ignored them and kept her focus on the parking lot ahead. She was sobbing, though she could not remember the last time she had cried. It was frustration more than the physical assault that had brought her to tears. She reached the parking lot, reached the car, opened the door and locked herself in. On the way out, her fender bumped that of another car parked near the exit, but she didn't care, she didn't stop and she kept driving until she was safely in her own garage and home.

Tony had to eat lunch alone. One by one, his friends had been recruited by the principal to become Tyler Scouts. Chuck was the most recent, tapped only yesterday, and now Tony was the last one left at their old table. The scouts trained at lunch—*and* before school *and* after school—so unless he found some new friends, he was probably looking at a lot of time spent by himself.

Tony glanced to his left at a table where a gaggle of hot girls were talking in low tones, heads together. If he had a girlfriend, he wouldn't need any guys to hang out with. But he didn't. He wasn't smooth, didn't have any game and hadn't even had a date since the beginning of the semester. There'd been a chick he'd fooled around with a little bit this summer, a skanky dropout who'd worked with him at Taco Bell, but he'd left that behind when he'd quit the job in August, and even if it was possible, he wasn't interested in starting anything up again with her.

Glumly, Tony opened his sack lunch, certain that everyone else in the eating area was looking at him and laughing. All the surrounding tables were crowded with students, and his pathetically empty table couldn't help but be the center of attention. He reached into the brown bag to pull out his sandwich—

And a strong hand clamped down on his.

"Hey!" he said, shoving the hand away and standing up quickly, prepared to fight off the intruder.

It was Chuck. And Logan. And Craig. They were grinning, and behind them stood a line of Tyler Scouts stretching all the way back to the classrooms. Now he definitely *was* the center of attention. But he didn't mind. In fact, he was pleased. "What is it?" he asked, hoping he already knew the answer.

He did.

Logan handed him a letter. "Principal Hawkes wants you to become a scout."

Tony melodramatically wiped his brow, as though he'd been sweating it out. "About time!" he said.

"You won't need this anymore." Chuck grabbed the brown bag containing his lunch and threw it as hard as he could. It flew over several tables, landing on the head of a fat kid, who leaped to his feet and swiveled around. "All right!" he bellowed. "Who did that? I'll kick your fucking—"

The scouts laughed derisively.

The boy grew pale and immediately sat back down.

"Respect," Chuck told Tony, making a fist.

"Yeah!" Tony grinned. This was going to be great. He didn't know exactly what the scouts did or what their purpose was, but they definitely did get respect. *Everyone* was afraid of them, and while he'd never been one of those kids who aspired to join the military or become a policeman, he found that the idea of being someone in authority appealed to him.

"Aren't you going to read the letter?" Logan asked.

"Oh," he said. "Yeah." Tony scanned the missive in his hand. It was a xeroxed form letter that said the principal was personally asking him to become a Tyler Scout because of his stellar scholastic record and personal qualities that had been vouched for by a minimum of two other scouts.

His stellar scholastic record?

Tony frowned, kept reading. Once he underwent the initiation ceremony and took the pledge, he would be awarded an official uniform and would become a duly sworn officer of the school.

"Initiation?" he said, looking up.

"It's kind of rough," Chuck admitted. "This is your chance to back out."

Tony couldn't tell if that was a statement or a warning. Still, this was a school-sponsored program put together by the principal. How rough could it be? "That's okay," he said.

Craig slapped a hand on his back. "Good." He grinned. "Glad to have you aboard."

"What do I—?" he began.

He was grabbed from behind, his arms pinned to his sides. A black hood was placed over his head and then tied loosely around his neck so that he could neither see straight ahead nor look down at the ground. His arms were let go. He could hear the normal sounds of lunchtime—students talking, laughing, eating—but they seemed to come from far away, and none of the scouts said a word at all. Someone grabbed his hand and pulled him forward. There were scouts on every side of him, and while that made for easier walking, since he knew he wouldn't bump into anything, it made it more difficult to tell in which direction they were going. After the first two turns, he was completely lost.

It seemed like they'd walked far enough to be off campus and halfway down the next block by the time they finally stopped. At one point, it had felt as though they were going down a ramp or an incline, and when the hood was removed from his head, he saw that they were in some sort of tunnel. It was rounded at the top and along both sides ran pipes and insulated cables. He assumed it was a passageway used for maintenance. A series of bare bulbs was strung above them, the ones behind and slightly in front of them lit, the ones beyond that dark.

Just behind the last illuminated bulb, suffused in its yellowish glow, was a slab of raw meat hanging from a hook. On the dirty cement below it lay a pile of clothes. He knew it was just one of those typical hazing rituals—they were trying to fool him into thinking that was *human* meat—but the bloody slab was odd looking, and he thought the crumpled shirt below it looked like Phil Cho's.

Phil had supposedly been transferred last week to another school.

Tony glanced around nervously. Chuck, Logan and Craig were nowhere to be seen, and the scouts surrounding him were all rather formidable and intimidating. They looked like football players, though he didn't recognize any of them.

Without a word, strong arms pushed him forward. His impulse was to dig in his heels and fight against the tide, but he knew that if he did so, he would never become a scout, so he allowed himself to be led to the hanging slab of meat. This close, he could see that it was too skinny to be cow or pig and had the vague contours of a human torso.

"It's lunchtime," the scout to his left said. "Eat."

A hand shoved his face into the meat. It felt cold and rubbery, and the smell was overpowering, a putrid stench that almost made him gag. But he didn't want to embarrass himself in front of these guys, didn't want to end up rejected by the scouts and back at the lunch tables eating alone like a loser. He tried breathing through his mouth so as not to smell the disgusting odor, but his senses were overpowered, and when the scouts started chanting as one, "Eat! Eat! Eat!" he opened wide and bit.

The taste was awful, sickening. The odd chewy consistency of the cold meat made him want to spit it out instantly, and it took every ounce of willpower he had not to throw up, but he managed to bite the small piece in his mouth in two and then swallow the individual halves.

The other boys had stopped chanting, and from the darkness behind the hanging meat, he heard whispering, what sounded like several voices talking at once. All the scouts were in back of him, and as far as he knew, there was no one in the tunnel ahead. But still he heard the whispers, and it sounded as though some of them were saying his name.

There was no longer pressure on the back of his head, and he turned around, feeling the wetness of blood on his face from where it had been pressed into the meat. The other scouts were backing up. They heard the whispering, too, and they were scared. Even in the dim light from the string of bare bulbs, he could see the fear in their eyes, and he started walking toward them. Not too fast—he didn't want them to think he was a pussy—but quickly enough to put some space between himself and the hunk of meat hanging before that black emptiness. Something was behind him—he could feel it—and it was all he could do not to bolt.

Several of the scouts were turning now, no longer just backing up but actually walking away. A few were starting to stride briskly down the tunnel the way they had come. The whispering was closer, louder. He could hear it above the noise of shuffling feet and the voices of the scouts, and maybe it wasn't behind them—maybe it was in front of them, or maybe it was all around.

Someone screamed. Tony didn't know if the screamer had seen something or had simply panicked, but all of a sudden they were running wildly, like little children, every person for himself, no longer a cohesive unit but a random collection of frightened individuals desperately trying to escape. Tony was last, and he kept expecting to feel cold claws on his shoulder, kept waiting to be dragged back into the darkness and hung up on a meat hook. But he ran as fast as his legs could carry him, shoved his way past two scouts, passed Chuck and was safely in the middle of the pack when the tunnel began sloping upward and he saw the light of day at the end.

The scouts in front of him stopped yelling, gradually slowed from a sprint to a march and regained the orderliness instilled in them by all their recent training. They emerged, surprisingly, from a sloping sidewalk that ran between the Little Theater and the band classrooms. Tony had not noticed the narrow space between the two buildings before and, if asked, would have said that there *was* no space between the buildings or, if there was, that it was a strip of bare ground littered with garbage, like the area behind the cafeteria. But he looked back beyond the last of the scouts and saw that the inclined sidewalk led to an underground tunnel that headed under the faculty parking lot.

At the top, the other scouts were all smiling and gathered around him, slapping him on the back and offering congratulations.

"*That* doesn't get any easier," Logan said.

Tony looked at him incredulously. "You mean that's happened before?"

"Every fuckin' time."

"Now just the blood oath and you get your uniform," Craig told him.

"*Blood* oath?"

Chuck put a shaky hand on his shoulder. "You're one of us."

Tony smiled weakly. "Gabba, gabba hey."

Seventeen

Minimum day.

Those words, previously so magical to both students and teachers, now caused Linda's stomach to knot with tension. Once a month, Tyler had a district-mandated minimum day, ostensibly to allow instructors time to perform nonteaching duties. Jody and the charter committee had elected to continue the practice, and as always, each period was shortened so that the school day ended at noon. The students went home. But whereas before teachers were given free time to catch up on grading, writing tests and preparing assignments, or even, if they so chose, allowed to go home themselves, Jody had made it clear that from here on in, the afternoon of each minimum day would be taken up with a mandatory meeting of the entire staff.

Though Linda had been calling every day to check in, there was still no news from the union. No news was bad news, she assumed, and her gut told her that Jody was going to win this one. Whatever happened, she probably could not count on the association for help.

After the students were gone, Linda met Steve and Diane in the English department office. They had fifteen minutes for lunch before the meeting started, and

Steve hurried off to grab some junk food from the cafeteria. Diane was still on a diet and skipping lunch, while Linda had left a thermos filled with soup and a sack containing carrots and grapes on top of the file cabinet. She found a plastic spoon in the upper right desk drawer and started eating.

"What is it?" Diane asked. "Even through all that soup slurping, I can tell you're dying to tell me something. Spit it out."

Linda wiped her mouth with a napkin. "People are changing. This school is affecting people and making them different, not themselves."

"I'm listening."

"You know yourself about Jody's disciples, and you know my opinion about some of the other things going on here."

"Yes, I do. I even agree with some of them."

"Well, something else seems to be happening. People are changing. And I don't mean just their loyalties or ideas or whatever. Their *personalities* are undergoing some radical transformations."

"Like who?" Diane asked. "Give me an example."

"Trudy Temple, for one. I saw her threatening a girl with a tennis racket yesterday after school. Her arm was cocked back, and it looked like she was going to beat the kid. It wasn't even some smart-ass punk, which might at least be understandable. It was Kim Nimura, who's about four feet high and who I don't think I've ever heard say a single word—she's so shy. I went over there to see what was going on, to make sure Kim was okay, and Trudy shot me this look that practically curled my hair. You know that saying 'If looks could kill'? Well, if they could, I'd be dead. And this was Trudy. Trudy! You know she'd never do anything like that. That's not her.

"Paul Mays, too. He's gone over to the dark side.

I saw him laughing and talking with Jody and Bobbi this morning."

"And you're blaming this on . . ."

"The school," Linda said. "The charter."

"Which has some sort of magical power to influence people."

"You're being sarcastic, and that's probably putting it too simply, but . . . yes."

"Then why aren't we affected?"

"I don't know," Linda admitted. "Maybe it's like voodoo. You know how voodoo only works if you believe in it? Maybe this is the same kind of thing."

"There's no bigger believer than you, my friend, and you're fine. Well, maybe not *fine* . . ."

"Come on."

"And my textbook allowance was slashed. That's an objective truth. It happened no matter what I believe."

"Things like that, yeah. Practical things. Concrete, material things. But I think you have to believe in the power of the charter in order for it to have any effect on you personally."

Diane closed her eyes. "I *do* believe in fairies! I *do* believe in fairies!"

"Knock it off."

"Well . . ."

"People here *are* different, a lot of them. No matter what you might think. And maybe the explanation isn't supernatural." She fixed her friend with a level stare. "Despite the *ghost* that I saw. But you have to admit that this charter is cutting the campus in two—supporters and opponents—and that divide is just getting deeper every day."

"That I agree with."

Steve walked in, chewing the last bit of something, a can of Coke in hand. "Made it with time to spare!"

he announced. He grinned. "What do you think Jody'd do to us if we were late? Hang us by our thumbs from the flagpole?"

Linda motioned toward him with a sweep of her arm. "I rest my case."

"Huh?" Steve looked confused.

"I never had any argument about Jody. I agree with you there."

Steve glanced from Linda to Diane. "What are you two talking about?"

"Linda thinks there's something in the water here at Tyler—"

"In the *charter*."

"—and it's changing people and making them into someone they're not."

"Oh, it's true," Steve agreed. "I was talking to Paul yesterday, and remember how he was all militant and angry and anticharter? Well, now he's a gung ho supporter of the administration. He's like one of those brainwashed cultists. Even though I think they're still going to phase out his EH program."

Linda shot Diane a look. "See?"

"Okay, maybe there's something to it," Diane agreed. She looked at the clock. "But you'd better finish your lunch and we'd better get going. Or Jody *will* have us hanging by our thumbs."

This time there were seat assignments. The principal wasn't taking any chances by allowing her opponents to sit together, so in a variation of the ever-popular boy-girl-boy-girl arrangement, the placement of staff members followed a supporter-opponent pattern. Bobbi was in charge of actually seating people, and smirking, she led Linda to a seat as far away from Diane and Steve as possible. Craning her neck and looking around, Linda saw that most of her friends and closest allies were scattered to distant sections of the room.

Bobbi ushered Robert Harris, one of the PE teachers, into the chair on her right. "I love being treated like a child," he told Bobbi. "Thank you."

Linda laughed.

Teachers were still entering the room, but the clock on the wall said it was one, and since Jody had said the meeting would start precisely at that time, she stepped behind the podium and tapped on the microphone to make sure it was working.

The podium.

Linda frowned. Was it the same one as before or had the principal bought yet another one? Because it looked different. It was just as elaborate, still ornately embossed with gold and silver, but there were carvings on its base she did not remember: the Tyler tiger, although far more frightening and ferocious than she had ever seen it before; a pile of books with a grinning skull atop the stack; and what appeared to be a one-room schoolhouse, with grotesque faces peering out of the two windows to either side of the door.

Whether the podium was new or had been altered, it was still disturbing, and Jody met her eyes and smiled as if knowing exactly what was going through her mind. Linda looked away, cursing herself the second she did so. The principal would take that as a sign of weakness, and in an effort to reclaim some traction, Linda casually glanced about the room, then once again returned her gaze to Jody's face, hoping the woman would think she'd merely been scouting around for friends and had met her eyes the first time by accident. No such luck. The principal wasn't even looking in her direction anymore.

The last few teachers were hurriedly seated as Jody

began to speak. "Welcome," she said. "I want to thank you all for making our great experiment such a huge success. Particular credit goes to our esteemed charter-committee members, who have taken on the role of advisers, consultants and school board as well as teachers. . . ."

The speech went on like this for some time, the bland self-congratulatory rhetoric that was mandatory at all meetings. Then things changed. Jody scanned the room and without preamble said, "In your mailboxes this week, each of you will receive amended contracts, which you are all required to sign. The new contracts state that previously ratified collective bargaining agreements are null and void, and that position-correlated pay scales are no longer valid. Salaries will now be calculated on an individual basis. Disciplinary action will be less codified, giving the administration more leeway in dealing with personnel problems. There are also no more open-ended or multiyear contracts. All employees must sign new contracts annually."

"The terms of this charter keep changing," Robert muttered next to her.

"Then you shouldn't have voted for it," Linda snapped. "I didn't."

The PE teacher looked at her in surprise. She expected hostility, a nasty comeback, since that's all she seemed to get from the charter supporters these days, but instead Robert looked downcast and discouraged, and said nothing. Linda felt a welcome and unexpected sense of hope. All was not lost. If people were starting to become disillusioned with the direction in which the school was headed, maybe it was only a matter of time before they would have enough votes to override the charter or even resubmit to district control. She wasn't sure exactly how that worked, but she made a mental note to herself to look it up.

Jody's smile had grown wider. She actually looked happy. "I also regret to inform you that although we had promised raises for all, specifically a five percent increase on your next paycheck, that will have to be postponed for the time being. Due to unexpected expenditures, we simply do not have the money in our budget to honor that promise."

"It *was* a promise!" a man yelled from the back of the room. His voice sounded muffled, and even when she turned around, Linda couldn't see who it was. "The only reason most of us voted to become a charter school is because we were promised raises greater than what the district was offering! Now teachers in the other schools are getting three point five and we're getting nothing!"

"Yeah!" Linda said at the same time as someone else. There were murmurs of assent, but not nearly as many as there should have been.

"*And,*" the man continued, "we were supposed to vote on everything and make these decisions together! What are these *unexpected* expenditures? I never heard a thing about this!"

"They are primarily security measures," Jody said patiently. "I'm sure you would not want to sacrifice the security of our campus for the sake of a few pennies, now, would you?" She smiled condescendingly. "As to the specifics, we have the wall, of course. It's slightly off schedule and therefore slightly over budget. We are also purchasing a new highly efficient, highly advanced monitoring system. The price tag is admittedly hefty, which is why we cannot afford raises at this time, but we'll be getting a lot of bang for our buck. There will be surveillance cameras in every room of the school as well as others mounted outside under the eaves of the buildings, and we will have a centralized command station located next to the custodians' office.

"We will be able to monitor everything. Every corner of the school and every person in it. At any given time, we will be able to pinpoint the actions and location of our most incorrigible troublemakers, which should lead to a significant drop in both personal and property crimes."

"Who's going to be doing the monitoring?" Diane asked from somewhere off to the left. "And what about faculty and staff? Are we going to be spied on every minute of the day? I don't want some pervert watching me go to the bathroom on his little video screen."

Jody chuckled. "Safeguards are in place. And, no, we won't be keeping track of employees."

Yet, Linda thought.

"When all is said and done, we will have not only the safest and most secure school in the district, but with our state-of-the-art technology in place, Tyler will be a model and example for all of the high schools in California."

There were questions, a lot of questions, and the principal answered them all, even Linda's pointed query about treating all students as though they were guilty of some crime and invading their privacy. But the more she heard, the worse Linda thought it sounded. Between the prison wall and the cameras, not to mention all those scouts marching about, they would soon be living in an Orwellian police state. She decided to add *Nineteen Eighty-four* to her syllabus and have each of her classes read the novel. Maybe they would get the hint. Maybe they would tell their parents.

Questions over, there was a low buzz of conversation among faculty and staff. But the tone seemed more resigned than outraged. Around her, she heard complaints from several teachers. They were not as upset as they should have been, though. Nor as defiant.

Jody raised a hand for silence, and like obedient children, everyone stopped talking.

"Next week," she announced, "we will also be instituting a new dress code. Study after study has shown that children who attend schools requiring uniforms perform significantly better than schools with a more laissez-faire attitude toward student attire. So beginning the first of the month, all Tyler High School students will be required to wear uniforms. Flyers and order forms will be going home to parents in the Wednesday envelopes."

"I'd like to see those studies," Linda said, standing. "Because I don't believe they exist."

The principal frowned. "Copies will be made available to all staff members who request them. But let me assure you that there are *many* studies on this subject and that they all—"

Ray Cheng stood up. "I don't believe that's true. There was an article last year in *Today's Education* that said just the opposite."

Jody was getting annoyed. "I'm not going to argue with you about this. The decision has been made."

"Unmake it," Ray challenged her.

"No," the principal said. She glared at Ray and Linda and other faculty members who must have looked like they disagreed with the new policy as well. "You're of Chinese descent," she said to Ray. "Why do you think all of those Asian countries are kicking the shit out of us academically?"

"You think it's because their kids wear uniforms?"

"You're damn right."

"This is high school," Linda reminded her. "These students are nearly adults. Some of the seniors *are* legally adults. They should be allowed to dress the way they want. Clothes, hair and fashion provide them with a safe, harmless way of expressing themselves." She looked around the room for support. "I hate to bring it up again, but these are good students here, for the most part. We aren't living in some gang-ridden neighborhood filled with crack addicts. These are normal middle-class kids. We can't keep treating them like they're criminals."

Jody's voice was stern. "We are treating them in a way that ensures they won't *become* criminals. All of our efforts are working toward the same goal, and they are methods that have been proven time and time again in both public and private educational facilities." She fixed Linda with a hard stare. "Now I suggest you sit down, Mrs. Webster. Unless you would like another reprimand added to your file."

She heard the intake of breath from several men and women nearby, a sound that indicated a more-than-passing acquaintance with reprimands, and she wondered how many other teachers Jody had disciplined lately.

"You sit down, too, Mr. Cheng. This is an announcement, not a discussion. It's not up for debate."

Jody's Stepford smile returned. "It's a win-win situation," she told the crowd. "We have entered into an agreement with a local uniform supplier. In return for giving them our business, the firm will donate to the school a percentage from each uniform sold. We will use that income to help fund some of our after-school programs. As for the specifics, the uniforms were designed by myself, with input from members of the charter committee, and are in the school colors of orange and black. Each teacher will be responsible for inspecting all students in his or her class on a daily basis to make sure that they are complying with the new regulations. A checklist detailing all of the dress code's requirements will be provided. As I said earlier, order forms will be distributed through the Wednesday envelopes, and by the following Wednesday, everyone will have been issued his or her uniform." She looked out at the assembly. "I don't expect there to be any questions."

Jody wrapped up her speech with some rah-rah platitudes, and the meeting continued with status reports by members of the charter committee, each of whom had been assigned the task of overseeing a particular area of the school. Without the principal's grand pronouncements, the discussed topics soon disintegrated into boring minutiae. Next to her, Robert dozed off, and Linda saw Bobbi, sitting in a chair in the front of the room and off to the right, watching him and writing in a notebook. No doubt he would be punished for this transgression later. Bobbi continued to scan the crowd, periodically writing notes, and Linda knew she was scrutinizing the assemblage for those who did not appear to be entirely on board.

How much worse was it going to be after the security cameras were installed?

And still the meeting droned on. A half hour. An hour. An hour and a half.

If the point was to numb them all into submission, Linda thought Jody might succeed. Even she felt tired and overwhelmed by the marathon session, and when they were finally released, it took her a moment to rise from her chair because her left foot was asleep. Around her, teachers filed out quietly. She met up with Diane by the door, and Suzanne sidled next to the two of them as they were walking across the quad toward the English department office. "I need to talk to you," she said. "About Yvonne Gauthier."

"What about her?" Linda asked.

Suzanne looked around furtively. "I'm telling you because I don't know who to trust. And I'm not sure anyone else would believe me." She waited for Scott Swaim to pass by, then leaned in closer. "I don't think Yvonne quit."

"You think she was fired?"

Suzanne shook her head. "More than that. She supposedly resigned on Back-to-School Night, right? But she left without taking any of her personal belongings. Her purse and coat and iPod were still in her room. I know. I saw them. I thought maybe she'd come back for them later, although that didn't make much sense—how could she have driven home that night without her purse, right?—but yesterday I was helping a student look for something in the Lost and Found, and there in a box was Yvonne's stuff. She never did come back for it. So I got her address from her emergency card and drove by her house. It's abandoned. There are newspapers piled up on the walkway, her mail's spilled out of the mailbox and now the postman's putting it on the ground in rubber-banded bundles. No one's mowed the lawn since, I would guess, Back-to-School Night. The grass is wild; the flowers are dead; there are weeds everywhere."

"What are you saying?"

"I don't know exactly. But I think something's happened to her." Suzanne looked around. "I think someone *did* something to her."

"I believe you," Linda said.

Diane nodded in reluctant agreement.

"Should I tell the police? Report her missing? What should I do?" Again, she looked around to make sure no one else was nearby. "I don't want Jody to know that I know."

"Call the police," Diane suggested. "Make it an

anonymous tip. Call from a pay phone. Tell them you think Yvonne Gauthier, a teacher at Tyler High, is missing. Give them her address."

Linda nodded. "Spice it up if you need to. You're anonymous. Tell them you heard screams from her house or something so they'll have a reason to go in there."

"Okay," Suzanne said.

It was three o'clock, the sun was out and they were in the middle of a high school campus, but Linda felt as chilled as if she were alone in a graveyard at midnight. The stakes, it seemed to her, had suddenly been raised.

"We should have a meeting," she said. "Away from school, where we can all talk freely and get everything out in the open. We need to get a fuller, more complete picture of what's going on and what everyone knows, instead of just piecing things together ourselves from the bits and pieces we hear at lunch or in the halls."

"And who knows?" Suzanne said. "Maybe if we all put our heads together, we can figure out something to do about it."

Diane was already consulting her day planner. "How does Friday night sound? It'll give us time to get the word out. And I mean spoken word. Nothing should be in writing. We don't want a paper trail."

Both Linda and Suzanne nodded.

One of the new custodians approached, pushing a flat cart piled high with folding chairs. They smiled politely at him, but waited until he was out of earshot before they spoke again.

"Let's do it," Linda said.

Frank groaned. "You know I hate going to teachers' parties."

"This is different."

"Will there be teachers there?"

Linda shot him a don't-be-stupid look.

"Then I don't want to go."

"I told you. It's not a party. It's a meeting. About the situation."

"I don't see how I can help."

She faced him, hands on hips. "Don't you care at all what's happening? I know it's just *my* job and it's not as important as *yours*—"

"That's not what I meant, and you know it. Besides, I may not even have a job pretty soon."

"All the more reason for you to get involved."

Frank sighed. "I wasn't entirely serious, you know. It was just part of the usual banter I thought we engaged in. Of course, I'm coming. And, of course, I care."

She put a hand on his arm, took a deep breath. "I know. I'm sorry. It's just that I'm under a lot of pressure lately. You're supposed to be the rock here. You're supposed to listen to my problems and reassure me and give me great advice."

"I will." He kissed the top of her head.

She couldn't help smiling. "But you really *don't* like teachers' parties, do you?"

"No," he admitted, "I don't."

Twenty minutes later, they were in Anaheim Hills, parking next to the curb in front of Ray Cheng's house. He had offered to host the meeting because he lived in a different city and they wanted to get as far away from Tyler High as possible.

Frank whistled as he looked at the giant two-story house with its professionally landscaped yard. "Nice place. What's his wife do? She's obviously not a teacher."

"Middle management for some company in Irvine."

"We picked the wrong occupations."

They got out of the car and started up the cobblestone path toward the front door. Frank was carrying a satchel, and she stopped him before he reached the lit porch. "What's that? Your laptop? Go put that back in the car. I want you to try and be social tonight."

He smiled. "Don't worry."

Before she could stop him, he was up the porch steps and ringing the bell. The door opened instantly, and Ray was there to welcome them, motioning for them to come inside. "Glad you could come," he said. "Nice to see you. Even if it is under these circumstances." He gestured toward the dining room, where a long table was sumptuously set. "Get yourself something to drink. Have something to eat," he said. "Mingle."

The interior of the home was as impressive as the exterior, and Linda found herself drawn to a picture window that held a spectacular view of half of Orange County. Below them, in the darkness, a river of red and white lights that was the freeway snaked through a randomly lit urban landscape that looked like a reflection of the star-studded sky above.

"Is this where you imagined Ray would live?"

Linda turned around to see Diane standing behind her and swirling a glass of wine. "No," she admitted. She looked around. "Where's Greg?"

"He didn't want to come."

"Smart man," Frank said under his breath.

Linda hit his shoulder.

Diane smiled. "Not only are teachers underpaid, but we get no respect."

"Is everyone here?" Linda asked.

"A lot of people are."

"Do you think there are any spies?"

Diane sighed. "You know what's sad—or scary? I was just wondering the same thing myself."

"Should we do some sort of head count? We pretty much know who's who, don't we?"

"Not necessarily," Diane said. "Why don't we just wander around, keep our ears and eyes open and find out what we can."

They started walking through the large living room, saying hello to their friends and colleagues, chiming in with their own criticisms when they heard teachers complaining about the school. Frank started talking shop with Winton Bremer, the computer science instructor, and Linda left him to consult with Steve Warren, who'd just arrived. A few moments later, she saw both Frank and Winton dutifully nodding their heads as Iris Royer, the oldest teacher at Tyler High, chattered away about what the school was like when it first opened.

A little while later, by the drink table, Linda saw Frank still nodding politely at Iris' reminiscences. Winton had somehow escaped, but Frank was trapped. "This is fun," Iris said, touching his arm. "We ought to get together like this more often."

Frank shot Linda a look over Iris' head. "Yeah," he lied.

Linda turned away, trying not to laugh. But she felt sorry for him, and smiling, she told Iris it was time for her to reclaim her husband. The two of them returned to the area next to the big window, where they met up once again with Diane.

"Where's Suzanne?" Linda asked worriedly. "I didn't see her."

Diane nodded. "She was supposed to be here."

"Maybe she's late," Frank offered.

Linda looked at her watch. "A half hour late? I don't like that. It's not like her."

Ray finally emerged from the entryway and, since it was his house, got the meeting officially started by tapping a fork on his wineglass and announcing: "Attention, folks!"

All heads turned toward him.

"I think we all know why we're here. So why don't we get down to it. The floor is open."

Suddenly everyone was talking at once, and Ray held up his hands and said in his sternest teacher voice, "Quiet!" There was scattered laughter, and he grinned. "Sorry. Habit. But it looks like we need a little more structure. So I'll start off. Then we'll go around the room and everyone can say their piece."

Nods of assent all around.

Ray told of finding the feces atop his desk after helping Linda look for a ghost that had appeared in her room the night before. At the word "ghost," Linda saw several teachers look at one another meaningfully. She wasn't the only one! Others had seen ghosts, too! She was filled with a sense of relief and a sudden feeling of unaccountable optimism.

Ray went on to talk about different stories he'd heard and various conversations he'd had.

The teachers who spoke after him had more specific incidents to relate. A lot of them revolved around the principal. Lisa Piccolo, who lived with and took care of her invalid mother, said that Jody had called her mother while she was at work, and that her mother had still been sobbing from the conversation when Lisa had arrived home hours later, although neither the principal nor her mother would talk about what had occurred. Joel Grazer told of a meeting with Jody and Bobbi two weeks ago in which he'd informed them that he was going to be taking a personal day on Friday in order to take his son to see Thomas the Tank Engine in Perris. The two women said that if he did so, they would both claim that he had sexually harassed them. He'd taken the day anyway. Nothing had happened yet—but he was still waiting for the ax to fall.

Each teacher who spoke was more open than the last. It was as if hearing the experiences of their coworkers gave them the courage and strength to reveal not just the facts of what had occurred to them but their feelings and impressions about the school overall. There'd been hints of this in some of their conversations in the lounge or in the parking lot, but never before had they shared so openly or so freely compared notes, and the effect was liberating.

"I don't like the library," Jackie Linden admitted. "I never have, and I don't think I've said two words to Janet Fratelli in the entire six years I've been here. But now I'm *afraid* to go in that building. It scares me. I won't take my classes there anymore, and I've changed my syllabus so that my students don't ever have to check out a book from the library."

Linda went even further. "Ray told you that I'd seen a ghost in my room, although I'm not sure he believed me at the time. But I did. And it was on Back-to-School Night."

A murmur went through the assembled group.

"I think Back-to-School Night was kind of a catalyst," she continued. "I think it's when the old school finally died and the charter took over completely."

A lot of the teachers were nodding. "Back-to-School Night," several of them murmured.

"That's the night Yvonne disappeared and that Carlos and Rakeem quit," Diane chimed in.

Linda nodded. "Something happened that night, something at the school that we still don't know about. But I think it's affected everything that's happened since. It's ratcheted everything up a notch."

"Speaking of Carlos and Rakeem, has anybody noticed those two janitors they hired to replace them?"

Lisa asked. "They're creepy. I get, like, a child-molester vibe from that one guy, Mel."

"Yeah," Jackie said. "I thought the district had some sort of screening process, a background check that they did."

Linda jumped in. "That's just it. The *district* does. Tyler does not. And ever since we turned charter, Jody and her committee are completely in charge of all new hires."

There was dissatisfied grumbling among the teachers.

"The question is," Ray said, "what can we do about it?"

Next to her, Frank cleared his throat. Opening his satchel, he took out a sheaf of papers. "I've been doing some research on charter schools. Do you know that, contrary to conventional wisdom, charter schools, on average, fare no better and even slightly worse in the percentage of students who graduate and go on to college? Dropout rates are almost identical. What's more, even though they're allowed to basically cherry-pick their students, scores on standardized achievement tests are lower overall than in traditional public schools. And they also have an unacceptably high failure rate. I've printed out a list of bankruptcies and cases of gross financial negligence or malfeasance. As the adage says, ninety percent of all businesses fail. Well, public institutions can't afford to fail. So maybe it's time to stop applying so-called business solutions to education and just accept that in some instances the for-profit model does not and should not apply."

Linda looked at him in surprise. Sometimes, he astounded her. Here she'd been thinking that he was being dragged here against his will and was going to sit alone in a corner and drink, and he had actually come prepared with facts and figures. All she had to offer were impressions and theories, but he'd done research. She shook her head, smiling. That was just like him, and at that moment she did not think that she had ever loved him more.

"It seems to me that that's the case you have to make," Frank continued. "You need to start compiling statistics, then go to the district and state boards and show them the deleterious effects this charter has had on Tyler High."

"But these . . . ghosts and things." Joel seemed embarrassed even mentioning it. "How are they connected with the charter?"

"I don't know," Frank admitted. "Maybe they're not. But it appears that nearly all of you can trace your problems with the school and your unhappiness over what's happening there to the beginning of this semester. And the only difference between this semester and last is that now you're a charter school."

Frank handed Linda the pages he'd printed out, and she passed them around the room. "Look these over when you get a chance. There's some other information there as well. I'm sure you can find additional data on your own. But from what Linda tells me, the good thing about your situation is that your school is not completely independent. There's still an affiliation with the district. Which means that no matter how dictatorial your principal gets, there's still the possibility of going around her or over her head."

They didn't get much accomplished at the meeting, but they came away feeling energized and inspired, and on the way home, Linda, for the first time in several weeks, actually felt slightly positive about the future. "I love you," she told Frank.

He smiled at her. "I love you, too."

It was a series of unusual coincidences that led to Suzanne staying late on Friday, and when she finally closed the door to her room, walked outside and saw how dark it was, she found herself wondering if those "coincidences" had been specifically arranged for just that reason. She'd been thinking a lot about such things lately, and looking at the school through that lens had brought her to a whole new level of awareness.

Suzanne glanced at her watch. Seven fifteen. She was already late. For all she knew, the meeting would be over by the time she drove over to Anaheim Hills, but she was determined to make it to Ray's house if she could. She'd call from her car and find out. She would have called already, but the phone in her room was dead, and as everyone knew, cell phones didn't work on Tyler's campus.

That was another thing that was very suspicious.

The school seemed empty. And creepy. Rather than pockets of shadows, there were pockets of light. She had no idea if the administration was trying to save money or energy, but the place was darker than it used to be, and the change not only had lent the grounds a sinister ambience but seemed to have reshaped the terrain. The trees looked strange, walkways were in the wrong place and buildings seemed forbidding and far too tall. She knew it was an optical illusion, but she almost had the sense that this was not Tyler High, that she'd somehow been transported somewhere else.

It was cold, and Suzanne wished she'd worn a jacket. Shivering, hugging her purse to her chest, she started up the walkway that led through the quad, trying to recall if the rather threatening-looking tree to her right had been there this morning.

A figure emerged from the shadows.

She gasped involuntarily, jumped back.

"Don't worry, Ms. Johnson. I'm here to help." The figure walked into a pool of light. It was one of the scouts, a boy in her third-period class named Hamilton Price.

"I'll walk you to your car," he said. His voice was flat, unemotional, and seemed more order than offer.

She did not like the idea of Tyler Scouts, nor did she like most of the students who had been recruited to become scouts, and Hamilton's company was the last thing she wanted right now. But she was afraid to say so, and she found herself nodding in acquiescence as the boy stared blankly at her. "Okay," she said. "I'm in the faculty lot."

They walked for a moment in silence. Their footsteps seemed loud in the stillness, but from one of the buildings—

the library?

—she heard other noises as well, low, barely audible sounds that made her think of small animals being tortured. "You're here late," she said to Hamilton, trying to engage him in conversation so she couldn't hear those faint indistinct squeaking sounds coming from the building.

"I was waiting for you," he said flatly.

She didn't like that response. As ambiguous as it was, none of its possible interpretations were good.

Suzanne quickened her step. "I'm late for a meeting," she explained, though there was no reason she should have to explain herself to him. "I was supposed to be there already. They're probably wondering what happened to me."

She sounded desperate now, scared, and she willed her mouth to shut up before she made even a bigger fool of herself.

Hamilton said nothing, keeping pace with her.

They'd been passing through the center of campus, and now she led the way through the closed corridor that bisected the math/science building and led to the lunch area. The corridor was supposed to be lit, but only one fluorescent bar on her upper left was on, and it was covered with moths and bugs whose fluttering wings sent manic flickers up the walls. Before them, on the other side, was a world of almost total blackness. Only a strangely moving light inside the cafeteria and the orangish overhead illumination from streetlamps in the parking lot far away offered any relief from the omnipresent gloom.

Suzanne wanted to turn back. It was an intuitive reaction, like that of an animal whose instinct warns it of danger, and if Hamilton hadn't been with her, she would have hightailed it back to her classroom and spent the night there, sleeping at her desk with all the lights on. But she knew the scout would follow her wherever she went, and she was just as afraid of him as she was of the darkness ahead. The best thing to do was to hurry out to the parking lot, get in her car and drive away from here as quickly as possible.

But what if Hamilton tried to get in the car with her? Or what if he tried to follow her home? At this point, neither possibility seemed that much of an imaginative stretch.

She'd kick him; she'd hit him; she'd rake her car keys across his face. She'd do whatever it took to get away from him. Suzanne was aware of what a bizarre train of thought this was—planning an attack on the student who was escorting her to her car—but desperate times called for desperate measures, and she had no doubts, no qualms, no reservations. Hers weren't the thoughts of an unstable, unfit teacher but the completely logical stratagems of an ordinary woman in an extraordinary circumstance.

They were through the corridor. As with the quad, this part of the school grounds looked unfamiliar to her, strange. She squinted into the gloom. On the west side of the lunch area, where the outdoor basketball courts were supposed to be, she saw what appeared to be a swing set, a slide and monkey bars. Instead of black asphalt, the ground was white sand.

Hamilton saw where she was looking. His voice, when he spoke, was a dull monotone: "That's where the dead kids play."

Her heart nearly stopped. She wanted to see Hamilton's face to determine whether he was joking, but she had the feeling that he wasn't, and she was too scared to check. She kept walking, picking up the pace, knowing that if all went right, she would be at her car in two minutes, three tops.

Except she couldn't see the lights of the parking lot anymore. There was no sign of any illumination in the murkiness before her. It was possible that a fog had rolled in, but although it was cold, it was not damp, and that seemed a slim possibility. She slowed her pace so as not to trip over unseen obstacles, and as her eyes adjusted, she thought she could make out shapes in the dark ahead.

She squinted.

In front of her was the playground.

Where the dead kids play.

That was impossible. She turned, this time toward the classrooms, or where she thought they should be, but there was the playground again: the swing set, slide and monkey bars.

And children were playing on them.

Suzanne started to run. She didn't know in which direction she was going, didn't know where the parking lot was, didn't know where *anything* was. All she knew was that she had to get out of here, had to get away from the school. Now.

From somewhere in the night she heard the sound of laughter. It was children's laughter, although it was anything but innocent, and it seemed to come from all directions.

Ahead of her was the playground again, and she turned to her left and ran as fast as she could—

But there was the playground again, and she turned in another direction and—

There was the playground again.

She stopped, frustrated and frightened, sobbing. Hamilton was still by her side. She was afraid to look at him, but she could feel his presence next to her, his shoulder pressing against her own. The playground seemed closer this time, and though the figures cavorting on its equipment were little more than shapes slightly lighter than the surrounding blackness, she could see that some of them looked more like teenagers than children. Some of them might have been high school students.

"Your car is gone," Hamilton said in his robotic voice.

She heard him through her sobs, and though she tried not to believe him, she did.

"You'd better tell the principal," he added.

"No!" Suzanne screamed. She pushed at the scout and ran as fast as she could in the opposite direction. He didn't follow her, and there was no playground before her this time, but the darkness grew heavier, more dense and claustrophobic, and within seconds she was all alone in a world that was jet-black and featureless. "Help!" she cried, screaming at the top of her lungs. "Help me!" Her voice died and went nowhere, as though the sound was absorbed by the gloom.

"Help!" she sobbed.

But the figure that emerged from the murk and took her hand was not there to help her.

And when she saw its face and felt the coldness of its touch, she could not even scream.

Eighteen

It had been a long time since Myla had hung out with Rachel Jackson-Smith. Since freshman year, probably. So it was a big surprise when her old friend came over near the end of lunch and asked if she could sit down with her. Brad had just left to drop some books off at the library before the bell rang, and Myla was reading over the minutes of the last student-council meeting to make sure all her objections had been typed up and were part of the record, when she heard a tentative "Hi." She looked up to see Rachel standing there in her usual jeans and a T-shirt, holding the straps of a backpack in her hands. She'd gotten new glasses sometime in the past few years, but other than that, she looked almost exactly the same as she had in ninth grade.

Myla couldn't remember the last time she'd actually talked to Rachel. What's more, she didn't know *why* she no longer talked to Rachel. The two of them had met during freshman orientation, and that first year at Tyler they'd been inseparable. But as sophomores, for some reason, they'd made other friends and gone their separate ways. Now Rachel was an editor on the school newspaper, the *Tyler Gazette,* and was getting quite a reputation for her fearless reporting, going up against the administration, the athletic department and a number of other sacred cows.

Even though she no longer hung out with her, Myla admired her.

"How's it going?" Myla asked once Rachel sat down. "Haven't seen you around for a while." She winced inwardly, embarrassed by her own banality.

Rachel wasn't much better. "I've been around."

They were awkward with each other at first, pathetically trying to reconnect by bringing up the most generic subjects possible, but when the bell rang and Rachel made no move to leave, Myla had an idea that there was something on the other girl's mind, some reason why she wanted to talk.

"Do you . . . need something?" Myla asked tentatively.

"Listen," Rachel said. "Can you get off this period? I mean, you're on student council. Can you write yourself a pass or something? Because if you can't," she added quickly, "I can. As an editor, I can write passes for my reporters, and I can do it for you, too."

"Why?" Myla asked.

Rachel was silent for a moment. "It's hard to explain," she said finally. "I think I'd rather show it to you than tell you about it."

"But what *is* it? And why me? I don't understand. You want me to skip class to . . . see something?"

Rachel sighed. "Let me ask you something. Have you noticed anything *strange* about Tyler this semester, since we became a charter school?"

"Who hasn't?" Myla said.

The other girl laughed in a way that sounded relieved. "Thank God. That's the part I didn't know how to bring up. Basically, I'm writing an article about everything that's going on, trying to tie it all together. For example, did you know that Mr. Carr has been harassing band members about their religion? He has a Christian club or Bible study group that meets before and after school, and he's trying to get all of the band members to join it. He's not just threatening them with hell—he's threatening to kick them out of band if they don't convert. Mrs. Habeck, on the other hand, is some sort of witch or pagan. And not one of those we're-all-one, worship-the-earth Wiccans. She believes in blood sacrifice, and she's been trying to recruit students to *her* beliefs."

"I thought you weren't allowed to do stuff like that at school."

"You're not allowed to do stuff like that at a *normal* school. But a charter school's a different story. And that's just the beginning of what goes on here. Anyway, I've been documenting incidents, talking to witnesses. It's a pretty well-researched piece, if I do say so myself. The editor in chief and our adviser have already approved it. We're going to get the word out."

"Where do I come in?" Myla asked.

"To be honest, I don't know, exactly. But I figure the student council might have some pull with the administration. Or the PTA. At the very least, you could help us by giving me an on-the-record quote. You're sort of in a position of authority, and your support might help get this ball rolling."

"So you want me to come with you?" Myla asked.

"I know you're on student council, but I *know* you." She lowered her eyes. "Or at least I did." She looked up again at Myla. "And you're not like the rest of them."

"Uh, thanks. I guess."

"I mean it. And the things going on . . ." Rachel shook her head. "I can't explain it. You just have to see it." She took a deep breath. "And that's what I want you to do. I was given a couple of tips this morning, and I'm going to check them out."

"Very Kristen Bell of you."

Rachel reddened.

"That was a compliment," Myla said quickly. "I'm sorry. I've been hanging around Brad and Ed too much. Their sarcasm's rubbing off on me. I swore it wouldn't, but . . ."

"I heard you were going out with Brad," Rachel said. "Congratulations."

"You knew that?" Myla was surprised. "And you know Brad?"

"I keep my ear to the ground," Rachel intoned with mock solemnity. "And I know everyone."

Myla laughed. "I missed you," she said.

"I missed you, too."

The second bell rang.

"You're definitely late for class now. I can write you an excuse, if you want to go back—or I can write you a pass if you want to come with me."

"I'll come," Myla said.

Rachel was suddenly all business. She opened her backpack, pulled out a notebook and took a pen from her right front jeans pocket. "First stop: girls' locker room. I got a report that something goes on there every fifth period. But we have to hurry." She started walking fast down the walkway that led to the sports complex. "A lot of these things I've uncovered are tied to certain teachers at certain periods." She was walking so fast that Myla was having a hard time keeping up. Rachel looked behind her. "Have you noticed anything specific in any of your classes, anything recurring?"

"No," Myla said, catching up. "Not that I can think of."

"What about the locker room or your PE class? Who do you have, by the way?"

"French. Sometimes Temple. And, no, I haven't noticed anything."

"I've heard bad things about Temple," Rachel said. "That's who we're here to see."

They were nearing the locker rooms. Off to their right, on the field, a couple of the boys had already suited up and were standing around, waiting. Ahead, through the entrance to the stadium, members of Tyler's all-white football team were walking in a circle around the all-Hispanic soccer team, singing obnoxiously at the top of their lungs.

"La cucaracha! La cucaracha! Stick some peaches up your butt!"

Both teams were in uniform, and Myla thought that strange. Why were they even here? They were supposed to practice after school, not during fifth period.

"La cucaracha! La cucaracha! Stick some peaches up your butt!"

"In here," Rachel said, drawing her attention away from the stadium. Turning to the left, Myla followed the other girl through the open double doors into the girls' locker room.

Open doors?

Myla frowned. Anyone walking by could see inside. Those doors were supposed to be closed. And there was also supposed to be a tiled barrier inside the entrance, a large square block the girls had to walk around that hid the interior of the locker room from view when boys passed by. What had happened to that? It had been there this morning.

But that was only the beginning.

Heads turned as the two of them walked into the locker room. Alva Ramierez, one of the toughest, meanest girls in school, scowled at them. "You're not in this class. What are you doing here?"

Rachel held up her notebook. "I'm writing a story for the school paper."

"On what? My pussy?"

There were a few titters of nervous laughter from the other girls nearby.

Alva fixed Myla with a hard stare. "What are you staring at, lez?" She threw a wadded pair of panties at her head.

Myla deftly stepped aside.

"You two come to get your jollies watching us undress? That why you're here?"

Elephants don't turn me on, would have been Myla's response, but before she could even open her mouth, the door to the coach's office opened, and Mrs. Temple walked out.

Completely naked.

The locker room grew silent. Even Alva seemed cowed. But there was no surprise on the faces of any of the girls, and Myla understood instantly that this was not something out of the ordinary. It happened a lot.

Rachel grabbed her arm and pulled her into the adjunct bathroom, out of the way. The bathroom was dark, and standing next to one of the sinks, they could see but not be seen.

The coach was walking naked between the lockers, up one aisle and down another. Some of the girls were in their gym clothes, some were still in their uniforms and others were in various states of undress, but all of them looked down or away, anyplace but at Mrs. Temple, who strode proudly past them, chest out, shaved crotch on display for all to see. One awkward-looking girl Myla didn't recognize was standing there in bra and underwear, about to slip on gym shorts, when the coach stopped in front of her. She pulled down the girl's underwear, turned her around, ran a finger into and down the crack of the girl's buttocks from the top to the bottom, then continued walking, smiling to herself.

Myla felt like gagging. Rachel was scribbling furiously in her notebook, though she couldn't possibly see what she was writing.

"In the gym in two!" the coach ordered, and girls scrambled to finish suiting up. "Bring your Ping-Pong paddles!"

Even Alva seemed to have forgotten they were there, and Myla and Rachel watched from the shadows as the locker room emptied out and the girls streamed through the open doorway on the other side of the room and into the adjoining gym. "Come on," Rachel whispered, sneaking out, and Myla followed.

In the gym, they could see the girls were huddled around the free throw line of the nearest basket. Mrs. Temple, still naked, was standing in the center of the court, hands on hips. As she'd ordered, all the students were carrying Ping-Pong paddles.

"Line up!" the coach said. She spread her legs, bent over and grabbed her ankles. "You each get three hits! Now, I want to feel those swings with some follow-through! Alva, you first! Paddle my ass until it's cherry apple red!"

Myla and Rachel watched as, one by one, the girls in the class stepped forward and smacked Mrs. Temple's bare bottom three times in quick succession while the teacher critiqued their strokes. "Pull your arm farther back!" she barked at one girl. "More uptilt at the end!" she told another.

A couple of times she quivered, moaned and said more softly, "Yes! That's nice!"

Rachel tugged lightly on her arm, and Myla followed her back through the locker room and outside.

"Oh my God," Myla said as they hurried down the walkway. "Oh my God."

Rachel's normally soft features were set in a grim expression. She did not speak until they were nearly to the lunch tables. "I was tipped off about that. One of the girls in that class told me to come and see for myself. I didn't know exactly what was going on, but I sort of had an idea. I just didn't think it was that . . . blatant.

"I should've brought along a camera," she chastised herself. "Visual proof is always better." She turned toward Myla. "But you're my witness, right? You know what we saw."

"I'll never forget it."

They stopped walking, and Rachel sat down at one of the lunch tables and jotted down a few more notes. "We have to go to room two eleven," she said as she wrote, "but we have a few extra minutes." She stood. "Let's stop by the Little Theater. There's something else I want to show you."

The two of them walked back toward the classroom buildings. There was a scout stationed in front of the corridor that led back to the quad, but Rachel showed him her press pass and that got them through. "Jarrod Helms," she said dismissively once they'd made it through the corridor. "The only thing more frightening than the thought of him in a uniform is the idea that someday he might get a badge and a gun to go along with it."

Myla smiled. Same old Rachel.

They walked past a row of classrooms. Ahead, the door to the Little Theater was open, and from within came the sounds of fast-paced country music. Not speaking, motioning with her hand for Myla to follow,

Rachel moved to the side of the door. She poked her head around the corner to look into the theater, then switched places with Myla and indicated that she was to do the same.

At first Myla saw nothing. Three-fourths of the auditorium, the area in which an audience would sit during a performance, was dark, the lights off. But she could still hear that hillbilly music, louder now and accompanied by a man's voice calling out square-dancing instructions, and when she craned her head farther, she saw a lit stage peopled with boys and girls dressed in Western attire. They were paired up and dancing, following the unseen caller's instructions.

"Swing your partner round and round. Sniff her where it really counts!"

As one, the boys twirled the girls, then lifted them up, shoving their noses straight into the girls' crotches. There was no giggling or squealing, as she would have expected, no cries of outrage or indignation. Indeed, the students performed the movement mechanically, dutifully, as though they had been through it many times before and were concentrating hard on perfecting their technique.

"With your feet upon the floor, grab her ass and yell for more!"

The girls bent over. Using both hands, the boys reached forward, squeezed the proffered buttocks and, as one, yelled, "Yee haw!"

Myla felt a tug on her arm and pulled herself away from the sight. She followed Rachel down the corridor until they reached the closed doors of the band room. "Gross, isn't it?" Rachel said.

Myla nodded slowly, looking around at the two-storied classroom buildings ringing the quad. "It makes me wonder what's going on behind some of those other closed doors, what things are happening that we don't know about yet."

"That's why I'm writing this article. That's why I'm asking for your help. We need students to get involved. We need to put a stop to this."

Myla was not even sure if that was possible. They weren't dealing with a single out-of-control teacher here, or one unfair rule that needed to be changed. Whatever was happening was affecting the whole school. She thought of that locker. There was a supernatural element to it as well, and that frightened her more than anything.

Rachel, though, seemed undaunted, and that gave Myla strength.

The reporter strode into the quad and down a walkway toward the social sciences building. "Last stop on the tour," she said.

Myla was not sure how much more of this she could take. "What is it this time?"

"For this we actually have to meet someone. My source."

"Clandestine stuff. Who?"

They'd reached Mrs. Habeck's room. "Chelsea James. I need to go in, get her out of her history class, and then she's going to take us to see something even most of the teachers don't know about: scout training. *Female* scout training."

Myla had seen the male scouts train before. It was hard to miss them. With their militaristic uniforms and their constant marching exercises on the lawn in front of the school, it was almost as if they *wanted* everyone to see and know what they were doing. Myla thought that it was part of an effort to intimidate the rest of the student population, something she'd told Roland Nevins at the last student-council session, though of course Roland had denied it.

The female scouts, however . . .

They were trickier. They wore the patches just like the boys, but they still had no uniforms and they never seemed to do things together. It was rare, in fact, to see two female scouts even speaking to each other. They were so secretive that they flew completely under the radar—a lot of people had probably forgotten that they even existed—and again Myla thought that was probably intentional.

Rachel had withdrawn a hall pass from the back of her notebook and was filling it out. "Wait here," she told Myla. "I'll be back in a sec." She walked into Mrs. Habeck's classroom, and Myla glanced around the quad. There was graffiti all over the short wall that bordered Senior Corner: insults and obscenities, crude depictions of male and female genitalia, symbols she didn't recognize but that reminded her of Arabic writing. Myla frowned. She was pretty sure none of that had been there before lunch.

Rachel emerged from the classroom with Chelsea, a girl Myla had seen around but didn't really know. Chelsea looked at her coolly but did not say hello. She was wearing a Tyler Scout patch herself, and Myla found herself questioning the girl's motives. *Why* had she come to Rachel in the first place? *Why* was she offering to take a reporter to a training session? She certainly didn't look like any sort of whistle-blowing ideologue. Indeed, there was something hard and cunning about her, an indefinable quality she shared with all the other scouts Myla had seen.

But then she let her guard down, and Myla saw that she was just a scared kid, a regular high school student caught up in something she didn't believe in or understand. "Thank you for coming," she told Rachel. "And writing about this."

"Thank *you* for telling me about it."

Chelsea glanced around the quad. "Come on. We'd better get going. This is the best time to show you what's going on."

"What if they catch us?"

"I'll say you're doing a story for the paper on how much better and more well-trained we are than the boys."

"Is there a rivalry between you two?" Rachel asked excitedly. "Are you competing with each other?"

"No," Chelsea admitted. "We just do what the principal tells us. The boys, too. But it *might* work."

What if it doesn't? Myla wondered. But she said nothing.

They walked through the corridor toward the lunch area. "We'll take a shortcut," Chelsea said, hanging a left. She led them past the auto shop, past woodshop and metal, around the side of the shop building to a dirt footpath that led through a narrow trash-strewn section of ground between the building and the fence that separated it from the sidewalk and street outside. They trekked up and down short small mounds of hard-packed earth, kicking aside beer bottles, Coke cans and potato chip wrappers. The path wound around the back of the building and joined a cement sidewalk that passed through an open area west of the sports complex. Ahead was a series of pens and corrals housing a couple of sheep, a few goats and a cow. Beyond that was a barn.

Myla had never been on this part of the campus. She didn't know how that was possible after nearly four years here, but it was. She was vaguely aware that the school had a Future Farmers of America program, the FFA, but she had no idea where they met or what they did, and it was a surprise to her to find this barn and these pens way out here in an area that she hadn't known existed. What made it seem even more remote was the fact that here the nine-foot wall that would eventually enclose the whole school was finished. They were cut off from the city outside. Neither the houses nor the street beyond was visible, and it reminded her in a way of Disneyland. There was that same sense of being in a hermetically sealed world.

From within the barn, they heard female voices. At this distance, Myla wasn't sure whether they were talking, fighting, laughing or screaming. Something suddenly occurred to her. "This is fifth period," she said. "Shouldn't they be in class?"

"Yeah," Rachel agreed. "You'd think they'd practice before school or after school or during lunch."

"We train in shifts," Chelsea said.

Myla still didn't like that "we."

"Someone is out here *all* the time. That's the way Principal Hawkes wants it. Every period of the day, a group of girls is out here practicing fighting techniques."

Rachel had her notebook out. "Who are you training to fight?"

"They haven't told us yet." Chelsea stopped walking. "From here on in, we have to be quiet. If someone sees us, let me do all the talking. Okay?"

Myla and Rachel nodded.

"We'll go around the side of the barn. There's a window there where you can see in, and it faces the backs of the girls."

"What about the teacher, the instructor or whoever's training you?"

"There is no instructor fifth period. That's why I picked it to show you." Chelsea lowered her voice. "That's also why it's more dangerous. Now no more talking."

They left the path and hiked around the corrals and

pens, crouching low and running across a section of open dirt until they reached the side of the barn. As Chelsea had said, there was a window in the wall, a small square just about eye level next to a hook holding a coiled rope. She peeked in first, then moved aside and let Rachel have a look.

Myla went last. There were far more girls here than she'd expected, probably close to twenty, and she did some quick math. Seven periods with twenty girls each. A hundred and forty girls? That didn't seem possible. There were only three hundred kids in the entire senior class. Maybe this was the peak, though. Maybe other periods had fewer recruits and that's why Chelsea had taken them here now.

Maybe not.

She saw a couple of girls who weren't seniors, and though she'd thought the scout program was open only to twelfth graders, it looked like that wasn't the case.

The girls stood silently in line in the center of the barn, facing away from the window, each of them clutching a spear in her right hand. Apparently, there were no left-handed scouts, a fact that was probably irrelevant but that she filed away in her brain nonetheless. Lying in front of them on a mound of hay, bloody and writhing, was a cow. It was, no doubt, a cow that the FFA kids were feeding or raising, but the scouts had appropriated it and seemed to be using it for target practice. Or, more accurately, torture practice. Standing before the animal, Tiffany Leung raised her left hand and used her right to jab the spear she was holding into the cow's shoulder. It lifted its head, bleated in agony, then let the head fall back again, too weak to fight.

Tiffany moved off to the left. The next girl in line stepped forward, thrust her spear into the cow's rear end, eliciting an even more horrible moan of pain, and then twisted it before pulling the spear out and following Tiffany to another station, where the girls were throwing their spears at the carcass of a chicken that had been affixed to a wooden post.

On the wall to the left of the tortured cow, Myla saw, were shackles. Two above and two below, their chains ending in manacles and fetters, they were clearly designed for human restraint.

She moved away from the window. "My God," she breathed.

Rachel was writing in her notebook.

Chelsea nodded somberly. "That's what they make us do. And they say this is just the beginning of it." She said no more, but Myla immediately thought of those shackles on the wall.

Silently, the three girls made their way back to the center of campus the way they'd come. Clutching her hall pass, Chelsea left them at the social sciences building. "Don't use my name," she pleaded. "Don't mention me at all."

"I won't," Rachel promised.

Myla looked at her friend, at a loss for words.

Rachel looked grim. "Worse than you thought, isn't it?"

It was and it wasn't, Myla decided. She could never have imagined the specifics of what she'd seen today, but it was definitely in line with what she'd suspected lay under the surface of the school this semester. Still, she nodded.

"Do you have a quote for me?"

Myla shook her head numbly. Her brain wasn't able to come up with a pithy response to all that she'd witnessed, and Rachel seemed to understand. "I'm going to write the article tonight. I'll show it to you tomorrow. Meet me in the morning before school. By Senior Corner."

"Okay," Myla agreed. "I'll try to think of something to say."

But Rachel didn't show up the next morning.

Although Myla got to school at seven thirty and waited until the bell rang, there was no sign of her old friend, and she had to run all the way across campus to make it to PE on time. At Nutrition, she told Brad she had something to do and went up to the school newspaper's office, the room adjacent to Mr. Booth's class. The adviser was there, proofreading pages along with the editor, and several students were typing on computers lined up on a table against the far wall.

"Excuse me," Myla said. "I'm looking for Rachel Jackson-Smith."

The students looked at one another, eyes wide, then turned to Mr. Booth. The adviser calmly finished proofing the paragraph he was on, then glanced over at her. His eyes were cool, unreadable. "I guess you didn't hear," he said. "Rachel was killed last night by a drunk driver."

She'd been hoping for the best and expecting the worst, but the words were still a shock, and they took a moment to sink in. "Rachel's . . . *dead*?"

Mr. Booth nodded. "We're working on a front-page tribute to her right now. Would you like to see it?"

There was something surreal about this whole scene: the unflappable instructor, the uninvolved students, the way the news of this tragedy was being treated like . . . news. Rachel was someone they knew and worked with and were supposed to have cared about, but her death might just as well have been the announcement of a new teacher's hiring or the score for Friday night's football game. Feeling stunned, she walked over to the adviser and read the article he'd been proofing. In it was the answer to every question she might have asked about the facts of the accident—it had happened at the intersection of West Street and Lincoln Avenue at approximately eight thirty; she'd been wearing a seat belt, but her car had no air bags and she'd died at the scene; the drunk driver was an unemployed construction worker with a suspended license—but it was all presented coldly, dispassionately, as though it had occurred in another state and involved someone none of them knew.

Not only did that seem wrong; it seemed . . . suspicious, and for the first time she looked at the newspaper office as though it were one of the stops on yesterday's tour, as though Rachel were showing her another example of something eerily off base here at Tyler High. She looked up at the adviser, took a deep breath. "Rachel was working on a story," Myla said. "About . . ." She realized she didn't know how to describe it. "About strange things that are going on here on campus."

"Don't know anything about it," Mr. Booth told her.

She looked at Richard Park, the editor, but he averted his eyes, found something to stare at on the floor.

"I went with her yesterday to look at a PE class, a square-dancing class and a training session for female Tyler Scouts," Myla said, exasperated. "The PE teacher was *naked* and making her students *spank* her, the square dance was *obscene* and the scouts were killing a cow in the FFA barn. Rachel was writing an article to expose all that and other things she'd uncovered."

Mr. Booth shook his head. "She would have told

me if that's what she was doing, but she never said a thing about it and there's nothing like that in her file notes or on her Web page. We checked her computer this morning for any work that remained outstanding, so we could reassign it to someone else."

"She okayed it with you!" Myla pointed to the editor. "And *you*!"

The editor looked at the floor.

"No," Mr. Booth said. "She didn't."

"Bullshit!"

The adviser looked at her coldly. "We're done here," he said. "I think you'd better leave."

Brad was worried. After break, Myla hadn't shown up for English. She never missed a class, and when he saw her empty chair, he knew in his gut that something had to be wrong. He wanted to call or message her, but even if students had been allowed to use them, cell phones still wouldn't work on campus.

He was so distracted that in PE he forgot to change his socks while suiting up for basketball. Both socks were white, so it shouldn't have made any difference, but ever since they'd started wearing these fucking uniforms at the beginning of the week, teachers—PE teachers especially—had been on the warpath, inspecting every aspect of their attire, from shirt tucks to shoelaces, punishing students for every minor infraction.

And he had forgotten to change from one pair of white socks to another.

Coach Nicholson called him on it the second he stepped into the gym. "Becker!"

Brad looked up at the sound of the raspy bark.

"Get your ass back in there and put on the proper socks or you'll be given ten demerits! I want you on the court and dressed appropriately! Now!"

Brad ran back into the locker room. But he stopped running as soon as he passed through the doorway. Something was wrong. He could feel it. It wasn't a change in temperature, but it was a physical sensation nonetheless, a sudden difference in the quality of the air, and it hit him instantly. And hard. He glanced first to his left, then to his right. The locker room was empty, but . . .

But it didn't feel empty. Dim gray sunshine shone through the clouded skylight in the center of the room, creating shadowed areas near the toilets and the coach's office where someone could be hiding. The locker room was silent, but it was a pregnant silence, too perfect to be real, one that seemed to be hiding something within it.

He walked forward slowly, warily, not thinking that someone would jump him exactly but aware that it was a possibility.

His rubber-soled gym shoes slapped loudly on the wet cement floor.

The coach was probably writing him up right now, marking him as tardy as well as piling on those demerits, but Brad approached his locker cautiously. The feeling that he was not alone in here had grown, and though his locker row was directly beneath the skylight, the weak illumination offered no comfort and served only to make the outlying parts of the room seem even darker. He looked toward the end of the aisle.

There was a figure standing in the shower.

Van Nguyen.

The boy was fully clothed, wearing jeans and a T-shirt, standing in the far corner of the tiled shower stall, staring down at a basketball at his feet. Even though Brad could not see his face, he knew it was Van. With the unfounded certainty of dream logic, he also knew that he did not want Van to look up, that if the other boy did and Brad saw his eyes . . . something would happen.

What, exactly, he did not know.

But . . . something.

Brad looked away, quickly spun the combination on his lock and took his gym socks out of his locker. He hazarded a glance back at the shower.

Van had moved.

Brad's mouth went dry. The boy was still looking down at the basketball at his feet, but now he was in the center of the shower stall, beneath the middle nozzle. Brad didn't know whether Van was a ghost or whether he was just acting strange, but either way, he was afraid of the other boy, and if he saw even the slightest bit of movement, he was going to haul ass back to the gym and take his demerits. There was no way he was going to stay here and wait for Van to do something.

Heart pounding crazily, Brad kept an eye on the unmoving figure while he kicked off his shoes. He sat down quickly on the center changing bench, still watching the shower, but he had to look away for a few seconds while he took off his socks. He looked up again.

Van had moved to the edge of the shower stall.

And was facing him.

Brad ran. He didn't bother to pick up his socks from the floor or close his locker—he just took off, grabbing his shoes and dashing through the locker room to the doorway that led to the gym. Ahead, he could see the rest of the class already playing basketball. Mr. Nicholson was standing behind the basket, whistle in his mouth, watching their performance. Brad was still afraid enough of the coach to not want to be yelled at, so he sat down at the edge of the gym to put on his shoes. He didn't have any socks on and would get in trouble for that, but it was nothing compared with what he would have to face if he returned barefoot.

He hastily untied the laces of his sneakers and slipped the first one on, but before he could put on the other shoe or even tie the laces of the first one up again, he heard a low *tap-tap-tap,* like the drip of water from a faucet. He turned around—

—to see Van standing directly behind him, unmoving, staring down at the basketball lying at his feet.

Brad jumped up, screaming, and, with only one shoe on, ran into the center of the gym. In that split-second glimpse, he had seen Van's face, and it was a sight that he would never forget. Van's skin was ashen, an almost whitish blue, and his mouth was open in a toothless O. His eyes were wide open and fixed.

The rest of his class stopped what they were doing and watched, several of them laughing, as Brad ran toward them, laces flapping on his one shod but sockless foot, his other bare sole slapping against the hardwood floor. The coach looked angry, and he blew his whistle, pointing. "Get your ass back in there and put on the proper footwear!" he ordered.

"Van Nguyen!" Brad shouted, still running forward, away from the locker rooms. "I saw him in there! His ghost or something! It's in there! It tried to attack me!"

Now nearly everyone was laughing as Coach Nicholson strode purposefully across the gym toward Brad.

"I'm not lying! You can look for yourself! He's—"

The coach grabbed Brad by the neck and twisted him around. The blunt fingers digging into his skin hurt, and Brad wanted to cry out, but Mr. Nicholson's grip was restricting his flow of air. The teacher pushed him angrily back into the locker room. "Show me!"

he demanded. "Show me why you came running out there with one shoe and no socks, crying like a pussy about ghosts!"

Brad's eyes darted around. The locker room was empty. There was no sign of Van or his basketball, and that feeling he'd had earlier, that sensation of not being alone, had completely disappeared.

Whatever had been here was gone.

He felt like a tool, a *cowardly* tool, and embarrassed, he tried to come up with a response. "I thought it would be funny," he lied.

The coach leaned in so close that Brad could smell his foul breath. "No, you didn't," he said derisively. And he smiled. "You were *scared*."

Brad didn't know what that meant. Was the teacher making fun of him? Or did he know what was really going on? It was impossible to tell, and Brad said nothing, just to be on the safe side.

The coach shoved him back toward the doorway, letting him go. "Get your ass back in the gym and shoot some baskets. You've got an F for the day, Becker. Be grateful I don't fail you for the week."

There was still no sign of Myla at lunch, but Ed was hanging out at the usual spot, and Brad threw his sack lunch onto the plastic table, sitting down across from his friend.

"What's up with you?"

"Myla wasn't in class. I don't know where she is." Brad looked around to make sure no one else was listening. "And I saw Van," he told Ed. "In the locker room."

"Was he hiding there or—?"

"I think he was a ghost."

There was no disbelief to overcome—they were beyond that now—and Ed nodded, leaning forward. "What happened?"

Brad told him the details, including the way Coach Nicholson had grabbed his neck and shoved him back into the locker room. "That fucker attacked me."

"I can still see red marks," Ed said, looking at the skin above his collar. "We should take some photos of it. Right now. You have a good case here. This is assault. We can get him fired. Shit, you might be able to get some big bucks from the school."

Brad shook his head. "You know that's not going to happen. Not here. Not now. In fact, what this really means is that the teachers aren't even afraid of that possibility anymore. They think they can do what they want without reprisal, and, hell, they probably can. We have to be really careful from now on. It's a whole new ball game."

"So to speak," Ed said drily. "By the way, do we know if Van's basketball disappeared with him?"

"My guess is yes," Brad told him.

"So that must have been his basketball's ghost that you saw."

"Are you making fun of me?"

"Just trying to keep it light," Ed said. He dropped his voice, made a show of glancing over at the next table and back again. "Little pitchers."

Brad held his neck, did a fake stretch and checked out the table. Four girls who could have been freshmen, or could have been sophomores, were eating in silence, obviously listening to the conversations going on about them—including theirs. All of them were wearing Tyler Scout patches on the sleeves of their shirts.

"Did I ever tell you that I have a really big dick?" Ed asked loudly.

"No," Brad answered, playing along. "But I bet those chicks over there would like some of that."

All four girls looked immediately in the opposite direction so as not to get drawn into the conversation.

"Yep. I got quite a chunk o' change hangin' here."

"That's not what your sister told me," Hal Gurney said. He walked by, slapped Ed on the side of the head.

Ed grimaced, holding a hand over his ear. "The perils and pitfalls of popularity."

Brad grinned. "It's nice to see that some things always stay the same."

They didn't know who those girls were, whether they were spies or, if they *were* spies, whom they were spying for. So Brad followed Ed's lead, kept the conversation light and ate his lunch. But he was still freaked-out about seeing Van, and each blur of movement in his peripheral vision made him tense up, conjured in his mind's eye that horrible ghastly face.

He was also still burning up about his treatment at the hands of the coach.

And he was worried about Myla.

If anything, his experiences in PE had made him even more aware of the possibility that something could have happened to her, that she could be in real, physical danger. He considered going off campus and using his cell phone to call her, but the wall was nearly complete, there were scouts patrolling whatever gaps were left and it was nearly impossible for anyone to leave school during the day anymore. Besides, even if he called her, she might not answer. Her cell might be off. She might be with her parents, dealing with some sort of family emergency. Or at a doctor's office.

Or a hospital.

He didn't want to go there.

He saw Myla after lunch, standing outside Mr. Grazer's class. Walking by with Ed, on the way to their lockers, Brad looked over and saw her standing alone next to the closed door. He hurried over. "Where have you been?" he demanded. He'd been concerned about her, but now he felt angry. Whether she'd had a dentist appointment or a student-council meeting or something else, she should have told him ahead of time, and he blamed her for making him worry.

"My friend Rachel was killed last night by a drunk driver. I just found out at break."

"Oh my God," Brad said, sucking in his breath. He could see the look of devastation on her face, and he felt guilty for his resentment. He hugged her, holding her tightly, holding her close. Her muscles were hard, tense. "How come they didn't say anything about it on the morning announcements?"

"I don't know." Myla sounded dazed.

"Holy shit." Brad was pretty shook-up himself, and he didn't even know the girl. He'd never been this close to death before, and it felt weird having a girlfriend who knew someone who'd died.

"Was that Rachel Papatos?" Ed asked.

"No, Rachel Jackson-Smith."

"The chick on the paper? You knew her?"

Myla nodded.

Brad was surprised, too. He probably didn't know all of Myla's friends, but he thought he knew most of them, and he didn't think she'd ever mentioned Rachel. He wasn't even sure he knew who she was, though the image in his mind was of a pretty, dark-haired girl in his Intermediate Spanish class last year.

"She was a good writer," Ed said. "She did that thing on the football players' grades. . . ."

"She was doing an article about the school." Myla's voice was low. "About what's really going on. I went with her yesterday to see some things she'd learned about." Myla shook her head. "You wouldn't believe it."

"Try me," Brad said.

She told them about the PE class and Coach Temple, about the square-dancing class and the female scouts.

"Why didn't you tell me about this last night?" Brad wanted to know. "We were on the phone for over an hour, and you didn't even mention it."

"You wanted to talk about that band and that book, and after that, we went over the homework, and you talked about colleges."

"Yeah, but . . ."

"I don't *know* why, okay?"

"Okay." He could sense that she was near tears. "I understand. But where were you this morning? I was worried."

"I was supposed to meet Rachel, but she didn't show up. So at break I went to the newspaper office to try and talk to the editor and the adviser. They're the ones who told me what happened. And they know more than they're saying. The adviser especially. Mr. Booth. Richard, the editor, almost seems like he wants to talk, but he's afraid. I was waiting, trying to get him to talk on his own, but then I just ended up wandering around, thinking."

"You weren't written up? No scouts found you and took you to the office?"

She shook her head. "I guess I was lucky. I wasn't even paying attention to what I was doing, really. I was just walking aimlessly."

Ed had been unusually silent. Brad would have expected some smart-ass remark from him, especially about the naked PE teacher, but his friend seemed surprisingly subdued.

Cheryl, Cindy and Reba passed by. "Harvest Festival meeting after school," Cheryl reminded Myla.

The three girls neither stopped nor slowed down. "Nice to see you, too!" Brad called after them.

"Sluts," Ed added.

As one, the girls froze, turning their heads to fix Brad and Ed with stares so cold and hard that they might have been looking at a pair of child molesters. Brad stared right back until the three turned away and continued walking. A shiver of fear tickled his back. "Don't go to that meeting," he told Myla.

"I have to. I'm on the committee."

"All those things you saw, all those things that are happening? They're part of it."

"I know," she told him. "But, theoretically, I'm one of them. And if I dropped out, if I wasn't one of them anymore . . ." She left the thought unfinished, but Brad knew she was thinking of her friend Rachel.

"Be careful."

"I'm always careful."

Students were walking more quickly, some of them sprinting, and it was obvious that the bell was about to ring. The three of them said hasty good-byes. He and Ed hurried to their lockers and then to their respective classrooms.

Brad and Myla met up again in economics, but there were too many people around—including three scouts—and they couldn't talk. There was also a pop quiz, which Brad wasn't really prepared for, that took up half the period and conspired to keep them apart. Outside class, before leaving her, he gave Myla a hug intimate enough to provoke whistles from some of their departing classmates and a "You'd better knock that off" from one of the scouts.

He held up a middle finger, then kissed her on the forehead, on the cheeks, on the lips. "Stay strong," he told her.

He met Myla by her locker after school, the way he

always did, but this time there was a pair of scouts positioned at the end of the hallway and the two uniformed boys walked slowly forward, holding batons, ordering students to stop talking, stop loitering and leave campus immediately.

"What's the problem?" demanded a kid several lockers away. "School's over. We can—"

One of the scouts shoved a baton into his midsection, and the boy doubled over. "Get a move on!" the scout ordered.

Brad and Myla hurried down the hall and off campus, walking through an opening in the nearly completed wall out to the sidewalk. Neither of them wanted to go home right away. They needed time to digest what had happened and talk it over, so they walked down the street to McDonald's, where they got two straws, ordered a single large Dr Pepper and commandeered a booth.

"I don't think it's safe to talk at school anymore," Brad started out.

Myla nodded. "You're right."

"So anything we have to say, anything important, we save for off campus."

"I just want to know what happened to Rachel." She took a deep breath. "I know this sounds crazy, and I can't even believe I'm saying it myself, but I think she was murdered."

"It doesn't sound crazy," Brad assured her. He paused. "You know, my friend Brian Brown's on the paper. He's a good guy. I'll talk to him, see what he knows."

"What are we caught up in here? Haunted lockers? Security walls? Bottomless cheerleaders? Girls with spears? Naked teachers? Missing students?"

"And I saw a ghost," he offered. "Van Nguyen's." He explained what had happened.

"A lot of stuff seems to be centered around that PE area, doesn't it?"

"And the library, Ed says. And the office."

"Who are we kidding?" Myla sighed. "It's everywhere." She jumped up suddenly. "Oh my God! The Harvest Festival meeting! I forgot all about it!"

"Don't go," Brad said. "I don't want you to—"

"I have to!" she called out, hurrying toward the exit. "I'm sorry! I'll call you tonight!"

"But—" he began.

And then she was gone. Through the window, he saw her dashing down the sidewalk back toward the school. Glumly, he stared down at his cup with the two straws. He was half tempted to follow her, or, at the very least, wait for her. He didn't like the thought of her being on campus after hours. It wasn't safe. Hell, it wasn't safe in the middle of the day with all those people around. But he knew she would get mad if he stalked her like that, and he didn't want to get in an argument with her. Her friend had died; she needed his support right now. The last thing he wanted to do was put more pressure on her or make things more difficult.

He finished the Dr Pepper, refilled the cup, then carried it outside. He took one last look down the street toward the school—that eyesore of a wall was visible even from here—then turned and headed in the opposite direction.

Brad arrived home just in time to see a Tyler Scout leaving his house through the kitchen door near the driveway. *What the hell?* His heart was hammering in his chest, and he watched from the back of a hedge as the scout strode boldly out to the street and then crossed it, turning north in the direction of the school. He couldn't make out who it was—Todd Zivney, maybe?—and he waited until the figure had turned the corner at the end of the block before he stepped out from behind the hedge. He wasn't sure why he was so afraid, but he was, and he hurried up the front walkway to his house.

"Mom!" he called out as he sped up the porch steps. "Dad?"

Were his parents even there? Both of them worked, and often he beat them home, especially since his dad had gotten a new job that required him to commute to L.A. every other day. He reached for the knob, turned it. The door was unlocked. Somebody was home.

"Mom? Dad?"

Why had that scout been here? What possible reason could he have had for visiting Brad's parents? Best-case scenario: he was dropping something off, delivering some sort of paperwork from the office or from one of his teachers. Worst-case scenario? Brad didn't even want to think about it.

There'd been no answer to his calls, and Brad sped through the living room toward the kitchen. The scout had been leaving through the kitchen door. Which meant that it had probably been his mother the boy had come to see.

"Mom?" he called, hurrying in.

She was sitting on the floor of the kitchen, her back against the refrigerator, her dress hiked up far above her knees. He could see bruises on her upper thighs, though that was a place he didn't even want to look at. Her eyes had been closed when he entered, and her mouth open, but she quickly opened her eyes, closed her mouth and tried to immediately rearrange the expression on her face so that it didn't look like she was in pain.

She attempted to smile. "I fell," she told him. "Slipped on water or something. Just give me a minute." Her eyes closed again, and he saw that there was discoloration in the skin around the left one. She was going to have a black eye.

"I've been thinking," she said weakly. "I'm going to volunteer to help out with the Thanksgiving food drive at your school next month. It's a good cause. And Tyler does a fine job of helping the community."

"Mom . . . ," Brad said, kneeling beside her. He was trying hard not to cry.

She patted his hand, then used his shoulder to help draw herself to her feet. "I'm fine. Just slipped."

"I saw him leaving," Brad said. "The scout. That kid from my school. Why was he here?"

An expression of fear passed quickly over her features but was gone before it even registered. "I don't know what you're talking about," she said.

"I *saw* him, Mom. He went right out that door."

"Thanks for helping me up," she told him. "I'd better get dinner started."

"You're not in any shape to—"

"I'm fine."

"Mom . . ."

"I'm going to be volunteering more at your school, I think. It'll be good. It's a good thing." She turned away, lurching over to the sink. "It'll be good for both of us."

Brad saw, on the tiled floor in front of the refrigerator, where she'd been sitting, a small drop of smeared blood.

This time he did cry. "Mom," he said. She turned toward him, and he grabbed her, hugged her and held her tight. She reached a tentative arm around him and squeezed, and then both of them were sobbing.

Nineteen

The phone rang, and as usual, Frank let the machine pick up. More likely than not, it was something to do with Linda's school, and he didn't want to get dragged into one of *those* conversations again. The last time he'd actually answered the phone, an angry PTA parent had threatened to castrate him for not showing up to the Dinner-with-Dads event. He'd tried to explain that he was not a PTA member, that he had no children attending the school, that he wasn't even a dad, but the furious woman had vowed to feed his genitals to her koi fish. The time before that, someone had called to confirm his address before dropping off a shipment of one hundred calf fetuses preserved in formaldehyde. When he'd politely pointed out that he had not ordered any calf fetuses preserved in formaldehyde, the man had become irate and said that he held in his hand an order form signed by Jody Hawkes that said one hundred of them were to be delivered to the residence of Frank Webster. The man was yelling obscenities when Frank hung up on him.

So lately he'd been letting the machine take the calls, although he always deleted the messages before Linda came home, and he never told her about any of them. She had enough to worry about already.

The answering machine beeped, and he listened in on the message as it was recorded. This time, it was a contest Linda had supposedly won. The pitchman's smooth voice said that out of all the teachers at John Tyler High School who had automatically been entered in a contest for a free, all-expenses-paid Las Vegas weekend, Linda had been selected. . . .

Frank ignored the message, went back to work. He stared for a moment at his frozen monitor. He was starting to get frustrated. Somehow, he'd gotten a virus on his computer, although he had no idea how such a thing was possible. He'd constructed a firewall strong enough to withstand almost any assault, and he was always ultracautious about what software he used and which Web sites he visited. Right now, he was using a series of utilities to try to locate the virus because if he didn't, all of today's work—which he hadn't had time to back up—would be lost. He was already close to a week behind on his current project, which, during these unsettled times at the company, could conceivably put him on the chopping block.

Chopping block.

Frank thought of all the other spouses of Tyler teachers who had lost their jobs or been transferred.

Or died.

He paused for a moment. He was not superstitious, but neither was he blind, and especially after that meeting at Ray Cheng's house, he knew that there were things going on that could not be explained by logic or rationality, aspects of the charter school that defied all reason and edged into what would probably be called the supernatural.

And it was dangerous.

There was no doubt about that.

Was he immune?

Other spouses with far-less-militant wives or husbands had been beset by tragedy recently, often under mysterious circumstances, yet he and Linda had remained pretty much unscathed. So while it was impossible to say for sure, it certainly seemed as though the two of them were exempt from the worst of it. And while he had no idea why that should be the case, he hoped that it was.

Linda arrived home some time later, tossing a white box down on the floor. "Do you know what that is? Do you want to hear the latest news? We have to wear uniforms, too. The staff. We've been told that we must conform to new standards of attire that have been voted on by the charter committee." She reached down, opened the box, withdrew an orange blouse and a black skirt. "And we've been assigned these stylish little getups in, as you can see, the beautiful Tyler High School colors!" She threw the clothes down in disgust. "I should have transferrred when I had the chance."

Frank shrugged. "Told you."

Linda stood straighter. "No," she said firmly. "Tyler needs me. And I shouldn't let anyone chase me away. This is my school, these are my kids and it's my duty as a teacher to fight for them."

Frank clapped. "Rousing! Where's the recruitment office? Where do I sign up?"

"Knock it off."

"Actually, speaking of Tyler, I found something that might interest you. Before my computer froze up on me."

"Your computer froze up?"

He waved her away. "Don't worry. I'll fix it." He picked up the top page from the messy stack of papers in front of his printer. "Ta da! Jody Hawkes' home address."

Linda seemed confused. "I don't see how that's supposed to help. . . ."

"Look at it. At the address. Don't you see where she lives?"

Linda blinked, looked up. "The school?"

"That's her home. She lives there."

"She's using that as her mailing address," Linda said. "She doesn't want people to know where she really lives. Some psychotic, computer-hacking kid with a grudge against her could track her down if her real address was made public."

Frank shook his head emphatically. "I checked it out. I'm not a complete novice at this, you know. And I do have a few contacts. Her old address was in Brea. A house that she sold three years ago."

"Three years ago is when she started the process for the charter application."

"Aha! Since then, Tyler High has been not only her mailing address but her official place of residence."

"But I've seen her leave. After school. I've seen her drive away."

"A screen. Or maybe she was going out to do some shopping. Or buy dinner. Or see friends."

"She lives there," Linda said, stunned.

Frank nodded.

"I need to call Diane and tell her."

"I'm wondering if it's even legal. That's a school, not a house, and I don't think it's zoned for residential use. There's probably someplace where we can file a complaint. A city agency, maybe even the school board."

"I'll be honest. The thought of Jody Hawkes living alone on campus, sleeping on some cot that she hides away during the day, is damn near the creepiest image I can think of."

"But it's information that we might be able to use. *Why* is she there? Is she homeless after a nasty divorce? Is she crazy? At the very least, this brings up troubling questions about her mental and emotional stability."

Linda nodded slowly. "You're right. It's creepy, but it might be used against her."

"Do you want me to find out if there's some way we can get her out of there?" he asked. "See if we can force her to move?"

"That wouldn't affect her position. She'd still have her job. *And* she'd be pissed off. Let's just sit on this and wait, use it when we need it."

Frank was glad. He would have been happy to help her, but he really needed to get back to his own work. If he couldn't dislodge this virus soon, he was going to have to find another computer, use his backup disk and then try to re-create what he'd done this morning. He pointed to the uniform box and grinned. "Fashion show later?"

"Drop dead," she told him.

Laughing, he returned to his computer.

"Line up!"

Like well-trained military recruits, the students moved quickly across the band room, stood next to one another in a row against the wall and remained unmoving, legs together, arms at their sides. This had become a recurring ritual, repeated throughout the day in several classes, and they were getting good at it.

Mr. Carr walked back and forth in front of the line, hands behind his back and holding his baton. Several students flinched as he passed by. Mr. Carr used that baton not just for conducting but for other things as well, and they knew it.

"Your blouse is untucked, Miss Kennedy."

Regina Kennedy quickly tucked in her blouse.

"Zip up, Mr. Palua."

Orlando Palua zipped his zipper.

The teacher stopped in front of Christy Pham. "Is that a regulation bra?"

The girl nervously nodded her head. "Yes, Mr. Carr."

"Let me see."

Christy unbuttoned her blouse and held it open, revealing an orange brassiere.

"A-cup?"

"Yes, Mr. Carr," she said, embarrassed.

With a slight smile, he walked on. He stopped at the end of the line in front of Jim Dudley, who stared at him defiantly. Mr. Carr remained in place, maintaining eye contact for what seemed like an eternity. Jim refused to look away.

"All right, Mr. Dudley, pants down."

"You can't—," Jim started to protest.

"Pants down! Now!"

"No."

"Do you want detention?"

At this, Jim paled slightly. He looked down the line at his fellow students for help, but they were all staring straight ahead, afraid to even watch the scene. After a brief pause, Jim unbuckled his belt, unfastened and unzipped his pants and pulled them down to his knees.

"All the way," Mr. Carr said. "Underwear, too."

The boy did so, and the teacher motioned for him to turn around. Moving awkwardly, the bunched pants making it difficult for him to maneuver, Jim waddled in a circle until he was facing the wall. Mr. Carr crouched down, examining the orange briefs on which black letters spelled out JOHN TYLER HIGH SCHOOL. He stood angrily and grabbed the student's shoulders, whirling him about. Jim nearly fell over but managed at the last second to maintain his balance. "Hey!" he objected.

"Your underwear is dirty," the teacher spit out.

"Yeah. So?"

Mr. Carr leaned forward. His voice was low and menacing. "When you don't wipe your ass properly, when your *shit* defaces the great name of Tyler High, you are showing disrespect to me, to the other teachers, to your fellow students, to everyone who is involved in trying to provide for you the highest-quality education in the country! Do you understand me?"

Jim snickered. "Yeah."

"What are you laughing at?" Mr. Carr's face was red with anger, the veins in his neck practically popping out. The knuckles of his right hand, gripping his baton, were white. "Do you even realize the seriousness of your offense?"

Jim Dudley was back to his usual cocky self, threat of detention or no. "Skid marks happen."

Mr. Carr hit him with the baton, a hard blow across the side of his neck. Jim cried out and fell sideways, his feet still tangled in his pulled-down pants. The teacher hit him again. And again. And again. On the head, on the arm, on the leg. The baton was drawing blood, and Jim was screaming obscenities as he tried simultaneously to scramble to his feet, pull up his pants and ward off the blows. He managed to grab the baton from the band teacher, and Mr. Carr stepped back and allowed Jim to stagger to his feet—

—before kicking the boy in the stomach with all his might and sending him slamming into the wall behind him. There was a crack, as of a stick breaking, and suddenly Jim collapsed onto the floor. His eyes were wide open, the whites visible, and a trickle of blood leaked out of his slack mouth.

Mr. Carr picked up his baton, smoothed back his hair. He looked down the line at the unmoving students. "Too bad he tripped," he said flatly. "Isn't it."

The kids glanced at one another.

"Isn't it?" he roared.

They nodded, scared. "Yes!" "Yeah!" "Yes!" "It sure is!"

"Go to the office and tell them to call the police," he told Christy Pham. "We have a dead kid here. The rest of you? Grab your instruments and start practicing."

Diane no longer sent students to the office.

She didn't want them to be given detention.

She'd been written up for that—punishment was encouraged in this new school order—but it was not a stance she was willing to modify. She no longer trusted the school administration, and if there was any discipline to be meted out to her kids, she would do it herself.

She'd learned that lesson the hard way.

There'd been more behavioral issues than usual over the past few weeks. She didn't know if students thought they could get away with more these days, if she, specifically, was being targeted because she was perceived as weak and ineffectual or if there was just a general mood on campus that was ugly and belligerent, but in more than one class, she had students who consistently challenged her authority and acted up. Finally, she'd had enough, and after Nathan Whitman not only showed up fifteen minutes late for third period but threw his textbook against the wall when she informed the class that they were to read one of the stories in it, she wrote up a referral and sent him to the office.

He did not return for two days.

Diane would have thought he was suspended, but there was no mention of that on the roll sheet, and when she went into the office during her free period on Tuesday and spoke to his counselor, Ms. Tremayne, she learned that he had been given detention.

"Detention?" Diane said. "He's been gone since Monday!"

The counselor looked uncomfortable. She closed the door to her office. "Detention is . . . different than it used to be," she explained, and Diane could tell from her voice that she did not approve. "The charter committee has redefined the term."

It certainly had. As it turned out, there was no more detention hall, that temporary and occasional requisitioning of one of the library's meeting rooms where poorly behaved students were punished by being forced to either sit in silence or do extra work for a specified period of time. There was instead the Penalty Space, a previously unused classroom that had been converted into a series of eight holding cells for students with discipline problems. Each cell was windowless and contained no furniture. Students could be placed in there indefinitely.

"So it's like solitary confinement?"

"Not exactly. There's someone in there with them."

"Someone."

Ms. Tremayne nodded. "It's a new position created by the principal and the committee: punishment facilitator."

"What does that mean?"

The counselor nodded meaningfully at her closed door, presumably toward the principal's office across the hall. "I'm not allowed to say."

"Do the students' parents know about this?" Diane asked.

The counselor cleared her throat nervously. "They are informed."

Diane frowned. "What does that mean?"

"I'm not trying to be evasive. It's just that the principal and the charter committee have made it clear that discipline and punishment are the exclusive province of the administration. Teachers are not supposed to be involved at all, beyond issuing the initial referral. In fact, it's more than a rule—it's in an addendum to the charter itself." She dropped her voice. "I may be breaking several rules right now by even having this conversation with you."

Diane understood. The counselor was unhappy with this new arrangement, wanted to get the word out about it and was doing it through her. "Just one more question: how long are students put in detention—I mean the Penalty Space?"

"It varies. From a half hour or an hour to . . . five days."

"Five days!"

Ms. Tremayne nodded but said nothing.

"And where is this room?"

The counselor paled. "You don't want to go there."

"Come on. Where is the Penalty Space? I just want to get a look at it."

"You won't be allowed in."

"I just want to see the outside." Diane had never encountered such resistance to such a simple request, and it unnerved her a little. More than a little. And she wondered what it was about the room that inspired such steadfast stonewalling.

"It's room one sixty-six," Ms. Tremayne finally admitted. "But it's . . . hard to find."

"How could it be hard to find?"

"It just is."

"It's right after one sixty-five, right?"

"Theoretically."

Talking to the counselor was getting her nowhere, and while Diane appreciated her help and obvious sympathy, she could not stomach all this fearful tiptoeing around any subject that had to do with disciplinary procedures. "That's okay. I'll find it." She stood, thanked the woman and opened the door to leave.

"Be careful," the counselor warned, her voice barely above a whisper. "And don't go *in* the Penalty Space. You can look at it from outside, but don't go in."

Diane nodded. *The Penalty Space can't be worse than this hallway,* she thought as she made her way quickly down the short corridor away from the counselor's door. Indeed, Linda was right—there *was* something about the office that seemed ominous, and it wasn't just the automaton TAs or the openly hostile secretaries. It was something in the building itself, and for the first time she thought that maybe she *shouldn't* go to the Penalty Space. At least not alone.

Still, it couldn't hurt just to look at it from afar, and she walked out into the quad and over to the science building. Room 166 was on the opposite side, down the narrow corridor that separated the science and arts buildings, and she headed up the walkway that led there. The room was at the building's far extremity, where the corridor dead-ended at the wall, and even looking at the spot from this far away, she felt nervous. That portion of the hallway seemed to be shrouded in shadow, and though it was broad daylight and the sun was shining overhead, it might as well have been night. This was the middle of the school day, and all the surrounding classrooms were filled with students, yet she felt as though she were all alone. There was no noise coming from any of the closed doors in the science building nor any sign of movement from within the closed tinted windows in the adjacent arts building. It was as if the school were empty, and thinking about Ms. Tremayne's warnings—

You don't want to go there

—she decided that maybe this was not the time to check it out.

She turned around, went back to her classroom.

When Nathan Whitman returned the next day, he was not himself. He was kind, patient, thoughtful, a model student. That should have made her happy—it certainly made a lot of his other instructors happy, if teachers'-lounge scuttlebutt was to be believed—but Nathan was no longer Nathan. He was a different boy in the same body. That alone was cause for consternation. But when Lisa Piccolo and Joel Grazer both admitted that two of their students had also been sent to the Penalty Space and had emerged brainwashed and different, Diane knew that this was not just a fluke. Something *happened* in there, something that worked consistently and that somehow turned problem kids into perfect little angels.

As convenient as it might be for teachers, she could no longer allow any child to be subjected to whatever sort of indoctrination or extreme behavior modification occurred in the Penalty Space.

So for the past week she'd avoided writing referrals for any student, no matter how badly they misbehaved. They *were* children, after all, and even the transgressions of the worst of them did not make them deserving of this treatment. She felt weighted down with guilt for what had happened to Nathan, and she even made a phone call to the boy's parents to discuss it with them, but they were thrilled with the change in their son and rather than condemning the school for transforming him into someone he was not, they had nothing but praise for it.

Lisa and Joel—as well as Steve and Ray—agreed with Ms. Tremayne that she should stay as far away from the Penalty Space as possible, but Linda understood both the horror she felt and the curiosity, and she suggested that they check out the room together.

"I mean, come on," Linda said. "Windowless prison cells where kids are kept for *days*? With an ever-present torturer—I'm sorry, 'punishment facilitator'? Can this even be legal?"

"We keep saying that, but we never follow up on it. No one does. No one does anything about what's happening here."

"It's time for us to change that."

"How?"

"First of all," Linda said, "you're a department head."

"Big whoop."

"That means," she continued evenly, "that you have a certain amount of clout or respectability or *believability.* Particularly to the outside world. Now, we've all been taking notes, right? Keeping detailed track of everything that happens?"

Diane smiled. "That husband of yours is something."

"He comes in handy sometimes. And he's right about this. We have to fight fire with fire. We have to beat Jody at her own game. She no doubt had facts and figures to show the district and the state that Tyler was a good candidate to become a charter school. And you see how obsessed she is with keeping test scores up. If she doesn't meet projections, our charter's yanked."

"Praise be."

"*We* need to show those same people the extent she's going to reach those goals. It's been, what, two weeks since our meeting? I think it's high time we have another get-together, pool what we've gathered so far and see what we have. Opinions, facts, all of it." She took a deep breath. "And it sounds like this Penalty Box—"

"Penalty Space."

"Okay, Penalty Space can be a real feather in our caps. *This* is the kind of thing that's going to hang her. *This* is what's going to help us get back to normal."

Diane thought for a moment. "What scares me is how scared Ms. Tremayne was. I don't know her that well—"

"Neither do I."

"—but she seems like one of the good guys, despite her position. She *really* didn't want me anywhere near that room, and I don't think it's because she was trying to hide something. She seemed genuinely afraid for me. And, let's be honest, what that place does is brainwash students. They come out different than when they go in. This is where Stepford students are made. And what I'm worried about is that if one of us goes in there, we'll come out . . . one of them."

"Which is why we're *both* going in."

"Oh no, we're not," Diane said firmly. "No, we're not. One of us needs to stay outside. This is one of those situations where you tell someone that you're going hiking so that if you don't return on time they can send a search party after you. I mean, who knows if we can even get in, right? But if we can, and we decide to go through with this and check it out, one of us needs to remain free. Because if we both get brainwashed . . . there goes the ball game."

"Okay," Linda said. "I see your point."

"And I'm the one going in."

"Wait a minute. I don't think you—"

"I'm the one who sent Nathan Whitman to detention. It's my fault he is the way he is. It's my responsibility to go in there, see what's happening and find out if there's some way I can set things right."

Linda nodded. "Okay," she agreed. "So what's the plan?"

"Tomorrow before school."

Linda smiled ruefully. "We're talking about this like you're going into some lion's den. It's a converted classroom in a suburban high school."

Diane smiled back. "Yeah." But neither of them believed that, and the next morning she found herself at the head of that hallway again, standing next to Linda and staring down at the shadowed area in front of room 166. It could have been her imagination, but the shadows seemed to be *swirling,* like mist, and she didn't mention it to Linda because she did not want her suspicions confirmed and did not want to chicken out. She looked at her watch. "It's seven fifteen," she told her friend. "If I'm not back by seven thirty, do something."

"It might not be open," Linda pointed out. "It's early. None of the other teachers are here yet. . . ."

"Kids are locked in there for *days,*" Diane reminded her. "Someone can let me in."

"I'll wait here until you *are* in," Linda said. "I'll let them see me. They might not screw with you if *they* know that *I* know you're there. After that, I'll go back to the department office and wait."

"I'm kind of scared," Diane admitted. "This is a lot of buildup."

"I'll go if you want."

Diane shook her head. "No." She started down the corridor, toward those swirling shadows, and with each step she took, the outside world seemed to retreat. There were classroom doors to her left, classroom windows to her right, but they seemed far away somehow and not really there. When she looked back toward Linda, *she* seemed to be the one in shadow, and when Linda said something to her, Diane could not hear what it was.

And then she was in front of the Penalty Space.

Room 166.

Taking a deep breath, she knocked on the door. She waited, knocked again. When there was still no answer, she tried the knob. To her surprise, it turned—it was unlocked—and gathering her courage, she pulled open the door and walked inside.

She was in a narrow hallway that stretched before her much farther than it should have, much more than the length of a classroom. The walls were dark but didn't look like wood or plaster or concrete, and when she touched her finger to the wall on her right, it felt cold, like metal. The door closed behind her, and on impulse, she tried the knob.

It turned.

She'd expected it to be locked, expected to find herself trapped in here, and just knowing that she could get out and escape if she had to gave her a boost of confidence.

Diane walked forward. There was no light in the hallway, but she could somehow see, and a few feet down the passage, she stopped in front of a door on the left. A white "A" had been crudely painted at eye level, and when she looked down, there was only a knob, no dead bolt, no padlock. She stood for a moment and listened, then pressed her ear to the door.

Nothing.

Silence.

Tentatively, she knocked. "Hello?"

There was no response and she tried again. When still she heard no sound, she reached for the knob and turned it. The door opened. Within was a narrow space barely bigger than a closet. On the short wall opposite her was a flat bench of the type found in discount-store fitting rooms. The tiny cell was otherwise devoid of furnishings or adornment. There was no toilet, she noticed, but perhaps the Penalty Space was less prisonlike than she'd originally thought and there was a bathroom farther down the hall.

Less prisonlike?

This little cubicle was *worse* than most of the prison

cells she'd seen. There was barely enough room in there for one person, and she wondered where the "punishment facilitator" sat or stood whenever he . . . did what he did.

Diane closed the door, looked down the hallway. "Hello!" she called out.

There was no answer: no voices, not even any knocks or thumps on the wall. The place appeared to be abandoned. Maybe that was good. Maybe she wasn't the only one who had stopped writing referrals and sending students to the office. Or maybe she'd just gotten lucky. There must have been some reason why Ms. Tremayne had not wanted her to come here—

Don't go in the Penalty Space

—and perhaps it was fortunate that she'd arrived at a time between incarcerations. Touching the cold wall, she tried to imagine what it was about this converted classroom that worried the counselor so. There were, of course, the shadows outside that seemed to permanently shroud the entrance. And there was the fact that the hallway seemed much longer than was physically possible. But despite all that, Diane felt braver and more confident than she had before coming in here, and she pressed forward, knocking on the next door, inexplicably marked "Q." When there was no response, she opened it.

Her mother was standing in front of the bench.

Diane gasped, slamming the door shut. She stood there for several seconds, catching her breath, then opened the door again.

Her mother was still there, and she was in her angry guilt-mongering lecture mode. Diane recognized the set of her mouth, the hard flatness of her eyes, the clenched right hand.

She slammed the door again. This was impossible.

Her mother wasn't dead, so this couldn't be her ghost. And she lived in Massachusetts, so she couldn't actually be here. Diane didn't know what was going on, but she understood now Ms. Tremayne's wariness.

Suddenly, the hallway was no longer silent. There were knocks and raps and tappings and thumps. Voices—some whispering, some screaming, some mumbling in a monotone—sounded from every direction, a cacophony of tongues so all-encompassing that it made her feel disoriented. The end of the passage was no longer visible but seemed misty and impressionistic, almost as though it was disintegrating before her eyes. Frightened, she turned to leave, and the door to the first cell—A—flew open, banging loudly against the wall. She ran past it, seeing *something* out of the corner of her eye, and shoved her shoulder against the entrance at the same time her hands tried to turn the doorknob.

It wouldn't budge. It was locked.

No!

"Help!" she screamed, pounding on the door. "Let me out!"

Behind her, she could hear movement. Heavy footsteps, scuttling claws, increasingly loud voices getting nearer and nearer.

"Help!"

The door opened.

It was Linda. Diane practically tumbled outside and quickly slammed the door behind her.

"I couldn't leave you here alone," Linda said. "I had the feeling something might happen."

Diane ran into her friend, hugging her gratefully, practically hyperventilating. "Did you see what was in there? Before I closed the door? Did you see anything behind me?"

Linda shook her head. "Just a dark hallway."

"Jesus," Diane breathed. "Jesus."

"So what did you see? What *was* there?"

She shook her head. "I'll tell you in a minute. Once we get out of here." Holding Linda's arm more tightly than was probably comfortable, she pushed her friend in front of her and hurried down the walkway to the end of the building. Passing the other nearby classrooms, she wondered if the students and teachers in them ever heard anything through the walls. She vowed to look up which teachers were in these rooms and talk to them.

They did not stop until they reached the quad, and Diane bent down, grabbing her knees and breathing deeply. Her heart was pounding as if she'd just run a race, and her hands were shaking.

"What was in there?" Linda asked.

Diane told her everything, from the beginning.

"So what was all that? What *is* in there?"

"I don't know, but I'm never going back in. *No one* should."

"Except Jody."

Diane found herself laughing, laughing much more than the joke deserved, laughing until there were tears in her eyes. "Except Jody," she agreed.

Linda smiled. "And maybe Bobbi."

Twenty

The evening was cold, and the dark clouds that had been gathering throughout the day now obscured all trace of moon and stars. A crisp wind, not too strong but not too soft, fluttered the flags and banners that marked the perimeter of the carnival and sent crinkly autumn leaves swirling about the grounds. From one of the houses nearby came the smell of wood from a fireplace.

They could not have chosen a better night for the Harvest Festival.

The festival was being held on the field near the sports complex. Not the football field in the stadium, where games were played, but the field adjacent to the gym where the outside PE classes were held. Each of the on-campus clubs and organizations that wanted to participate and passed what Myla said was a strict and biased screening process could take part, and this year a record number had sponsored games and activities. An army of volunteer students, along with teachers and parents, had spent the better part of the week making decorations and planning the booths, and everything had been set up earlier today. It looked terrific.

There was to be a Sadie Hawkins dance in the gym

afterward, a retro tradition that Tyler honored each year and that seemed to be perennially popular. Girls asked boys to the dance, rather than the other way round, and they also bought the tickets and corsages and arranged for pictures. Myla had asked Brad, of course, but no one had asked Ed, and although he professed not to care, Brad could tell that it hurt him. Still, Ed accompanied them to the festival, allowed in under Myla's auspices. "Who knows?" he said. "I might get lucky and run into some dateless troll so desperate to go to the dance and be seen by her friends that she'll give me a last-minute pity invite."

"Don't get your hopes up," Brad warned.

Ed snorted. "Don't worry, dude. They're not."

As Myla had promised, there *were* no dateless trolls at the festival. These were the beautiful people, the campus elite, the rich, attractive and predominantly white. Brad felt like a gate-crasher, unwelcome and unwanted among the prom queens, athletes and Tyler Scouts, but he refused to allow it to bother him, and he bought a bunch of tickets at the ticket booth, giving half to Myla, and they went around to various games, attempting to win prizes. Ed, too cheap or stubborn to participate, watched.

It was kind of fun, Brad had to admit, as he won a stuffed Shrek at the pep squad's ringtoss game and a jack-o'-lantern Frisbee at the German Club's beanbag throw. But as the evening wore on, he began to notice a growing crowd of people outside the chain-link barrier that had been erected around the field. There were only a few at first, but each time he looked past the lit booths to the gloom outside, he saw more and more peering in. They were students, many of them kids he knew, the ones not allowed to participate, only there was something about the darkness that made them seem odd, alien, unfamiliar, and for some reason he was reminded of dirty street urchins in an old Charles Dickens novel. There was a hunger in their faces, and a desperation, and though he couldn't see what they were wearing, in his mind they were garbed in torn raggedy clothes. It was a strange reaction, one he didn't understand, but it haunted him, and he kept looking back and forth between the wealthy, well-dressed Harvest Festival attendees playing carnival games and preparing for the dance, and the silently staring mob on the other side of the fence.

Myla was talking to one of her friends over by the dunk tank, and he and Ed had cornered Brian Brown and were grilling him about why he had been avoiding them and wouldn't answer questions about Rachel's death. ("What the fuck are you talking about?" he yelled. "It was a drunk driver! No one on the newspaper had anything to do with it!") Then the lights that had been strung over a series of poles around the field flickered on and off several times. A power chord and a drumroll sounded from within the gym as the band inside indicated that it was nearly time for the dance to start.

Students started walking toward the open entrance of the gymnasium, and Brad glanced over at Myla. Brian took the opportunity to escape into the crowd, and Brad turned toward Ed. "What's your plan?"

His friend shrugged. "Hang out, hug the wall."

"You could go home if you want."

"Are you trying to get rid of me?"

"No," Brad assured him. "But this *is* a dance. I just thought it might be less awkward for you."

"Doesn't bother me. Awkwardness and I are old friends. I'll just watch all the shiny happy people and plot my twisted revenge."

"All right. But after the festival, you go home alone.

Myla and I need some private time, if you know what I mean."

"We drove separate cars. Of course I'm going home by myself."

"I just meant don't expect to meet up with us somewhere after we leave. We want to be by ourselves."

"Don't worry. I'll head home to twang my tater and you can park somewhere and bend her over the backseat."

Brad turned away. "Asshole."

"Sorry," Ed apologized. "Habit."

Myla came over, her friends' dates having found them. She offered her arm. "Ready?"

"Ready as I'll ever be."

The carnival area was emptying out as students filed into the gymnasium. Arm in arm, Ed at their side, Brad and Myla trekked across the trampled grass to the gym. They walked inside. The interior of the gym had not been decorated so much as sponsored. There were banners depicting fall leaves and pumpkins, streamers in yellow, orange and brown, and balloons in bunches arranged strategically around the perimeter of the dance floor. All of them sported logos for various chain stores and eateries. The symbol for a well-known bank adorned the curtain behind the stage where the band was playing, and above the drink table were ads for the companies that had supplied the drinks.

"Welcome to the Microsoft Harvest Festival Dance in the Tyler High Starbucks Gym," Ed said wryly. "Over in the Pepsi-Cola Corner you can sign up for the Apple iPod song request. . . ."

"Amazing," Brad said, looking around. He turned to Myla. "Did you know about this?"

"I knew about it, but I didn't think it was going to be this blatant. Or tacky."

"A night to remember," Ed said, "courtesy of our student council and Taco Bell."

"It's not that bad," Myla said defensively.

"It's pretty bad," Brad admitted.

"Let's just dance," she told him.

Brad was not much of a dancer. In fact, he didn't dance at all. But he held Myla on a couple of the early slow songs, swayed back and forth and faked it. When the tempo picked up, he went to get them both drinks. He grinned at Ed, standing alone by the drink table and nursing a cup of punch. "Having fun?"

"Tons."

"You can still go home."

"You'd like that, wouldn't you?" Ed shook his head. "I'll never cave in to public pressure."

"Masochist." With a salute of his cup, Brad returned to the edge of the dance floor, where Myla was talking to Reba and Cindy and their dates. The last thing he wanted to do right now was socialize with those two snots, but he put on his best fake smile and handed Myla her drink. "How goes it, all?"

Either Myla sensed his true feelings or she was looking for a way out herself, because she took a sip of her drink, put a hand on his arm and said, "I want to get our picture taken."

"Okay," he said. He nodded a quick good-bye to the rest of the group, and the two of them headed toward the rear of the gym where a photographer had set up shop behind a curtained partition. As they got closer, Brad took a look at the long line of waiting couples and shook his head. "I'm sorry. I'm not going to wait for twenty minutes just to have some guy overcharge us for some badly posed picture with a corny backdrop."

Myla's grip on his hand tightened. "Oh yes, you are. For one thing, this is our first dance. It's important to me, and I want a memento. Secondly, it's Sadie Hawkins. I'm paying. So get your butt in line and shut up."

Laughing, he allowed himself to be dragged over to the photo queue.

The couple in line in front of them, a boy from his PE class and a girl he'd seen around campus but did not know, were talking about how maybe they shouldn't have come here tonight.

"I kind of wish we'd gone to a movie instead," the girl was saying. "This whole elitist thing rubs me the wrong way."

"You, too?" Myla jumped in. "That's what I was fighting against. I was on the Harvest Festival committee," she explained.

Another couple—Ray Sandy and Anita Begole, who were both in his and Myla's English class—had gotten into line behind them.

"We saw a whole bunch of kids outside the fence," Anita said. "I don't know if they were trying to get in or what, but there was definitely a *Tale of Two Cities* vibe to it."

"I'm sorry," Brad said to the girl in front of them. "I don't know your name." He pointed to the boy from his PE class. "Dane, right?"

"Yeah. This is my girlfriend, Laurie. You're . . . Brad?"

He nodded. Introductions were made all around, and the six of them started comparing notes not just about tonight but about the entire semester so far. They were all concerned, all unhappy with the state of things, and the criticisms Brad heard made him feel much better. He'd felt like a spy behind enemy lines tonight, and in his mind all the people on the other side of the fence had become the exploited and all the people on this side the exploiters. It gave him hope to know that everyone here tonight was not of one mind, that he and his friends were not fighting against a monolithic enemy.

Fighting?

What fighting had they done? None. They'd talked about it a lot, but there'd been precious little action, and while he knew that was partly because there were only so many hours in a day and in addition to these troubles they had to deal with family and homework and the ordinary stresses of everyday life, part of it was also because they didn't know *what* to do.

That had to change. It was up to them to make more of an effort.

Dane and Laurie were called behind the partition by a woman behind the curtain, and he and Myla moved to the front of the line. Brad craned his neck and looked over Myla's head to scan the gym. He wondered where Ed was, hoping his friend hadn't gone home. It suddenly occurred to him that it might be dangerous to exit through the carnival gates. He recalled the hunger he'd seen in the eyes of those massing outside and found himself pondering why they were there in the first place. They couldn't have come just to watch, and in his mind he saw them ganging up on Ed as he tried to leave, a horde of angry disenfranchised kids setting upon his friend and attacking him. He hated himself for even considering such a thing—was he becoming one of *them*?—but the scenario was not that far-fetched, and he could definitely see the evening ending in some sort of class riot as the revelers started to go home. And not class as in freshman-sophomore-junior-senior, but class as in upper and lower, haves and have-nots.

His gaze fell upon Ed, still standing alone by the drink table, ignored by everyone, and Brad felt a sense of relief.

"Next!" the woman behind the curtain called.

They walked around the edge of the partition to where the photographer was taking pictures of Dane and Laurie.

Only it wasn't a professional photographer. It was Mr. Swaim, the art teacher. And he was lying on the floor in front of the couple, clearly trying to shoot up Laurie's dress. The two students were awkwardly posed on what appeared to be a crate with a sheet draped over it, and they were obviously uncomfortable with what was going on. Both were attempting to hold fixed smiles that were strained far beyond any comfort level, and their eyes kept darting down to the teacher on the floor. Laurie pressed her legs closer together as Mr. Swaim shifted his position. The backdrop behind them was a blown-up photo of a decomposing pumpkin.

"You have a choice of three packages," the woman who'd called them said robotically. She was seated behind a table on which were strewn order forms and pens, and had the white-trash look of a stripper gone to seed. He thought he'd seen her working in the office. "Package number one includes one eight-by-ten, three four-by-fives and six wallets. Package number two—"

"Spread your legs a little, dear," Mr. Swaim told Laurie.

She stood up, kicking at the photographer. "Go to hell!" she shrieked. "I'm not going to let you do this!"

"This is bullshit!" Dane said, trying to sound strong but coming off more than a little scared. "We don't want any pictures!"

Mr. Swaim sat up and grinned suggestively. "That's okay. I think I got what I need." He looked over at Brad and Myla. "Your turn."

Brad grabbed Myla's hand and pulled her back behind the partition as the two of them strode away.

"Next!" the woman called.

"I don't believe this," Brad said. Still holding Myla's hand, he dragged her over to the drink table, where he told Ed what they'd seen.

"No shit?"

"The good thing," Brad said, "is that we were talking to some other couples in line and word's getting out. *Everyone's* unhappy with the school this semester."

Ed gestured toward the dance floor with his cup. "Really? It doesn't look like it."

Brad frowned, looking beyond the dancers. "Wait a sec," he said. The doors of the gym had remained open, and from outside he could see flames. It looked like the carnival area was on fire. Leaving Myla and Ed behind, Brad ran across the gym floor and over to the doorway to see what was happening.

It was a bonfire. While the rest of them had been at the dance, someone had taken down the booths and banners and had built a large fire in the center of the field. Sticks, branches and lengths of lumber were piled into a high pyramid as tall as a house, and volcanic flames were shooting up from the burning pyre and into the sky like birds released from captivity. A group of students—he couldn't be sure from this far away, but they looked like scouts—were dancing around the blaze.

Myla and Ed had come up behind him. A whole host of students were now moving toward the open doorway to see what was going on, and some of them were pushing past him and heading outside.

"Let's check it out," Myla said.

The three of them joined the crowd and started across the grass.

"Did you know about this?" Ed asked.

"No," Myla said, and Brad couldn't tell whether she was angry or afraid.

It *was* the scouts who were dancing around the bonfire, he saw as they got closer. He could see their uniforms lit by the flames. There were girls as well, although whether they were dates or female scouts he could not be sure. Other kids from the gym were starting to join in, and while it appeared spontaneous, it could just as well have been rehearsed. There was a uniformity to the movements that suggested this was all part of some preplanned ritual.

Brad, Myla and Ed stopped several yards in front of the fire. They could feel the heat even from here, and the brightness of the blaze made the surrounding darkness seem that much darker. The flames were growing higher, and Brad turned his head to the left to look toward the fence. Flickering orange firelight glinted in the eyes of the kids pressed against the chain link. If before they had seemed hungry and feral, they now seemed sad and doomed, and there was an eerily similar look of resignation visible in all their faces.

More and more students joined the group dancing around the bonfire. They were singing. Or chanting. It was hard to tell which above the roar of the flames. The wind had picked up and was now biting rather than crisp, its cold sting drawing even more people to the heat of the blaze. A couple of the jocks, he saw, had taken off their shirts, and when the dancers had come around again, one of them was completely naked.

Brad's muscles stiffened. This was getting out of control.

One of the girls from the dance had pulled down the top of her dress, exposing her breasts, and was frolicking wildly about the perimeter of the bonfire.

All the adults seemed to have disappeared. There were none around anywhere, not a chaperone or a club adviser or even a janitor. They were probably all at the dance, but Brad had the feeling that they had chosen not to be here at this time. There was a genuine feeling of anarchy and violence in the air, the sense that anything could happen here tonight, and Brad had never been more afraid of anything in his life. If something happened here this evening, it would wash over them like a wave, and there would be nothing they could do about it.

He wanted to drag Myla and Ed back into the gym to protect them—he could hear the faint sound of the band through the open doors; the dance was still going on—but he also wanted to see what was going to happen, and he knew that his friends would not allow themselves to miss whatever was coming next.

The students dancing around the fire were no longer singing *or* chanting. They were screaming. Primal frenzied cries that bore no resemblance to any form of human speech. From somewhere in another part of the field, through what sounded like a portable amplified speaker, came the voice of a man who seemed to be reciting a prayer. Brad thought he heard the words "thankful" and "sacrifice."

There was a sudden commotion at the fence, movement and jostling, along with additional cries and shouts, these definitely more earthbound and angry.

Ed elbowed him, pointing toward the bonfire. "Look!" he shouted above the noise. "It's Cheryl! She's naked!"

He was right—she was, though the sight was more disturbing than erotic. She seemed to be performing some type of cheerleading routine, but there was a desperation to her exaggerated movements that made Brad think of one of those hamsters running on an exercise wheel.

A group of scouts was heading toward the bonfire

from the part of the fence where the dustup had occurred. They were moving through the darkness, and he couldn't be sure, but it almost looked as though they had someone with them, a prisoner who was being hemmed in and herded toward the fire. It was Brad's turn to elbow Ed. He squeezed Myla's hand to get her attention. "Look over there!" he told them.

But just then the scouts disappeared around the other side of the bonfire. Brad looked back toward the portion of the fence from whence they'd come, and saw that all the kids outside the chain link were gone. There was only emptiness and blackness beyond the border of the festival grounds.

More and more students were joining the wild dance. More and more of them were stripping off their clothes.

Suddenly Myla's grip in his tightened. Her nails dug into his palm, and her other hand reflexively clutched his arm, digging into the skin. Her eyes were wide with horror, and she was saying something, but he couldn't make out what it was amid the tumult all about them. He looked to Ed on the other side of him. Like Myla, he was staring at the blaze, and Brad followed their eyes, his own gaze fixed on the conflagration, trying to make out whatever it was that they were seeing.

And there it was.

A figure in the flames.

A boy.

His hair and clothes were gone, and he was little more than a black shape within the raging incandescence. He was writhing in torment and against all odds appeared to be trying to crawl *through* the fire and out. A burned hand reached up as if to call for help or clutch a rescuer's arm, and then he collapsed, his still form joining the pile of blazing wood on the pyre.

Brad ran forward, Ed at his side, trying in vain to swat at the leaping flames, looking desperately around for water or a fire extinguisher or something to dampen the raging inferno. "There's someone in there!" he yelled. "He's on fire! He's burning up!" He wanted to reach in and grab the kid, but he could feel his eyebrows singeing and the hair on his arms scorching as he got too close. He backed away helplessly. "Put out the fire!" he cried. "Save him!"

A girl he didn't know, naked and dancing, leaped past him, her breasts brushing his arm.

"Get a hose!" he called, trying to grab a boy who was cavorting by. "Get some water!"

"Help!" Ed screamed next to him.

But no one heard them, no one cared and the celebration continued. Looking into the fire now, he could not even tell where the boy had been. The blaze was so hot it had already eliminated any trace of him.

Brad was still yelling for help, but he stopped in midscream. It could have been his imagination, *must* have been his imagination, but in the darkness on the far side of the fire, he thought he saw Principal Hawkes.

Staring into the flames.

And laughing.

Twenty-one

Ed punched his locker, feeling not just angry, frustrated and scared but an emotion so far beyond any of those that there was not even a word for it. "Someone died out there, dude!"

"I know it," Brad said.

"Then why . . . why . . . ?" Ed was at a loss for words. "Why isn't anyone *doing* anything about it? Why aren't the police investigating it? Why isn't it all over the news? Why isn't this place crawling with cops? Why isn't the school shut down? Why aren't people being arrested?"

"My mom wouldn't even believe me about it," Brad said. "She's pissed off 'cause she thinks I was drinking."

"My parents won't believe me either!" Ed fumed. "I don't know who that was, but that was a kid in the fire. He burned up and he died. And we were there, man. We were witnesses. Fuck, we were part of it."

"I know."

"His parents must know about it. He has to have been reported missing by now."

"Maybe someone should check it out," Brad suggested. "Go to the police station and see if anyone has filed a report."

Ed snorted. "Who? Your reporter buddy Brian Brown? That worthless piece of dog shit?"

"Us, I guess. After school, we could head over there, ask some questions."

"Then what?" Ed shook his head. "Who's going to believe us?"

"Someone will."

Ed was not so sure. His faith in institutions had never been strong, and after everything that had been happening this semester, he didn't trust anyone. If the administration could form its own militia and build a prison wall around the school without anyone in the community batting an eye, then what hope did they have of alerting the public to anything that went on here? Besides, most of the things that were happening were not of the type that could be remedied by inspections or citations or even arrests. Like that skeleton captain said in the first *Pirates of the Caribbean* movie, they'd better start believing in horror stories. They were in one.

The morning was foggy, with a thick mist that cut off the tops of the buildings and hid everything beyond a twenty-yard radius behind a wall of white. Students walking through the quad looked like ghosts, and Ed thought that was entirely appropriate. It was like a Dorian Gray thing. This was what the school was *supposed* to look like.

As impossible as it seemed, he and Brad got lost. They weren't really going anywhere—they were just wandering around waiting for the first bell to ring like they usually did—but the fog was so thick that his sense of direction had been knocked out. He couldn't tell which way was east or west, north or south. Even the glimpses they got of the buildings made it seem as though they were in the wrong places, and within minutes they found themselves in what appeared to be a flat stretch of blacktop with no building in sight. There were also no students passing by them, no sign of anyone around at all. Ed didn't like it.

Brad was still talking about the Harvest Festival.

"This has gone too far," he said. "We've got to do something about it."

Ed agreed. "But what?" he asked.

Instead of answering, Brad stopped walking. He looked around. "Where are we?"

"I was just wondering the same thing."

"This school . . . ," Brad began, but trailed off. He was peering into the mist, and Ed looked, too. At first he saw nothing, but gradually, a series of irregular shapes came into focus. He couldn't place them at first. They were outlines, silhouettes, and some of them were moving, and he finally figured out that he was looking at a little kids' playground, like the one they'd had at their grammar school. He saw a slide, a swing set, monkey bars, a teeter-totter. Children were playing there, flighty figures running and swinging and sliding and climbing.

"What is that?" Ed whispered.

Brad shook his head. "I don't know."

Slowly, carefully, they moved closer. There was a bigger figure among the small ones, riding alone on the teeter-totter, up and down, up and down, and as they approached, as the fog became less thick, they could see more details. The little kids, Ed noticed, all seemed to be dressed in old-time clothes. *Ghosts* was the word that came to mind, and the chill he felt while watching them play had nothing to do with the weather. The big figure, the one on the teeter-totter, was—

Burned.

He lifted one weak arm. Just like the boy in the bonfire.

"Fuck!" Ed yelled.

And then the playground was gone. The fog was still there, but what had looked like a vast expanse of blacktop turned out to be the sports complex, and to their left he could see the cafeteria. The bell rang, and students who'd been getting oatmeal-bar breakfasts from the vending machines started hurrying to their classes.

"Holy shit," Ed said. "Did you see that?"

"Of course." Brad looked around. His face was blanched. "I wonder if anyone else did."

"I don't think so."

"It's a hint," Brad said.

"Of what?"

"I don't know. But we were given a glimpse of something. Something I'm not sure we were supposed to see."

Ed's heart was still thumping loud enough for him to hear the pulse in his ears, and his skin was a pelt of gooseflesh. "It's not the most useful knowledge on the planet."

"No," Brad admitted. "But we have it and we can use it. If we can just figure out how."

They started walking toward the classrooms. Neither spoke for a moment.

"That was that guy," Ed said finally. "The one in the fire. The one who died."

"I know."

"I think he was trying to signal us."

"I think so, too."

"You think that's what Van was trying to do when you saw him in the locker room?"

Brad shivered. "No," he said. "Van . . . Van was something else."

They talked about it some more at break and even more at lunch with Myla, but none of them could figure out exactly what was going on or what they were supposed to do about it.

The day seemed to drag on forever. How could he concentrate on classwork when he'd seen a kid burn to death and then seen his ghost playing with other ghosts in some alternate world they'd stumbled into? Ed was tempted to ditch seventh period—why *had* he signed up for library TA?—but his absence would definitely be noticed, and who knew what sort of punishment Mrs. Fratelli would mete out to him? The one thing he'd learned about the librarian from working with her was that she was really hard-core.

Although he'd known that going in.

It was one of the reasons he stayed in the library, one of the reasons he hadn't transferred. Mrs. Fratelli was not an administrator, not a secretary, but not really a teacher either. She was ostensibly on the periphery of the school, but she had her own building and her own staff, was queen of her own private realm, and he had the sneaking suspicion that she was closer to the center of things than anyone suspected.

Ann was already at her post behind the counter by the time he arrived at the library. He had never cracked her secret, had never discovered why she and the other TAs seldom spoke and walked around like they were more zombie than human. He still suspected some brainwashing effort on the part of the librarian, but she had never tried anything on him, so he could never be sure.

"Where's the old lady?" he asked Ann. He liked to act cool around the other TAs. It was the only place he could get away with it, since they were among the few kids at school even dorkier than he was.

The other girl ignored him.

Ed shrugged. "That's okay. I'll check out her office."

That was bold. Mrs. Fratelli didn't like anyone in her office when she was not there, and if it turned out that she was somewhere else in the library, he would be breaking cardinal rule number one. But still Ann didn't respond, just continued to stare straight ahead in that spooky blank way she had, and he walked behind the counter and knocked on the librarian's door.

No answer.

Feeling brave, he let himself in. Mrs. Fratelli wasn't there, and he took the opportunity to scope the place out, though he still remained in the doorway. His gaze alighted on a book lying on the flat empty part of her desk. The leather-bound cover was black, and he couldn't read the red-lettered title upside down, but the sepia-toned photo beneath the words was of the library. Sort of. He took a few steps forward. He recognized the blocky ugliness of the square structure even upside down, but there were no other buildings anywhere around it. There was, however, a line of dead trees in the front, and hanging from each tree was a bound black teenager who had obviously been lynched.

Ed stepped back into the doorway, feeling guilty. He looked behind him to make sure there was no sign of Mrs. Fratelli and saw only the back of Ann's head as the other TA stared silently into the heart of the library.

Ed thought for a moment. Brad and Myla seemed to blame everything on the charter, and it was true that Tyler had seemed to be a pretty normal high school for his freshman-through-junior years, until the charter conversion this semester. But he had the feeling that whatever was going on here was deeper than that. Yes, the charter seemed to have brought everything to a head, but this library had been a dead zone ever since he'd started attending the school. *No one* wanted to go here. And Mrs. Fratelli had always been the way she was. She hadn't changed this semester. This was her.

He glanced again at the book on the desk and thought about some of the other odd books he'd shelved, the ones with pictures of deformed men and naked women, butchered corpses and dead babies, the ones with titles simultaneously gruesome and pornographic. And those were the books that were on public display, the ones that anyone could check out.

What about the ones that were hidden?

Special Collections.

Maybe there was something in there that could shed some light on Tyler's secrets.

Ed hesitated. He knew where Mrs. Fratelli kept the key to the room. It would be easy for him to take it right now and go there, putting it back when he was through. It would be wrong . . . but it would be easy.

Which was the bigger wrong, though? A boy had burned up in that fire. Other students were missing and, if Van was any indication, probably dead. Some teachers might even be missing if the rumors he'd heard were true. Wasn't it his responsibility to find out all he could, even if it meant breaking a few rules?

The librarian could return at any second, so without further hesitation, he strode into the room, picked the key ring from its hook under one of the shelves and quickly stepped back outside, closing the door behind him. Still no sign of Mrs. Fratelli. He pocketed the key ring and walked over to Ann. He tapped her on the shoulder. It was the first time he'd ever touched her, and he expected her to turn slowly and dully like she always did, but to his surprise, she jumped, startled, and let out a short yelp.

He jumped, too, but was encouraged by the fact that she could still have a normal human reaction. "Where's Mrs. Fratelli?" he asked.

"She went to the office to see Mrs. Hawkes. She told me to hold the fort until Miss Green came."

Ed had still never seen the elusive Miss Green, and he was beginning to doubt that the library assistant even existed. He didn't want to be too obvious, but he had to know, and he asked Ann, "Did she say when she'd be back?"

The TA shook her head.

He thought quickly. This might work, but he'd have to move fast. "I'm going upstairs. Let Mrs. Fratelli know if she returns."

Ann was once again her normal, nonresponsive self, and he hurried down the center aisle, then up the stairs that led to the second floor. He hadn't told the TA why he was going upstairs because he had a plan. Sprinting down one of the aisles, he reached the far wall and hung a right. Going past the row of empty study carrels, he reached the alcove containing the permanently locked door marked SPECIAL COLLECTIONS. Hesitating for only a second, he unlocked it, opened it a crack, ignored the foul odor that seemed to come from within, then hurried back downstairs to replace the key.

Mrs. Fratelli had still not returned, thank goodness, and luckily, no classes or individuals had yet come to the library to check out books or work on the computers. He was sweating and breathing hard, but he tried to control both as he sauntered up to and around Ann and the front desk. "Mrs. Fratelli?" he called, pretending he was looking for her. As he'd hoped, Ann didn't turn around, and with a furtive look back at her, he opened the door to the librarian's office, put the key away and closed the door behind him.

"That place is a mess up there," he told the TA, gesturing toward the ceiling and by extension the second floor. "I just wanted to tell Mrs. Fratelli about it. I'll probably be up there the entire period. Do you think you can let her know where I am when she comes back?"

Ann said nothing, staring straight ahead, so he got out a scrap of paper from beneath the counter and grabbed a pen. "Never mind. I'll write her a note."

"I'll tell her," Ann said.

"Are you sure?"

Ann nodded.

He paused. "That's okay. I'll write her a note anyway. Just make sure you give it to her."

"I'll tell her you were in her office."

Ed froze, his heart leaping in his chest.

Ann's head pivoted on her neck, making her look for all the world like a robot. "If you don't let me give her your message myself, I will tell her that you went into her office. Twice."

He had no idea what was going on here, no clue what Ann was thinking or what her motives might be. He was not even sure he understood the substance of her proposal.

"You want to tell her yourself?" he asked carefully.

She nodded in that familiar dull way.

"And you will *just* tell her that the second floor is a mess and I'm up there cleaning it?"

She nodded.

What kind of game was she playing? He didn't know, but if he didn't play along, the shit would hit the fan. It might anyway, but he had no choice, and it was a chance he had to take. "Okay," he said, adding a conciliatory, "Thanks, Ann."

She didn't respond, and he was off again, walking briskly down the aisle and up the stairs, running like crazy once he reached the second floor. He hurried past the study carrels to the alcove.

The door to Special Collections was wide open.

Ed stopped. He had opened the door just a crack.

And there was no one else on this floor except him.

The room beyond the open door was like a black maw. Waiting.

"Hello?" he called.

There was no answer, no sound, but he thought he felt, coming from within that darkness, a soft wind, like an exhaled breath, carrying that foul odor he had smelled in the first second after he'd opened the door.

He didn't have time to fool around. The librarian could be back from the office at any moment. Either he was going to do this thing or he wasn't. Steeling himself, prepared to run away at the slightest hint of danger, he approached the open door, reached his hand around the side of the jamb and felt for a light switch. He thought for a moment that he wasn't going to find one. But then his fingers touched what felt like a rounded knob, and he turned it.

Lights flickered on.

He walked inside.

The smell wasn't as bad as he'd first thought. It wasn't great, but it wasn't unbearable. It was a damp scent, more like must or mold than the odor of rotting flesh that his mind had first conjured. He stepped forward slowly. The room was big, much bigger than he would have expected, given that this was the library's northernmost extremity. He'd anticipated finding a narrow chamber that ran the length of the building, but the windowless room in which he found himself was a perfect square larger than any of the school's classrooms.

And it contained only a single wooden bookcase.

Ed walked over and perused the titles on the

shelves. There were no call letters, nothing to indicate they were library books, and they were all part of a set, not only bound in the same black leather as the volume on Mrs. Fratelli's desk, but imprinted with the same red-embossed title: *The Academy*. Intrigued, he pulled one randomly from the middle of the second shelf. The photo on the cover was of—

The playground he and Brad had seen in the fog.

Like the picture on Mrs. Fratelli's book, it was old and sepia-toned, and while there were no children visible and it had been taken on a clear day, he recognized immediately the placement of the swing set and slide, the monkey bars and teeter-totter. In fact, the photograph appeared to have been taken from exactly the same angle at which he and Brad had stood. He opened the cover, flipping quickly through the pages. The volume was a yearbook, of sorts. Although it certainly wasn't the type of yearbook meant for students. It seemed more like a yearlong documentation of a school's inner workings aimed at some future generation. Titles of chapters included "Administration," "Instruction" and "Discipline."

There were photos as well, and he paused to glance at a few of them. One showed a scowling, heavily bearded man wearing antiquated clothes who looked as though he would have been just as at home on a whaling ship or a judge's bench. The ID line underneath read: "Principal Hawkes."

Principal Hawkes?

Ed stared for a second at the hard dark eyes of the man. He could see no resemblance, but coincidence or not, the fact that there'd been another Principal Hawkes sent chills down his spine. He continued turning pages. There was another picture of the playground. It was occupied this time, but the barely clothed children playing desultorily on the equipment looked battered and bruised as well as poor, and even through the blurred focus of the primitive photograph, Ed could see what appeared to be bleeding wounds on the arm of one rag-clad boy.

Toward the back of the book was a picture of the schoolhouse, an old-fashioned *Little House on the Prairie* building. What caught his attention in this one was the background: rolling hills in front of far-off mountains. He would have thought nothing of it but for the fact that he recognized that view. Although the hills were bare grass and had no buildings on them, they were the hills above Brea, and the mountains behind were the San Bernardinos.

It was the same view he saw daily from the PE field.

The school in the photograph was Tyler.

A long, long time ago.

As far as he could discern with his quick perusal, the name of the school was mentioned nowhere, but he didn't have time to read the book in detail. The librarian could return at any time, and whatever happened, he didn't want to get caught in here. He put the volume back and counted the titles on the top shelf. Twenty-five. There were six shelves altogether, which meant there were 150 volumes here. If one volume represented one year, the school's history went back 150 years.

But they'd been told that Tyler High had been founded in 1950.

That's what the plaque at the front of the school said as well.

Maybe that's when it became a high school, he rationalized. Before that, perhaps, it had been some sort of K-through-twelve institution.

Or *academy*.

Whatever the hell that meant.

He promptly reached up and took out the very first

book. The photo on the cover of this one was of that bearded man—

Principal Hawkes

—and once again he was glowering, staring into the camera with a hard angry glare. Ed took a look behind him at the doorway to make sure no one was coming, then began flipping through pages. John Joseph Hawkes was apparently the principal's name, and Ed made a note of it, intending to go online later and see what he could discover about the man.

There were fewer photos in this book, but there were several drawings, and from what he could tell, they were John Hawkes' sketches of the school and proposed future expansions. The man was nothing if not ambitious, and in addition to the one-room schoolhouse, he envisioned what appeared to be an entire community built around his ever-growing Academy. Ed glanced at some of the accompanying text. From what he could tell, the focus of the Academy and the surrounding utopian community was to be three-pronged: spiritual, mental and physical. That meant that students and the adults they would grow into were expected to keep themselves fit spiritually, mentally and physically, according to John Hawkes' rigid standards. Ed didn't know about the spiritual aspect, but the descriptions of "physical activity" and "mental activity" made him think of the sports complex and the library—two locations on campus where strange occurrences seemed to be concentrated.

He wished he could stay here and read all these volumes all the way through, but time was running out. Mrs. Fratelli could show up at any moment. He quickly flipped through the rest of the book, skimming it. In a chapter titled "A Spiritual Education," he read that John Hawkes stressed the importance of teaching religion in school, although *what* religion was a mystery, since the references to it that Ed read all focused on the appeasement of ghosts. The man also seemed to claim some sort of divine right. From what Ed could tell, John Hawkes believed he had been chosen by God to educate the youth of the United States. He had established the Academy, he was its sole director and after his death the job could be handed down only to his descendants.

Ed frowned.

John Hawkes?

Jody Hawkes?

Could it be?

He didn't have time to think about it. In another chapter, "The Eternal Academy," Ed saw that John Hawkes believed his school would last forever, that God had willed it to be so and that the increasing number of graduates and their offspring would eventually spill over into other communities, other states, until their influence was overwhelming and impossible to ignore.

Weird, he thought, and put the book away. On impulse, he bent down and took the last volume from the bottom shelf. This cover photo was in color and showed Tyler as it looked today. He flipped the pages, saw pictures of teachers he knew and kids he recognized. He stopped on a chapter titled "The Charter."

"Obtaining charter status for the Academy is the top priority," he read. "Independence will allow for the reinstitution of the Academy's original curricula and will enable us to reach our ultimate objective."

He heard a noise behind him.

Someone was on the second floor.

Ed swiftly replaced the book. Hurrying, he turned off the light and shut the door, moving quickly but quietly, making a special effort at the last second to muffle the inevitable click when the latch slipped into place. Once out of the alcove, he stopped, listened. He didn't hear anything, but that meant shit. He was pretty sure someone was up here.

He just didn't want to run into whoever it was.

Especially if it was Mrs. Fratelli.

The least likely path for a person to take would be around the west side of the floor, where the unused reference desk and the small room with the old microfiche reader were located. Everyone usually came down one of the center aisles or along the wall with the study carrels. He quickly made his way between the stacks.

And almost ran smack into Mrs. Fratelli.

It was pure luck that he didn't scream. The librarian looked at him with her unchanging expression, at once dead-eyed and severe. "I came to see what you were doing. I heard that you were cleaning something up here. I wasn't aware that there was a problem."

"Oh, there's not," he said. "I fixed it. I mean, I cleaned it up. It looked worse than it was, and it turned out not really to be anything at all. I was just on my way downstairs to do my shelf reading."

She stared at him silently. He was aware that he was babbling, probably making no sense and no doubt digging himself into an even deeper hole, but he was not good at thinking on his feet.

"Show me what you did."

He was scared. Mrs. Fratelli was intimidating under the best of circumstances, and he didn't like the fact that she seemed suspicious. He wondered if she knew what he'd been doing. He wondered if Ann had said anything about him going into her office.

The second floor was silent.

They were the only ones up here.

Mrs. Fratelli stared at him.

"It's all cleaned up. Everything's fine. I really need

to start on that shelf reading or I won't get it done." He walked away, turning and heading in the opposite direction so she couldn't see his tense, wincing face. It was a bold gambit and one that paid off. He was prepared at any second to be stopped in his tracks, but she didn't yell at him, didn't say a word. She didn't follow him either, and that made him think that she was going to go back, retrace his steps and try to find out exactly what he had been doing up here.

Was there any way she could tell? Had he made any mistakes? Had he disturbed anything? Had he put everything back in its proper place?

What would she do if she caught him?

Ed was worried and still scared, but he felt he'd been given a new lease on life as he walked down the steps and saw the front door of the library. He was safe now. Even if the librarian came after him, he could escape outside. He was no longer trapped.

He even smiled at Ann as he made his way to the fiction stacks to start on his daily shelf reading.

"Check this out, dude."

Brad looked at the computer screen over Ed's shoulder. They had Googled "John Tyler High School," "the Academy" and "John Joseph Hawkes." Nothing worthwhile had come up for the first two, but after scrolling through page after page of unrelated entries for similar and sometimes not-so-similar names, Ed had finally found some concrete information about John Hawkes.

According to an article on education in frontier California that was published in *American Heritage* magazine in 1956, John Joseph Hawkes was a pioneer in the establishment of standardized instruction in the United States. Now a forgotten figure, he was once hugely influential, having served as an adviser to President Franklin Pierce, an early advocate of universal education. A former army captain, Hawkes later became a minister in some weird offshoot religion that believed in God but not heaven or hell. In its theology, the dead did not go anywhere after death but remained on earth as ghosts. It was Hawkes' wish that schools be built to accommodate the needs of both the living and the nonliving, since they were destined to coexist in the same physical space.

His religious beliefs, as well as a scandal involving the death of a child at his school, which was alluded to but not spelled out, led to Hawkes' very public downfall, and he died penniless and unknown in 1865.

Brad straightened up. "That sounds like our guy."

"Anything there we can use?"

"Not really," Brad admitted.

"I didn't think so."

"We've got to keep looking."

"Yeah."

"You're not going to like this," Brad said. "But if we don't find anything online, maybe there are books in the school library that can tell us something."

Ed shook his head. "No way in hell, dude. No fucking way."

"That's where you found that Special Collections set. And those other books with deformed people and stuff."

Ed was already trying another search engine. "I won't give up the quest."

"I know. But think about that playground we saw. And this guy believed that people just became ghosts and hung around after they died? The answer's here somewhere, and if we have to scour the school for clues, then that's what we have to do."

Ed ignored him.

"You hear me?"

Ed scrolled through a list of unrelated topics and sighed. "Loud and clear, bud. Loud and clear."

The editor of the school newspaper was standing in front of one of the vending machines in the lunch area, getting a package of chocolate-chip cookies, when Myla saw him. It was break, and Brad and Ed were in the library. Ed had discovered some strange books in the secret Special Collections room yesterday afternoon, and they were in there now, searching the regular stacks, the ones not often used, looking for other books that might give them additional clues as to what was going on. She'd begged off because her period had come, and she'd needed to use the restroom. Now she was all alone, so she walked up to the editor and cleared her throat loudly. "Richard. Richard Park."

He turned around, and she saw the look of panic on his face.

"What happened to Rachel?" she asked. "You never told me the truth about that."

His voice was high and whiny. *Nervous,* she thought. "Yes, we did. She was killed by a drunk driver."

"What about the article she was working on?"

"I don't know anything about it."

Myla looked him in the eye. "We both know that's not the case. Rachel told me that both you and Booth approved it. And she wasn't a liar. Or are you saying that she was?"

"No!" he protested.

"Then what's the story?"

He opened his bag of cookies, trying to pretend there was nothing wrong, but she saw that his hands were shaking. "I have to go."

She stood in front of him. "What are you planning to do about coverage of the Harvest Festival?"

"What do you mean?" He licked his lips.

"Were you there? Did you see what happened?"

He shook his head. "The student council banned us. You know that."

"Did you *hear* about what happened?"

"I heard it was a huge success and the festival raised nearly twice as much money as last year. . . ."

She moved in closer. "Someone died. Someone was killed. He was burned in a bonfire and everyone wants to know who it was and how it happened."

Richard backed up.

"I smell Pulitzer here. You break this story open, you'll have your choice of any journalism school in the country. This is big. And you have the power to get it out to the public."

She'd touched a nerve. She could see that the idea grabbed him, but the spark in his eyes died the instant it appeared, fear immediately trumping ambition.

"What happened to Rachel?" Myla pressed again. "You know. Why won't you tell me? Is it Booth? Is he making you keep quiet? You know you don't want to live with this for the rest of your life. Why don't you just come clean?"

Richard's eyes widened as he looked past her, and then two muscular scouts came from behind, pushed her aside and grabbed him by his arms, practically lifting him off the ground. Myla didn't recognize either of them, and to her eyes they both appeared too old to be in high school.

"The principal wants to see you," the one on the left said.

"I didn't tell her anything!" Richard cried. "I swear!"

"You didn't hear that," the other scout said, pointing at her, and then they were gone, striding quickly back toward the quad, Richard held between them, his legs scrambling as he tried to keep up.

I didn't tell her anything.

Myla wanted to go after them, but she knew that was imprudent. She wouldn't be allowed wherever it was that they were headed. Besides, she was scared. The other kids using the vending machines and hanging out around the tables had not batted an eye when those two fascists had carried off the newspaper editor, and the fact that she went to a school where broad-daylight abductions were accepted as a matter of course frightened her almost as much as the act itself.

Richard had dropped his bag of cookies, and she picked it up, staring numbly at the blue foil package.

"Myla."

She looked up to see Cheryl, Reba and Cindy walking toward her. The three girls were smiling, but in a smirky self-satisfied way that did not bode well. She braced herself. "What?"

It was Cheryl who spoke. "We had a student-council meeting last night—"

"No one told me," Myla said.

"Yeah, well, it was *about* you. We took a vote and decided to excommunicate you from our ranks. As of last night, you are no longer a member of the council."

"It was unanimous," Cindy added spitefully.

She no longer wanted to be on student council, really, but it would still look good on her résumé, and the fact that her so-called friends had gone behind her back in such a malicious and underhanded way made her want to fight for her position.

"I was elected," she said. "You cannot 'excommunicate' me." She smiled tightly. "Besides, the student council is not a religion. It is an extracurricular school activity. I think the word you were looking for is 'impeach,' not 'excommunicate,' although I believe there are processes and procedures you would have to go through in order to do such a thing. One of them would be to inform me of your intent so that I could be there to defend myself."

All three were taken aback. Reba and Cindy looked toward Cheryl for guidance.

"I'm not a novice," Myla said coldly. "I know what I'm doing. And if anyone has proven herself unfit for office, Cheryl, it's you. I *will* be at the next council meeting. Try to remove me from office then."

She smiled. "By the way, how are things going with Mr. Nicholson? To be honest, he's a little old and paunchy for my taste. But, hey, that's just me."

Turning her back on her three *ex*-friends, Myla started for the classroom buildings just as the bell rang. She felt proud of herself; she felt good. But then she saw the two scouts who had taken Richard away, the editor nowhere to be seen, and she slunk toward fourth period feeling like the weight of the world was on her shoulders.

Twenty-two

"I told you I wanted macaroni and cheese!"

Kate Robinson ducked out of the way to avoid being hit as Tony threw the plate of food across the kitchen. She was afraid of her son. A terrible thing to admit, but there it was. He'd been acting like a macho bully ever since he'd joined that scouting program at school, and over the past week or so he had turned *mean.* It wasn't just his newly found seriousness or his obsessive need for order and discipline; it was the anger, hatred and cruelty she'd seen in him that made her so anxious, that caused her to lock the door to her bedroom at night.

"Can't you do anything right?" he demanded.

"We were out of cheese," she said patiently, "and I know you don't like the kind out of a box, so I decided to save that for tomorrow and make spaghetti tonight."

"Stupid bitch."

"What did you say?" Anger flared within her, and she advanced on him. "Don't you *ever* say that. Do you hear me?"

"I wish I lived with dad instead of you." He looked at her with unconcealed hostility. "Stupid bitch."

She crossed the rest of the kitchen in three quick steps—

And Tony slapped her across the face. Hard. There was satisfaction in his eyes as he did it, and though her own eyes welled with tears, she refused to let him see her cry. She sucked it up, forced back her emotions and calmly walked past him and out of the kitchen. More than anything else, she wanted to retreat into her bedroom, lock the door and hide. But she couldn't show any more weakness than she'd already shown, so she went out into the living room and sat down on the couch.

Lying on the coffee table, mocking her, was Tony's white envelope. He must have dropped it there after school. She wanted to ignore it, wanted simply to turn on the television and watch the news until Tony retired to his own room, but she could see it in her peripheral vision, bright against the darkness of the table, and after a moment's resistance she succumbed.

She reached for the envelope, opened it. There were a good thirty or forty pages in there this week, and on top was a yellow photocopied sheet that had her name scrawled in marking pen in the upper left-hand corner. The rest of the page was a form letter, and she picked it up and read it:

Dear Unfit Mother,

Your complete and utter failure to participate in school activities on behalf of your child has left us no choice but to level a fine against you for noninvolvement. Please come to the office at your earliest convenience to pay the $359.62 you owe John Tyler High School for the abdication of your parental responsibility. Interest will ac-

crue daily at a rate of 19.5% until this amount is paid in full. Visa and MasterCard accepted.

The preprinted signature read: "Jody Hawkes, Principal."

Astonishment was her first reaction. Anger was her second. How dare the principal try to make her feel guilty? *Unfit mother?* She was going down to the school tomorrow and give that woman a piece of her mind. She refused to pay a single dime, and if that bitch didn't back down, she was going to talk to Tony's father and the two of them would fight this to the bitter end, even if it meant hiring a lawyer and using up every last dime they had.

She didn't even bother looking at the other pages in the white envelope. She picked them up, dumped them in the recycling bag with the old newspapers, then pushed in the envelope itself for good measure, squishing it down.

From the kitchen, she heard the sounds of Tony rattling dishes, loudly closing cupboards and slamming the door of the refrigerator in an effort to show her how he was fixing his own dinner because she had not done so to his specifications. *Fine,* she thought. *Let him throw a tantrum.* She turned on the television to watch the news. Sometime later, he stormed past her into the hallway and slammed the door to his bedroom as hard as he could. She waited awhile, until she was sure he wasn't coming out again, then went into the kitchen to see how bad the damage was.

It took her until nine o'clock to clean the place up.

She took a shower and went to bed, but her mind was active, and it was well after eleven when she finally fell asleep.

She was awakened in the middle of the night by Tony.

He was standing at the foot of her bed with three other Tyler Scouts dressed in those identical quasi-military uniforms. In the dim illumination of her night-light, they made her think of Hitler Youth. Tony was carrying what looked like a pillowcase, and before she could ask what he intended to do with it and what they were doing in her bedroom at this hour, he had pulled it over her head, and hands were all over her, grabbing, groping, lifting. A cool breeze swept between her legs as her nightie flipped up.

"Let me go!" she shouted.

One pair of hands gripped her right arm and shoulder, one pair her left. She hoped one of those pairs belonged to Tony because the other two were holding up the lower half of her body, and the scout on her lower left side had one hand on her calf, the other buried deep in the crack of her buttocks. The scout on her lower right held both hands together on her upper thigh, one of his thumbs pressed hard against her vagina.

Kate didn't know which was greater, her fear or her humiliation, but she kept her wits about her, and while this seemed to be a kidnapping, the fact that one of the kidnappers was her son gave her a distinct advantage. "Wait until your father hears about this," she told Tony, although she couldn't see which one he was. "Your father is not just going to be angry—he's going to be disappointed. This is not the way we raised you. This is not how you are supposed to behave. Do you hear me?"

She kept up a running lecture as they carried her what felt like down the hall, through the living room and out the front door.

"We're going outside? I didn't hear the door close.

Did you close it? Did you lock it? What if someone comes in while we're gone and steals everything?"

If her goal was to embarrass him in front of his friends, it didn't work. Her comments were met with stony silence. She was carried into what had to be a van and placed inside, the same hands holding her as the vehicle sped down the road, although at least the fingers had been removed from her inner thighs and butt.

It was amazing how acute her other senses seemed since the pillowcase had temporarily deprived her of her sight. She felt every small bump in the road, every acceleration and deceleration of the van, heard every breath of her otherwise silent captors, every creak and groan the vehicle made.

Then they stopped, then they were there, and her nightie flipping up once more, unfamiliar hands shoved once again into inappropriate places, she was carried somewhere through the cool open air before finally entering someplace warm and put down. The pillowcase was removed from her head.

And she was in the Tyler High School office.

It had to be after midnight, but it might as well have been midday. All the lights were on and all the desks appeared to be occupied. Secretaries were typing on computers; clerks were on the phone. She even saw a student assistant walk by carrying a stapler to one of the offices down a short hallway at the rear of the room.

The hallway.

She found herself staring at the short, seemingly unremarkable corridor. Something about it made her feel uneasy, and Kate realized that despite her tough stance earlier in the evening, she was afraid.

A door in the hallway opened, and Jody Hawkes emerged, walking toward her and smiling. Another woman, with a belligerent face and the mien of a lapdog, accompanied her. As the two of them drew closer, Kate could read the woman's name tag. BOBBI EVANS, it said, ADMINISTRATIVE COORDINATOR.

"You've come to pay your fine," Bobbi said. It wasn't a question but a statement.

"Yeah, I have my checkbook hidden here in my nightgown." Kate turned away from the woman and faced the principal. "What the hell do you think you're doing?" It was hard to be dignified when she was nearly naked in someone else's workplace, but anger saw her through. She looked behind her to find Tony and tell him that they were both going to get out of here and go home, but all four of the scouts had disappeared.

"You are here," Jody said, "because you failed to volunteer, as required by the Tyler High School Charter and the contract which you yourself signed."

"As a matter of fact, I did volunteer, but your art teacher is a pervert and your PTA is a bunch of psychotics. I was going to volunteer again in Tony's math class later this week. But of course you didn't even try to find that out."

"Do you want to see what a *true* volunteer looks like? A *real* involved parent?" Motioning for her to follow, the principal led Kate to a door to the right of the hallway that sported a plaque reading CONFERENCE ROOM. The administrative coordinator followed close behind.

The principal opened the door. Inside, a long table had been pushed against the back wall, and a handful of women were kneeling on the carpet, facing forward. In front of them stood a woman with a shaved head, wearing a long simple peasant robe. She looked like a medieval penitent, only her robe was black with an orange belt—Tyler's colors—and on the back of her head was a similarly two-toned tattoo of the Tyler tiger. She was leading the other women in a chant: ". . . I hereby renounce my religion, my friends and my family. With full heart and serene mind, I dedicate myself to the PTA and pledge my troth to John Tyler High School."

Kate turned away.

"It shames you, doesn't it?" the principal asked.

Kate turned on her. "No, it's crazy. And it doesn't make any sense. Renounce their families? Their kids are the reason they're here! How could they renounce them?"

"Because they've gone *beyond* that." There was a fanatic glint in the principal's eyes that made Kate realize that the woman might very well be insane. "Their loyalty is no longer to *their* children but to *all* of our children, to the *school*. This is the type of mother who deserves to have her child in a charter school, and this is the type of charter school that deserves to have such a mother volunteering for it. This is the wave of the future. This is where *you* should be."

"Drop dead," Kate told her.

Bobbi stepped forward. "Then you must pay the fine."

Kate leaned forward. "I'm not paying you a red fucking cent."

The principal smiled. "Let's go into my office."

Kate smiled back. "Let's not. You had your goons break into my house—"

"Tyler Scouts."

"Your *goons* break into my house, kidnap me, then bring me here, where I consider myself to be imprisoned. You are looking at not just a civil but a criminal lawsuit, and when I'm through with you, you won't even be able to get a job cleaning toilets at a Kwikee Mart."

"Let's go into my office."

It wasn't a request but an order, and astonishingly, the administrative coordinator *pushed* her from behind and forced her to follow the principal around the corner and into the short hall. Immediately upon passing through the entryway, she was overcome with a dread so palpable that she nearly froze in her tracks. Then the principal was opening the door to her office, Bobbi was pushing her from behind and they were walking inside.

One look at the room and Kate knew she was in deep trouble. This was like no office she had ever seen. The floor was hard dirt pocked by holes and piles of clumped excrement that could have been animal but appeared human. The walls were a mélange of dark colors—black, purple, brown—that looked as though they had originally been stripes and had melted into the mess she saw now. Taped over what had to be a window were irregularly cut pieces of white and yellow construction paper on which were drawn crude crayon renderings of male and female genitals. On the ceiling was painted one of those yellow happy faces, but the paint was old and faded, dull rather than bright, and instead of a curved-line smile, there was a black circle from which hung a cord and a single bare lightbulb. A frowning face was drawn on the bulb in marking pen.

"That will be all," the principal told Bobbi. "Leave us alone."

The administrative coordinator left—reluctantly, Kate thought—and closed the door behind her.

"Sit," the principal said.

There was no place *to* sit. The office was completely devoid of furniture save for a couple of twisted pieces of metal that could conceivably have been chairs at some point in their existence, and a broken wooden table on which were stacked various whips and knives and weapons.

Kate remained standing.

"I said *sit*!" Jody Hawkes picked up a bamboo cane and made slashing motions in the air with it.

Kate made no effort to move.

Suddenly, the principal was no longer alone. There was a man behind her, a tall, full-bearded man in an old-fashioned topcoat. Kate had no idea where he'd come from. He could have been there all along—his dark clothes blended in with the muddy colors of the walls—but she was pretty certain that he had simply appeared. She was not even sure the principal was aware of him. For a brief second, she thought he might be there to punish or harm the other woman, but it became instantly clear from the fact that he was shadowing her, mimicking her every movement, that he was on her side, that in some terrible way he was part of this room.

The principal cut a swath through the air with her cane. "You will not leave this office—"

Until you pay the fine, Kate expected her to conclude. But there *was* no conclusion to the sentence. That was it.

You will not leave this office.

She'd had enough. Kate turned to open the door.

The cane struck her across the shoulders. The impact was excruciating, and Kate felt a warm wash of blood trickle down the cold skin of her back. She cried out reflexively, automatically, an instant response to the infliction of pain, but she did not falter, did not stop and continued reaching for the knob.

Another cane smacked hard against her hand. Bones broke this time, there was once again blood and she saw out of the corner of her eye the bearded man wielding a cane of his own, one of dark wood with a silver head that looked like something Dr. Jekyll and Mr. Hyde would use.

Before she could even scream, both figures were attacking, blows raining down upon her from all sides as they circled in, canes flailing. She dropped to the floor, her chin landing in excrement, and she was vomiting even as the two canes beat the life out of her.

It was the principal who struck the final blow.

"You're not a real parent," she said, raising her arms high.

And then there was only blackness.

Brad told his parents that Ms. Montolvo, his Spanish teacher, wanted to talk to them. She wasn't his worst instructor—that would be Mr. Connor or maybe Mr. Myers—but she'd definitely been acting very peculiar lately. She was the teacher who had changed the most since the beginning of the semester, and her behavior was strange enough that an encounter with her might enable his parents to see how bad things were getting.

And while she was freaky, she was not yet dangerous.

Unlike Mr. Connor or Mr. Myers.

It was a risk, a gamble, but he'd called both Myla and Ed last night when he'd first thought of it, and they'd both agreed it was a good plan. All three of them had attempted to tell their parents about what was happening at Tyler High, but to no avail. After all, what ordinary person would believe an honest account of the horrors they'd experienced? His parents and Ed's had been so irritated by their constant barrage of stories that it was almost a boy-who-cried-wolf situation, and their failed efforts to contact the police had only further put them in the doghouse. It was doubtful that their parents would believe *anything* they had to say on the subject. So he'd come up with the idea of telling his mom and dad that he was having trouble in Spanish and that his teacher wanted to have a conference.

His dad had e-mailed Mrs. Montolvo and set up an appointment for a meeting in the morning before school.

His mom had to work at the last minute—another nurse called in sick—but his dad had the morning off, so the two of them drove to school early and Brad purposely took his father through the gate in the wall that led to the lunch area. He was hoping for a glimpse of that ghostly playground or even some dead birds by the backboards, but nothing unusual was visible at all, and he directed his dad through the corridor that led to the foreign-language classrooms.

Ms. Montolvo's door was open, the light on inside, as the two of them approached. Brad wiped his hands on his pants, nervous all of a sudden, unsure why he had thought such an idiotic idea might work. His dad knocked on the doorframe. "Anybody home?" he asked jovially.

Ms. Montolvo stood. "Mr. Becker, I assume. Come in, come in. You, too, Brad."

This was not going well. She looked normal today, and was acting like a regular teacher. Yesterday, she had been wearing what looked like clown makeup, which appeared especially odd against the two tones of her uniform, and when Tami Yoshida had mistakenly used the masculine rather than feminine form of a word in a sentence, she had inexplicably and nonsensically started railing against what she believed were the evils of computer animation.

"So," she said, offering them both a seat at the table near the window, "what did you want to see me about?"

Brad's heart lurched in his chest.

His dad frowned. "I thought you wanted to see me."

Laughing lightly, she touched his hand, lowering her eyes coquettishly. "Oh, I do."

Thank God. The craziness was starting.

"So how *is* Brad doing?" his father asked.

"Oh, he's a fine student. We just had our first test last week, and he did very well. He also raises his hand and participates in class."

Brad felt like he was in first grade.

His dad frowned again. "So there's no real problem?"

"No, not at all."

His father looked at him. "Well . . . I guess that's good." He checked the clock above the blackboard and stood. "I'm sorry to run like this, but I'm sure you have a class to prepare for, and I only came by to check on the status of my son here. . . ."

"Mr. Becker?"

"Yes?"

Ms. Montolvo leaned across the table. "I'll lick your ass until you beg for mercy," she whispered.

Brad didn't know whether the teacher thought she was being quiet, or whether she didn't care about being overheard, but he saw his father's face redden. His dad glanced over at him, and Brad quickly looked away. He had never felt so embarrassed in his life. Inwardly, however, he was rejoicing. His old man would *have* to believe him now.

"I really have to go," his father said stiffly.

Brad followed him out the door. "See?" he started to say.

But the moment his dad walked out of the classroom, it was as if he'd forgotten what had happened. He smiled at Brad. "Looks like everything's fine. Glad to hear you're doing well."

"Uh, Dad . . . ?" he prodded.

His father looked at him blankly. "Yes?"

"Don't you remember what she said in there?" *She offered to lick your ass,* he wanted to say, but he couldn't bring that up.

Was he so pathetic that he'd let a little embarrassment keep him from opening his old man's eyes to the truth?

No.

The campus was starting to get crowded, so he kept his voice low. "I think she wanted to have sex with you, Dad."

His father chuckled. "That's a good one, Brad."

Brad felt himself starting to panic. *His old man had forgotten already!* Was the school getting to him? "She did," he insisted. He took the plunge. "She said she'd lick your ass until you begged for mercy."

His father's face hardened. "That's enough."

"Look around you! There's the wall I told you about! And my teacher's crazy! There are ghosts here, Dad. And people are dying and disappearing. Everything I tried to tell you is true! You can see it for yourself!"

"I have to go. And you have to get to class." His dad smiled, but the smile came too quickly, as though a switch had been flipped and it had been turned on by someone else. "I'll see you this afternoon, buddy."

And then he was gone, striding down the walkway toward the parking lot. Brad watched him go with a sinking feeling in the pit of his stomach.

"Your father's a nice man."

Brad jumped at the sound of Ms. Montolvo's voice. She put a hand on his shoulder, spoke softly into his ear. "And I *would* lick his ass until he begged for mercy. I'd tongue his balls, too. And use his pubic hair for dental floss."

Heart pounding, Brad hurried away from her as fast as he could without running and drawing attention to himself. Spanish was his first class, but now he was not even sure he was going to go. He didn't see how he could sit there listening to Ms. Montolvo talk about conjugating verbs after what had just happened.

He couldn't ditch, though. The teacher knew he was here today, and if he didn't show up, she would e-mail his dad about it.

He didn't want that to happen for *several* reasons.

He walked across the quad, going nowhere in particular, just needing to keep moving. Over in Senior Corner, there were no seniors. He saw on the small patch of grass what appeared to be a dog impaled on a stake embedded in the ground. Through the center of campus marched a squad of Tyler Scouts, swinging their arms in unison and heading toward the lawn at the front of the school, singing a military song.

This school was sinking fast. And they were going down with the ship, with no rescue in sight.

The bell rang, and while the thought of returning to Ms. Montolvo's class put butterflies in his stomach, he was more afraid to not go than go. He waited until the last minute, however, making sure the room was filled with other students before he entered, and he sat down in his chair just as the final bell rang.

Ms. Montolvo spent the period ranting about the evils of rotoscoping.

Brad was glad Myla was in his biology class third period. Seeing her always gave him a lift, no matter what was going on. Yet something felt wrong from the second they walked in. He couldn't put his finger on what it was, but the classroom seemed weird and uncomfortable to him, the air thick and heavy. He met Myla's eyes. She felt it, too.

He wasn't sure anyone else had noticed. The two

nerds in the back row were discussing comic books; the slutty girls in the corner were whispering and giggling among themselves; the majority of the students were staring into space or doodling on their notebooks the way they always did.

Brad sat down slowly, feeling like an astronaut trying to maneuver around in one of those bulky space suits.

Mr. Manning, seated at his desk, was staring at the back wall of the room, smiling. The last bell rang and the students waited, but the teacher remained where he was. There were a few muffled giggles and some restless movement. Brad watched the teacher. There was no mirth in that smile, he thought. It was grim—angry, even—and it looked as though it could snap off at any second.

In the center of the class, Antonio Gonzalez made a snorting noise. "Hey, dude," he said. "You gonna teach today or what?"

Several kids laughed.

The teacher stood. Still smiling, he walked down the aisle and, without warning, grabbed Antonio by the hair, yanking him out of his seat.

"Oww!" the boy screamed. "What the fuck—?"

Mr. Manning punched him hard in the stomach.

The entire class watched as Antonio doubled over, seeming almost to deflate as he did so. He was a big kid and Mr. Manning was not a tall man, but in seconds those dimensions seemed to have been reversed. "Faces forward," the teacher ordered. His voice was loud—harsh and angry enough to brook no resistance. Brad shot a quick look at Myla before following the rest of the class and complying. He stared at the blackboard as from behind came sounds of hitting and slapping, followed by grunts of pain.

Heads were turning, and Brad couldn't resist the

temptation either. Slowly, surreptitiously, he shifted in his seat, looked back and saw Mr. Manning shove Antonio to the rear of the room. There was an alcove there with a sink and counter beneath a series of shelves containing chemicals and scientific paraphernalia. "You'll stay there for five minutes!" the teacher ordered.

Only . . .

Only the alcove was dark. The lights in the room were on, and banks of windows faced the sun in the east, but somehow the alcove had become suffused with shadows so murky that Antonio seemed almost to disappear within them. Brad didn't want to think about how that was possible, and he faced forward once again, reminded for some reason of that playground he and Ed had seen in the fog.

The teacher strode to the front of the class and, as if nothing had happened, began writing on the board. "Take notes!" he ordered, and there was a rustle of papers as everyone opened their notebooks, grabbed their pencils and began copying down what the instructor was writing. As always, Mr. Manning did not lecture but simply filled the blackboard with outlines and definitions that he expected his students to duplicate in their notes.

He filled the first half of the board, then the second. Erasing what he'd initially written, he picked up a new piece of chalk and began writing on the first half of the board again.

Finally, he put the chalk down, dusting off his hands. "You can come out now, Antonio," Mr. Manning said pleasantly, addressing the rear of the room.

The boy emerged from the shadows, stumbling into a desk, his legs wobbly and uncertain, as though he were just learning to use them again after a long time off his feet. He seemed to have wet his pants—there was a large stain on the crotch of his jeans—and the expression on his face was one of complete befuddlement. He was drooling. Students scooted their desks aside, giving him room as he lurched up an aisle toward the front of the class.

He reached the teacher's desk, leaned against it and moaned incoherently.

"Joey?" Mr. Manning said. "Patrick? Would you come here, please?"

Two boys stood, looking at their classmates with trepidation as they stepped up to the front of the room.

The teacher pulled Antonio away from his desk, taking one of his wrists and giving it to Joey, handing the other one to Patrick. "Take him to the special-ed room," Mr. Manning said. "He's aphasic."

"Aphasic?" Patrick asked. "What does that mean?"

Mr. Manning grinned. "It means he's a retard."

Brad looked over at Myla, saw fear on her face that mirrored his own.

"The rest of you open your books and turn to chapter three. . . ."

Linda arrived home feeling good, bearing sandwiches from Pepino's Italian Deli, although she realized that she should have called Frank ahead of time, because she found him in the kitchen taking a baking dish of Pasta Roni out of the microwave.

"Where were you?" he asked. "You were late, so I figured I'd better make dinner."

"You call that dinner?"

"You knew I couldn't cook when you married me. Where were you?"

"We had another meeting. After school."

"And how are things coming?"

"Not bad," she admitted, putting the sandwiches

down on the counter. "I also heard from the employees' association. The Ninth Circuit's agreed to hear their case. We might have union representation once again."

"Or it might be tied up in court for years."

"Or that."

He picked up a fork and tried a bite of his clumpy pasta. "So what happened at your meeting?"

"Everyone's been following your suggestion: keeping notes, saving memos, writing down dates and times."

"Good."

"Several teachers have been doing further research, and it may interest you to know that this is not an isolated occurrence. Or at least part of it isn't. Several charter schools have been beset by megalomaniac principals. We've been in contact with teachers there, and some of them have managed to have their principals removed. Others have had their charters revoked."

"Bravo!"

Linda unwrapped one of the sandwiches. "It's not all good news. Tyler has some problems to deal with that these other schools don't."

"Your ghosts," Frank said.

"That's a simple way of putting it, but, yes."

He carried his baking dish to the breakfast table and sat down. Linda followed, bringing her sandwich. "But that seems to be charter related, too," he said. "Right? Nothing strange or supernatural was happening before this semester."

She gave his cheek a pinch. "I just love the way you matter-of-factly list the supernatural as one of several factors we need to consider."

"I know, I know. You love my Spock-like brain."

"It's reassuring somehow." She took a bite of her sandwich.

"So what's your next step?"

"We have the first round of standardized tests next week."

"Yeah?"

She put down her sandwich. "Yeah. The thing is, if our test scores go down from last year, on top of everything else we've gathered, I think we have a good shot at getting this charter revoked. I called Sacramento this afternoon, and that five-year trial period is not set in stone. If the benchmarks Jody promised to have us meet are not met, there's a chance that we can get the charter nullified. Proof of malfeasance or misbehavior on the part of the administration or the charter committee would help as well. That's what one of the other schools said, too."

"I don't understand." Frank looked at her. "You're going to ask your students to put their futures at stake and do poorly on their tests? Doesn't that seem slightly unethical to you? Isn't there some educators' version of the Hippocratic oath that precludes that?"

"We haven't worked everything out yet. But those achievement tests measure school performance, not individual performance. They're blind. They wouldn't affect the kids at all."

"Still . . ."

She sighed. "It's a dilemma. But it might be our only hope."

After dinner, they did the dishes together—what few there were—then relaxed, vegging out on the couch in front of the television until the late news came on. Frank checked his e-mail one last time while she took her vitamins and turned out the lights, and they met up again in the bedroom.

Linda took off her blouse and bra, then pulled off her skirt and looked down at herself, grimacing. "I have to wash these panties. They're filthy. They need to give us at least three more pair."

Frank grinned. "You want me to lick 'em clean?"

"I've been wearing them for two days already!"

"That's how I like 'em."

"You're sick." She paused, smiling. "Okay, you're not. You're actually sexy. In a dirty, nasty kind of way. And I probably would let you lick them if they didn't have our charter school pledge printed there. Panty worship's fine. Charter worship . . . that I will not tolerate."

"Take them off, then, and let's get down to business."

She kissed his nose. "I really do want to shower first. It's been a long day and I feel unclean. Working at Tyler will do that to you." She kissed his mouth. "Don't go anywhere."

"Don't worry. I'll be right here."

He was asleep by the time she got out of the shower, and she smiled as she watched him. His eyes were closed, his mouth was open and he was snoring.

Pulling down the covers, she crouched between his legs and took him into her mouth. He awoke, stretching and smiling, running his hands through her hair. When he was hard enough, she climbed on top of him and guided it in, riding him slowly and gently.

They came together.

And fell asleep in each other's arms.

Greg went to bed early, but Diane stayed up late to correct papers.

It was going to be a long night. She still had creative-writing assignments from last week to grade, as well as today's essay test, and if she hoped to have any kind of weekend, she needed to finish them all by Friday. It was her plan to grade all the stories tonight and all the tests tomorrow night. She prided herself on her quick turnaround, and despite everything that had been on her mind lately—

the Penalty Space

—she had no excuse for falling so far behind. She vowed to stay up all night if need be and get this job done.

Following her usual ritual, she shut off the television, made herself a pot of tea and turned off all the lights in the front of the house save the one over the dining room table where she worked.

The first story was by Kelly Hong, her best student. Diane smiled. If she were a less-conscientious teacher, she could just slap an A on that assignment without reading it and move on to the next one. Kelly had never turned in anything less than A work, and Diane knew that the girl's obsessive perfectionism would not allow her to slack off this time. But she refused to cheat. It wouldn't be fair to Kelly or the other students. Besides, she genuinely wanted to read the girl's story. Taking a sip of tea, she opened the blue folder's cover.

"Ms. Brooke Must Die!" read the large-font title.

Diane frowned. That was odd. And very uncharacteristic of Kelly. She read the title again. It felt weird seeing her own name used in such a context.

She read on:

I don't know when I decided that my English teacher, Ms. Brooke, had to die, but decide it I did, and nothing had ever felt more right. I finished my test and looked toward the front of the classroom, where the teacher sat at her desk, looking over the homework we'd turned in that morning. What I wanted more than anything was to slit her throat, to feel the blade of my knife sink into her flesh and sever the artery that pumped the blood into her twisted brain. . . .

Diane kept reading. Despite the distasteful subject matter, the story was well-done, and there was no real reason for her to give the assignment anything other than an A, although next to the grade, she wrote, "Disturbing."

Diane picked up the next creative-writing assignment and looked at the title: "Assfuck Redemption."

Assfuck?

A heavy weight seemed to settle in her stomach as she turned the page. Halfway down the paper, she spied her own name, and her gaze went immediately to that paragraph.

Ms. Brooke adjusted herself, pushing her buttocks out farther and higher in order to take him more deeply, her fingers fluttering between her legs as she manipulated herself from underneath. Her asshole was tight and soft and warm, and he grunted with animalistic pleasure as he drove it in hard. His orgasm was coming, and she cried out, too, as her furious fingers brought her to climax. With a feeling of great release, he thrust manfully, spurting deep into her willing ass as her sphincter muscle tightened around the base of his massive erection, squeezing out every last drop of his hot thick sperm.

Diane grimaced in revulsion. She refused to read any more. There was no way she could give this sickening fantasy anything resembling a decent grade. Frowning, she thought about Kelly's story and picked up another paper, opening it at random. She read a few lines, did the same with another. And another. And another. They were all filled with graphic sex and appalling violence. As she sifted through the pile, glancing at sentences here, paragraphs there, she saw that they each had her as a main character. It was embarrassing and frightening and disgusting all at the same time. What made it even more disturbing was that each of the stories seemed to be fairly accomplished. Even her worst students, the ones who could barely string together a coherent sentence, had written pieces that were impressively detailed and relatively well executed.

Dispirited, she let the folder in her hands fall onto the table.

She couldn't do this. Not tonight. She was tired, was disheartened and couldn't even think clearly enough to decide what needed to be done. She certainly wasn't going to correct the papers the way she ordinarily would. For now, she was going to go to bed, and tomorrow she would pretend to her class that she hadn't read any of their work. Maybe by tomorrow evening some sort of solution would come to her.

Diane stood, finished the last cold dregs of her tea, put her cup in the sink, then turned off the dining room light and felt her way through the darkness to the hallway. In the bedroom, Greg's nightstand light was on and he was on his side, lying sacked out in the center of the mattress. He often fell asleep while reading—"The best sleeping pill's a good book," he liked to joke—and she walked over to the bed to take off his glasses. He wasn't wearing them, though, and she saw almost instantly that they had fallen off and he had rolled over and broken them.

"Greg," she said. She tried to push him over, but there was something strangely heavy about his body.

It had no give, and there was no reaction to her prodding. She felt his cheek.

His skin was cold.

"Greg!" she screamed. Using all her strength, she moved him onto his back, ripped open his pajama shirt and straddled his chest. She felt for breath, listened for a heartbeat, felt nothing, heard nothing and tried to remember her CPR as she pinched his nose, blew into his mouth and then pressed rhythmically on his chest. "Don't die," she sobbed. "Don't die." But she knew in her heart that he was dead already.

Still, she wouldn't give up, and she kept administering CPR, pumping and blowing, pumping and blowing, pumping and blowing. . . .

She gave up at some point, her arms hurting, her lungs raw. She was crying hysterically, but some part of her thought that it might still be possible for him to be saved, and she reached over his body to pick up the phone and dial 911. Maybe the paramedics had machines she wasn't aware of, or knew techniques that she didn't, and would be able to bring him back.

She looked down next to him on the bed and, by his squashed glasses, saw the bound volume he'd been reading. She was staring at the title even as the police dispatcher answered the phone and asked her to please describe the emergency.

It was the John Tyler High School Charter.

Twenty-three

Afraid to attend most of their classes and needing time to plan, Brad, Myla and Ed ditched school for the rest of the week. They alternated their time between the public library and Ed's house, where they went only when they were absolutely positive that neither of his parents was there.

Their research had finally paid off. They'd found an obituary for John Joseph Hawkes in an old newspaper, stating that he had died here in Santa Mara of "unnatural causes." They'd also located a monograph Hawkes had written on the importance of discipline in learning, where he argued that dividing students into teams of scouts, teaching them each different survival skills and pitting them against one another in physical contests resulted in the students' becoming more self-sufficient and motivated.

"Scouts!" Ed said excitedly, pointing at the computer screen. "See?"

"I see," Brad said.

They'd uncovered as well, in a collection of Franklin Pierce's documents that had been made available to the public through a virtual library, a letter John Hawkes had written to President Pierce. In it, he had described his plans for establishing the Academy and its support community. The most interesting line, however, was an unclear sentence that stated, "Mrs. F. has Agreed to Become Librarian."

Ed pushed himself away from the computer as though it were emitting toxic rays. "Mrs. F.?" he said.

"It can't be," Brad told him.

"It might be," Myla disagreed.

"It is," Ed said.

Unfortunately, none of the information they'd discovered helped them in any practical way, and the only worthwhile idea they'd come up with was starting a blog in order to get the word out about what was happening at Tyler High. Since Ed was the most computer literate of the three of them, he set up an interactive home page, with Brad and Myla doing most of the actual writing. The hope was that others would add to their postings with examples of their own, and to this end they'd sent out anonymous e-mails to everyone they could think of, informing them about the existence of the Web site.

They'd even sent e-mails to the school district offices, the police and every media outlet they could think of.

It couldn't hurt.

But by Saturday, they were getting restless. With Brad driving his mom's Honda, they drove by the school, making several passes along the front before gathering the courage to drive around the block that contained the campus. Unfortunately, they could see little beyond the tops of the buildings over the brown brick security wall.

"Hey," Ed pointed out. "They were right. There's no graffiti."

"Everyone's *afraid* to write on that wall," Brad said.

"You know, we could get expelled." Myla's voice sounded nervous.

Ed snorted. "For skipping a few classes? That's one of the privileges of being a senior."

"There's an official senior ditch day. It's in May. And we didn't just skip a few classes. We were absent from all of our classes for half a week."

Brad drove around the school once again, looking at the gates to see if any were open. For all three days—Wednesday, Thursday and Friday—Brad had expected his parents to yell at him when he'd come home from Ed's, having been informed by the school that he had not been attending any of his classes. But no one from the office called; no notices arrived in the mail; no e-mail was sent.

It was as if, he thought now, the school didn't care that they were gone.

He slowed the car.

Or was *glad* that they were gone.

"Myla's right," he said. "We can't stay away forever. I think we've already pushed this thing to the limit. Right now, we can forge notes from our parents, turn them in and probably get away with it. Any longer, and we'd probably need a doctor's signature. Then we'd be screwed."

Ed pointed at the wall. "You really want to go back in there?"

"No. But I don't think the school wants us back either." He pulled to the curb and parked, turning to face them. "Think about it. Our teachers have been marking us absent for three days and no one from the office has bothered to call our parents to find out why. Doesn't that seem suspicious to you?"

"Not necessarily," Ed said.

"I think it is. We're a threat and they know it. That's why they're happy we're not there. I think we're on to something. I think we can make a difference."

"We've done all we can on the outside," Myla added. "The Web site's up. We need to go back and spread the word in person. Besides, it's test week." She sounded almost embarrassed. "I can't miss that."

"Those tests mean nothing," Ed said. "They don't count toward your grade. They don't mean shit." He ran an exasperated hand through his hair. "And have you forgotten already? Tell me again what Antonio was like after he came out of the corner. You want that to be you?"

"We need to be careful," Brad stressed. "But we need to go back."

Ed sat back in the seat, arms folded. "No way, dude. No fuckin' way."

"Way," Brad said.

Myla smiled. "Way."

Ed sighed. "Shit."

After nearly a week's absence, Tyler, in their minds, had grown into a fearsome boogeyman, a place of monolithic evil on the order of Mordor, so it was somewhat surprising when they returned Monday morning to see kids carrying books and wearing backpacks, chatting in the halls, doing all the normal things high school students did.

But the wall was still there, hemming in the campus, and they had only to scratch the surface to find evidence that all was not right with the world. Scouts were now posted at both ends of every hallway as well as at various points around school: in the quad, in front of the office and the library, by the lunch area, on the walkway to the sports complex. Senior Corner was filled with some unidentifiable type of rotting meat, and the cowed students walking to class were so silent that the buzzing from flies on the meat sounded like the noise of a lawn mower.

"I told you," Ed whispered. "I told you."

A full can of Red Bull sailed through the air from the direction of the Little Theater and struck Ed in the back.

"Ow!" he cried, turning.

Todd Zivney, standing in front of the theater entrance, grinned. "Hey, wimpy! Where's Popeye?"

Ed ignored him and tried to slink away, but Brad held his ground. The scouts were placed so deliberately around the campus that he suspected they had assigned posts they were not allowed to leave. "Popeye can't be here!" Brad called. "He's fucking your mom! Or at least he's one of the thirty men standing in line for it!"

Zivney shouted a torrent of obscenities, but just as Brad suspected, he didn't move from his spot.

Ed smiled.

"Are you laughing at me? That'll be your last laugh, you little faggot!" Zivney threw another can.

Ed easily sidestepped it and turned away, facing Brad. "I'm feeling a little better now," he admitted. "I'll probably get my ass kicked at break and lunch and possibly PE, but that will almost have been worth it."

"There are good teachers here and good students," Myla said. "We need to find them and stay with them. There's safety in numbers."

The three of them went into the office, gave their fake notes to the attendance clerk and were met with a surprising lack of suspicion—despite the fact that they had come in together and had been absent the exact same amount of time. They emerged moments later, free and unscathed.

"If I'd known it was this easy," Ed said when they came out, "I'd've been doing this more often."

Brad and Ed walked Myla to PE—"Be careful,"

Brad warned her; "I will," she promised—and then Brad dropped Ed off at his chemistry class.

He waited until the final bell rang before he went into Ms. Montolvo's room, and for the rest of the morning—

Everything was fine.

It was almost as if this were a normal school, with normal teachers and normal students. Even Mr. Manning behaved like a regular person.

It was his favorite teacher, Mrs. Webster, who brought him back to reality. One of the kids asked about the achievement tests on Wednesday and whether they were going to be on their usual seven-period schedule or an all-day testing schedule, the way they were when they took the SATs and the PSATs. The teacher didn't answer right away, and when she did, her voice was uncharacteristically serious. "It's a modified all-day schedule," she said, speaking slowly. "You will remain in your first-period classes until lunch and, after that, go to your regular afternoon classes." She paused. "But you are not actually required to take the examination. The school is required to administer the exam and turn in the results, but there is no law stating that you must take it."

What was going on here? Brad wondered. Was she telling them not to take the test?

He looked at Myla and their eyes locked. She was thinking the same thing he was.

Mrs. Webster spoke carefully. "As I'm sure you are all aware, ever since Tyler High became a charter school, there has been a renewed emphasis on standards and accountability. In fact, one of the requirements the state put on us is that we meet a series of stated educational goals. If we do not, our charter could be revoked."

She was.

The teacher looked around the room, and what Brad saw when her eyes met his was that she hated the charter.

And feared it.

The discussion ended there, and they moved on to talk about George Orwell's *Nineteen Eighty-four,* which was not much of a stretch and which he was now beginning to think had been a deliberate choice on her part. He was encouraged not just by her suggestion but by the fact that, apparently, they now had an ally on the staff. There were probably others as well, and he tried to go over in his mind the instructors he knew, placing them in categories of friend or foe.

After class, instead of walking out with the others, he and Myla stayed behind in the room, waiting until everyone else had gone.

"Is there anything I can do for you?" Mrs. Webster asked pleasantly.

What if he was wrong?

"Is it true that there's no legal requirement for us to take the achievement test?" he asked cautiously.

She nodded slowly. "There is not," she said, equally cautious.

"So if I stayed home that day or I just left the test blank and didn't fill in any of the bubbles, it wouldn't affect my grade?"

"No," she said, and he thought he heard a note of gratitude in her voice. "It might affect the standing of the school, but it would not reflect on you. No one would even know it *was* you. The test is administered anonymously."

Another teacher, Mr. Cheng, poked his head in the doorway. "Almost through here?" he asked.

Mrs. Webster waved. "I'll be right out." She turned

back to Brad and Myla. "Do you have any more questions?"

Brad looked at Myla, who shook her head. "No," he said. "Thank you."

"*Now* there's something we can do," Myla said enthusiastically as they hurried down the stairs. "We have to get this out. We have to blog it."

Ed, when they told him, was not quite convinced.

"Well, that's fine for Mrs. Webster's first period," he said. "But if I tried that excuse in my class, I'd be in the principal's office so fast my head would spin." He motioned toward Brad. "You really think Ms. Montolvo would let you squirm out of taking the test because it wasn't a legal requirement? I think not, bud."

"You're right," Brad said. "But what if we try something else? What if we flunk the test intentionally? What if we do our best to get every answer wrong and we can convince other students to do it as well? It wouldn't take many. A handful of good students screwing up would seriously throw off the curve. And if what Mrs. Webster said is right, the fact that Tyler's overall score went down instead of up would mean that the charter could be in jeopardy."

"I hate to burst your bubble here, but remember that guy who burned up in the bonfire? Remember our haunted playground? Remember what I saw in the library? Not everything is the fault of the charter. This is just an evil fucking place."

"But they're connected," Myla insisted. "The only question is, is this a charter school because it's evil, or is it evil because it's a charter school?"

"Chicken or egg," Brad said. "Six of one, half a dozen of the other. All we know for sure is that this is a combustible mixture, like fire and gasoline. Haunted, charter . . . what we have here is a perfect storm, and the combination of the two has gotten us where we are today. Break apart that pairing and I think we're safe."

"I hope you're right," Ed said.

Brad glanced across the quad to where a unit of scouts was marching through the corridor that led to the lunch area. "I hope so, too."

He hadn't liked the idea at first, but the more he thought about flunking the achievement test, the more Ed thought it was a good plan. As crazy as it sounded, it might actually work. It also appealed to his more rebellious sensibilities. But before they posted it online, before they dragged other kids into this, they needed to bounce it off someone besides Mrs. Webster.

He thought of his counselor, Ms. Tremayne. He'd been to see her only that one time, when he'd transferred out of woodshop, but she'd seemed like one of the good guys.

You have any problems, you come to me. That's what I'm here for.

Since he was planning to transfer out of the library anyway—there was no way he was going back into that building, not with things the way they were—he went to the office at the beginning of seventh period, thinking he could talk to the counselor, drop his TA gig and then hit her up about the test idea.

There were still scouts guarding the entrance to the building. Not Zivney or his buddies but two boys Ed had seen around and who he thought were in the marching band. Without Brad and Myla at his side, he wasn't sure at first how he was going to get past the sentries, but neither made any effort to stop him and he simply walked inside.

A witch of a secretary asked him angrily what he wanted, and Ed replied in a calm voice that he needed to see his counselor, Ms. Tremayne.

"What for?" the secretary demanded.

He was slightly intimidated by the woman's aggressiveness, but he held his ground. "That's between me and her. Can you tell her I'm here?"

The secretary opened the counter gate. "See her yourself."

Ed walked quickly through the office. It hadn't changed, exactly, but it was *more* of what it had been, and the place felt not just uncomfortable now but slightly dangerous. The elements in place were all what they should have been—desks, clerks, computers, copiers, phones—but they were not in the right combination or something, like chemical ingredients that were benign on their own but if mixed turned toxic.

He kept his eyes focused straight ahead, pretending he didn't see the TA with a bandage across her face, the secretary intently coloring a piece of paper completely black. He walked into that horrible short hallway and opened his counselor's door without knocking, stepping in and closing the door behind him. He was breathing hard as though he'd been running, and there was the pressure of a headache at the front of his skull.

Ms. Tremayne looked up from her computer screen, surprised. "Hello," she said.

He took a deep breath, sat down. "Sorry to barge in here like this," he said. "My name's Ed Haynes. A few weeks ago, I transferred from my woodshop class to library TA."

"Yes. I remember."

"I need to transfer out."

She swiveled her chair toward him. "I see. Is there any reason—"

The headache was pressing against his forehead. "I just need to get out of there," he said.

"Do your parents—"

"Listen." He leaned forward, putting his arms on her desk, squinting against the pain. "Do you have an aspirin or something? All of a sudden, I have this huge headache."

"The nurse's office is right next door." She stood. "Do you want me to get her?"

Ed shook his head, and for some reason the shaking motion made the pain lessen a little. "Maybe I'll transfer out tomorrow," he said. "That's not really the important thing right now. The real reason I'm here is because I need to ask you a question. It's about our charter and . . . and everything that's going on here right now."

Ms. Tremayne looked at him. "All right," she said after a long pause. She was nervous, he could tell, and wary about what he might ask. But the counselor hadn't been co-opted, she hadn't been beaten down and he knew that she was still one of the good guys.

"We were thinking," he said, "and I know you can't condone this or anything, but we were thinking that if, for some reason, Tyler's students did really bad on this achievement test Wednesday, wouldn't that kind of screw things up for the school? I mean, the whole reason we became a charter school is that it was supposed to be better for us and raise our test scores, right? So if our scores didn't go up, if they went down instead, people would have to take another look at the whole charter thing, right?"

"Yes," she said carefully. "That is true."

His head felt heavy, and he wanted to put it down on the desk, but instead he leaned backward in his chair. "We don't like the charter," he said. "Me and my friends. A lot of the students. Teachers as well."

"I don't either," the counselor said softly. She looked at the closed door. "It's why I'm leaving," she confided. "Tomorrow's my last day. I got a job with the Orange Unified School District. That's the only reason I'm telling you this."

That was a surprise. As a student, he had no choice but to attend school; it was mandatory. He and all the other students were a captive audience, prisoners in a sense, and because of everything going on at Tyler, he had assumed that the faculty and staff were trapped here as well. At least those who weren't *part* of the problem. It had never occurred to him that they could just up and leave the way they could with a regular job, and the fact that she was able to do so made it all seem more surreal somehow.

Ed shook his head again. It didn't exactly clear the cobwebs as the descriptions said in books, but it definitely lessened the intensity of the pain.

The counselor seemed to know what he was doing. "I get headaches in this building, too," Ms. Tremayne admitted. "Bad ones, sometimes. Although today I feel okay."

"What if students staged a protest," Ed asked flat out, "and purposely flunked the test? Do you think that would do anything?"

There was a long pause. "It might," Ms. Tremayne finally admitted. "And it's worth a try. Those sorts of standards tests reflect on the school as a whole, not the individual students." The door was closed, but she still leaned forward conspiratorially and pitched her voice low. "There's been a lot of talk around the office about making sure our test scores go up. It's a major concern around here."

Ed felt better. Not physically—his head was still thumping—but in regard to their plan. "Thank you," he said.

"You know, your parents can petition the district to have you transferred to another school. You don't have to stay here."

"But what about everyone else? What about my friends?" He shook his head. "No."

"But keep it in mind. It's an option."

He nodded. "Good luck in Orange," he said.

She smiled wanly. "Thank you."

Ed sped through the office, focused only on the exit as he strode past the cubicles and desks, and it was with a great sense of relief that he burst into the open air. He wanted to breathe it in, to savor it, but those two scouts were still standing to either side of the door, and he hurried past them into the quad.

It was the middle of seventh period, and he had no place to go. He couldn't just hang around and wait for Brad and Myla to get out. The scouts were charged with punishing loiterers. He glanced at the library. And there was no way he was going back there. He was done with that place.

He'd get off campus if he could, but he was pretty sure the gates in the wall were locked.

He opted for walking. As long as he kept moving, it looked like he was going somewhere, and he took a piece of homework paper out of his backpack, pretended it was a note from a teacher and went up and down the corridors studying it. He avoided the scouts, keeping a sharp eye out for Todd Zivney, and he was left alone. The period passed slowly, and several times he thought his cover might be blown, but finally the bell rang, classes were released and he was allowed to blend into the crowd.

He waited by Brad's locker until his friend showed up.

"I ran our idea past Ms. Tremayne," he said.

Brad frowned. "Your counselor?"

"She's cool. And she's out of here. She got a job at another school. She knows what this place is."

"So what'd she say?"

"She said it might work."

"What if we're wrong?" Myla fretted. "What if this *doesn't* work and we *can* be punished, and all we're doing is screwing up our GPAs so we can't get into decent colleges?"

Ed laughed. "It's tearing you up, isn't it? This goes against everything you are."

"Yes," she admitted.

"Not me. I feel free."

"Let's put it on the blog," Brad said. "We've got a day and two nights. Let's see what happens."

Twenty-four

Diane felt numb. Emotionally, spiritually, physically. All the time. She was not on any medication, but it felt like she was, and her short-term memory was shot to hell. She did what she had to do to get through the day, focusing on practical tasks at hand, making decisions that needed to be made, but everything that had happened since Greg's death was a blur. She remembered some of yesterday but not the day before, and she knew that by tomorrow that would be gone, too. It was as though her mind was protecting her by erasing everything connected to that horrible event as soon as she didn't need it anymore.

Linda and Frank were there for her—*all* her friends were there for her—but as well-meaning and understanding as they were, this was not happening to them. The anguish was hers and hers alone, and when everyone else left and went home and the house was empty, she had to face it by herself.

Greg had not wanted a funeral but had wanted to be cremated with only her in attendance, and that was an easy wish to honor. She didn't have to make arrangements or invite coworkers or deal with relatives. She didn't have to converse with lapsed friends or barely known acquaintances. The truth was that his plan seemed designed more for her benefit than his—he had never believed in any sort of afterlife—and when she figured out that that was probably the case, that he had done this for her, she broke down.

For about the millionth time.

She had his ashes placed in a box rather than an urn, and since he had expressed no preference as to what should be done with them, she decided to keep them in the house. Temporarily, until she could find a better, more permanent location, she placed the box on his side of the long oak dresser. It was where he liked to put his wallet, keys and change when he emptied out his pockets after coming home at night, and in a way, having the box of his ashes at that spot in the room was almost like having him there. She could see it as soon as she walked in; she could see it when she dressed and undressed; she could see it while she was lying on the bed.

On the day after she brought his ashes home, Diane received a letter of condolence from Jody Hawkes and the charter committee. It was not a Hallmark card they all had signed but rather an ink-jet-printed missive that none of them had signed but that featured a letterhead bearing all their names. It was as cold and heartless as she would have expected, made even more so by the fact that after a too-brief statement recognizing her loss, it mentioned that although district policy provided bereavement leave, under the charter, Tyler High School did not, and any days of work she missed would have to come out of her pool of personal days.

She tore up the letter in a fit of anger. She would have burned the damn thing if there'd been a fireplace in the bedroom and it had been turned on, but as it was, she threw the pieces on the floor, shouting as she did so, then gathered them up after the fact, threw them in the toilet and flushed them away.

The burning idea was a good one, though; it remained in her mind, and she opened the door to Greg's office to get her copy of the Tyler High School Charter. She'd put it in there not for safekeeping but because she was afraid of it, and there it had lain, on the top of Greg's desk, for the past several days. In her mind, it was reading the charter that had killed him, and though she hadn't known what to do with the document before, she did now.

She took the booklet out to the living room, dropped it in the fireplace, then turned on the gas, lit a match and started the fire. The flames, yellow and blue and unnaturally uniform, flared up and around the stack of bound paper. It took a moment for the pages to catch on fire, but finally they did, the white sheets blackening and curling back. It felt good to watch it burn, cathartic, and she stood there, staring into the flames, until there was nothing left of the document but a pile of disintegrating ashes.

She smiled as she turned off the gas, feeling as though she'd accomplished something.

Soon after, Linda called with the latest news from school. Diane was planning to return to work tomorrow, and she asked her friend if they could carpool.

"Of course!" Linda said.

"I just don't want to face it all alone. I'm not even sure I want to face it at all. The thought of going back, seeing everyone, having to answer their endless questions or endure their sympathy . . . I don't know."

"Maybe you're not ready," Linda suggested gently.

"No, I'm ready. I'm going stir-crazy here. And I know that once I get back to work and back to my normal routine, everything'll be fine. I *need* some semblance of normalcy."

"You don't want to wait until Monday? It might be

easier returning at the beginning of a week rather than in the middle. And this is test week."

"No," Diane said firmly. "I need to do this."

"Then I'll pick you up early," Linda promised. "Seven. That way, you can get through the campus and to your classroom before the hordes descend, kind of ease your way into things."

"You're a good friend," Diane said, and started to cry.

"Are you *sure* you'll be all right?"

"I'll be fine."

Linda was indeed at her house by seven—a few minutes early, in fact—and by the time her friend rang the doorbell, Diane was ready to go. She'd been ready since five, actually, having endured yet another sleepless night, and while her lack of sleep might catch up with her later in the afternoon, at the moment she felt fine.

There were a few cars in the lot when they arrived but not many, and Linda parked as close to the exit as possible. "So we can make a quick getaway," she joked.

Only one of the gates in the wall was open, and after getting their book bags and briefcases out of the backseat, the two of them walked through the archway and onto campus.

Bobbi came after her the second they stepped through the gate, rushing over from a spot in front of the office where she'd obviously been waiting. "What did you do to her?" she demanded. "What the hell did you do?"

Diane was in something of a fog and couldn't quite understand what was happening, but Linda stepped out in front of her and held up a fist. "Back off! Now!"

Bobbi stopped short.

"Diane just lost her husband. I don't know what you're going on about, you insensitive bitch, but if you say one more thing to her, I swear I will punch you so hard I'll knock you out!"

"Jody—" she began.

"What'd I say?" Linda advanced on her.

Bobbi ran away. Well, she didn't actually run, but she turned back the way she'd come and strode as quickly as her heeled shoes would allow her. They watched, unmoving, as the administrative coordinator nearly tripped over a low step on the walkway before continuing into the office.

"What the hell was that about?" Linda asked, turning to her.

Diane shook her head. "I haven't a clue." She chuckled. "You were going to knock her out?"

Linda smiled. "Anything for a friend."

From across the quad, Enrique waved at them. He was holding a broom in his hand, and it batted the branches of the tree next to him, causing a smattering of brown leaves to rain down. He called out, "Sorry to hear about your husband, Mrs. Brooke!" But he didn't sound sorry at all, and there was a huge grin plastered on his face.

Diane looked down at the ground. "Let's go," she muttered. "Before anyone else arrives."

By break time, she was feeling better. Being in front of a class again, teaching, was exactly the medicine she needed. She was craving caffeine, though, and since no one had bothered to get a new filter for the coffeemaker in the department office, she and Linda made a quick trip to the lounge. A group of teachers were gathered around the counter near the microwave. "Did you see her face?" Lisa asked.

"She looked scary," Jackie Linden said, and for a

moment Diane thought they were talking about her. But they must have realized that she could misinterpret the conversation, and Jackie clarified, "We're talking about Jody. Something happened to her yesterday. She looks really bad."

Somewhere in the fog of her brain an alarm bell sounded. There was a ray of clarity amid the haze, and she thought of Bobbi coming at her this morning.

What did you do to her? What the hell did you do?

The teachers were starting to gather around, offering their condolences, expressing sympathy. Diane felt claustrophobic all of a sudden, and she backed away a little. "What did Jody look like?" she asked.

The tide of sympathizers relented, everyone secretly relieved by the change of subject.

"Plastic surgery gone awry," Joel Grazer opined.

There was nervous laughter from some of the other teachers.

"It looks like she was in an accident," Lisa Piccolo said, "and is healing,"

"I haven't seen her today," Steve Warren offered, "but I saw her yesterday at lunch, and she looked fine."

"I saw her yesterday after school," Jackie said, "and she didn't."

So whatever happened to the principal had occurred between twelve thirty and three.

What did you do to her? What the hell did you do?

There was the germ of an idea in the back of Diane's mind, and she excused herself and walked out of the lounge without even getting the coffee she'd come for. Linda hurried after her. "What is it?"

"It's crazy," she said. "What I'm thinking is crazy."

"What?"

"Remember when Bobbi came after me this morning?"

"How could I forget?"

"She was yelling at me, blaming me for something. She said, 'What did you do to her?' "

Linda frowned. "*You* think *she* thinks you did something to Jody?"

"Maybe I did."

Linda shook her head. "Now I'm confused. What exactly are you talking about?"

"Remember I told you I burned my copy of the charter? The one that . . ." She trailed off, swallowed hard, willed herself not to cry.

"Of course," Linda said quickly. "I remember."

"I burned it after lunch sometime, after the mail came and I got that letter from Jody and the committee. That's the same time that this thing, whatever it is, happened to Jody's face."

"You're saying . . ."

"I'm saying that when I burned my copy of the charter, it did something to Jody."

The theory was a leap, but Linda had no problem taking it, and Diane could already see the wheels turning in her friend's mind. "We need to get a look at her," Linda said.

"Yes."

"We need to see her sometime today. So we'll know if there's a change when I go home and burn *my* copy of the charter."

Diane smiled. She was feeling suddenly hopeful.

"In fact, I'm going to call a meeting this afternoon. We need to talk about this. *Everyone* needs to burn their copies. If it doesn't work, if nothing happens, that's fine. But if it does . . ." Linda nodded to herself. "I have some other ideas, too, other things I want to bring up."

"I want to see her," Diane said. There was malice in the wish, a desire for revenge. She had no real proof that Greg had died of anything other than a heart attack, and there was certainly no proof that the burning of her charter had in any way harmed the principal, but in her mind they were all connected, and she was energized by the possibility of avenging Greg's death.

The bell rang, signaling the end of break, and groups of gathered students began splitting apart as they headed off to their individual classrooms.

Diane looked toward the office. "Let's take a quick peek," she said. "Really fast."

Linda nodded, and before either of them could change her mind, they walked down the concrete path to the administration building, ignoring the two pairs of scouts they passed along the way. There were butterflies in Diane's stomach as they reached their destination and she looked at the tinted glass door in front of them, unable to see anything inside.

Linda reached for the door handle, pulled it.

They looked in.

Jody could have been in her office or in the bathroom or in a conference or somewhere else on campus. The door could have opened upon an empty front counter and a collection of clerks at their desks.

But she was standing alone behind the counter staring at them.

Linda gasped and let go of the handle, allowing the door to close. Diane gasped, too. Partly because she was surprised, because it appeared as though Jody was waiting for them, because they had been caught.

And partly because of Jody's appearance.

Even from here, Diane could see what looked like hardened scar tissue on the principal's grotesquely swollen cheeks. It made her look like a completely different person, an uglier, meaner person, and Diane's first thought before the door closed and cut off her view was that this visage was much more in keeping with the true personality of the woman.

Could this really have happened because she had burned her copy of the charter?

It didn't seem possible, but then a lot of things didn't seem possible, and she turned to Linda and said, "What do you think?"

The quad was emptying out as students dashed to their classrooms before the bell rang, and although they were both going to be late, neither of them made a move. "I don't know of anything that could change a person's face like that between lunch and the end of school."

"Allergic reaction?" Diane speculated.

"I don't think so."

"I don't either."

The bell rang, and they finally started walking.

"It looked like she knew we were coming," Diane said.

"She saw us walking up. We can't see in through those doors, but the people in the office can see out."

"Do you really think that's why she was staring at us?"

"No," Linda admitted.

"She looked mad. That's a good sign."

"I think so, too."

"Do you think she was scared?"

"I don't know." Linda smiled grimly. "But she'd better be."

Every seat at Denny's was filled with a teacher.

If there had been other patrons, they were gone, and Linda stood in the center of the coffee shop and looked around her, feeling strong. Weakness and doubt were still there—they were *always* there—but she was filled with more hope than she had been for a long time. She looked at Diane, seated next to her, and reached down to give her friend's hand a reassuring squeeze.

"We are gathered here today," she began, "to fight the charter."

A cheer went up, and she couldn't help smiling.

"Many of you, most of you, probably, have seen or heard about the altered appearance of our fearless leader."

There were titters all around.

"There's no need to play games or tiptoe around this. What we believe caused this to happen is the fact that Diane burned her copy of the charter booklet. I know this sounds crazy, but whatever happened to Jody happened sometime between noon and three yesterday. Steve saw her at lunch; Jackie saw her after school. That's the same time period when Diane burned her copy of the charter."

"It's no crazier than anything else!" Alonso called out.

"Right. Exactly. So what we want you all to do tonight is go home, find your own copies of the charter and burn them. Every single one."

"Are we trying to kill her?" Lisa asked.

"No," Linda said. *Yes,* she thought. "But let's be honest here. If the principal is someone or something that can actually be harmed by our burning documents, then . . ." She left the thought unfinished.

"Are we all agreed?" she asked. "Is there anyone who doesn't think it's at least an idea worth trying?" She scanned the restaurant. No one raised a hand or made an effort to speak. "Good.

"Now, I have another idea. Also a little wacky, perhaps, but also worth a try."

Diane nodded her encouragement.

"Originally, Jody submitted a charter application to

the state and the district. The charter was written and we were asked to vote on it, to ratify it. When it was approved—by the slimmest of margins, I might add—that was when Tyler officially became a charter school. *And* when most of our problems seemed to start. What I propose is that we take another vote. It wouldn't be official, of course, and it wouldn't be under the auspices of the school. Jody would not allow that. But I believe we have a quorum here. Why don't we take another vote on whether we as teachers would like Tyler High to remain a charter school? We can record the results, give a copy to the administration and submit copies to both the district and state agencies that sanctioned the charter to show them our lack of faith in the current system. Kind of a no-confidence vote."

"I think that's an excellent idea," Ray said.

"There are teachers missing," Steve pointed out. "We're not all here."

"And what about classified staff?" Joel Grazer asked.

Linda hadn't thought of that. "We can still send a strong message—," she began.

Ray consulted with some of the teachers around him and did some quick calculations. "This isn't exact, but I believe Tyler High has a workforce of seventy-six all total, faculty and staff." He did a head count. "There are forty-two of us here. We should still have a quorum, but before we send off results to anyone, we can look up the correct numbers and fill in the blanks."

Linda nodded. "Very well. Let's do it. All those in favor of rejecting the Tyler High School Charter?"

The show of hands was unanimous.

"All those opposed?"

Nothing.

"Forty-two ayes, zero noes and thirty-four abstentions," Ray announced. "Give or take a few, the ayes have it."

A cheer went up.

"There's one last thing," Linda said when the noise died down. "Something else we can do. This one might be more difficult, because technically it may be grounds for dismissal, so we need to discuss it. But I don't think we should proctor the achievement test tomorrow." There was mumbling among the teachers. "I know this is last-minute, but hear me out. One of the stipulations made by the state and the district, one of the promises made by the charter itself, is a measurable increase in Tyler's scores. If that goal is not met, there's a reasonable expectation that the charter could be rescinded. Improved scores was one of the conditions of acceptance. We have a chance tomorrow to really make an impact on that front. In fact, I've been telling my students for the past two days that they are not legally required to take the test. I realize that that's probably unethical, and I've wrestled with myself over it, but I've decided to go with the greater good."

"I overheard a few of my students whispering," Marcia Williams said. "I pretended not to hear, but apparently there's a plan by some of the students themselves to purposely flunk the test. For the same reason. Wouldn't that be more effective?"

"We can't take a chance," Linda told them. "We don't know how many students would actually go through with it. We also have Jody's ringers to contend with. Not only are some of our worst-performing students now gone, but they've been replaced by aces, which could very well balance out some of the poor scores. We need to make *sure* that Tyler does not do well on the test. And even if our vote and our protest isn't enough to swing it, just the fact that we *did* vote and *are* protesting should make the district and the state rethink its commitment to Tyler's charter. If Jody Hawkes cannot control her staff, they might think it time to reestablish district control."

"I hate the district," Ray said regretfully.

"But not as much as you hate the charter."

"No."

There was much more controversy over this subject—it was not a theoretical fairy-dust solution but a tangible tampering with legitimate educational duties that could have real-world consequences—and after much discussion, they finally agreed to leave it up to the conscience of individual instructors whether to administer the test. Even if only some of the teachers rebelled, Linda reasoned, it could still cause a sizable ripple.

By the time they adjourned, it was dark outside and irate patrons were milling about the area near the door, impatiently waiting for tables. The restaurant staff, too, was irritated—most of the teachers had ordered only coffee—and Linda left an exorbitant tip for her server to make up for the inconvenience.

"Remember," she said before they left, "we *all* have to go home and burn our copies of the charter."

They split up, said their good-byes.

"What do you think's going to happen?" Diane asked as they made their way out to the car.

"I guess we'll find that out tomorrow," Linda said.

Twenty-five

Brad called Myla before he went to bed. He called her every night. In fact their phone calls were becoming so epic that his mom had taken to putting a kitchen timer outside the door of his room and when it rang after an hour, he was supposed to hang up. But tonight they spoke longer, nearly two hours, and while there was bravado in their talk, it masked a lot of anxiety. Ed had installed a counter on their Web page, and their blog had registered over five hundred hits since Monday evening, which was pretty good but not spectacular, since the population of the school was somewhere around twelve hundred. There were a few anonymous postings, but not many, and while Brad put on a brave face, his fear was that their plan was dead in the water and the only thing that would come of it was their own expulsion.

Or worse.

He dreamed that night of the ghostly playground, and in it were his family and all his friends, dead because he had endangered their lives with his ill-conceived schemes.

As they had been doing all week, Brad, Myla and Ed walked to school together the next morning. They had no idea what was going to happen today, but the moment they turned the corner onto Grayson, they knew that something big was afoot. Not only were there two yellow buses lined up and waiting to get into the parking lot, but the sidewalk and street ahead were overflowing with people.

"What's going on?" Myla said.

"I have no idea." Holding her hand, Brad walked a little faster.

Ed, already several yards ahead, was the first to spot the television cameras. "Look!" he said.

Someone had alerted the media. Ed crowed that it was their blog, and he could very well have been right, but it had mushroomed from there. Walking through the crowd, listening in as a reporter not from one of the UHF Orange County stations but from one of the big Los Angeles stations, a woman they all recognized, interviewed both Eric Van Gelder and his dad about their opinions on the fairness or unfairness of achievement tests, Brad realized that today's action was being framed as a protest against standardized testing. A reporter for another local news station solicited a quote from Brad's suddenly loquacious friend Brian Brown, who came down squarely on the side of the school administration in his insistence on the efficacy of such tests.

Still, the fact that such attention was being drawn to their school could only be good, and Brad's hopes for success were raised considerably.

The outside of the school looked like a three-ring circus. A crowd of parents, pundits and curious onlookers was milling about the sidewalk and parking lot, not allowed past the wall, and Tyler Scouts were roughly escorting students through the throng and onto school grounds, pushing aside anyone who stood in their way. The scouts, both male and female, were sporting weapons and looked prepared for battle as they wielded blackjacks and clutched batons.

"I'm not going in that gate," Ed said, watching the scouts manhandle a girl and shove her through the entrance.

"We'll go around," Brad suggested.

They stepped into the street, walked between the buses and trekked down the block to a different gate where a bunch of other students were avoiding the crowds and going in.

On the campus, it was chaos. The second they passed through the gate, the sounds of cars and human voices from the street and sidewalk outside disappeared, replaced by weird noises whose origins could not be determined: a curious rumbling that sounded like an earthquake in midtremor; short, sharp cries that were loud and shrill enough to cause earaches; an odd mewling that could have come from cats or infants or something in between. Groups of students were huddled together for protection in front of the locked doors of their classrooms, waiting for teachers to open them, while male and female scouts were throwing spears at one another by Senior Corner.

The three of them remained close to the gate should they need to beat a hasty retreat.

Coach Nicholson, brandishing a whip, ran through the quad, chasing a pair of female students wearing only black underwear with orange letters that read I SHOW FEALTY TO JOHN TYLER HIGH.

"Is that what your underwear looks like?" Ed asked.

Myla blushed.

"Mine just says 'John Tyler Charter High School.'" He grinned. "Want to see it?"

Brad hit him.

He stood there, watching all the frantic movement with a sense of detachment. There was a desperation to it all, he thought, as though the school knew it was going down and was pulling out all the stops, utilizing everything it had in an effort to go out with a big bang.

If just one of those reporters or cameramen got a view of what was going on in here right now, it would be all over.

"This can't last," Myla said, as though reading his thoughts. "It's too much. They're going to get caught."

Then the first bell rang.

And it all stopped.

As though someone had flipped a switch, the mayhem halted midstream and everyone began walking to their lockers and classrooms in an orderly fashion. The strange sounds disappeared, replaced by silence, and even the scouts picked up their weapons, straightened their uniforms and headed off to their first-period classes.

"Wow," Ed said.

"We'd better get going, too," Myla declared.

Brad nodded, gave her hand a squeeze. "This is it," he said. "Wish us luck."

"Not so fast!"

All three of them halted at the sound of the voice. Brad knew who it was without looking, but he turned around anyway to see Todd Zivney standing behind them and holding a knife. Behind *him* was the principal's secretary, Mrs. Evans, wearing a fiendish smile on her face. "Principal Hawkes knows what you've done!" she said gleefully. "Principal Hawkes knows everything!"

"You three," Zivney announced with satisfaction, "are going to the Penalty Space."

"What is the—?" Ed started to ask, and was

promptly cuffed on the side of the head with the butt of the knife handle. "Fuck!" he yelled.

Zivney hit him again. "Say another word, and I'll slit your goddamn throat."

"Put them in there for a year," Mrs. Evans said. "That should teach them a lesson."

A year? Brad looked at Myla. That had to be a joke. If they weren't home this *evening,* their parents would be all over this, not only calling the police, but making sure that no stone was left unturned in the effort to find them.

"Move!" Zivney ordered, punching Ed in the back.

They followed the scout's directions through the center of the school to the far side of the science building, where they went down the narrow corridor that separated the science and art rooms. "You're almost there," Zivney said, and Brad could hear the cruel delight in his voice.

But they never made it to the Penalty Space. Shadows engulfed them halfway down the hall, swirling formless tendrils of darkness that had no weight or heft but that obscured the world around them and made them feel as though they were being sucked into an endless black hole. Zivney ran away screaming, leaving them to fend off the onslaught alone, and Brad reached for Myla's hand but found only air, the end of his arm seeming to disappear in the twisting inkiness.

"Myla?" he tried to call. "Ed?"

But his voice made no sound.

And he found himself in another place.

Linda was supposed to be proctoring the test, but she had not passed out any booklets or Scantron forms and had told her students they were free to go home if they wished.

They wished.

The spectacle outside the walls had given the kids the confidence to be defiant, and the madness within the walls had left them feeling frightened, so when she informed her first-period class that they could leave with no repercussions, nearly all of them bailed. Hector Alvarado, who was not her best student but was definitely the most conscientious, offered to remain and take the exam, thinking that was what she wanted, but she told him kindly that he could go, and he took off, too.

Now she sat there staring at the unused tests, waiting. When the time came for the exam to be over, she would take the pile of unused Scantron forms and turn them into the office. She had thirty kids in her first-period class. That was thirty kids who would get zeros on the exam.

She wondered how many other teachers were doing the same thing. Diane, for sure. And Ray. And Steve.

There was an odd noise in the hallway outside the classroom. Her spine tingling, Linda stood up, walking over to the doorway to investigate. She poked her head around the corner of the doorjamb.

Jody was standing at the far end of the hall.

Her heart froze. This time, the principal was not smiling. She looked furious, and rage had distorted her features to such an extent that she no longer looked like herself. *No,* Linda thought. *Not just rage.* For the entire underlying bone structure of the principal's face had changed, making her into a monster, and with an uneasy combination of elation and terror, Linda realized that it was because so many of them had burned their copies of the charter.

It hadn't done enough, though. It hadn't stopped her. And Linda understood that, for that, they would need to find and burn the original.

Why hadn't she thought of that before?

Where was the original kept? In Sacramento? Here on campus?

Jody moved. But instead of turning and going down the stairs the way she had previously done, the principal strode forward. Glaring, eyes focused like a laser on Linda, she advanced quickly. Her mouth was open in a wide toothless O and the sound that emerged from it was the howling of wind. She'd become something no longer human, and instead of remaining to face the woman, Linda turned tail and ran.

She took the steps two at a time. She had no idea where she was going, only that she had to get away, and when she reached the bottom of the stairs, she hesitated for a moment, unsure whether to hide in the department office and lock herself in or dash outside. Like a squirrel in the roadway, she moved first to the left, then to the right, before finally deciding that her chances were better out in the open.

Hearing a noise from the stairwell above, she pushed open the door and ran.

Outside, it was a different world.

There was fog, though there had been no fog previously, and swirling through the white mist were dark shadows that reminded her of those shrouding the entrance to the Penalty Space. There were no people about, neither students nor teachers, and the campus seemed to exist in a strange realm of eerie silence.

Only she was not sure that it even *was* the campus. There were no indications that there was a classroom building off to her left, or that there was a tree and a garbage can directly in front of her, or that any of the school's familiar landmarks even existed. Turning around, she could see neither the door she had just walked through nor any outline of the building. The mere fact that Jody might still be coming for her, however, spurred Linda into moving forward. For while the fog itself was spooky, it was not half so spooky as the thought of the hideously mutated principal striding through it with the roaring of wind issuing from her open toothless mouth.

Linda strode ahead, encountering nothing, no trees, no walls, no bushes, only what seemed to be a flat empty space. She knew that she should be in the quad, but she clearly wasn't, and she decided after the first few seconds that she was lost.

Suddenly a building loomed out of the mist.

The library.

It was the only thing visible, and in the haze of white, its square bulk looked like nothing so much as a box in which something had been trapped. Linda frowned. That was a strange reaction, but this semester she had learned to trust her instincts. Some of her strangest reactions had been the ones most on the money.

She approached the library warily. She was almost upon it now, less than a few feet away, but the details of the building had not grown clearer or more distinct. Indeed, the structure retained a curiously blurred vagueness, as though it were an idea that had only just been conceived and had not been entirely thought through. She could see a fuzzy rectangle of light, however, at the spot where there appeared to be an open door. She walked up to it, intending only to peek in and see what was there. But before she knew what she was doing, she stepped inside—

And was in a one-room wooden schoolhouse.

She stopped, blinked.

The schoolhouse was old. It was not just old-fashioned but dilapidated, and in the corners were layers of cobwebs and pieces of broken writing slates. JOHN TYLER SCHOOL, read the barely visible letters on the crudely carved sign above the blackboard. The teacher's desk, illuminated by a blue light that came from nowhere but seemed to suffuse the room, was covered with dust and had on it some crumbling books, the core of a rotted apple and, on a stick, a small shredded flag whose colors were so faded she could not make out what it was. Behind the teacher's desk, in a glass case mounted on the wall, was a yellowed document of some sort.

But she was not alone, and that was the scariest part. Seated in the rows of antiquated writing desks, facing forward, were students, several of whom she knew. She saw Van Nguyen, who'd been missing since before the beginning of the semester, as well as Kyle Faber and other kids who had supposedly been "purged" from the attendance rolls. Together in the rear of the class were Myla Ellis, Brad Becker and one of Brad's friends. A couple of other students looked familiar to her as well, and while she thought she knew them, she couldn't be sure. All the kids seemed pale and faded, their faces white, their clothes drained of color. The only exceptions were Myla and Brad and Brad's friend, who looked just as they always did, and she wanted to go to them, but she was afraid.

At the front of the class stood a teacher, a heavily bearded man wearing a dusty black topcoat and a stern expression. He carried in his hand a switch, and it was clear that he was ready to use it on anyone who misbehaved.

Except . . .

Except no one was moving. They might as well have been wax dummies or figures in a museum diorama. Everyone in the classroom was locked in place. Like the schoolhouse itself, they seemed frozen in time.

There was movement outside, though, and through the windows she could see a playground in the fog where children were running about, laughing, screaming. They appeared to be having fun, but their voices were old and far from innocent, and the laughter to her ears sounded mocking, derisive and decidedly sinister.

Linda wanted to leave, wanted to get out of here and find some way back to the real world. But the fact that Myla, Brad and the other boy still seemed so alive gnawed at her, and she would not be able to live with herself if she didn't try to help them. She took a tentative step forward, and when no one moved, when the teacher did not bellow at her or attempt to hit her with his switch, she gained confidence. "Myla!" she whispered. "Brad!"

There was no response, but she hadn't expected any, and she reached out and touched Myla's shoulder. It felt normal, with some give beneath the clothes, but there was absolutely no reaction on the part of the girl. Linda looked into her face, waved a hand in front of her eyes. Nothing. As an experiment, she touched the faded shoulder of the girl to Myla's left. It was hard and cold, like an ice statue.

Frowning, Linda looked at the face of that girl more carefully. She was one of the students Linda had thought she'd recognized but had not been able to place.

She recognized her now.

Suzanne Johnson.

The social studies teacher was a teenager here rather than an adult, but Linda could still tell it was Suzanne, and she was filled with not only horror but sadness. She took a closer look at two of the other boys who seemed familiar. One was Carlos as a high school student, the other Rakeem.

These were the people the school had captured; these were the people the school had caught.

There was the sound of nails scraping across the chalkboard.

Linda jumped, startled. Jody was now standing at the front of the class next to the bearded man. She looked, if possible, worse than she had in the hallway outside Linda's classroom only moments before. Her hair, never her most attractive feature, was falling out in clumps, and the bones of her face protruded in freakish and unnatural ways. Her mottled skin looked cracked and rubbery, her eyes were pulled into menacing slits and her mouth remained permanently in that perfect O shape, tiny teeth now abutting two big fangs inside. The principal's hands were clawed, one considerably larger than the other, and her legs seemed to have grown simultaneously shorter and thicker.

She used her right claw to once again scrape across the chalkboard. "Caught you," she said. Her voice was slurred and raspy. "Bitch."

The principal was not yet done changing. Before Linda's eyes, what appeared to be the nub of a fledgling horn pressed out from the middle of her wrinkled forehead. In the real world, Linda realized, Tyler High School students were supposed to be taking their tests right now. Many of them were not, and of those who were, some were intentionally failing. Jody's right cheek turned red, split open. Every second that the school's overall test scores continued to drop, the principal grew more monstrous. She *was* the charter school, and anything that helped bring it down affected her.

"We voted to rescind the charter," she announced.

"You can't do that," Jody spit out. "Only I can authorize a vote."

"Oh, we did it, all right. You're finished. And so is your charter."

"*You're* finished!" Jody yelled, her voice thick. "Why do you think you're here?"

Here.

The sides of Jody's deformed mouth crept upward into something approximating a smile. She gestured around her at the interior of the schoolhouse, at the unmoving students in their seats, at the cobwebbed corners.

Linda suddenly understood.

This was where Jody had hidden everything. All of the school's secrets were in this schoolhouse.

Here.

Linda's eyes went to the small glass case on the wall behind the teacher's desk. With sudden insight, she realized what the yellowed document in there was: the original charter.

This was where it had been hidden.

She had to get over there somehow, grab it and burn it.

Burn it? With what?

She had no lighter, she realized, no matches, nothing that could conceivably be used to start a fire. Assuming she could make it past Jody to steal the charter, there was nothing she could do with the manuscript except try to tear it into pieces, which she was not sure would even work.

And she was afraid to go anywhere near the principal. She didn't even want to look at her.

The bearded man frightened her, too.

Jody laughed wheezingly. "Is this where you thought it would end? Is this where you thought you would wind up?"

Linda's heart lurched, and a bolt of panic shot through her. *End? Wind up?* She hadn't had time to think about it, hadn't even considered it until this moment, but how *was* she going to escape? She looked behind her to make sure the doorway was still there and still open.

It was.

And she saw something else at the same time.

To her left, built into the back wall of the schoolhouse, was a fireplace. Like those pioneer prairie schools, this room was heated by wood. Careful not to let her gaze linger too long lest the principal get suspicious, Linda quickly scanned the hearth. She saw a small pile of chopped wood, some tongs.

And a tin of matches.

Once again, she directed her attention to the front of the room, her mind racing. They were long matches, the kind that could usually be struck anywhere and still light up. But how could she take one of them without Jody seeing it?

Still afraid to look at the principal for any length of time, she focused on the sign above the chalkboard: JOHN TYLER SCHOOL. Somehow, it gave her strength.

In the real world, Tyler's test scores were still dropping. The principal winced, crying out in pain, as another horn pushed its way out of her forehead. At the same time, Brad's arm moved slightly on his desk.

Jody was losing control! She was getting weaker, and as she deteriorated, her hold on the school and everything in it slipped. The dead were dead—those faded people weren't going anywhere—but Brad, Myla and the other boy were still alive. Trapped here like her, incapacitated somehow, but still alive.

"We all burned our copies of the charter!" Linda said.

"No!"

"Yes!"

Brad swiveled his head. So did Myla and Brad's friend. She touched them, pushed them. "Help me!" she yelled. "Get up!"

Jody lurched toward her. The principal could no longer walk normally, but she could still propel herself forward on her thick unbending legs, and wheezing heavily, she started down an aisle between two rows of students. Behind her, the bearded man moved, fixing Linda with a piercing gaze and cutting the air with his switch.

"Help!" Linda screamed.

"What?" It was Brad's friend who spoke first, and he looked around in confusion, not knowing where he was or what was going on.

She didn't have time to get the kids up to speed. Jody would be upon her any second, and the bearded man was right behind her. "Stop them!" she shouted. "Don't let them get me!" And then she was running over to the fireplace, grabbing a handful of dusty matches and hurrying on. She didn't have time to look behind her to see what was happening; she could only move forward and hope she wouldn't be stopped. Running along the side wall, past the windows overlooking the foggy playground where the dead children frolicked, she slipped behind the teacher's desk, yanked open the glass case and pulled out the charter.

The pages of the document were not secured or fastened together in any way, and a few stray sheets escaped from her clutches and floated to the ground independently, but the bulk of the charter held together as she dropped it on the floor. Out of the corner of her eye, she saw the bearded teacher changing directions and trying to return to the front of the room as Brad and his friend shoved their desks into his legs. Linda struck a match on the side of the desk, praying it would work.

It did, and when she touched the flame to the corner of the top page, it instantly started to burn.

"No!" Jody yelled, and her voice was echoed by that of the bearded man.

Linda scrambled to pick up the stray pages and touched them to the growing fire, dropping them onto the pile once they'd caught.

The schoolhouse was dissolving around them. With each page that burned, something disappeared. The children outside first, their voices suddenly cut off and silent. Then the fog, as the world on the other side of the windows turned black instead of white. The students faded away, and their desks. The walls, the ceiling—all the physical elements of the schoolhouse seemed to run like paint and be absorbed into the floor.

Jody and the teacher were the last to go. Clutching each other and screaming in tandem as though their bodies were being torn apart, they merged into one, and as the flames devoured the last of the charter, and the charred and blackened pages crinkled into ash, they, too, were consumed, fused into a black square that looked like a book.

Another world came into focus around them. The real world. They were in what looked like an empty storeroom completely devoid of furniture save for a bookcase in the middle of the floor. There were books on the shelves, and one on the floor, all of them smoking and smoldering. Linda looked around, confused, not knowing where they were.

"We're in the library," Brad's friend said in wonderment. "Special Collections."

Myla pointed to the book on the floor and the black smoke seeping out from between its covers. "That's them," she said fearfully.

Linda still had the rest of the matches in her hand, and she moved over to the book and kicked it open.

The front cover flew back, and the blank pages inside started to burn more easily. She reached down, put the heads of the matches in the fire and, once they caught, dropped them on the book.

There didn't seem to be any sprinkler system in this room. A logical, responsible part of her was outraged—this was a *library*! At a *school*! How could it not have a sprinkler system? But another part of her was grateful.

Brad's friend had gone over to a door and opened it, and Brad and Myla hurried out, coughing. Linda waited a moment longer, using her arm to cover her nose and mouth, watching the book burn. When she was certain the fire was not going to go out, she exited the room as well.

She closed the door behind her, faced the students. Smiling, she addressed the boy next to Brad. "And your name is . . . ?"

"Ed," he said.

"Thank you, Ed. Thank you all."

"Do you think she's dead?" Myla asked, looking back at the closed door.

Dead. It was a harsh word, a final word, but in this instance she liked it and was glad that it fit.

"Yes," she said. "I do."

She took a deep breath. "Now let's find a phone and call the fire department before this whole place burns down."

Epilogue

It took over a week to sort everything out. As far as anyone knew, Jody Hawkes had disappeared, along with several hundred thousand dollars of the school's money, reason enough for the district to revoke Tyler's charter status and reestablish control.

After Jody, Linda thought, even those rabid fundamentalists didn't seem quite so bad.

Besides, there was an election coming up.

Janet Fratelli had disappeared as well, and to Linda, her whereabouts were a complete and utter mystery. Her office in the library had been cleaned out, stripped of anything personal, and no one knew where she had gone or why.

Bobbi Evans had been found dead by her own hand in the horrific hellhole that had been Jody's office. In a cruel irony, Bobbi was listed both in an article in the *Orange County Register* and in an obituary in the *Santa Mara Sentinel* as a "secretary" rather than an "administrative coordinator."

Although things were gradually getting back to normal on campus, it would be quite a while before all was as it should be. Several teachers had quit, several more had been fired and it seemed at times as though there were more substitutes on campus than full-time employees. An interim principal had been hired, an old district hand coaxed out of retirement, and he not only had disbanded the Tyler Scout program but was conducting an investigation to determine whether any of the former scouts should be suspended or expelled.

Both Linda and Diane, as well as most of the other remaining teachers, had been questioned extensively regarding what exactly had gone on at Tyler, not just on that last day but for several weeks prior, and though they hadn't met ahead of time to get their stories straight, their accounts must have been similar enough that no red flags were raised.

It would have been very difficult to talk about ghosts and moving shadows and anything supernatural to the law-enforcement officials and district bureaucrats to whom she'd spoken, so Linda kept it simple and direct, leaving most of that out—although she did bring up the missing students and teachers. After what she'd seen in that schoolhouse, she doubted that any of them would ever be found, but she felt she owed it to them to make sure that someone in authority made the effort.

Brad, Myla and Ed had filled her in on what they'd discovered through their own research, and Linda was astounded by their knowledge of the school's history and their description of John Hawkes and his academy. She had not known about any of this, but hearing it now made pieces of the puzzle start falling into place. She was very impressed by the students' fact-gathering skills, which put those of many teachers to shame, and she vowed to talk to their other instructors about awarding them extra credit. Initiative like theirs deserved to be rewarded.

By the end of the second week, life was starting to get back into a more normal routine, and while Linda was still far more tired than she had any right to be, she was very glad that the worst of it was behind her.

The horror was over.

Snuggling close to Frank as they lay in bed watching Bill Maher on HBO, she touched him under the covers, her hand sliding down his bare chest and under the elastic band of his underwear. "Want to do it?" she whispered.

"Okay," he said, looking over her shoulder at the television. "But can we wait until the show's over?"

She gave him a quick kiss. "Sure we can," she said. Leaning back on the pillow, she smiled, feeling good, feeling happy.

Feeling safe.

About the Author

Born in Arizona shortly after his mother attended the world premiere of *Psycho,* **Bentley Little** is the Bram Stoker Award–winning author of numerous previous novels and *The Collection,* a book of short stories. He has worked as a technical writer, reporter/photographer, library assistant, salesclerk, phone book deliveryman, video arcade attendant, newspaper deliveryman, furniture mover, and rodeo gatekeeper. The son of a Russian artist and an American educator, he and his Chinese wife were married by the justice of the peace in Tombstone, Arizona.